The Borgia Kiss

Kurt Heinrich Hyatt

Published by Rogue Phoenix Press, LLP
Copyright © 2020

ISBN: 978-1-62420-454-8

Credits
Cover Artist: Designs by Ms G
Editor: Sherry Derr-Wille

Dedication

To my wife, Rosa.

Chapter One

The flames from the burning tanker bellowed greedily behind her. Falle crouched beside a pile of rubble, her heart pounding as she watched green tracers arch overhead and geysers of dirt and flame from incoming beams.

She wiped at tears streaking the grime on her face. At the parapet another defender clutched at his chest and fell back among the dead, his scream thin above the noise of battle. His force pistol rolled down the slope and came to a stop at her feet.

The incoming beams had stopped. They were almost here.

One of the raiders appeared and climbed over the parapet. He caught sight of the little girl beside the pile of rock and stopped. The grin which swept his face was an evil thing, sharp and wide as the assault knife he slid from its sheath.

Falle picked up the force pistol. The raider was reflected in a myriad of light patterns and images; a bead of sweat running through the beard stubble on his chin. Gore smeared the ornamental lacework of the knifeguard and a torn shred of cloth fluttered on his combat vest. The smile he wore was wider than the horizon, coming closer.

The force pistol jerked to life in her hand. She saw, as if a spectator looking over her shoulder, the raider performed a deep bow around the neon pencil from her weapon before flipping backward to lie still on the sand.

More raiders appeared on the horizon. Again and again she fired, a little figure wreathed in smoke.

Abruptly, they turned and ran, their yells fading out across the valley. There was the whine of a hoverplane starting up, growing faint in the distance.

Falle lowered the pistol and stared at the barrel glowing red, at flames behind her reflecting from the polished tristeel. She held it to her breast while she climbed the dune and looked out over burning wreckage and sprawled bodies.

She was alone. From this moment on she would always be alone.

~ * ~

Mr. Chang drummed his fingers on the padded armrest of his targhide office chair and gazed out the plexglass window high above the busy workings of the aurumite mine. A faint clatter of machinery could be heard over the quiet drone of his suite air-conditioning. He watched spirals of dust rising from the pit to paint graceful shapes against the pink Dustball sky.

There was the swish of his office door and footfalls moving across the carpet. He swiveled the chair to face his visitor.

Standing on the tan plush was a mass of veined muscle, a roadmap of scars, the mean red-rimmed eyes of a wartpig. Facing the little man behind the huge desk, his meaty paws trembled and sweat ran down the back of his combat vest. He nervously cleared his throat. "You wanted to see me, boss?"

For a long moment Chang fixed him with a cold glare. He pushed a glass of water and a square of red stone to the front of the desk.

"Here before you is a twenty gram piece of refined aurumite, worth about two hundred creds on the New Earth market. Beside it is a simple glass of water." Eyebrows lifted above the antique spectacles. "Which do you think is the most valuable commodity on this planet, Mr. Gorth?"

Gorth swallowed heavily. He knew where this was going. "Um, the glass of water, Mr. Chang."

"Very good, water. Without water, nothing on this windblown desert of a planet, including you, myself, the happy colonists of Haboob City and of course, this little mining enterprise of the Aurumite Corporation of New Earth would survive." He tapped the rim of the glass. "There are only five known aquifers drawing water from fossil deposits

2

although there are bands of sandcrawlers, otherwise known as water prospectors, continuously searching for more. What aquifers they do locate and file claim on, Haboob City pays a price our operations budget cannot support. Which is why I depend on you and your raiders."

A silence descended on the room, broken only by the faint cry of the wind and patter of sand against the plexglass.

"Tell me about the raid on Zak Braddock's new find in Kilometer Twelve?"

Gorth ran a dry tongue over his lips. "Yeah, the family of sandcrawlers and their crew. Well, they had the shaft drilled down to the aquifer, their equipment set up and ready to start pumping into their tankers," he explained. "We hit them hard and fast before they could get off a distress call to the city." "So you were able to take over the claim and start filling up our tankers?"

"Um, not exactly." A drop of sweat hung trembling from Gorth's nose. "We were taken on by heavy and accurate pulse gun fire from behind the dunes. Lost five of my best men before we were able to make it back to the hoverplane and get away."

"Heavy and accurate pulse gun fire," Chang repeated calmly.

He touched a row of buttons and a screen came to life on a far wall. Framed against a burning tanker, a little girl in a torn and dirty dress held up a pulse gun, firing at an approaching band of Gorth's raiders.

"I understand she's the daughter of the claim owner, Zak Braddock. What would you say this child's age would be? Ten, maybe twelve?"

Gorth paled beneath his tan.

"Perhaps you've forgotten your past employment digging at the mine face at its lowest levels. Perhaps you would care to be reassigned back there?"

"Nossir, Mr. Chang."

"Surveillance from our company satellite monitoring the water prospectors," Chang continued. "Just before it passed out of range it showed your little antagonist wandering off into the desert. Do you know what this means, Mr. Gorth?"

The raider looked away from the now blank screen. "Um, nossir,

Mr. Chang."

"It means it is now safe for you and your brave lads to return to the claim, take it over and start pumping out water."

~ * ~

It had not been a good day for Hal and Ernie. The possible aquifer indicated by their sensing equipment turned out to be a glitch in the calibration after an hour of drilling probes through rock-hard sandstone. The comm set on the terratrax, necessary to monitor frequent and violent sandstorms, expired after a series of asthmatic wheezes. To crown a glorious day, a pillow block bearing on the starboard track runner seized, necessitating an emergency teardown under the blazing pink eye of Dustball's sun.

Hal wiped his face with a greasy rag and squinted at the rolling dunes on the horizon. "Hey, is that smoke I see?"

Ernie dropped a wrench into the toolbox and peered at the horizon. "Yeah. Say, ain't that the direction of Zak Braddock's new claim?"

"Pretty close to it. Why don't you finish up here while I take a look-see?"

Hal hiked down a canyon of shattered sandstone monoliths and slogged up the side of a huge dune to look down on a valley below.

Smoke oozed lazily from a wrecked service truck parked next to an overturned water tanker. Scattered around the wellhead machinery were the bodies of raiders and defenders of the claim. With a chill, Hal noticed from the torn clothing and position of the body the woman had been raped.

A lone droning arose and the dagger shape of a hoverplane drifted over the hills. A line of tracked vehicles followed, pulling to a stop at the wellhead.

"Claim jumpers," Hal whispered, easing himself down the dune.

Ernie had just completed repairs when Hal arrived, sweating and out of breath.

"You gonna have a coronary on me?" Ernie demanded.

"Claim jumpers over the hill, just showed up at Braddock's

claim," he panted. "We gotta make ourselves scarce in this vicinity."

"I found a cracked race in the bearing housing. It'll last until we get back to Haboob City and pick up a new…holy shit!"

A strangely familiar hum came from behind them. *Sounds like a blaster ramping up to full charge*, Hal thought and turned to see a little blonde girl in a ragged and smoke-stained dress standing a few feet away. The force pistol she held in her tiny hand seemed enormous. He groped with the unreality of it all until he saw the crazed blue fire in her eyes sighting along the barrel.

"Don't fire, we're the good guys," Ernie squalled, his hands reaching heavenwards. "Gimme a break, willya!"

The girl seemed to ponder his request before switching off the safety catch.

"Let's just back off a moment, honey," said Hal reasonably. "We're not claim jumpers."

"I don't wanna die." Ernie wailed. "Look toots, just gimme three steps and you won't see me no more."

The muzzle of the blaster lowered slightly. The girl looked from Ernie to Hal. "Who are you?"

"Just a pair of sandcrawers; water prospectors," said Hal. "Had to stop here and make repairs on our rig. I'm Hal Chavez and the guy over there on his knees crying is Ernie Potts."

"I'm Falle Braddock," she said after a moment's consideration.

"Your family had claim to the aquifer over the dune, right?"

The blue in her eyes darkened.

"Yes."

Hal nodded in sympathy. "Look, we're headed back to Haboob City and you're welcome to come along. Why don't you toss me your little toy and hop aboard?"

She glared, mouth set in a determined line.

"Not a chance, mister."

"Okay, Miss Blondie," Hal drawled. "You're in the middle of the Firestone Desert, about thirty clicks from toy stores, ice cream and a nice clean place to go potty. You wanna ride or walk?"

With reluctance she walked over and handed him the weapon.

5

"Thank you ever so much, Miss Braddock."

He turned to his partner. "Ernie, you want to show the lady a seat on our rig while I fire up the engines?"

"Um, I need a few moments first," he replied uneasily.

"What the hell for?"

"I think I pooped my pants."

~ * ~

"Boss, we have a problem."

Flasco chewed the plastic end of his spindriver and contemplated the ominous red light on the pump console. A line of tankers was parked by the wellhead behind him, veiled by smoke from a burning drill rig.

"Okay Flasco, what kind of problem?" said Gorth, looking over his shoulder while he rolled out pump hoses.

"Old man Braddock set up a really nice surprise for claim jumpers. State of the art booby trap on the pump controls." He shook his head in admiration. "Looks like he had time to arm it before your boys took him out."

"Well, stop farting around and disarm it," said Gorth impatiently.

"Not so easy. See the pad by the panel? It reads the DNA of the operator. Wrong DNA and something very bad happens to life forms in the vicinity."

Gorth eyed the control box warily. "What kind of booby trap we talking about here?"

"No way to tell until it goes off. Could be flesh-eating gas, lethal pulse of neutron X radiation, even a nest of sand wasps." He stood up, dusting off his knees. "I could work through the alarm codes, one by one."

"How long would this take?"

"About two weeks."

Gorth scowled. "Okay, the pump control security system is deactivated by a DNA reading of Braddock's hand on the pad, right?"

"Sure, but that crispy critter in yonder terratrax is what's left of him."

"A blood relative would have the same DNA reading, right?"

"Sure, but what…"

"Get a team out in the hoverplane and find the little girl, his daughter. Honk up Chang's mine security staff in Haboob City on the off chance she makes it there."

"Big sandstorm moving in, boss."

"How far can she go? Just find her."

~ * ~

The terratrax rode the storm like a ship in a heavy sea, swaying at each blast of wind-driven grit, riding up each dune and plowing down the slope. Hal eased around a dagger of basalt, which loomed suddenly though the murk on his infrared screen.

"Wonder why the raiders at Braddock's claim left then came back," he mused aloud. "Probably forgot to bring beer for the party." Ernie flinched as the storm lashed grit across the windshield.

"Yeah, some party. Murder, rape, destruction. I can imagine what that kid had to go through," said Hal. "Must be a traumatizing experience for a child."

"She's traumatized," Ernie snorted. "When I saw her blaster aimed at my nuts…"

"Okay, okay. Why don't you drive the sled while I go back and check on her?"

"Hey, I bet the first thing she says is 'Are we there yet?'"

Hal picked up a snackbar and a juice tube from the galley and made his way down the narrow corridor to the crew's quarters.

Falle had her nose pressed against a porthole watching the sand hurrying past. She greeted Hal's arrival with a blank reptilian stare.

"Are we there yet?" she demanded.

"You'll be the first to know. Listen, I thought you might be hungry."

He held out the snackbar and juice tube.

She turned the bar over in her hand with distaste. "What's this? A dried gomph dropping? Am I supposed to eat it?"

"You're very welcome," Hal retorted. "I planned to escort you to

7

the restaurant in our cargo hold but I remembered our French chef is off today."

With a surly grunt she peeled off the wrapper and stuffed it into her mouth.

"All right, I need to discuss what we're gonna do with you." He knelt in the aisle by her seat. "We're about ten zaks from Haboob City. You got any relatives there? Maybe back in the Homeworlds?"

Finishing off the snackbar she twisted the top from the juice tube and shook her head. "Just my father, Aunt Dee and Uncle Brad. They're all dead back at the claim." She stared moodily out the porthole. "I'm glad I shot them."

Hal blinked. "Excuse me?"

"The claim jumpers; they kept coming over the dune and I shot at them with the gun thing until they left." She looked up at Hal, the doll face and pale blue eyes hard. "I liked it, especially the one with the knife."

"The knife?"

Falle reached under her dress and unsheathed a serrated assault knife. She ran her fingers lovingly along the blade. "He's the one who did bad things to my Aunt Dee. I shot him in the crotch."

Hall took a deep breath. Picking up this lone survivor perhaps wasn't the most life-extending decision he had made of late. He held out his hand. "Maybe it would be a good idea if I kept it for you, huh?"

She graced him with a blend of defiance and scorn. "Okay, turn around, bend over and I'll give it to you."

"Whoa, hostility. I can see you're gonna make lots of friends when we get to…" He peered out the porthole at a line of winking lights. "Speaking of which, I think we've arrived."

The terratrax joined a line of hovertracks, tankers and sundry vehicles moving down a busy street. The sandstorm was winding down, revealing the polydome shapes of office buildings and brightly-lit storefronts. They pulled onto a sidestreet and killed the engines.

"Ernie, why don't you head to the part depot and pick up our bearing. See if they know anyone who can fix our comm set while you're there."

He looked over his shoulder to see Falle coming down the aisle.

"I gotta make tracks to the Peaceforce Station, fill out a report about the raid on Braddock's claim and find out what to do about little Miss Sunshine here."

The girl poked Hal in the ribs. "Can I have my blaster back?"

"Not a chance, kid." he retorted. "Why?"

"Because I want to point it at baldy here and see him poop his pants again."

Ernie glared at her and lurched from his seat toward the hatch. "I'll pick up the parts but I need a pit stop at the Sandcastle Bar first for a cold one."

"Don't get shit-faced, we need to get back to work. What say we meet back at the 'trax about six?" He studied Falle. "Why do you always have to be such a gomph's ass?"

She favored him with a smile. It was the first time he had seen her do this and he decided he didn't like it at all. There was something really...feral...in her smile.

~ * ~

"Look, buddy, we already got five reports of claim jumpers all over Dustball to investigate, plus eight murders, thirty armed robberies and the hijacking of an aurumite shipment in Haboob City alone." The sergeant behind the cluttered desk looked tired and overworked. He pushed a stack of forms toward Hal. "Just fill out a statement and we'll assign a case number. Now what about the kid?"

"I guess she's the lone survivor of the raid on her father's claim," Hal explained. "Anyplace I can take her?"

"Well, the City Shelter for Displaced or Abandoned Children has a long waiting list. Check with them tomorrow. You're gonna have to hang onto the kid until they have an opening."

"You have to be kidding." Hal sputtered. "Do I look like some kind of babysitter?"

"You accepted legal responsibility for her when you rescued her out in the desert. That's the law here on Dustball." He turned his back and began punching reports into a viscreen. "Have a nice day."

Standing at his side Falle snickered. "Seems like you're stuck with me."

"I was about to say the same thing to you," he retorted.

Hal sighed. He took in the torn dress and grimy face. "I suppose if we're going to be seen together, I should be doing something about you looking like a rag doll someone dragged out of an interplanetary landfill."

~ * ~

The bartender at the Sandcastle Bar and Grill watched the end of shift workers from the mine surge through the doors whooping and shouting to friends. Soon there would be spilled beer, bar fights, passes at his new and highly nubile server and hopefully…tips.

"Need another refill, pal." Ernie dropped an empty shot glass into the pile before him.

"Coming right up." The bartender hated whiny drunks but they were usually the best tippers, worth a little forced sympathy. "So, you're giving up water prospecting, huh? Working here in the city for your brother?"

"Danged right. Called him up at his tanker repair shop and heard he's looking for a good wrench turner. No more sweating my brains out in the desert for me."

"Hey Danny, how they hangin'?"

A tall woman in the uniform of mine security slipped into the stool beside Ernie.

"Elaine Dante, long time no see."

The bartender beamed at the new arrival. Elaine was one of the good tippers. "What'll it be?"

"Schooner of Fresian ale, nice and cold."

"You still angling for the job of security chief at the mine?"

He placed a foaming mug before her.

"I guess you're still hunting for the guys who hooked your aurumite shipment, huh? Promotion in the bag if you can nail them."

"Nah, old Chang has us out combing the entire city, looking for some little girl." She took a long pull at her mug and belched appreciatively.

"What did she do, hijack the shipment?"

"Hell, if I know. He just sent out an order to find her and turn her over to some spacer named Gorth."

"Snotty little blonde brat," Ernie announced to his pile of empty shot glasses.

Elaine looked over at him with interest. "This is funny. Chang didn't say nothing about her being blonde."

"Had a blaster pointed right at my family jewels," Ernie slurred. "Good old Hal decided to be Mother Theresa instead of leaving her little smart mouthed butt in the deshert."

"Say mister, you mind if I buy you a drink?" said Elaine, grinning.

Ernie blinked at her myopically. "That would be real shwell of you, buddy."

"Bring my friend a shot of whatever he's having," she said to the bartender. "Him and me got a lot to talk about."

~ * ~

The dressing room door opened and the saleslady ushered Falle past racks of children's clothes into the waiting area. "Here's the little lady, all shiny and new like a Homeworld penny," she gushed.

It was indeed a vast improvement with the new blue dress, a ribbon in her hair and freshly scrubbed face. "Would she be your daughter?"

Hal pushed himself off the uncomfortable and cushionless couch and groped for his wallet. "No ma'am. I was blessed by a benevolent fate she is not," he replied.

"Anyone can see he isn't my father," Falle huffed. "If he was, I'd be butt ugly and smell bad like him."

The saleslady seemed bemused. "My goodness, if it wasn't for the age difference, I would swear you two were married."

They took the transport shuttle across town. As they got off at the side street she tugged at his sleeve.

"Listen, about what I said in the clothing store."

Hal appraised her thoughtfully. She seemed abashed about something, chewing her lower lip and fidgeting.

"Well, don't be shy. Spit out what's on your mind."

"It's about my new dress and stuff."

"What about the new dress and stuff?"

"I kind of forgot...to thank you." She twisted her fingers together. "I'm sorry I called you ugly."

Hal was completely taken aback. "Wow, gratitude and common courtesy. I didn't know you had it in you, blondie."

She flushed. "Okay, you're not the best example of good taste and personal hygiene. In fact..."

She peered over Hal's shoulder. "I think we should leave now."

He followed her gaze and noticed the black tailfin of a hoverplane behind the terratrax.

"If it isn't Miss Braddock and Mr. Chavez." Gorth and four of his raiders stepped from a side alley. They had their hands resting on the butts of their force pistols. "How about a nice scenic flight into the Firestone Desert," said Gorth. "I hear its right pretty around sunset."

~ * ~

The sun was low on the horizon, painting a red tableau of parked water tankers and the group of raiders. Walking down the ramp from the hoverplane with Falle close behind him, Hal was relieved to see the bodies of her family had been removed. There was still a lingering trace of sun ripened corpses overlaid by smoke. Gorth gave him a final shove in the direction of the aquifer pump controls.

"Flasco, I'd like you to meet Miss Braddock and her friend Mr. Chavez." He grinned at the little man loaded down with toolbelt and meters. "The little lady has volunteered to help us with our small problem."

"Sure, some small problem."

He took in the little girl staring at him with cold blue fire in her eyes. *Damn, she's got a mean set of peepers,* he thought.

"Your father showed you how to arm and disarm the DNA reader on the pump controls, right?"

"Of course he, did," she replied sullenly.

"Glad to hear this. Tell you what, lots of candy in store for you if you disarm dear old Dad's booby trap."

"Lots of candy, huh? I'm almost eleven years old, you little pile of puke," she retorted. "Go take a hike."

"Kinda thought she'd say that." Gorth jerked out his force pistol and shoved it against the side of Hal's head. "Care to make any dumber decisions, Miss Braddock?"

Falle contemplated the circle of grinning raiders. The expression on her doll face could have been carved from marble. She walked over to the pump console and began pushing buttons. A siren began to scream while a red eye blazed into life. She placed her hand on the DNA sensor pad and twisted a switch. The siren squelched off and the red eye segued to a mellow green. She looked up at Gorth.

"It's safe to operate now," she declared. "I have to go potty really bad."

Gorth smugly holstered his weapon. "Flasco, get the tankers over here and start up the pumps. I'm gonna escort the kid over by them sandstone slabs so she can have a tad of privacy. Oh yeah, why don't you tag along too, Mr. Chavez?"

The whine of water tankers starting up echoed back and forth among the crags.

"This is far enough."

Hal saw Gorth had his weapon out and a determined set to his jaw. He grabbed Falle and pushed her behind him.

"Getting ready to tie up some loose ends, huh, dirtbag?" he said.

"Well, we can't have Miss Braddock here showing up in Haboob City claiming beneficiary's rights to Mr. Chang's new aquifer, can we?" he snorted. "Okay, which one of you gets it first...?"

A flash of green incandescence lit up three silhouettes on a sandstone slab. A wave of superheated air washed over them. The group of raiders about the well became transparent before blossoming into fountains of emerald gas. Faint cries drifted across the valley.

"What in the goddamned blazes of hell." Gorth snarled and then uttered a thin scream as the assault knife slid into his vitals. He took a single palsied step before falling on his face on the sand.

Hal watched with utter disbelief while Falle jerked the knife from the body and with surly contempt wiped it clean on his shirt.

"You know, I'm not complaining," he said after a moment's contemplation of the silent water tankers clustered about the well head. "But I thought you disarmed Dad's booby trap at the pump?"

"I didn't disarm it because I couldn't," she said. "I'm Zak Braddock's *adopted* daughter. My real father was Mike Crandell."

Hal whistled silently. "Looks like Mr. Chang of the Aurumite Corporation was so eager to get his mitts on this aquifer he neglected to check out some facts."

A hot wind sighed over the valley floor, heralding the coming sunset. Falle raised her face to Hal, dropping her gaze downward.

"So, what's going to happen to me now?" she asked. "I suppose…we'll be heading back to the city. Maybe they have room now at the Center for Displaced or Abandoned Children."

Hal realized he was no longer looking at the feral eyes of a vengeful survivor but the face of a lonely and frightened child.

"Actually, I was thinking of how swell we get along together. Since good old Zak Braddock thought what a bright idea it was to adopt you maybe I could put up with doing the same."

Hal felt her hand slide into his. From the corner of her eyes two tears slid down her cheeks. She smiled a soft and happy smile.

~ * ~

The new chief of security for the Aurumite Corporation on Dustball stood on the tan plush in front of Mr. Chang's ornate desk. She had her thumbs hooked into her gunbelt and was idly watching the busy workings of men and machinery through the plexglass. She appeared almost bored.

Mr. Chang felt a worm of unease. He loved browbeating subordinates, especially the late Mr. Gorth whom he enjoyed reducing to a state of quivering jelly on occasion. It appeared if Ms. Elaine Dante was any more relaxed, she would be asleep.

"The aquifer on Kilometer Thirty has run dry and the contract with the one on Kilometer Eight is about to expire." He assumed his sternest expression. "We have at best two days of water left to sustain our mining operations."

"Yes, sir, I've read the reports," she said.

"Our surveillance satellite has shown the claim at Kilometer Twelve is up and running at full blast. Do you have an explanation Ms. Dante?"

"Evidently the young Miss Crandell inherited the claim. She and her partner obtained funding from a major New Earth bank when it was discovered the aquifer held millions of deciliters of fossil water."

"I promoted you to security chief as a reward for locating Miss Crandell and now you tell me she is running the operation there?" His scowl deepened to no avail. His attempt to intimidate Ms. Dante was going nowhere. "So, what's this about a partner?"

Elaine shrugged. "The partner is a Mr. Hal Chavez and the operation is called the Crandell and Chavez Water Company."

Chang's mouth fell open. "Are you serious?"

"Yes sir. In fact, our finance department contacted them regarding a possible purchase of their water output."

A faint flicker of hope arose with another spasm of heartburn. "What was their reply?"

An enigmatic smile played over her face. "I really don't think you want to hear their reply, Mr. Chang."

A chime sounded from a ceiling speaker. "A priority one communication is coming in from New Earth," crackled a metallic voice.

A jowled and stern-looking executive wearing a tailored grey jumpsuit appeared on a wall screen.

Chang turned to the screen, pushing his glasses farther up his nose. "Good morning, Mr. Calomini. What a pleasure it is to see you," he said, affecting a weak smile.

A priority one call from the Senior Director of the Aurumite Corporation was unusual - Ominous.

"Good morning to you, Mr. Chang, although perhaps it won't end that way; The Board of Directors has decided to terminate your employment at the mine on Dustball."

Chang jerked as if he'd been slapped. "Terminate my employment at the mine?" he sputtered. "You can't do this, I have seniority…"

"Dustball is a Right To Work planet. We have the option to terminate at will." The face on the wall screen looked impassively down.

"But…why?" Chang groped for an argument which would avert this catastrophe.

"Seventy percent of the shares in this mine have been purchased by a local investor."

"Local investor?"

"Crandell and Chavez Water Company; Part of the agreement was your termination, effective immediately." Mr. Calomini's lips moved slightly in an expression of sympathy. "Deep regrets, Mr. Chang, and best of luck."

The wall screen went blank.

Two burly security guards appeared on either side of Elaine Dante. She nodded toward the big desk.

"Escort Mr. Chang to the main gate," she ordered.

Voicing threats and shrill protests to no avail, he was hustled to the elevator, past gaping office workers to the steel exit gate on the grounds.

"I have a final message to deliver, Mr. Chang," Elaine said, as they stood on the dirt road.

Angrily shaking off the guard's hands, Chang straightened his suit, glaring at her.

"Well, what is it?"

She looked at one of the guards who spun Chang about and planted a number fourteen size boot on his rear, sending him sprawling face first into the gravel.

"Miss Falle Crandell sends her regards," said Elaine Dante.

Chapter Two

CONGRATS HABOOB CITY GRADS! The banner proclaimed high above the auditorium floor where celebrating students gyrated. Orion basshorns vibrated walls where colored beams pulsed to the music. Groups of students clustered around tables where snacks and bowls of fruit punch had been set out.

A gangly youth approached a cluster of boys gossiping about a table and nudged one in the ribs.

"How's the fruit punch, Sann?" he asked.

Sann made a face. "Tastes like fruit punch. Wanna swill some, Dik?"

"I got something here to give it a little bite." He slipped a flask from his tuxedo.

"Dik. You the man."

Sann furtively eyed the group of parents and school administrators at a far corner of the room and held out his cup.

Dik tipped the flask into his friend's cup and took in the festive atmosphere. "Seems the whole school showed up," he mused. "Say, who's the cute wedge?" He nodded his head at a slender blonde sitting in an alcove, staring moodily at the dancers.

"That's Chavez' stepdaughter, Falle Crandell," he explained. "They live to hell and back, out by the Firestone Water Plant."

Dik studied the slim form in the blue satin dress. "Hmm, nice legs, perky little tits. How come we never seen her at any of the other dances?"

"Ah, she's not too sociable, doesn't have many friends at school. She's probably here because Admin put it out the grad dance is a mandatory event."

"She does have a bedroom bod. I think I might mosey over and ask her for a dance."

"I noticed she's turned down a couple of guys already who asked her. Like I said, she's not too sociable."

"Hey, not only am I the hottest jock in the place but also the son of the mayor of Haboob City. How can she refuse?"

"Knock yourself out then, superjock."

~ * ~

Falle shifted her position on the uncomfortable bench and glanced at her timeband for what seemed the hundredth time. Twenty more zaks to endure this bullshit. She noticed Hal had disappeared down a hallway with his arm around her biology teacher. *Right, biology.* She sniffed and glanced again at her timeband.

A youth wearing an immaculately tailored tuxedo suddenly stood before her. "Say, you got time for a dance?" he asked.

"Sorry, I have sort of a sprained ankle," she replied, eyeing him warily. "Thanks, anyway."

"See the old guy standing by the redball hoop? He's Mr. Blunt, the school president," Dik smiled winningly. "He sent me over to remind you one dance is mandatory at the grad night celebration. By the way, my name is Dik Smedlap."

Falle took in the almost handsome face above the tuxedo and shrugged. "Well, if I must." She rose, smoothing out the creases in her dress.

The music had segued into a slow waltz as they moved out onto the floor among the crowd of dancers.

"You must be Falle Crandell," he essayed, taking a peek at her cleavage. "I like the perfume you're wearing. Smells expensive."

"It is," she replied, moving to the sway of the music. "My dad had it shipped from New Earth City."

"You mean, your stepfather, Hal Chavez," he observed.

"He raised me, which makes him my father."

Falle was aware of a trace of condensation on the hand inching downwards.

"I suppose so," Dik nodded. "So, what happened to your real parents?"

"They were both killed when a Umas raiding party dropped a firebomb on the settlement out by red Vista. I was told I was the only survivor."

"So, you're planning someday to change your name to Falle Chavez?"

"Getting a little personal, aren't we?" She sensed the hand was approaching the proscribed zone below her panty line. "You want to move your paw up where it belongs? That's getting personal too."

"Ah, I think you like where my paw is, sugarbowls," he grinned, giving her cheek a squeeze.

"Get your hand off my ass, squort snot," she hissed.

"You know, I had a wet dream last night about someone just like you. Wanna help me make it a reality?"

The next moment he found himself flat on the dance floor, blood dripping from his nose, spotting his white cravat. The dancers around them stopped to gape, before erupting in a storm of laughter.

Dik scrambled to his feet. He took in the hooting faces, his own face reddening with rage and embarrassment.

"Why, you little bitch," he sputtered. "I autta slap your lips to the moons."

Falle unsnapped her timeband, tucking it into a dress pocket. She smiled, flexing her fists.

"Anytime you're ready, Mr. Head," she invited.

~ * ~

School security officer Gradski was leaning back in his office chair, feet resting on a cluttered deck when Hal was led into his office.

"Good evening to you, Mr. Chavez," he greeted. "Took my boys a little time to track you down. You know, a classroom desk ain't the most comfortable spot for a romantic encounter."

Hal gave him a sheepish grin. "Yeah, I suppose so. Listen, I need to pick up my daughter."

"Ah yes, the gentle and meek Miss Crandell."

"So, what the hell happened at the dance?" Hal demanded. "All the info I got from your two goons when I asked was a lot of dumb sniggering."

"You might say she provided the evening's floor show." Officer Gradski leaned farther back in his chair and smiled sardonically. "She beat up the mayor's son."

Hal's mouth fell open. "She did what?"

"Busted jaw, broken nose and a couple of cracked ribs I'm told," he explained. "She been taking advanced lessons in karate or something?"

Hal shook his head. "She pals around with the mechanics and well diggers at the water plant. Some of them are pretty tough spacers."

"Well, I just got off the horn with Mayor Smedlap." His grin widened. "He was screaming like a ruptured sandcat. You might wanna scoot outta Dodge before he shows up with an army of personal injury lawyers."

"So where is she now?"

"My two goons are bringing her in right now. And by the way…" He gestured at Hal's pants. "Might be a good idea to zip up before she arrives."

A moment later Falle was escorted into the office. She was wearing a torn dress, a bruised cheek and a truculent smirk.

Officer Gradski chucked a thumb at the door. "You two have a nice trip back to the boonies."

The twin moons of Dustball cast bisecting shadows over rows of parked aircars and terratrax on the school parking lot while Falle and Hal wound their way to their sandskimmer. She stole a furtive look at her stepfather.

"It wasn't my fault, you know," she said.

"Okay, I don't wanna know all the details about you providing the graduation class evening entertainment," Hal sighed. "I think your future employment prospects in Haboob city are pretty much down the toilet."

Falle stared morosely at a meteor painting a crimson line over distant hills. "Dad, he had his hand so far down my…"

"I'm sure you had a reasonable complaint before wiping the dance floor with the mayor's son. Since we're now on the subject of a career path after graduation, any bright inspirations occur to you?"

"You mean like applying for admission to universities on New Earth? I've been receiving non- subtle hints from you the past few months."

"Something along those lines."

"Boring, boring." She kicked at a clump of dirt on the treads of a terratrax. "I can't see me warming a chair whilst staring at a comp viewscreen the rest of my life. I want something with a little more, you know, action."

Hal chuckled. "So, what university on New Earth has a curriculum on beating up people?"

"Come on, Dad. It's not like I crippled the jerk for life."

"Okay, okay. Just kidding."

Falle chewed her lip, looking up at him with eyes luminous from the glow of the Westering moon. "So how about me signing up with the Colonial Marines?"

"You're only eighteen."

"Could they…"

A low drone vibrated the loose rivets on the terratrax beside them. An expanse of night sky and stars was blotted out by a passing bat-like shape. They watched it descend over the city, red and blue landing lights flashing from wingtips.

"That's not a supply freighter." Falle exclaimed excitedly. "It's a space liner."

"Pan Galaxy just started a weekly run to Dustball, returning from their usual tour of Verdana and Swampworld," Hal explained. "Seems a bunch of tourists on New Earth have taken an interest in visiting the exotic desert scenery here. Remember Mayor Smedlap throwing up his luxury hotel last month?"

Floodlights on the space liner cut in. It came to a hover and dropped from sight with a distant whine of turbines.

Hal eyed the rapt figure at his side. "I did hear something about Pan Galaxy starting an intern program. You begin as a flight attendant, work your way up to astrogater and get in line to take the starpilot test."

Falle's voice radiated excitement. "You're kidding? Really?"

"Okay, I see you're not interested," Hal smiled. "I do have an opening for pump mechanic at the water plant…"

~ * ~

"Ms. Lizardo will see you now," the secretary announced, holding open the door to the executive office.

Falle took a deep breath and smoothed out the creases in her blue astrogater's uniform. She rummaged mentally through a file of possible misdeeds which would entail a summons from the Pan Galaxy Director of Operations.

Ms. Lizardo occupied an antique speerwood desk so enormous it appeared to make her dwarfish. Behind her a wall of plexglass displayed a panorama of New Earth city spread out far below. Seated beside her desk was a tall captain, wearing a starpilot's uniform.

"Good morning, Ms. Crandell," Lizardo greeted her. "Won't you take a seat? May I introduce Captain Rann Glassford of the Starpilot Academy."

Falle shook his hand and nervously perched herself on the edge of the chair. She watched Lizardlips, as she was known behind her back, rifle through a file.

"I can see you've almost completed your probationary period as a Class B astrogater and have applied for training as a star pilot." Lizardo peered bleakly over the folder. "I see no demerits aside from a certain lack of smiling courtesy in dealing with difficult passengers. You do have a commendation for thwarting the attempted hijacking of Flight 167 out of Planet Dropoff. However, knocking the miscreant through the plate glass window of the terminal was a bit excessive."

"Um, I can explain…"

"You have been accepted for the star pilot training program," Lizardo announced. "Captain Glassford here will be the instructor for the course which starts next quarter."

Falle swallowed hard. "Thank you, Ms. Lizardo. I appreciate your confidence in me."

She felt a glow flood her body. A chance for a career as a pilot for the largest space fleet…

Something was wrong. The atmosphere in the room seemed to thicken. She felt a shiver of dread when she noticed Lizardo and Captain Glassford exchange somber expressions.

"One more thing, Cadet Crandell," Lizardo began. "Earlier this morning, I received a hyperspace message from the coroner's office of Haboob City on Dustball. It would seem your stepfather's sandskimmer struck an old Umas personnel landmine. I'm sorry to say he did not survive."

A dagger of pain lanced Falle's heart. She felt suddenly sick, lightheaded and fought down tears welling up in her eyes.

"If you need time to return home, this can be arranged before your enrollment in the program."

Lizardo suggested gently.

They were both watching her. She sensed this was her first test. Star pilots were expected to endure stress and crisis situations with calm professionalism.

"The only time I need, Ms. Lizardo, is the time to enroll for training as scheduled," she replied in a voice which sounded alien to her.

"I understand. Captain Glassford will escort you to your new quarters."

In the hallway outside the executive office Falle leaned against a wall. A single tear slid down her cheek to drip onto her Pan Galaxy flight pin.

"Are you feeling all right, Cadet Crandell?"

Falle gazed into the craggy face and deepset sympathetic blue eyes. "I'm just weighing my two options, Captain."

"Excuse me?"

"Option one is finding a closet in which to cry my eyes out," she replied. "Option two is heading for the spaceport bar and getting totally shitfaced."

Captain Glassford chuckled. "Then you might consider an option three."

"Option three?"

"I know a nice bistro overlooking Grissom Falls which serves a superb gorth steak and vintage wine."

Falle straightened up, quickly wiping a sleeve over her eyes. "Is this some kind of request for a date, Captain?"

Glassford effected a shocked expression. "Of course not, cadet. It's more in the line of social orientation for a new student."

"Dutch treat, then."

"Certainly, Cadet Crandell."

~ * ~

A vast jungle swept below the cruising space liner; a carpet of featureless green, broken only by winding brown creeks and an occasional pond choked by colorful water plants. Ominous grey mists swirled over muddy banks.

"Attention passengers of the Swampworld Excursion," announced speakers throughout the Pan Galaxy tour ship. "We are now a few zaks from landing on the observation pad where you can stretch your legs and experience the flora and fauna of this amazing planet far below. Through the viewport to your right is Blackmud Lake, the breeding waters for the dreaded snakeoids."

"I don't like the vibration coming from the port stabilizer, Captain DeGras," observed Falle, scanning the dials on the console before her.

"We pick up vibrations from this planet's humidity and high oxygen content," DeGras replied, punching in the landing sequence. "Nothing to soil your panties about."

Falle considered what next to say, watching a gauge ease into the red zone. She and DeGras had not been on the best of terms since she had beaten him at arm wrestling during a company party.

"I'm picking up a high temperature reading on the stabilizer plasma feed also," she persisted.

"Ah, we get this every now and again. No big deal, honey."

"The readout is half way into the red zone, Captain. I think we should abort the landing and get back into orbit so we can sort out the problem."

Captain DeGras shot her an annoyed glance. "I didn't know you'd been promoted from co-pilot status, Crandell. Tell you what, if you still remember how, kindly activate landing struts before we…"

A sharp detonation rocked the ship. With a sickening lurch to starboard the space liner dropped like an anvil. Throughout the huge vessel passengers began screaming.

~ * ~

This was the desert of Dustball: A sea of red sand stretching out the horizon with endless kilometers. A pale light from the setting sun warmed the red crystal spires of Garnet Peaks in the far distance, turning them into ruby daggers.

A breeze tossed blonde hair around Falle's six-year-old shoulders while she sat on a carpet of red sand, spreading her dress over tiny spring flowers studding the gravel like jewels. All around her was stillness, a deep, timeless void of peace.

There came the intrusion of sharp hospital odors; disinfectant, bleached linen, newly waxed linoleum. From an enveloping fog came voices:

"So how is the sole survivor from the spaceliner crash on Swampworld coming along today, Nurse Theodorus?"

"Ms. Crandell's bioscan shows some puzzling abnormalities from yesterday, Dr. Bell."

"Let me see her chart. I take it the search party removed the final bodies from the crash site?"

"As of last night, Doctor."

Memories floated from the fog; the crippled starliner leaving a fiery trail through the atmosphere. The impact to the jungle below, the flames and screaming passengers and an explosion throwing her into a pool of stinking swamp water, she, floundering helplessly in green mud.

"The snakeoids didn't leave much after they finished feeding. Family members were warned not to open the caskets."

"Yes, I've been to the morgue. It's probably what saved her life, being trapped up to her neck in swamp mud. No heat signature for the snakeoids to home in on."

"Blood test just came back from the lab, Dr. Bell. I think you should see them."

"Oh my, that's not good. I hope this isn't what I think it is, Nurse Theodorus."

The fog rolled in. She began to drift off to a darkened void. Drifting….

~ * ~

The view from the window was fantastic. The twin suns of New Earth shone down on the city below, lines of speeding aircars winding between tall office spires, the lush green rectangle of Buzz Aldrin Park nestled by a tiny lakelet. She was in a private room, no less.

Falle frowned. How, when her company health insurance was becoming more rapacious each year? She was sitting up in bed, the remains of a breakfast tray on a table beside her. Behind a long glass window, a constant stream of white-clad orderlies, nurses and technicians hurried past.

The door opened and a gloved and masked nurse bustled in. "There you are, Ms. Crandell," she greeted her. Eyes above the surgical mask exuded cheer. "How are we doing this morning?"

Falle considered the question. "Actually, I feel great. How long have I been enjoying your hospitality?"

"About five days." The nurse ran a scanner across her chest and checked the readouts on the stasis board over the bed. "I'm glad you enjoyed your breakfast. Dr. Bell will be in to see you shortly."

"So, when can I leave?"

"Dr. Bell will be discussing this with you." The eyes above the mask looked troubled, then brightened. "My goodness, it would seem you have a visitor."

A starpilot in a Pan Galaxy uniform stood outside the window. He smiled, holding up a bouquet of flowers.

"Rann." cried Falle happily. "There's my boyfriend. Can he come in?"

"Not quite yet: doctor's orders." The nurse seemed flustered and turned to gather up the breakfast tray.

"Doctor's orders? Why?"

"He'll be talking about that shortly, Ms. Crandell."

Behind the glass Rann smiled and blew her a kiss.

~ * ~

"Why does everyone keep asking how I'm feeling? I usually feel with my hands and sometimes with my toes."

Falle was sitting on the edge of the bed wearing the standard peekaboo hospital gown. Boredom from the long wait to see the doctor who was now finally perched on a chair opposite her was raising her level of irritation. She noticed with a whisper of dread he was wearing surgical gloves and a mask.

"It's just one of the usual pleasantries this hospital requires us to use," Dr. Bell replied affably. "Informing our patients they look like something the cat dragged in sometimes interferes with their recovery."

"Is this an attempt at humor?" she asked acidly. "Well, have I recovered to the point where I can find some clothes and get back to my life?"

"That is something we need to discuss." The eyes over the mask held her with a level stare. "We haven't finalized all our tests yet and recommend you remain here for observation."

"Tests for what?"

Falle sensed something bad was coming her way. She wished he would remove the mask so she could read the message on his face.

"We think you may have the hydrophis virus."

"The what?"

"A nasty little bug we see a few people picking up on Swampworld. It's a type of blood disease, very little of which we understand."

Falle felt a chill gather about her heart. "I feel great. Actually, more than great."

"I'm sure you do," he agreed. "You're just a carrier. What the hydrophus virus does is release a class M neurotoxin into all the host's body fluids; a toxin powerful enough to kill in seconds."

"I feel fine," Falle protested. "Look, Doctor Bell, I just want to go home."

"We're hoping the final tests come back negative, Ms. Crandell. But if they don't…"

"Well, what if they don't?"

Doctor Bell drummed his fingers on the armrest of the chair. "In the event of a positive report we encourage the infected person to enter the treatment facility on Asteroid IXV."

Falle fought down panic. "What if I… or, the infected person refuses to go?"

"Entry into the treatment center is voluntary, of course."

Doctor Bell's sigh of regret was muffled by the mask. "Unfortunately, at this time the hospital, under the Alien Disease and Infections Protocol, is required to inform all persons who may come in contact with this individual of the potential hazards."

This last statement hung in the air like a scalpel. "Isn't there some medicine available, some kind of serum?" she persisted.

Dr. Bell rubbed his nose under the mask. "Rivergreede Pharmaceuticals have an experimental detoxant serum with a high success rate. Unfortunately, it is quite expensive."

"Um…could you define expensive?"

"Somewhere in the neighborhood of thirty thousand creds. I don't think your current medical insurance would cover an expense this extensive."

"You don't think?" For the first time Falle noticed a strange symbol imprinted in her left palm. "What is this?"

"It's the hazmat symbol. Hospital policy requires us to identify hydrophis carriers," Dr. Bell explained. "Also, it's for your protection."

"My protection?"

"If you were to receive a blood transfusion of your current type it would kill you."

Falle slipped off the bed and stood up. "Doctor Bell, would you be so good as to contact my boyfriend to pick me up. Some clothes and shoes close to my size would be nice."

"Very well," he shrugged. "In the meantime, I strongly recommend you avoid physical contact with him."

At this moment the one thing Falle desired was to be enveloped in Rann's strong and protective arms and to feel his lips on hers. She looked questioningly at him. "What kinds of physical contact to avoid?"

"*All* physical contact."

~ * ~

Rann's aircar lifted from the hospital flight deck and swooped down into the stream of commuters on the Western Flyway. He handled his craft the way he kissed her, Falle thought in the seat beside him. Smoothly, with an expert touch on the controls.

"You've been quiet as a falmouse since I picked you up at the hospital, hon," he said, glancing over at her. "It must have been quite an ordeal for you on Swampworld. I saw your picture on the Interworld News."

"Uh huh, I saw it on my room viscreen," she replied. "Maybe I'll become rich and famous."

He smiled. "Are we heading to my place for dinner?"

Falle winced inwardly, clenching her fists. "It might be best if you'd just drop me off at my apartment."

"Huh?" He looked startled.

"They're still running some tests on me."

"Tests for what?"

"Doctor Bell thinks…" She swallowed hard. "I might have the hydrophis virus."

"Holy shit!" The craft inadvertently dropped, causing a warning siren and another aircar below to swerve to avoid collision.

"Obviously you've heard about it."

"Yeah, I have." He leaned forward, gripping the control tightly. "It's very rare and incurable. New Earth has an isolation facility on Asteroid IXV." He made a wry face. "I hear it's like an Old Earth leper colony."

Falle placed a hand on his arm. "What if the tests come back positive?"

He looked over at her, managing a weak smile. "I'm sure it will turn out fine, hon. Yeah, not to worry."

She stood before the slidedoor to her apartment on the ninety-first floor of the Yuri Gagarin Building, rummaging through her purse for her passcard. It was the only item of hers the rescue team had salvaged from the wreck of the starliner and it still felt damp and smelled faintly of jungle plants.

"Nice to see you again, Ms. Crandell," said a voice behind her.

She turned to see Jinghua, her neighbor from across the hall. There was always something about Jinghua which made Falle uneasy. Perhaps it was the tight black bodysuit she always seemed to wear, or the reptilian glint in her obsidian dark eyes.

"Yeah, thanks."

"How are you feeling?"

"You know, everyone asks me that and the answer is just peachy." She fished the passcard from her purse. "Well, I gotta get ready for work tomorrow."

"I would think you might wish to take it easy for a few days." Jinghua's voice was like a snake gliding over dry grass.

"I feel like I've been taking it easy in the hospital for a year," she replied, jamming the passcard into the door slot.

"Now I need to get back to my life."

~ * ~

The cake was a masterpiece of sugared art. The little plastic girl in the Pan Galaxy uniform floated in a swamp of green icing surrounded by a menacing circle of candy snakeoids.

"Welcome back, Falle." The crowd of pilots, flight attendants and baggage clerks chorused as she entered the employee lounge from the arrivals tube.

"Guys, you really shouldn't have," she beamed at them, dropping her flight bag.

"We know," a second shift navigator grinned. "Any idea of how hard we had to work covering your butt while you lounged about in the hospital?"

"Well, go ahead and cut the cake," ordered a pilot, handing her a knife and a stack of plates. "I see you made it back from the cargo run to Lexan without navigating the ship into the ground like you did on Swampworld."

"Pretty harsh remark from someone who forgot to extend the landing struts before touchdown on Parsus IV, Mr. Grete," Falle smirked, stabbing the knife into the cake. "Who wants one of the candy snakeoids?"

"Attention," a voice barked from an overhead speaker. "Would Flight Officer Falle Crandell please report to Ms. Lizaro's office."

"Hey, Lizardlips wants to award the raise Falle's been whining for all season," Grete exclaimed.

"Only in your dreams, Phil," Falle smirked, pushing a plateful of cake into his hands.

~ * ~

Ms. Lizardo looked bleakly over the top of the folder, clearing her throat. "I'm sorry, Ms. Crandell, but I'm afraid its company policy."

"Two weeks' notice?" Falle stared across the ornate desk cluttered with commdiscs, reports and scattered memo tabs. "I have seniority here at Pan Galaxy with eight years of service."

"New Earth is a Right to Work planet. Seniority or years of service are not applicable here."

"Two weeks' notice…"

"Interstellar travel has been down due to the rebellion in Zabo's Belt, you know."

She seemed unable to look Falle directly in the face. She chewed nervously on her lower lip. "I see you've been reassigned shuttle duty to a Mr. Vox on the country of Euphoria, on the other side of New Earth."

"Not Big Vox?" Falle exclaimed, her voice tight with outrage.

"He's one of the most notorious druglords in Methtropolis City. Fairyspit, dhungweed, moondust, you name it."

Ms. Lizardo dropped the folder onto her desk with an air of finality. "I'm sorry, Ms. Crandell. That's the way it is."

~ * ~

The first sight to greet Falle on her return to her apartment that evening was rain beating on the front room window, perfectly matching her mood. She trudged over to check the messages on her autotalk, the flight bag over her shoulder feeling like a lead weight.

"Good evening, Falle," a disgustingly cheerful voice announced as the wall viscreen came to life. "You have two new messages."

"Greetings from United Mediscam, your insurance healthcare provider," came from a grimly smiling woman in an executive jumpsuit. "The initial bill for your five day stay in New Earth General Hospital has been processed at United Mediscam. Medications, tests and doctor consultations have been covered under your usual eighty-five per cent copay. Items not covered under your existing plan is the private room required by the hospital, air ambulance transportation, bed linen, towels, shower water and miscellaneous toiletries. Please submit your balance of eight thousand, four hundred creds before the end of the month. Thank you for being a member of United Mediscam, your partner in health security."

Falle let her flight bag drop to the carpet. She was looking around for the nearest seat to collapse into when another face popped onto the viscreen. It was Ms. Sanchez, the apartment manager.

"Hi Falle, how are you?" The welcoming smile looked frayed. "I'm so sorry to have to give you notice of termination of your lease. You've been a great tenant and we at Uri Gagarin will certainly miss you. A copy of the Hazardous Tenant Act will be included with your deposit refund. Best of luck."

The viscreen went blank.

Falle stood transfixed before the rain streaked window. So, this was why she lost her job at Pan Galaxy, she realized with a shock. Doctor

Bell must have notified all her business and personal contacts under…what did he call it? The Alien Disease and Infection Protocol. She didn't have, couldn't have the hydrophis virus. She felt great.

Frantically, she dialed Rann's number on the autotalk. She could hear the signal buzzing on the speakers, over and over, then a mechanical voice.

"I'm sorry, the person you are attempting to contact is not available."

Never in her life had she felt so abandoned. She fought down a wave of panic and forced herself to think. Rann was probably out with another pilot and had forgotten his palmreader. She had a passcard to his suite and the citywide transit tube was on roof level three. She grabbed her purse and fled the apartment.

The rain increased, slanting past the lightglobes lining the roof. Rows of glistening aircars dripped water onto the polyasphalt, black rain-spotted puddles collecting in the gutters.

She reached the overhang leading to the transit tube when a sleek aircar swooped down, settling with a descending whine of turbines. The hatch opened and Jinghua emerged. She spotted Falle and walked over.

"You know, there have been two rapes, five muggings and two murders at this level this time of night," she observed.

Falle pulled the collar of her jumpsuit tighter as a trickle of icy rainwater ran down her back. "Well, I didn't do them," she retorted, scanning the transit departure schedule on the wall. "The rapes, anyway."

"You seem upset."

"Life was never better for me, really."

She looked into black eyes, unblinking and reflecting glints from the overhead podlights.

"Can I give you a lift?"

"Well… perhaps you could…"

Two shadows emerged from the night. Falle felt a forearm encircle her throat from behind, choking her. She struggled, clawing for air.

"You take the chinkette, Radnor, I'll have this little blonde. Damn, she's a fighter!"

She tore at the muscular arm choking her, flashes of red before her vision. In desperation she forced her chin down and sank her teeth into the man's forearm.

Suddenly, she was alone on her hands and knees on the wet deck. Coughing, she looked up to see her assailant lying face down beside her. With disbelief she watched Jinghua calmly thrust a knife into the belly of the second assailant and jerk it upwards, disemboweling him. She strolled over to the body beside Falle, turning it over. Blank, staring eyes looked upwards into nothing. "Zog's Ass, he's dead as a smelt," she observed, wiping her blade clean on his shirt. "What did you do to him?"

"Nothing. He just grabbed me from behind and I..." She gasped, suddenly knowing why he died.

Several shadows were closing in from the dark recesses of the garage.

"Uh oh. Looks like their friends have arrived," said Jinghua.

She helped Falle to her feet and led her to her aircar. "Get in," she ordered, opening the hatch.

~ * ~

The rundown little bar was on the lowest level of the city, its clientele mostly dockloaders, starfreighter crewmen and assorted characters who seemed to have no obvious means of employment.

From a dim alcove Falle tossed down her third Faux Manhattan with a shaking hand. She looked across the table where Jinghua was studying her with a fixed feline stare. "Shouldn't we be calling the Peace Force about what happened at the garage?" she demanded.

"Why? They find dead muggers all the time, smart not to get involved," Jinghua replied slowly, as if explaining to a child. "Do you want to lose your job?"

Falle snorted. "Funny you should bring that up, I just did."

"You did?"

"For the next two weeks until my termination date, I'll be navigator on the shuttle to some dirtbag druglord named Big Vox."

"Mr. Vox. Yes, the name does sound familiar." Jinghua lifted a carafe from the battered table and refilled their glasses. "So, tell me how your mugger died." Her eyes bored relentlessly into Falle's.

"I suppose by now everyone on the planet must have heard. I have the hydrophis virus."

"Ah yes," Jinghua nodded. "The 'kiss of death'."

"Would you like one?" Falle suggested bitterly. She took another deep swallow and coughed. She was vaguely aware she had far exceeded her limit and her vision was starting to blur. "Wash with the knife you're packing. Thash illegal, you know." She slurred.

"Because what I do is illegal. I'm a contractor for the Borgia Guild."

"Great. You kill people for a living."

"I prefer to regard it as the removal of unpleasant obstacles in other people's lives." She took a slow sip from her glass. "In fact, since you're soon to be unemployed, we may have a job for you."

Falle blinked. "Exshush me?"

"We could use a woman of your talents in the Guild. Beautiful, but capable of causing instant death from the neurotoxins in a kiss."

"Funny. You're trying to be funny."

"The pay is more than good, as is the health insurance."

"Forget it."

Jinghua leaned back in her seat, pushing her long hair from her face. "You mentioned your last assignment will be as navigator to a shuttle assigned to Big Vox?"

"Dirtbag druglord taxi driver. Thash what I've come to." She watched the rain streaming down the windows at the entrance to the bar.

Jinghua regarded her with sympathy. "Yes, that's sadly true but Mr. Vox and I go back a long way to the time we were friends. Would it be too much of an imposition for you to deliver a little personal note from me?"

"Shure, no problem." The room tilted sideways. "Now…I shink I have to go home."

~ * ~

"This is United Mediscam with another billing update," announced the tight-lipped clerk in hospital scrubs from the wall viscreen. Falle leaned against the entertainment cabinet and watched stolidly. A dressing gown hung over her shoulders and a trail of discarded clothing led from the front door.

"Additional charges incurred by your recent stay in New Mars General Hospital not covered by our premium insurance plan come to three thousand, eight hundred creds for tests involving bone density, glaucoma, blood sugar and latent megalomania. In our continuing quest to provide quality health services at the lowest cost we have adjusted your premiums twenty percent upward in order for us to offer you an incredible six percent discount on pediatric examinations. Have a wonderful United Mediscam day."

"This is all the bad news I can handle for today," Falle moaned, wilting against the cabinet. She was wrong. A familiar face flashed onto the viscreen.

"Hi sweetheart, it's me, Rann. Sorry to record this message on your autotalk but I have to leave town on business for the next few days...um, weeks."

His toothy smile reminded her of the salesman who had sold her the aircar which blew all the gravitors a block from the sales lot.

"I'll call you when I get back. Bye!"

Before the image faded from the screen, she noticed a woman's nightdress hanging over the back of his chair. It wasn't her size, color choice or style. In short, it wasn't hers.

~ * ~

The shuttle circled the pad and gently touched down on the penthouse roof. Below was the city of Methtropolis; a carpet of lights stretching to the horizon.

"Really nice approach vectoring, Crandell," the pilot grinned. "So glad you didn't have me auger in like you did on..."

"Just park it while you still have lips, Bill," Falle retorted. The lingering hangover from the previous night was giving her a world-class headache.

"I suppose it would be too much to ask for the big jerkoff to be ready and waiting for us," he remarked, peering out the cockpit at the empty roof.

"I'll go get him. I need some fresh air, anyway." She had no sooner climbed down from the shuttle when a giant hulk emerged from the darkness.

"What you do here?" the hulk demanded in a bass voice. "Oaff need see you invite to party."

"Sorry, I forgot to check my morning mail," she replied. "I'm part of the shuttle crew here to take Mr. Vox to his meeting in Cannibis City."

"Ah, you here for Big Vox, my boss. I take you."

He led her through the foyer into a huge room where a riotous party was in full swing. Music from Oron basshorns vibrated the air filled with dhungsmoke while couples necked on sofas or gyrated on a raised dance floor. Stepping over a drunk passed out at the foot of a spiral staircase they climbed upward to a door at the top.

A long moment after the hulk pressed the entry chime the door slid open revealing a wizened dwarf wearing a pink bathrobe. Draped over the dwarf's shoulder was a pneumatic blonde wearing a miniskirt sized for an eight-year-old girl.

"Hey, sugarbowls, welcome to the party!" exclaimed the dwarf. "Zog, the escort service sent me a real fox this time. Wanna snort Banzai or a hit of Moondust before we start?"

Falle felt his little eyes slide over the curves of her body. "Um, you're Big Vox?" she blurted. "I mean, Mr. Vox?"

"Hey, size only matters in bed. How about a pipeful of dhung, then?"

"Sorry sir, I'm with the shuttle crew to take you to your meeting."

"Oh yeah, the meeting with the boys from Sector XII to discuss neovalium production, almost forgot."

Falle suddenly remembered the message Jinghua had given her. She pulled a crumpled envelope from her flight jacket and held it out. "Your old friend Jingqua asked me to give you this."

Vox's eyebrows contracted in thought. "Old friend Jinghua?

Never heard of the spacer." He grabbed the envelope, tore it open and scanned the note inside. Abruptly his pink jowls darkened and the little porcine eyes blazed up at her.

"Grab her, Oaff!" he barked.

Huge paws gripped her from behind, pinning her arms to her sides. Vox pulled out a force pistol from under his bathrobe, shoving it under her chin.

"Oh yeah?" he sneered, "You got less than five seconds to live, wedge."

Falle struggled against the animal strength holding her helpless, the pain of the weapon pressing into her larynx. In an act of either desperation or instinct she leaned forward and spat into Vox's upturned face.

With a guttural scream he lunged backwards and fell to the carpet, squirming. He lay still.

Oaff released her and knelt beside him, turning him over. Blank, lifeless eyes seemed to stare upwards at a crystal chandelier high overhead.

"What happen Big Vox?" He scratched the top of his massive head. "He no breathe, he no talk. Me think boss go bye-bye."

Falle sucked air into her lungs, sagging against the doorway. The note Vox dropped caught her eye. Picking it up, she read the neatly handwritten lines. *You are looking at an assassin from the Borgia Guild, Vox. You have five seconds left to live.*

"Sonofabitch." she hissed, crumpling it up.

The pneumatic blonde peered down at the sprawled body. She looked wistfully at Falle. "I guess this means the party is over, huh?"

~ * ~

Falle tilted her head, examining herself in her living room window. The bruise under her chin from the force pistol was a dark oval. *Perhaps a little face cream will help,* she thought. Her hands still shook when she recalled the scene at the party. The Methtropolis Police performed a perfunctory interrogation of all partygoers who failed to escape through various doors and windows after learning about Big Vox's untimely demise. It would seem he wasn't a particularly loved man. The official conclusion- so far- seemed to indicate he died of a heart seizure caused by excessive drug use.

The sound of chimes came from the doorway. To her shock the door hissed open revealing Jinghua standing before her.

She looked into the black feline eyes and felt the rage building up inside her.

"I can't believe you had the nerve to show up on my doorstep," she snarled.

"Good evening to you also," Jinghua replied with a pale smile. "Do we have time to talk?"

"Yeah, we unemployed people have plenty of time to talk."

She shrugged, indicating the chairs. "Well, why not, take a pew. I'm dying to hear the explanation for the slimy little trick you played on me today."

They settled into chairs, Jinghua dropping a black carry all onto the table before them. "Explain what you mean by unemployed?" she asked.

"Unpaid administrative leave, per company policy, until the inquiry over Big Vox's death is concluded. I'm sure *you* know how he died."

Jingqua nodded. "Quite. That won't be a problem for you."

Perversely, Falle felt like laughing. "No, he didn't die from ingesting a class M neurotoxin someone spat into his eyes. He choked to death on a bread crumb."

"I've been doing a little research on your condition," Jingqua continued. "It would seem the venom from the hydrophis virus becomes inert soon after it enters the victim's body. The symptoms and result are indeed identical to heart seizure."

"In that case, be sure not to borrow my toothbrush."

Jingqua opened the carry all and began stacking up one hundred cred plasticards.

"What exactly are you doing?" Falle demanded.

"A rival drug cartel contacted the Borgia Guild last week to eliminate Big Vox. Since you've completed the contract for us, here is your share; twenty thousand creds."

Falle gaped at the pile of plasticards and swallowed. "You have to be kidding," she managed to whisper.

"We would very much enjoy having an associate with your talent in the Guild," Jinghua continued smoothly. "In fact, we have a contract which just came in from a wife who would love having her wealthy and cheating husband expire to, how shall we say…something like a heart attack?"

With an effort Falle forced her eyes from the stacked creds and back to reality. "I somehow can't picture myself as a hired assassin. I'm a Certified Starship Pilot, for crying out loud. That's who I am."

There was a glass vase on the table holding a spray of crystal butterflies. Jingqua picked one up, turning it over in her hand.

"This butterfly reminds me of something they salvaged from the wreck on Swampworld. A porcelain antique vase from Solitaire, unscathed among the wreckage," she said, gazing at Falle with a trace of compassion which sat strangely on her hard yet lovely face. "I think it's time you think about what you can salvage from the wreckage of your life."

"I suppose that's one way of looking at it." Falle rummaged mentally through her file of options, more unsettled by Jingqua's analogy than she chose to dwell on. "I can always find another job. The hydrophis virus, I'm sure in time they'll find a cure I can afford."

"Perhaps they will." Jinghua shrugged and returned the butterfly to the vase. "Well, if you change your mind, there is a sizeable contract fee on this individual at United Mediscam."

"What did you say? Who?"

"The CEO of Accounting, a former corporate tax evasion specialist named Bob Weimer." She raised an eyebrow and looked steadily at Falle. "Don't tell me you are acquainted with him?"

"The company name does ring a bell in my pocketbook." She picked up one of the creds, savoring the smooth finish and the gold one hundred embossed in the center. She pursed her lips thoughtfully. "Chief CEO of accounting, huh? How interesting."

~ * ~

He was definitely making progress. The little blonde in the pink bodysheath was hanging on his every word, open admiration in her limpid blue eyes. The crowd in the hotel lounge swirled about them; secretaries just getting off work, business travelers, execs' ordering the first martini of the night.

"Of course, getting a corporate bonus isn't easy these days," he said, taking a sip of his Aghaid Fizz. "I had to raise the copays and bump up the deductions of our policyholders. I landed a thirty million cred profit for United Mediscam this past quarter."

"That's wonderful, Bob," said Falle, leaning closer so he could get a better look at her cleavage. "Tell me more about your new Porsche aircar."

"Well, it's not the top of the line Model J5, but it has targhide upholstery, hologram navigation and can top out at two hundred KPH." Weimer managed to lift his eyes from the depths of her bosom to an inviting smile. Based on past experience of similar encounters he sensed the timing was right for a familiar line. "Say, maybe you'd like me to take you for a spin? We could even stop by one of my penthouse suites for a nightcap."

"I'd love to, Bob," Falle cooed, sliding her hand along his leg. "I can guarantee you a goodnight kiss."

Chapter Three

"Services were held today in the Chapel of Interplanetary Memories for Senator T'ong Glokk of the Interworld Federation. From the Verdana swamp where he spent his embryonic childhood to the Federation's highest council, T'ong will always be remembered as an amphibian with style and gusto. 'If you have to croak, croak with a song on your lips' he was often wont to say.

"The controversial but beloved senator was found dead as a result of a broken neck in his private pond last Zarday in what New Earth crime investigators suspect was a botched robbery attempt. The only item of value taken was a gold Federation signet ring from his left flipper. City forensic investigators were puzzled by bite marks on Glokk's neck which appear to have been made by human teeth.

"Senator Glokk is survived by pondmate B'lurpp and tadpoles too numerous to mention. In lieu of worms, donations may be sent to SPAPS, the Society for the Preservation of Algae and Pond Scum. Farewell, our beloved T'ong."

"Actually, I heard he was a total jerkoff," Taragon remarked, staring through clouds of dhungsmoke to the viewscreen on the far wall.

The seedy little bar was packed with carousing miners and dockloaders, all eager to squander their Kasday paychecks. She turned her attention back to her companion seated across the battered table. "I hate to say this, but when I contacted the Bogia Guild for a hired assassin I was expecting someone who looked a little more...experienced."

She had a valid point. Falle was a petite blonde with a doll-like angelic face. The only feature spoiling the picture of a college cutie in a black bodysuit was her eyes. They were pale blue and utterly devoid of expression.

"You've seen my references from the Guild," Falle replied.

Her voice was low and without tone or inflection.

"Yeah, I once had good references from a housemaid I hired who broke more dishes than she washed."

Taragon took a sip of her whiskey and coughed. They must have distilled it yesterday with water from sewage in the Zardorian reclamation tanks, she mused.

Falle stretched her hand across the table. A gold signet ring bearing the crest of the Interworld Federation rolled onto the battered speerwood.

"Gorth crap!" Taragon grabbed a napkin and hurriedly covered it. "Okay, you've made your point."

"So, are we going to talk about the job?"

"The job, yeah." She glanced surreptitiously over her shoulder, leaning closer. "There's someone I'd like to see stinking up a vault like our lamented Senator Glokk."

"Perhaps you'd also like to invite your friend over to join in our conversation."

Taragon was taken aback. "What?"

"The rather large gentleman at the far end of the bar." Falle nodded in his direction. "The one having no neck and the bulge of a force pistol showing through his jacket."

"Well then. You do have sharp eyes," Taragon admitted, somewhat chagrinned. "He's my bodyguard. In this part of the city…"

"Hey, two foxy wedges all alone and waiting." A drunken miner emerged from the crowd and stood by their table, weaving.

"Beat it, nerf nuts," Taragon ordered without looking up.

"Hey, sugarbowls, you look like the type what wants to date a real stud, huh?"

"Let me know when you find one."

"Ah, come on, sweetcheeks…" The next instant the mass of Taragon's bodyguard loomed over him, exuding menace. The drunk blanched and raised his hands in supplication.

"Hey, I'm walkin', I'm walkin'," he whined and melted back into the dhungsmoke.

"Now you see why I wanted Jukebox along." She looked up. "Now disappear." Jukebox grunted and slouched off to his place at the bar.

"So, tell me about the security around this person you want stinking up a vault?" Falle picked up the drink before her and tossed it down as if it were water.

"Airtight. Security has installed proximity attack sensors on every wall. The slightest fast move toward our friend and a particle beam turns you into ionized gas."

"Weapon sensors too, I imagine."

"You bet your tush. Programmed to detect any metallic object they sense as a weapon, vaporizing whoever is carrying it." Taragon picked up the bottle and refilled their glasses. "Palace security hired this little runt with a droopy mustache named Stillborne. He designed the system for the Dhungsmoke Cartel on Planet Euphoria. Knows his stuff, though."

She sighed and ran an unflattering glance over her drinking partner, unable to relate a petite blonde and a doll face to a hired assassin. "Are you really sure you're up for this job?" she ventured. "Maybe the Borgia Guild can send me someone a bit more, how can I put it...lethal?"

"Lethal." Falle took a sip of her glass, got up and walked to the bar. She went to the drunk Taragon's bodyguard had run off and sat down beside him. The drunk was entranced when she ran her hand over his thigh. They chatted companionably, then Falle pulled his face to hers, kissing him on the lips. Without farther ado she eased herself off the barstool and returned to her seat at the corner table.

"You want to tell me what that was all about?" Taragon demanded.

The drunk, startled at the abrupt departure of what he hoped was his future bedmate lurched up, pushing through the noisy crowd toward them. Halfway across the floor he stiffened, clutched at his throat and began to gag. With palsied steps he made for the door and vanished.

"He'll be dead in about five minutes." Falle leaned back in her seat, crossed her legs and savored the expression on Taragon's face. "I picked up the hydrophis virus from a space liner crash a year ago. It won't kill me, I'm just a carrier. All my body fluids contain a class M neurotoxin." Her grin was feral. "That was only a little peck on the lips I gave your drunk. He should be glad he didn't end up in bed with me."

Taragon swallowed and edged back. "I guess your love life must really be in the toilet, huh?"

A flicker of emotion passed over the doll face. She seemed to stare through Taragon at some distant dream lost in time and space. "Let me just say when you lose something of yourself you simply find something else to replace it."

"So, you kill people for money?"

"I prefer to think of it as the removal of inconvenient obstacles in other people's lives." The blue eyes became ice. "Shall we discuss the inconvenient person in yours?"

"Yeah, him." Taragon took a quick glance about her, lowering her voice. "The person happens to be Chancellor Tomerlane, the Beloved Tyrant of the Six Cities in Zardoria, wise and noble leader, idol of the people, pure in thought and deed. My husband."

~ * ~

"It's party time!" the girl in the pink micro bikini squealed, jumping into the hot tub, sending a cascade of water over two figures seated at a nearby table. Over the vast balcony of the Grand Hall Girax basshorns blasted out music to the gyrating dancers around them.

Chancellor Tomerlane wiped water from his face and leaned toward his companion. "Look, Leonard, you designed and installed the security system in Taragon's boudoir. All I'm asking is for you to disable a window in the hall so one of my boys can scoot in there some night and do the job."

Stillborne thoughtfully chewed the end of his mustache. "I donno, Tom…you any idea of the heat an assassination of the First Lady is gonna bring?"

"Come on pal, didn't I get you the contract for the palace job?" he continued. "Didn't I fix you up with the Countess you were drooling over since you got here?"

Stillborne smiled in recollection of the wild night. "Yeah, she was great. I know all the strings you had to pull about the contract."

"You'll do it for me, pal?"

"Well, lemme see about setting up a scheduled glitch in the system and I'll get back…"

"Wise and noble leader, there you are!" A little man wearing a velvet court outfit was bending over Tomerlane. "It's time for your evening selection."

With a guilty start Tomerlane recognized Packenheid, his Grand Chamberlain. "Hey, Peckerhead, what's happening?"

"Time for the evening selection, Beloved Tyrant," he explained.

"Oh yeah, the evening selection." He got up and winked at Stillborne. "Duty calls. I'll talk to you later, Leonard."

He was led over to the balcony where a line of girls waited. "What's all these wedges doing here, new cleaning crew or something?" he asked.

"Oh no, Great One. These maidens are all volunteers to be your companion for the evening." He bent closer. "The First Lady has retired for the night."

"Oh yeah. Man, you sure are an efficient flunky, Peckerhead."

"I'm honored, Beloved Tyrant."

Pursing his lips Tomerlane considered them, the girls smiling with nervous anticipation. A night with the Chancellor usually promised generous monetary compensation. "Those two on the end might do. Oh, and I'll take the third on the left with the nice set of shabooms…"

High above in the vaulted ceiling, a shadow moved down a marble column on a gossamer-thin line. A carbon fiber crossbow gave off a muted hiss of gas as it was loaded. Instantly, a security sensor in a darkened alcove sent out a searching beam which passed over the deflecting material of the shadow's black bodysuit.

"Last one for the big head, one more for the little head," Tomerlane grinned, draining a wineglass and tossing it aside. "Now for those lucky wedges awaiting their master's touch."

"Yes, Great One, I will escort you…"

Packenheid stepped in front of Tomerlane in time to intercept a barbed crossbow shaft. He squalled in pain, flailed wildly to reach the burning agony between his shoulder blades, and slammed into his patron. There were screams and a collective cry of horror from the crowd when they toppled over the balcony railing to the floor of the Grand Hall a hundred feet below.

~ * ~

It was almost closing time in the bar and with the musico system shut down for the night the place held an almost funereal stillness. A sleepy barkeep was wiping down the bar top around a solitary drunk passed out among spilled beer and overturned glasses. In a corner table two figures sat in the gathering gloom.

"I was to be paid two thousand creds for the death of Chancellor Tomerlane," Falle hissed. Her voice was low, dark with latent menace. "Are you saying you're stiffing me on my contract fee?"

"He died from a fall from the balcony of the Grand Hall," Taragon retorted. "All you took out was Packenheid, his chamberlain."

"The crossbow shaft would have found Tomerlane's heart if the chamberlain hadn't stepped in the way. Regardless of how, he died because I was there."

"I'm not paying out two thousand scoots because you perforated a foot-licking flunky. Forget it." On cue, Jukebox emerged from the shadows and stood behind her, his hand fondling the butt of his force pistol. "So, you can take the finger from your mouth and drop the bad look from your face."

The air seemed to thicken while Falle stared across the table. Under her basilisk gaze Taragon felt a worm of unease. She reached into her blouse and held out a hundred cred disc. "Listen, here's a small retainer for your trouble. That okay with you?"

With startling suddenness, a smile brightened Falles' features. "Of course, it is. I'm afraid I've been remiss in offering you my congratulations."

"Excuse me?" said Taragon, flustered.

"You are now in line for the leadership of the Six Cities." She reached over the table and patted her forearm. "My warmest best wishes, Chancellor. Now, if you'll excuse me, I must be on my way."

"Yeah... thanks." With no small relief Taragon watched her walk across the deserted bar and disappear through the door.

Outside, the night rain slanted past flickering streetglobes to turn the cracked walkways a glistening illusion of newness. Water sluiced in the gutter before the seedy bar where in the mud and scattered garbage lay a crumpled hundred cred disc.

~ * ~

The woman reflected in the ornate boudoir mirror wore the flimsiest of negligees artfully concealing rolls of middle age fat and supporting in their proper positions a pair of heavy breasts. Wearing a complacent smirk Taragon centered a diamond tiara on her head. Tomorrow was her coronation and her first day as ruler of the Six Cities of Zardoria. She mentally checked the list of Tomarlane's ministers and councilors she would be sending into exile to the farthest corner of New Earth. Deadwood, all of them.

She picked up a jar of ointment and began rubbing it over a red rash on her forearm. *I must have got bit by some kind of bug last night at the dirtbag bar,* she mused. *They should have the place fumigated or better yet, burned to the ground.*

"I hope you're not planning to wear this to bed." A handsome young Captain of the Guard, wearing even less than her, joined the reflection in the glass. He put his arms about her, nuzzling her neck.

"You mean the tiara or the negligee?"

"I was thinking of the tiara, Your Grace."

"I'll be wearing only a smile when we start pounding the pillow, hot rod."

She turned and pulled his face to hers for a wet and lingering kiss.

He drew her closer, then abruptly stiffened, broke off the kiss. She looked up in surprise.

"Banistair... what is wrong?"

His face drained of color, his hands shook and he gave a strangled cry as he staggered back and collapsed, writhing on the marble floor. He lay still.

"Banistair. What's the matter?" She knelt by his side and turned him over. Blank, sightless eyes stared without seeing at the vaulted ceiling.

Taragon jumped up and backed into her dressing table, cosmetics and perfume scattering. Her heart hammering, she looked to the angry red rash on her forearm. It all came back to her in a rush, the scene in the bar where Falle had taken the finger from her mouth and stroked her arm, the scratch of a fingernail over her skin.

"The hydrophis virus," she whispered, dropping to her knees in despair. "She infected me."

Chapter Four

"Well, there I was, fifteen years with Cyrus Nanotextiles, all ready to step into old Greenwald's jumpsuit when he finally cashed in his chips. They bring in this young weenie from Orion Tech, just graduated. Bet he hasn't even started shaving yet and they gave him the job I was in line for, sweated for and kissed ass for all these years."

They were seated in a deserted corner of New Earth Spaceport lounge. Throngs of travelers hurried along ramps past plexglass windows to the departure tubes. Falle studied the exec in the tailored jumpsuit sitting across the table from her; jowls spreading over his cravat, narrow porcine eyes shifting nervously about.

"How did the Borgia Guild contact you?" she asked.

"They didn't. I was talking to some rep at a corporate seminar and he brought up the subject of how the Guild was shortening the list of cheating husbands, obnoxious bosses and mothers-in-laws." He paused as the thunder of a departing spaceliner vibrated the building. "He got your comm number from a friend who had his ex-wife's divorce attorney disappeared."

Expertly, Falle scanned the empty tables and faces in the crowd moving past the entrance to the lounge. "So, let's go over this new president of Cyrus Nanotextiles."

"Yeah, the weenie from Orion Tech," he sighed despondently, leaning to one side to lift a buttock and discretely break wind.

"The Corporate Council voted and I lost to him by one vote. One vote."

"Why did the vote go against you?"

"Somehow word got out about my alleged embezzlement of funds for the Aghaid Humanitarian Aid Project on Satellite." He took a deep breath and stared at her. "So, tell me what it's going to cost to set things right in my world?"

A starpilot captain and a young flight attendant had just emerged from the arrivals tube. With a dull shock Falle recognized the pilot as Rann. They were holding hands and, receiving a needle of pain in her heart, she noticed the sparkle of an engagement ring on the girl's finger. Nursing a dull ache, she watched them vanish in the departing crowd.

"Excuse me, am I boring you?" the prospective client demanded crankily.

Falle eyed him coldly. "Give me your card and I'll get back to you with a fee and details of the operation."

The client blanched under the blue fire in her eyes. He fumbled in his vest and slid a square of plastic over the table. "Um, thanks for meeting with me. Talk to you later."

He lurched heavily to his feet and headed for the lounge entrance.

Falle watched him depart with distaste. The comm bracelet on her wrist began to chime. A fierce yet beautiful face appeared in the tiny screen.

"I trust I didn't interrupt a torrid lovemaking session with a pair of dockloaders," said Jinghua.

"A sense of humor," Falle retorted. "When did you pick it up?"

"Where are you?"

"I'm in New Earth City Spaceport. Just got back from the Six Cities on Zardoria."

Jinghua's black inscrutable eyes stared from the screen. She seemed to be pondering her next words.

"Well, is this an official call or were you just lonely and needed someone to talk to?" said Falle.

"The Borgia Guild has a new contract out."

"Really? Will it be assigned to you or me?"

"Actually, the contract is out on you."

Falle blinked. With an instinct which was becoming second nature she shot a glance over her shoulder. "You're kidding. Why would they…"

"Chancellor Taragon of the Six Cities has put up twenty thousand creds for the first member of the Guild to deliver your behind to her dead or alive. She expressed her preference as alive."

"Look, I sent the Guild a report about Taragon welching on the contract to take out her husband," Falle protested.

"Very true, but in addition to the Guild she put out the word to every lowlife bar thug and druglord this side of the planet. It just came down to economics." Jinghua smiled. "I would suggest you do your drinking at home from now on."

Falle studied the face on the screen, searching for truth on an expression of inscrutable calm.

"Twenty thousand creds, huh?" she mused. "I'm kind of surprised you took the courtesy to call. I would have thought by now I would have felt your knife sliding into my ovaries."

"Very astute guess, but not entirely altruistic on my part. As your trainer and sponsor the Guild barred me from pursuing the contract." She toyed with a strand of her black hair. "The truth be told, I've become rather fond of you."

Falled nodded. "Which is why I'm getting this call from you."

"Exactly so."

It was true there was a bond between them, a shared ferocity, and the attraction of physical opposites. The older woman had become a model for her, a mentor and rare for Falle, a friend.

"I hope this call doesn't blow back on you," she said.

"I have the transmission blocked on my end. You might want to dump your comm band before the Guild gets a fix on your location."

"Thanks, Jinghua… I appreciate the heads up."

"No problem, Blondie. Good luck." The screen chimed, went blank.

Alone in the corner of the spaceport lounge Falle considered her options. There weren't many. By now the Guild had her profile and known hangouts spread through half of New Earth. Hired thugs would be roaming the streets and alleys. Her apartment in the city would now be a deathtrap. Eyes would be watching all public transportation tubes and if not the spaceport where she sat it soon would be.

Falle unsnapped her comm band and dropped it into an abandoned drink on an adjacent table. She had one chance. If she could get off New Earth planet before the baying hounds started snapping at her heels…

"When does the next flight for Haboob City on Dustball lift off?"

The lethargic and patently underpaid clerk behind the desk perused the screen "Lemme see…we got a United Starlines flight leaving oh three hundred at gate twelve."

"I'll take a one-way flight."

"Six hundred creds. Executive or coach?"

"Coach will be fine." Falle pushed the required creds across the counter. The departure waiting area had ultra high security screening. Perfect. No thug or Guild assassin could make it past the gate with any weapon. The dagger concealed in her boot would have to go before then.

"There you are, sweetheart," announced a male voice behind her. "I've been looking all over the spaceport for you."

Falle felt someone seize her arm and a sharp object piercing her skin. She made a lunge for her concealed blade but paused with her fingers on the hilt. A dreamy fog swept over her. A face swam from the mist, one she recognized as Gordo, a fellow Borgia Guild member. His specialty was poison or paralysis venom, concealed in an ornate signet ring.

"Sorry, buddy, my wife here sometimes gets confused. What we need are tickets not to Dustball but to the Six Cities on the other side of New Earth. Departure in ten zaks? Great. Thanks for your help, buddy."

It all became a dreamlike trance. Boarding the spaceliner escorted by Gordo, the limousine ride past the ramparts of the ducal palace. A familiar face and a voice laced with triumphant hate.

~ * ~

"So nice to see you once more, my little Miss Fangs. Here is where you pay for the thirty thousand creds I had to shell out for the serum to cure me of the virus. Excellent work, Gordo. Have you received your fee yet?"

"Yes, thank you, Chancellor Taragon."

"How long will she be under the influence of your mind-numbing drug?"

"At least another dozen talls. You mentioned another assignment for me?"

"As the new ruler of Zardoria I believe I need an example made of anyone thinking of crossing me. What is the most inhospitable planet in our system?"

"This would have to be Swampworld; endless jungle, mud, snakeoids, tropical diseases. Pan Galaxy used to take tours there, built a landing tower and observation deck. They discontinued service after the big spaceliner crash last year."

"Excellent. Put her on one of our shuttles and dump her off to be eaten or to starve. Another thought just occurred to me…"

"Yes, Your Grace?"

"The little shit Tomerlane used to pal around with, the one we caught sabotaging my boudoir alarm system. I think Miss Hydrophis could use some companionship."

~ * ~

Stillborne watched the shuttle shrink into the greenish sky until it became a tiny speck before becoming a splash of white light when it kicked into timephase.

He got up from the landing pad where he had been thrown, brushing off leaves and swamp flotsam. The observation booth stood forlorn at the tower's edge, moss growing around broken windows framing the jungle far below.

Pure bad luck, he grumbled to himself. *Dumb maid had to stroll into Taragon's boudoir with an armload of freshly-pressed sheets while he was buttoning up his toolbox after sabotaging the window alarm sensors. Tossed into the dark hold of a space shuttle by a pair of palace goons then thrown out onto this tower platform along with the wedge.*

He walked over to where she lay. Not bad looking, he observed with approval. Petite, blonde and wearing a tight black bodysuit. She was plasticuffed hands and feet and for some reason had a tight-fitting mask over her mouth. He discovered pale blue eyes boring into his.

"Hey, lemme give you a hand," he said, dropping to a knee and unsnapping the plasticuffs and mask. "You okay?"

Falle messaged her wrists and ankles, wobbling to her feet. Something was horribly familiar. She staggered to the railing and gazed out over the jungle.

"Oh no…" she whispered, sinking to her knees. In her ears she again could hear the screams from passengers, the awful symphony of rending metal and shattering plexglass. Once again, she could feel the furnace blast throwing her from the ruptured hull to land stunned in the mud.

"Whatsamatter, you sick or something?" a voice floated from nowhere.

She gulped in air and stood up.

"Yeah, I'm fine," she said, taking in her companion. "I always get a little under the weather when I'm drugged, trussed up like a turkey and thrown into the bilge of a space shuttle."

"Glad to hear it. Thought for a moment I was going to have to do CPR on you."

Falle gave the little man a slow smile. "You have no clue how bad an idea that would be."

Stillborne peered over the railing. "You got any idea of where we are?"

"I know exactly where we are," Falle replied. "This happens to be Swampworld and about two clicks to the West is a wrecked spaceliner."

He squinted over the endless jungle. "Don't see nothing. How do you know there's a wreck out there?"

"Trust me, there is."

"Hey, I know who you are," he declared. "You're the wedge from the Borgia Guild."

"Give the man with the droopy mustache a contraband cigar," she said. "With whom am I sharing this delightful vacation excursion?"

Stillborne snorted in disgust. "Name's Stillborne. You might say I was in exactly the wrong place at the right time when…Zog's Ass."

An enormous serpentine shape slithered from a clump of ferns far below, half snake and lizard. It lifted a blunt head and yawned, revealing a cavern of serrated fangs.

"A snakeoid," Falle explained. "I'm told they resemble lizards on ancient Earth when they began to lose their limbs and evolve into snakes. Notice it only has hind legs."

"One ugly spacer," Stillborne muttered, watching it crawl off into the swamp. "What are we gonna do now?"

Falle considered the derelict observation lounge and a gate leading to a catwalk spiraling downwards. "Our best bet is to head for the wrecked spaceliner. At least we might find some food and water."

"Go down there?" said Stillborne, appalled.

"Well, you can always hang around this tower. I think after a few days you'll be as hungry as the snakeoids always are."

Reluctantly, Stillborne followed her down the rusted and creaking stairwell to the mat of rotting foliage on the jungle floor. Falle went to the nearest pond and began smearing her body with mud.

"What in Zog's Jockstrap are you doing?" Stillborne demanded.

"Snakeoids have no eyes. They track their prey by sensing movement and body heat. Care to join me?"

"Geeze, what about the smell?"

"Can't be much worse than the way you smell now."

"Funny, Crandell, real funny."

They carefully fought their way through the fern tangle, slipping into pockets of mud and slime, watching for any ominous movement around them. A wall of dark clouds rolled in above them with a distant grumble of thunder.

The wreck lay in a blackened clearing like a broken and discarded toy. Scattered snakeoid skeletons revealed the ferocious battle rescuers to the site had to put up to recover bodies. Abruptly, after a flash of overhead lightning it began to rain, hard.

"Drog's Left Nut, the mud is washing off!" Stillborne yelled as they forced through a tangle of vines.

"I know, I know."

Falle made it to a hatch in the crumpled hull and punched a keypad. "Hope this baby still has power left."

A low hum and the hatch slid open. They scrambled inside and powered it closed. Outside, the rain drummed on the hull of the ship, streaking the grimy plexglass.

Making their way past a jumble of cables, insulation and broken seats they came to the first class galley where they found sealed packets of food and water tubes.

"Seems enough for a few days at least," Falle mused, stacking them on a dented counter. A flash of lightning lit up a monochrome still life inside the derelict space liner, overturned serving carts, scattered luggage and ominous stains on the deck carpeting.

Their refuge was the tail of the craft which had broken off on impact, the exposed front buried in a low hill giving them a somewhat secure redoubt from weather and fanged menaces roaming outside.

"Hey, a bottle of Emperion '92," Stillborne exclaimed, rummaging through an overhead compartment. "Those First-Class pukes sure knew how to live."

He snapped off the cap, taking a healthy swallow. "Damn, I needed that." He belched appreciatively and passed it to Falle who was making a comfortable nest from seat cushions.

Falle examined the label with approval and took a pull. "So how are you with advanced hyperspace electronics?" she asked, studying the bottle.

Stillborne's puzzled expression was lost in the dim light of the cabin.

"What are you talking about?"

"Space liners have emergency rescue beacons on their hulls which are activated on crash or emergency situations. There's one behind the access panel to your right."

Stillborne groped in the darkness, found a catch and flipped open a cover. "Yeah, this must be it. Battery's deader than a smelt, though."

"The battery in the door activator is still good."

"Sure, I could rig a bypass through the liner transducer," he considered, running his fingers over a keypad. "Bet I could get off a signal to New Earth and honk up a rescue party."

"This might not be a good idea."

"Huh? Why not?"

"What if the 'rescue party' they send happens to be from the Six Cities on Zardoria?" Falle took another thoughtful pull from the bottle.

Stillborne had a sharp memory of the two goons dragging him from Taragon's boudoir and giving him a very professional workover.

"Gorth crap," he muttered.

There was a scrabbling outside the hull. The blunt snout of a snakeoid was silhouetted against a plexglass viewport. A sharp questing tongue flickered out before it slid from view.

"Okay, can you set the signal frequency to a select receiver," Falle continued. "Say, a particular planet in the system?"

Stillborne was staring in fascinated dread at the empty viewport. "Yeah, I can program the signal to do that." He affected a smug grin. "I can do better. Find me some tools and I'll resignal the unit as a hyperspace transmitter."

Falle's opinion of the insufferable little prong went up a few points.

"Are you sure?" she asked.

"Who are you thinking of shooting the shit with?"

~ * ~

"Interplanetary message just came in for you, Ms. Dante, from a Falle Crandell," her executive secretary announced from the doorway leading to the office of the Director of Dustball Aurumite Corporation.

"Thanks, Roger." She pointed to a chair before her desk. "Take a seat; we have to go over some production estimates." Elaine Dante dropped her stylus, steepled her fingers. "Falle Crandell. She dropped out of sight on New Earth a year ago after surviving the spaceliner crash on Swampworld," she ruminated.

"I heard she turned over management of her water pumping station to one of her brighter repair techs," said Roger.

"What was the message about?"

"Well, it would seem she's back on Swampworld. Pan Galaxy sent her back there with a special investigator..." he consulted a speakwrite tablet in his lap, "a Dr. Leonard M. Stillborne, regarding new evidence of possible sabotage resulting in the crash. Evidently the company shuttle hasn't returned to pick them up and their hyperspace radio can't get through some type of solar interference to reach New Earth."

"Interesting situation. What does she want?"

"She wants to know if you can locate any space craft in the system close enough to evacuate them."

Elaine Dante raised her eyebrows. "Very strange Pan Galaxy would just drop them off and leave. A nasty place to hang out."

She turned to a desk screen and scrolled through readouts. "Okay, I see a space freighter en route to Asteroid DBIX with a stopover on the Terminax Space Station, a few parsecs from Swampworld. Give Captain Planque on the freighter a call and see if he can make a slight detour."

Elaine's executive secretary made a face. "Ms. Dante, this request of hers is really off the wall."

"If you feel we have an issue here, Roger, just spit it out."

"I think we should give Pan Galaxy on New Earth a call and find out exactly what is going on. Nobody just drops people off on a planet like this."

Elaine leaned back in her executive lounge chair and tapped her stylus on the blotter. "Ms. Crandell is the sole owner of the Firestone Water Plant here on Dustball. The contract to supply water to our aurumite mining operation is due to be renewed on generous terms next month. See where this is going?"

Roger fidgeted, looked uncomfortable. "I believe I catch your drift, Ms. Dante. I'll make the call to Captain Planque."

Elaine Dante beamed at her subordinate. "Very good, Roger. I see you are learning."

~ * ~

Captain Planque was not in a good mood. Even with the decent retainer he received from the pushy manager of Dustball Aurumite, he dumped nine hours off his flight schedule on the detour to Swampworld to load up the wedge with the mean eyes, and the little runt and his big mouth. With no small degree of satisfaction, he watched them walk down the ramp from his freighter into the busy Terminax Space Station.

In an equally bad mood was Stillborne. Two days in a tiny cabin with a nubile female who showed not the slightest interest in a horizontal contact sport and being fed table scraps left over from the crew's meals. He was hungry, horny and apprehensive of what misfortune might be next.

Standing beside him, Crandell was a study in calm detachment watching the swarm of travelers on their way or returning from flights to various planets in the system, service trucks hauling loads of cargo to the waiting freighters. Far overhead viewports revealed a constellation of stars. Huge panels on the walls displayed information on scheduled flight times.

"I'm hungry," whined Stillborne. "You got any creds on you?"

"Not much," she replied. "We also have no passcards, visas or travel permits allowing a flight to Dustball."

"Dustball? Why in Zerid do we wanna go to Dustball?" he demanded truculently. "Ain't nothing there but sand and rocks."

"Because it's more or less my home planet and I have friends there so I can lay low until this Six Cities thing blows over." She eyed him coldly. "What's this 'we' business? After I hook up transportation, our brief but less than enjoyable association will be a fading memory."

Being reminded of Taragon's wrath and possible future retribution put the situation in a whole new light for Stillborne. No doubt the lovable Captain Planque would blab and word could filter back to New Earth about their departure from Swampworld. Also, to be associated with an ally and possible protector of such obvious ferocity might be the salvation of his gluteus maximus.

"Falle, I know I can be a gomph's ass sometimes, but I wanna tag along with you," he pleaded meekly.

"Oh, so we're on a first name basis now. Forget it."

"I promise to mind my attitude from now on. I mean it."

"It's not your attitude, it's your mouth."

The little man seemed to droop in concert with his mustache. He gazed up at her with sorrowful eyes, reminding her of, what was it? Oh yes, an extinct beagle dog of ancient Earth. She exhaled wearily.

"Okay, you're on probation." Colored lights and a throb of music behind her beckoned. "Come on, at least we have enough for a drink."

The crowded bar catered to a noisy crowd of dockloaders, miners and very tough-looking individuals with the butts of assorted weapons protruding from vests and pockets. In a far corner a group of scarred and tattooed toughs were throwing knives at a picture of a Umas Sandtrooper tacked to the wall. Shouts of glee or derision accompanied each toss followed by an exchange of creds.

"I'll have a schooner of Zardorian beer," Stillborne announced to the comely female bartender appearing through a fog of contraband cigar and dhung smoke. "Hey, Crandell, what do you want from the lady?"

"Maybe later, I see an opportunity." She probed her boot and pulled out a slim dagger. With Gordo happily counting his reward for shanghaiing her and Taragon gloating over the sight of her trussed up, they'd overlooked the chance to do a thorough frisk. She pushed her way through the raucous crowd to the knife throwers.

"Hey guys, mind if I join the action?"

The group of toughs turned to regard the newcomer with patronizing grins. Secretly to herself, Falle also grinned. After untold centuries it was always the same…the weak and ineffectual female versus the brute competent male. Well, they would soon discover they were pigeons about to be plucked.

"No problem, honeycrack." A bearded hulk with a scar running from nose to jawline held up his blade. "Whatya say to old Bullock we agree to ten creds a throw?"

Falle favored him with her own patronizing grin. "Ten creds? This some kind of kid's game? Let's make it fifty creds a throw."

The giant rose to the bait. "It's your funeral, sugarbowls, you can have the first toss. Try not to hit the ceiling or walls."

Falle's dagger flashed through the air and landed quivering in the center of the target.

"Say babe, nice day if it don't rain," said Stillborne, ogling the bartender's tube top.

The nubile bartender set the mug down before him and gave out a pained look. "Is this the best hookup line you've got, short stuff? Geeze,

I thought I'd heard them all."

"Hey, sweetcheeks, got your attention though?" He leered at the exposed melons bobbing upwards, ignoring a loud argument from the rear of the bar and subsequent crash of furniture and breaking glass. "Anyway, size only counts in bed. Whatya say you and me get together after closing?"

"That'll be one cred fifty for the suds and ten points toward me whistling up the bouncer and having your scrawny ass booted out the door," she threatened wearily.

A tall stack of creds was placed on the bar top. Falle passed the bartender one embossed with a gold hundred. "Keep the change," she said.

The girl in the tube top did a double-take. "Well, thanks. It's been kinda a rough night with them loggers on their way to Dropoff."

"You only had to deal with this guy a few minutes. I had him for several days."

Stillborne scowled at her then his eyes bulged when he took in the pile of creds. "Zog's Holy Jockstrap, Crandell. You hold up the cashier at the spaceport terminal?"

"Proceeds in giving out lessons in knife throwing." She looked smug. "I also had to give out lessons in facial lacerations when two of them baulked at paying off their bets."

"I think I know your face," the bartender declared, staring intently at Falle.

The two behind the bar stiffened like hunting dogs on point.

"I doubt it," said Falle cautiously. "I have kind of a common face…"

"No, no, I saw your picture on the Interworld News," she persisted. "Yeah, the sole survivor of the space tour liner what crashed on Swampworld last year. You're Falle Crandell, right?"

"My fifteen zaks of fame." Falle relaxed into a smile. "I believe I will have a beer now."

"Sure, coming right up, Ms. Crandell." She filled a mug and dropped it before her with a flourish.

"We dodged another silver bullet this time," Stillborne remarked, wistfully eyeing her shapely rear undulated to the end of the bar.

Falle picked up one of the creds and fondled the embossed surface. "These aren't New Earth issue," she observed. "These look like Bank of Satellite stuff. This is strange..."

She recalled Satellite was the pariah world in their system, the least habitable planet closest to the sun. Colonized by the Umas race from the Outer Rim, home to a primitive indigenous people considered to be religious fanatics. A desert planet so arid as to make her Dustball a sylvan paradise and having only one resource. The heartstone; the most valuable gem in the star system.

"Excuse me."

Falle turned to see a tall, muscular individual wearing a combat vest. She recognized him as one of the two knife throwers with whom she had the gambling dispute.

"Let me guess," she drawled. "You'd like another lesson in what happens to people who welch on bets with me?"

The rugged face cracked into a grin. "The name is Kris Walderspan. I'm here to invite you to have dinner with me in the Chandelier Lounge."

Falle stared at him.

"You have to be kidding."

~ * ~

Candlelight sent a ruby glow through the glass of wine in Falle's hand. She gazed over the elegant silverware and the remains of a poulet a la moutard et au miel to her dining companion.

"So now that we're finished with our romantic dining experience, perhaps we can move on to the bullshit," she purred.

"Ah yes, the bullshit." Walderspan took a sip from his glass and considered her over the rim. "I heard tell you're a certified starpilot?"

"Somehow I feel you wouldn't be swilling this excellent La Cochon Blank with me if I wasn't."

He nodded. "We had a stabilizer line holed by a meteor which got past our screens just past the outer marker. Killed my whole flight crew

63

except for myself and Jon Bullock. We barely managed to limp to the space station on autopilot."

Falle took another sip of wine and nodded. "So, you need another starpilot. To go where?"

He rolled a red crystal over the tablecloth. Falle picked it up and cradled it in her palm. It suddenly emitted a red pulsing light, keeping time to the beat of her heart.

"Zog's ass," she breathed. "This is a heartstone."

"No one has yet figured out how it draws a person's energy to do this," he said.

"Where did you get it?"

"On planet Satellite. Got it from an Aghaid native who said he found it where a Umas cycled out into the sand."

The crimson pulse reflected in Falle's eyes. "It's beautiful," she murmured. "Kind of looks like you could dive inside and swim in red wine." The la Cochon Blanc '29 was starting to get to her.

"The Aghaid said he knows where they cache the jewels from their mine. Five million creds stored in a rickety warehouse just inside a perimeter fence."

The Umas. The invasion of her village on Dustball when she was a child. An image imbedded in her mind of her parents engulfed in the flames of their burning home.

"Forget it, Kris. Find another pilot."

"Your glass is empty. Let me pour you a refill."

"So, what's with the macho tattoo?" she asked, pointing to his left shoulder. "A ram's skull, crossed assault knives and some kind of scrolled motto. *Vincere Aut Mori?*"

"It means 'Conquer or Die'. We're an organization of mercenaries from the Outer Rim," he explained. "We work security for rich patrons, settle disputes on developing planets, all kinds of fun things. I just might let you sign up."

"Sign up to do fun things. Sure." The room was starting to swim around her.

The dinner went on to dessert, more glasses of wine and ended in the cabin of his ship. In the dim light she felt hands running over her body, exploring, and heat building up in her loins. His fingers caressed her face, his lips moving towards hers.

"Kris, stop." she gasped, writhing away from him on the bed.

"What's the matter?" Questing hands paused, surprise and a degree of annoyance in his eyes.

"I just...can't."

"Tell me what the problem is?"

"Look." She held up an extended palm, the hazmat imprint clearly visible in the compartment lighting.

"Holy gorth crap." He recoiled to the other side of the bed. His expression of fear and revulsion was a splinter in Falle's heart. She closed her eyes and got up.

Rivergreede pharmaceuticals Serum number 95. Thirty thousand creds.

At the door to his cabin she paused and looked back. "You have yourself a new starpilot, Walderspan. Let me know when you plan on leaving for Satellite."

~ * ~

The Umas mining operation spread out over the valley under the desert night. The Blue Lady had not yet risen over the Western horizon and the three shadows on the hill crouched in dim starlight.

"Someone mentioned the heartstones were stored in 'a rickety warehouse'," Falle observed, taking in the well-lit enclosure, ringed by guard towers and slicewire.

There were lines of mine cars now silent leading from the dark opening of the mine and rows of shacks holding Aghaid slave laborers.

"See the building on the far left? That's where they store the gems," said Walderspan. "The security neutralizer Stillborne built for us will get us past the alarms."

"I just knew the little runt would bug out on us before we left town," Bullock groused. "No nuts at all."

"Else he had better smarts than us." Crandell was getting a bad feeling about Walderspan's little scheme. It didn't seem to be the walkover he so blithely described when they arrived in New Seattle, what passed as a city on Satellite. Still, she reasoned, there was a chance. A chance for the thirty thousand she needed for a new life.

"You guys ready to get rich?" Walderspan asked.

"Let's do it," she replied.

They wormed their way passed the ropeweed, drawing nearer to the slicewire and roving pencils of searchlight beams. A wind began to sigh over the valley, growing stronger. In the far distance an ominous black wall rolled in.

Falle crouched, her long blonde hair whipping her face. "This is not good," she whispered. "We have to go back."

Both men looked at her. "Huh? Why do we have to go back?" Bullock demanded.

"A haboob is on its way."

"A what?"

"A big and dangerous desert sandstorm."

"Dammit, Crandell, we're almost there." Walderspan eyed the approaching cloud with skepticism. "It's only gonna be a little wind and sand, for Zog's sake."

The haboob slammed into them with cyclone force. In an instant they were choked, blinded by flying sand. They stumbled, turned to retreat, unable to guess which direction they had come. Hands shielding mouth and eyes they staggered through the cataclysm.

They were suddenly bathed in the glare of a searchlight. From driving sand and darkness, a squad of Umas appeared, pulse rifles at the ready.

Chapter Five

The whip cracked in the still dry air. The cart moved on again, creaking under its load of ore, plastoid wheels churning up dust which coated the sweat-soaked bodies of the prisoners. The sun was a molten god, gloating over the lines of carts and the sufferers winding down the canyon, sucking out their very lives with its heat. The whip cracked again. Blood mingled with sweat dripping onto the sand.

Falle turned over on the bedroll and opened her eyes. It was almost dawn. She reached out and touched the charged particle rifle by her side as would a lover, drawing strength and security from the polished tristeel. Strange, she pondered, watching the Blue Lady hanging close over the hills, that she would return to another desert, another time and another life.

This dawn had the feeling of another, on this planet known as Satellite, when three wraiths crawled through the trench under the slicewire, dragging broken chains from their ankles. Falle waved her companions down and watched Bantannomen, the Umas camp commandant, walk past the cone of the gatelight. She noted the halting stride and caught a ripeness in the air and guessed he was close to the start of his embryonic cycle. Very close. She tested the edge of the tristeel bar she had kept hidden under her bunk and ground to a flat blade through the long nights. Slowly she came to her feet and balanced herself, measuring the distance along the compound. The blade caught a flash of starlight before it tore through the rotting body of the Umas, killing the unborn nightmare within and scattering organs and body parts. Cautiously the three shadows continued on their way past the guardhouse toward the pad and the parked Umas jumpships.

She fell into half sleep, letting blue shadows wash her body, caressing with shade and light the thin dark bands of whip scars. She moved an arm over her breasts and the light flowed over a tattoo burned into her left shoulder. The skull of a ram and an emblazoned motto: *Third Galactic Rim Mercenary Batallion. Vincere Aut Mori. Conquer or die.*

Prophecy.

~ * ~

The Umas sandskimmer flew high above rock spires and undulating dunes far below. Falle lounged behind the cockpit controls and admired the silver banks of gauges set in polished speerwood. It was an almost new model and she wondered where Bantannomen obtained it, considering the interworld embargo on dealing with the Umas League. She and Fan-tonn would be celebrating when it went up for auction in New Seattle.

"By the Holy Manprobe and Sacred Sack of Agonn, stink very bad," gasped Fan-tonn, returning from the tail of the craft with a rag tied over his face. He had been opening aft viewports to vent the lingering odor of its former owner.

"Better to dump the stink now before the prospective buyers come aboard with their pockets bulging with creds."

Fan-tonn grinned in happy agreement then squinted past Falle at the forward viewport.

"Cran-dall…something down there."

"Where abouts?"

"By pile of grey rocks." He jabbed a finger to her left. "There, see. It looks like sandcrawler."

Falle dropped the craft into a lazy spiral. "Drog's Ass." she exclaimed. "This has to be the one belonging to Troll and Walderspan."

Falle set the skimmer down in a blizzard of sand. The first thing she saw after emerging cautiously with her particle rifle was the sprawled and mutilated body of Troll.

"About time a waiter showed up in this restaurant," complained a weak voice from the gloom of a rock overhang. "Hope nobody in this greasy spoon is expecting a tip for such crappy service."

A face covered in dried blood appeared. "About time, waitress. I'll have the filet mignon, medium rare and a bottle of Chateau Figeac to go with it."

Falle lowered her rifle. "It's Walderspan and he's delirious," she observed correctly. "Give me a hand, Fan-tonn, and we'll get him in the ship before he croaks on us."

Inside the sandskimmer Falle found a universal medikit and programmed it for blood loss and trauma while Fan-tonn helped Walderspan onto a bunk and removed his gore-soaked shirt.

"Subject experiencing severe dehydration, mild concussion and depleted blood level," announced the medikit from the center of his chest. "Commencing intravenous fluid and restorative measures."

Falle sat by his side, gently wiping the remains of sand and blood from his handsome face.

"Seems like you might just live, Kris," she smiled.

Her mind went back to the time they almost made love, the sensation of his hands on her body, the growing fire in her loins.

"Hey waitress, you sure remind me of Crandell," Walderspan announced, his voice slurred. "One hell of a wedge. Meanest eyes you ever seen but beautiful body. Great lady in a firefight. Kick any spacer's ass any day of the week." His eyes wandered to the cabin ceiling. "I tell you, waitress, sometimes I think she's more man than woman with them muscles and scars. Wonder if she'd drop her Aghaid loincloth and we'd see a dick and a pair of nuts."

Fan-tonn watched Falle stiffen and walk to the viewport to stare out at the desert. Under her tan her face was deathly pale. Something was very wrong with Falle Crandell.

"Cran-dall...you come sick?" he ventured.

"I'm fine, Fan-tonn," she replied without looking at him. "Walderspan is fine, you're fine, everybody's fine. No question at all, it's great to be fine."

~ * ~

"One more dune. Yep, only one more dune and there'll be a well fulla water."

Stillborne was crawling on his hands and knees up the hill of red sand, his face caked with a red talc, his lolling tongue blackened. Then he found himself contemplating a tiny sandaled foot. He looked up to see himself surrounded by a silent circle of sandwomen.

"Hot damn, two hunnert creds a head back in New Seattle."

His eager grin of incipient greed faded when he noticed spears topped by slivers of obsidian they were carrying.

"Hey babes, nice day if it don't rain," he greeted them with a watery smile.

Then he passed out.

"He is one of hunters from the city," one of the sandwomen remarked. "We should leave him to die in desert."

A second sandwoman measured with her eyes a wooden post flying a red strip of cloth. "He within the boundaries of our shelter, Aila. It is law of Agonn, blessings and peace be upon His Sacred Loincloth, to extend his life."

"Take him to sixth cave," the first sandwoman shrugged. "We will give him food and water."

~ * ~

"Okay, Phil, crank it up another notch. Easy, now drop it!" The two men were using crowbars to wrestle a reluctant tread onto the front sprocket of an ancient sandcrawler.

"Hell of a job, Walderspan," Phil grinned, wiping a sleeve over a sweaty forehead. "Hey, looks like you got a visitor."

Fan-tonn stood in the doorway of the ramshackle shop, watching the two men work. This was a different Fan-tonn who trudged through the desert in a ragged loincloth of rockpup hide. This one was resplendent in a red cloak with matching sandals and harness, his hand resting easily on a jeweled assault knife.

Walderspan tossed the crowbar onto a workbench. "Hey, Fan-tonn, long tongue, no flee. Nice duds I see you wearing." He nodded his approval. "I hear you and Crandell picked up a fat stack of creds when the Umas sandskimmer cleared auction."

"We also find two heartstones in cabinet." Fan-tonn smiled in acknowledgement but looked troubled.

"What's she up to, anyway? Haven't heard from her since I checked out of the hospital."

"She leaving to go Planet Verlatta to take new job." He looked glum. "She leave today, I lose friend."

"You mean Verdana?" Walderspan asked. "What job is she thinking of taking?"

"Not know. She wear funny clothes now."

"There's an interplanetary flight scheduled to lift off at New Seattle spaceport this afternoon," Phil volunteered.

Walderspan's brow wrinkled in puzzlement.

"Funny clothes?" he asked.

~ * ~

A gust of desert wind blew trash and sand over the floor of the seedy departure lounge of the spaceport. A listless crowd gathered before the security gate, awaiting the announcement to board.

"Why are women always late?" Walderspan sat on a sagging bench leaking stuffing and checked his timeband against the feebly glowing schedule on a wall panel.

He idly watched a shapely blonde wearing a white sheath dress, satin blouse and heels, slink across the floor toward to departure gate. His eyes widened in shock. It was Falle.

"Crandell, hold on." He scrambled to his feet and hurried after her. "Where in Zog's Ass are you going?"

She hauled the wheeled carry all she was pulling upright and regarded him with the fixed reptilian stare he knew so well.

"Damn, what's with the fashion model ensemble?" He was taking her in with a large measure of disbelief. "Fan-tonn told me you're heading off to Verdana? Is this right?"

"I've accepted a job offer with United Starlines," she replied.

"Job offer? Pan Galaxy voided your starpilot's license."

"Flight Attendant. I don't mind starting at the bottom again."

"Let's talk." He led her away from the crowd before the gate. "Listen, I've talked to Major Grange at Rim Mercenary headquarters over on the Outer Rim. He wants to meet you. The Umas are up to their usual antics on Planet Dropoff and he needs a good hand with a charged particle rifle."

Falle responded with a sullen glare. "I'm going to be late for my flight, Walderspan."

"Flight attendant? For United Starlines, the notorious low budget space liner service?" he persisted. "You know how many crashes they've had due to cutting corners on maintenance this year?"

"So? Life is full of risks," she sniffed. "Can't be worse than a harebrained scheme to steal a warehouse full of heartstones from the Umas."

"Look, I know you need creds for the serum to cure, um…your condition."

"I'm a carrier for the hydrophis virus." She spat out the words. "Don't go asking me for a goodbye kiss, Walderspan."

"Can't you sell your water pumping facility on Dustball…"

"Not for anything close to thirty thousand. Also, my plant manager tells me the aquifer will run dry in less than two years."

Walderspan raised his hands in a gesture of frustration. "Okay, but soon as Interworld Security sees the name of Falle Crandell on a passenger list unpleasant people on New Earth are gonna know."

"Who is Falle Crandell?" She fished in her purse and held out a passport card. "Note the name and personal info is for Falle Chavez. Amazing the expert forgers you can find in a back alley here in New Seattle for the right amount of creds."

"Falle, is this really the future you want?" he asked, knowing he was fighting a losing battle against her iron determination.

"My future wants a normal life," she replied. "Maybe I can't hump a man's brains out without killing him with a kiss but under these silk thong undies I'm wearing I sure don't have a dick and a set of nuts."

She stuffed the passport back into her purse, pulling the carryall back onto its wheels. "Have a nice life, Walderspan."

Walderspan watched her join the line winding up the ramp to the waiting starliner, unable to think of anything to say.

~ * ~

The mouth of the cave framed a busy communal scene of sandwomen gathering seedpods from ropeweed bushes, a hunter returning with a brace of rockpups over her shoulder, an occasional child playing in the sand.

Stillborne turned over on his grass pallet and groaned. He was feeling groggy and vaguely remembered shadowy figures bringing him food and water. They inexplicably decided to save his life. He was troubled by the memory of numerous sandwomen he had captured, abused and hauled to the city to be sold to wealthy Aghaid males. It occurred to him if he managed to return to New Seattle a career change would be in order.

The entrance to the cave darkened. A sandwoman knelt by his side holding a gourd of water.

"I am Tann," she said. "You look much stronger."

"Yeah, thanks." Stillborne drank deeply from the gourd and panted. "Damn, that tasted better than a bottle of Emperion."

"We have a deep well in the shadow of the Red Cliff."

"You speak pretty good terran," he observed.

"My mother served as maid to human miners before the Prophet Priff, the Sniffer of Powders, sent the holy word of Agonn to the Aghaid males we were to be driven out into the desert." She took the empty gourd from him. "When you are stronger yet we will show you way to reach human city."

"Must be kinda lonely out here in the boonies with all them women." Stillborne eyed her slim figure in the scanty rockpup loincloth.

"The nights are long." She was taking him in, her luminous eyes bright with invitation. "You are very handsome," she said.

Outside, before the line of caves carved by the wind in the cliff face, Aila put down her basket of pods. "Oahh, where is Tann?" she asked her companion.

"She went to take the human food and water. Gone long time now." Oahh replied. "It was her day to draw water for us all. Perhaps she tired and became sleep."

"There are folsox berries by the well." Aila winked knowingly at her friend. "Perhaps she seeks happy dreams."

Before they could make further comment, Tann emerged from Stillborne's cave. Her hair was disheveled, her face sweaty and radiated satiated contentment.

"The little man we save from desert," she sighed. "He has long manprobe."

Oahh and Aila looked at each other. Leaving their baskets on the sand they marched toward Stillborne's cave.

~ * ~

United Starlines flight 109 en route from Verdana to New Earth had just left orbit around the planet. Passengers were relaxing after an unusually rough liftoff through Verdana's dense and unbreathable atmosphere and were peering out of viewports, admiring the stars spread out on the vast black velvet. Abruptly, the stars fused into a blizzard of streaking white as the ship kicked into timephase flight. Service carts made their appearance in the isles, dispensing drinks and snacks.

"Would you like moco or san tea?" Falle inquired of a businessman in the Executive Class section. She was adjusting to her new life on Verdana. She had a nice apartment in Lifedome Four, one of nine set in the planet's dense jungle. Less enjoyable was her present position as an aerial waitress for a run-down spaceline staffed by underpaid and disgruntled employees. Still, she consoled herself, she was off Satellite and no longer sweating her brains out merely to survive.

"Thanks, miss, but I think I'll have a Blackhole Fizz with a twist of lemon," said the businessman, eyeing with approval the long, shapely legs under the ridiculously short and tight flight attendant uniform. "Say, I'll be staying at the New Earth City Hilton when we arrive," he ventured. "Maybe we could hookup later, go to dinner?"

Falle popped the cap from a bottle and restrained the impulse to spill the contents into his lap. She noticed the indentation on his finger where he had surreptitiously removed a ring.

"That would be nice," she cooed. "First I'd like to see a note."

He brightened with anticipation, and then looked puzzled. "You'd like a note?"

"From your wife. Saying it's okay to date strange women when you're off-planet."

The businessman scowled and she smiled angelically, moving down the aisle to the galley to refill her cart.

Her fellow attendant Doris was unpacking a crate of bottles. "Falle, could you take this load of beer down to the Economy section." She made a face. "Be careful when you bend over. Real randy crowd of miners back there."

Falle smiled at her. "Trust me, it's not much better in the Executive Class section."

"There's a job opening for a waitress at the spaceport cafeteria on Verdana," Doris groused. "Really thinking of applying…"

A tremor ran through the hull of the liner, a muted cry of pain from assorted metal components.

"There it goes again," said Falle. "Is this a normal thing when the ship goes into timephase? Doesn't sound good to me."

"Well, I mentioned it to the flight crew when I brought them some beer. They just laughed and told me not to soil my panties."

"Took them some beer." Falle rolled her eyes. "Bet the Interspace Commission would like to know what goes on here at United Cheaplines." Another tremor rattled the glasses in her cart. "I think I'll drop by engineering when I'm through with Economy and check things out."

"Try not to bend over when you're in Economy," Doris reminded her.

Mr. Lamb, the ship's ancient chief engineer, was hunched over a console below the enormous black hulk of the fusion drive. He was nervously snacking on his fingernails. "Dammit, look at the fluctuation," he whined to Falle. "Ten cycles above normal."

She looked up at a confusing tangle of pipes, cables and dials.

"So, what do you think is happening?"

"I figure we got an obstruction in a feed line close to the outer hull."

"What could this mean?"

"What could it mean?" Mr. Lamb looked at her with his rheumy eyes. "Goddammit, girl, could cause a rupture of the hull. Any idea of what happens if we lose hull integrity in timephase flight? Kablooee."

"I'm assuming you let the captain know of your concerns?"

"Hell yes." He returned to snacking on his fingernails. "He told me no big deal. The ship is old but she'll hold."

When Falle made her way up from engineering to the cockpit she found a party atmosphere with the ship cruising along on autopilot. The captain was leaning back in the command chair, feet propped up on the main console, the copilot and astrogater swilling bottles of Aghaid beer.

Falle nervously cleared her throat, aware of her lowly status as spaceliner waitress.

"Hey guys, I just had a conversation with your chief engineer," she ventured. "He thinks there might be a major problem with the fusion drive."

"Nah, there's always some problem with the old barge from time to time," the captain replied, taking a healthy swig from his bottle. "Not to worry, sweetcheeks."

His casual waving away of her concerns irritated Falle. "Well, he's running out of fingernails to chew. Any chance you're sober enough to give him a call?"

"Oh, my gosh, I really must apologize, Miss Chavez," said the Captain with a sarcastic drawl.

"I had no idea United Starlines had just promoted you to command of this spaceliner." The copilot and astrogater exchanged grins and began to giggle.

Another tremor ran through the ship, stronger and more alarming than the previous ones.

She had been through all this before, Falle realized. A similar scenario with an arrogant captain ignoring her warning of imminent catastrophe.

"Could I have a little of your beer, Captain?" she asked, holding out her hand.

"Well sure, sugarbowls," he smirked. "Nothing like a bottle of suds to straighten out a bad attitude."

"You're right, nothing like a bottle of suds." In a single move she smashed the bottle against the captain's head, drove her foot into the astrogater's crotch, and held the jagged bottle neck under the copilot's chin.

"Drop the ship out of timephase," she ordered him. "Like right now."

The copilot blanched, a trickle of blood spotting his shirt. "Ss...sure, Chavez, great idea," he stammered. "You should have asked us sooner."

Doris came rushing into the cockpit. "Hey, the liner is dead in space. What has...?" Her mouth dropped open at the sight of Falle standing over two sprawled bodies, the bloody end of a broken bottle pressed into the neck of the copilot.

Before she could rationalize what was happening, there was a muted bang somewhere in the bowels of the spaceliner. Instantly, her ears popped painfully as cabin air pressure sank.

"Attention. The ship's hull has been compromised. Please access emergency oxygen units," a metallic voice announced amid hooting alarms and the screams of passengers.

Abruptly, air surged into the cockpit. There was the sound of emergency panels snapping into place.

"Hull integrity restored, oxygen is now at safe levels," the metallic voice declared. "Thank you for flying with United Starlines."

Doris studied Falle, still holding the broken bottle. "Well, it seems to me one of two things is gonna happen. You're either gonna get promoted or canned."

~ * ~

Gloom pervaded the board room of United Starlines annual meeting. Executives sitting behind the long table contemplated their water glasses, not meeting each other's eyes.

The suite door glided open and the company president, Emile Barnsmellow, strode purposely into the room followed by an attractive young woman and a slinky individual who had *salesman* embedded in his fixed smile.

"Good morning, people, glad you could all be here," Barnsmellow announced. "Before we begin, allow me to introduce Mr. Brad Conster and his associate Ms. Anne Plastikote of Universal Cybernetics here on Verdana who will be delivering a presentation later in the meeting."

He nodded to his two companions who smiled dutifully at the board members.

"As you can see by the ladder graph behind me, our profits for the last four quarters have been in a steady decline," he began.

"Excuse me, sir, but the ladder graph seems to indicate a steady rise in profitability," an executive observed nervously.

Barnsmellow scowled, glanced over his shoulder. "The display board is placed upside down. Would someone please mount it correctly?" A junior executive scurried from his seat to make the correction.

"Now then, despite our emergency adjustment downwards of wages and qualifications for our starpilots, mechanics and operational staff we continue our financial decline," he continued. "As always, the biggest impact on our profitability has been expenditures for wages and benefits. Does everyone here agree?"

One of the executives at the table coughed nervously. "Mr. Barnsmellow, the wages and benefits at United Starlines are now the lowest in the space liner business."

"Precisely. Wages and benefits." Barnsmellow pounded a meaty fist on the board table. "We have a plan to outsource all our profit-draining employees. Let me now turn the meeting over to Mr. Conster and his associate."

The representative from Universal Cybernetics took his place at the head of the table. Highly polished speerwood reflected a face wearing a classic I-wanna-be-your-friend-for-life salesman smile reeking of false bonhomie.

"As you must have heard, my company has been manufacturing

here on Verdana the finest cybernetic androids for home and office. All of our models have advanced polycarbon and protoflesh bodies with full sensory inputs. Their basic programming is embedded with all the most desired human emotions such as loyalty, affection, commitment and desire to please." He paused to beam at his audience.

"Our recommendation to Mr. Barnsmellow is a gradual phaseout of your human employees starting with flight attendants and moving upwards to starpilots."

The Director of Operations raised a hand. "But skills above dockloader require more than a Level Five intelligence," he objected. "The Verdana Department of Artificial Persons has forbidden creation of cybernetics above this level."

"We have come to…how shall I put it…a financial agreement with the director of this department." He winked slyly. "We have been cleared to introduce Level Seven and above cybernetics to replace all human employees. After all, Verdana is a Right To Work planet."

The atmosphere along the table relaxed, smug grins were exchanged as a rise in executive salaries, bonuses and stock options appeared on the horizon.

"Exactly how close in human appearance will these cybernetic replacements be?" queried the Director of Finance.

"As close as myself." Ms. Plastikote took the floor with a smile. "I am a Level Six, Model HK25 Sales Associate."

All around the table were suitably impressed. Especially impressed was the Director of Finance appraising Ms. Plastikote's well-filled executive pantsuit.

"As mentioned, I recommend starting with the flight attendants," she resumed. "Rather than incurring the expense required to craft different facial features and physiques from scratch we suggest using one of your current attendants as a template. Could you recommend a particular candidate who might be suitable, Ms. Himmelfhart?"

The Director of Human Resources pursed her lips. "What comes to mind is the little blonde, Falle Chavez, who on Flight 109 brought the ship safely out of timephase just before the hull ruptured."

Barnsmellow rubbed his chin thoughtfully. "Well, if we're going to use her face and body to create several score cybernetic flight attendants, we have to be certain about her background. After all, we don't want a horde of former safecrackers, shoplifters or ex-Borgia Guild members running riot through our spaceliner fleet."

"Oh, I can vouch for her background after a thorough examination of her passport," the Director of Human Resources assured him. "It seems she was raised on Dustball, immigrated to Satellite and used her background living on a desert planet to become a tour guide for Desert Adventures."

"Hmm. How about her personal life?"

"Lives quietly in a modest apartment in Lifedome Four. Attractive as she appears, no known intimate relationships, male or female. Likes to target practice at Shooter's Universe, pumps iron at the gym daily."

Barnsmellow nodded his approval. "Schedule an appointment with Ms. Chavez. I think we should make her an offer."

~ * ~

Falle fidgeted in the uncomfortable chair before the desk of the Director of Human Resources, Mrs. Himmelfhart. The director was taking her time sorting through paperwork before giving Falle her attention. It was an old managerial technique she recognized intending to disconcert a troublesome employee.

Furtively, Falle glanced at her left palm, ensuring the permaplast coating she daily applied to hide the hazmat imprint was intact. She had a very good idea what this interview with Mrs. Himmelfhart would be about.

So far, United Starlines upper management had made no official response to the cockpit drama on flight 109. She did hear the pilot was in a coma for two days from the beer bottle she had broken over his skull. The co-pilot required surgery to repair his left testicle and the astrogater was in a clinic recovering from 'extreme emotional trauma'. The prospect of applying for the waitress job at the Verdana Spaceport seemed to beckon.

With an air of finality Mrs. Himmelfhart dropped a folder and looked across her desk at Falle.

"I'm sure you will be relieved to hear the Spaceline Review Board has examined the report regarding the incident on Flight 109 and has exonerated you of all charges brought by the flight crew," she said.

"I'm very glad to hear this, Mrs. Himmelfhart." Falle felt like wilting with relief. A future of taking lunchtime orders began to fade.

"In fact, management is contemplating a reward for your life saving actions on the flight," Mrs. Himmelfhart continued.

Falle brightened. A larger apartment in Lifedome Nine would be nice, with a view of Vedanette Lake, or at least an interweb subscription to *The Force Pistol Review.* "Are we talking about a raise in salary?" she asked hopefully.

"Unfortunately, this is not in the budget," said Himmelfhart with regret. "Are you familiar with the use of cybernetic androids here on Verdana?"

Falle nodded. The maintenance man at her apartment complex was one and she had noticed others doing the work of kitchen maids and landscapers. They always seemed to be smiling.

"United Starlines is planning a test program to have Universal Cybernetics create, say, one or two cybernetics to be programmed as flight attendants." She extended Falle a congratulatory smile. "We have chosen you to be the template for the new line."

The image of sunbirds floating above Verdanette Lake below her new apartment vanished. "Excuse me, template?"

"A copy will be made of your face and body for the cybernetics to be manufactured. When you report to the factory sales outlet you will enter a scanning chamber, sort of like a 3D printer, and a precise record of your physical attributes will be created."

Silently, Falle digested the Director's offer. She had heard rumors since her arrival on Verdana about corporations pushing for more cybernetic workers, creating labor unrest among unemployed humans. Also, what other of her dark secrets might the scanning process reveal?

"I'm sorry, Mrs. Himmelfhart," she said at last. "I'm really not interested. My sincere thanks to management, though."

The Director frowned, tapping her stylus on her blotter. "What would it take, then, for you to accept our offer?"

"It's not that I don't consider it an honor, but..."

"We of United Starlines are prepared to consider any request from you, other than monetary, of course."

"Any request?" Falle recalled the first time she had regarded herself in a mirror after graduation from Pan Galaxy's flight school; reveling in the gold wings of a starpilot on her new uniform.

"Does United Starlines have an entry program for pilot trainees?" she inquired. "I just might be very interested."

~ * ~

"Welcome to Universal Cybernetics Factory Outlet. Check out all the latest models."

Falle walked past the neonglow sales logo reflecting off the gleaming syntheteak floor. They appeared to be doing a brisk business, flocks of mostly chunky middle-aged women perusing the male models, lonely and balding single men having the dejected air of the newly divorced browsing the female lines. Passing a willowy female cybernetic in a pink nightie she turned over the price tag. *Wow, these things are pricey,* she silently mused.

"Hi, I'm Tori, a Model SX12 Wind Overnighter," Pink Nightie declared with a dazzling smile.

"You can take me home tonight for a two hundred cred down payment, pending credit approval."

"Here for the big sale, huh?" said a salesman arriving at her side like a shark sensing chum. "I can tell a smart buyer when I see her."

Startled, Falle dropped the price tag. "Um no, I'm here from United Starlines."

"I'm self lubricating and my programming includes forty-one intimate positions," Tori continued, taking a deep breath to better display her cleavage.

"Hey, we sold a Model ST9 Gladiator to a lady from there yesterday," the salesman declared, thrusting out his hand. "Tomm Hucksmore here and…"

"I can lick the chrome from a launch trailer hitch and suck a sportsball through…"

"Take a hike, tin tits," said Hucksmore without looking at Pink Nightie. "Sorry Ma'am, didn't catch your name."

"I'm Falle Cran-, er, Chavez," she looked vaguely around. "I was told to report here to be, um, scanned for your new line of cybernetic flight attendants."

Hucksmore's anticipatory sales grin slipped a notch. "Oh yes, Ms. Chavez. Go through the door at the end of the sales floor into the factory. Ms. Anne Plastikote is expecting you."

The cybernetics factory reminded Falle of a cross between a jetwing assembly plant and a butcher's shop. A conveyer belt carried polycarbon human skeletons to waiting tanks of protoflesh organs. Falle peered into a long line of crates containing completed male and female cybernetics. All were missing hair and facial features.

"We usually add hair and human features after a client places an order," said a voice behind her. She turned to see a tall brunette smiling at her.

"I'm Ms. Plastikote and you must be Ms. Chavez from United Starlines."

"Yes, that's me," Falle replied nervously.

The long line of crates holding faceless human bodies was making her uneasy.

"Excellent. Follow me please."

The room was an antiseptic white with banks of electronic gear stacked against the walls. In the center was a table leading to a narrow tube reminding Falle of an ancient MRI device.

"Remove your clothing and any jewelry, please," ordered Ms. Plastikote. "We can't have anything to interfere with your bioscan recording."

"I have some scars and, er, tattoos," said Falle, stripping off her flight attendant uniform. "Will this be a problem?"

"The bioscan device will not register non-living items such as scars, tattoos, dental or surgical implants. The transfer should be pure as the driven snow on Darkworld." She studied the faint lines on Falle's back. "My, you do have some scars, somewhat like whip marks. I'll bet there's an interesting story behind them," she smiled.

Ms. Plastikote always seemed to be smiling.

"You're a cybernetic," Falle accused.

"Of course, I am." She handed Falle a pair of darkened goggles. "Wear these to protect your eyes and lie down on the scanner bed."

~ * ~

Excerpt from the
New Earth City Inquirer
Your News Today!

Residents of the Six Cities in Zardoria, Planet New Earth were forced from their homes last Tarday to celebrate the marriage of Chancellor Taragon and Count Duefuss at the Chandelier Palace. Citizens of Zardoria, spurred by the electrolashes of Taragon's Citizens Guard, cheered wildly at the motorcade winding through the capitol to the Zardorian Spaceport where the Chancellor and her new husband will be departing later this day for their honeymoon in the luxurious Lifedome Nine on Planet Verdana. A pro-democracy demonstration at the spaceport was put down by the usual efficient brutality of the Citizens Guard.

~ * ~

"United Starlines? You have booked our flight to Verdana on this low budget tramp steamer carrier?" Taragon demanded.

She was sitting in the spaceport executive lounge surrounded by a mountain of her luggage. Count Duefuss hovered nervously at her side. He was getting an education in her short temper. He had just turned twenty-two; the Chancellor was in a collision course toward sixty.

"Beloved Tyrant, all the other spacelines including Pan Galaxy have embargoed Zardoria due to alleged human rights abuses," her Grand Chamberlain explained. His face was slimed with sweat. "I have reserved the entire First-Class section of a flight for you and your suite."

"The supreme ruler of the Six Cities on Zardoria departing for her honeymoon on a low budget carrier," Taragon fumed. "If the New Earth press finds out about this…"

"A Zardorian reporter who took a holo of the arriving United Starlines ship has been arrested and executed, Adored Despot," the Grand Chamberlain soothed.

Count Duefuss bent close to her ear. "Please, beloved, our flight is due to depart in ten zaks."

"Very well, let's get on with it," she scowled. "The First-Class section had better exceed my expectations for comfort and service or I'll have the entire crew executed."

~ * ~

United Starlines flight 320 knifed through the black velvet of space in timephase mode. Seat restraint signs winked off and flight attendants moved from the galley along the isles, serving passengers.

"Why can't we see the stars anymore?" Taragon was peering out the huge viewport at a snowstorm of streaking white light.

"I believe in timephase mode we are actually outspeeding the stars, beloved," replied Count Duefuss at her side on the luxurious couch.

"Would you two care for some champagne before dinner arrives?" said a voice above them. "I am told the main course is prime rib of ardex."

Taragon looked up into the face of flight attendant Falle Chavez. There was an eternity of mutual shocked recognition.

"Champagne would be fine," Taragon finally managed to croak.

Silently Falle filled their glasses and returned to the galley where Doris was fussing with an array of dishes.

"Doris, could we switch duties on this flight?" she asked. "I'll service the Economy Section and you can take First Class."

"Huh?" Doris looked at her in surprise. First Class was always considered a plum, with often generous tips from wealthy passengers. "What's up with you?"

"I think I just destroyed someone's appetite for the prime rib of ardex."

~ * ~

The tiny jetwing dropped from the night sky and landed on the snow in a miniature blizzard of flying ice crystals. A hatch slid open and chief engineer Klutz emerged, the hatch gliding shut behind him. He pulled his hood tighter against the arctic cold and walked to the huge geodesic dome outlined against the stars, his boots crunching on patches of ice.

He came to a door displaying a weathered plaque reading *New Earth South Pole Research Station* and jabbed a gloved hand at a button. A moment later the door slid open revealing a wizened elf wearing a white lab coat.

"Dr. Chatham, how nice to see you again," he greeted him jovially, stamping the snow from his feet. "I just thought a horny handed son of toil such as myself would stop by for a friendly chat with you two learned gentlemen."

Dr. Chatham was not overjoyed to see his visitor. "For the monthly extortion," he retorted.

"Ah, a small retainer to ensure my power plant in Glacier City continues to provide electricity for your little station so far up the mountain," he chuckled. "After all, to lose power this time of year with the ice bears coming out of hibernation so mean and hungry…"

"I'm sure you're very concerned about myself and Dr. Calomini up here with the ice bears," Dr. Chatham replied drily.

Dr. Calomini was nursing a cup of moco at a small table surrounded by lab equipment and electronics. He watched bleakly while Klutz lowered himself into a chair and pulled out a pocket compad.

"Let me see, last month's retainer…" he began.

"Last month's extortion payment," Dr. Calomini muttered.

"Please, Dr. Calomini," Klutz chided him. "Let's try and remain cordial or I might find reason to increase your remittance. My boys at the power plant have families to support, bills to pay."

"Assuming they're receiving a share of each month's 'retainer'."

"Ah, the good doctor has arrived with the filthy lucre," Klutz grinned.

Dr. Chatham sat down at the table and pushed a stack of creds to his visitor. Klutz carefully counted the stack and shoved them into his jacket pocket. He pushed himself away from the table and gave the two scientists a mock salute.

"Until next month, gentlemen, I bid you a fond adieu."

Dr. Calomini watched the door of the research station slide shut on their unwelcome guest and eyed his companion. Dr. Chatham was wearing a smile similar to the cat who had just devoured the canary. "What on New Earth are you so joyous about?" he demanded.

"Arrangements have been made to deal with this 'small monthly retainer situation'," he grinned.

"Arrangements?" asked Dr. Calomini.

Outside in the snow Klutz crunched his way back to the waiting Jetwing. A faint band of orange on the horizon signaled the reluctant coming of dawn.

He had no sooner reached the craft when something red came out of the night to land with a soggy thump on the hood. Klutz walked around to find a bleeding haunch of meat lying beside the windshield. For the first time he noticed fresh blood had been scattered on the snow around the jetwing.

"What in Zog's left nut is going on?" he breathed. A low moan came from the darkness, followed by several more, then the sound of heavy footfalls breaking the crust of snow, coming nearer.

"An ice bear pack!" Klutz gasped. He scrambled around to the entry hatch, tore off a glove and frantically punched the code into the access pad. Nothing. Then he saw torn wires hanging from the base of the pad.

Chief engineer Klutz screamed in terror. He jerked around to see an enormous head covered in shaggy white hair emerge from the darkness. He was able to scream one final time before the ice bear pack engulfed him.

Behind a hill of snow, Gordo listened with satisfaction to the final scream and night stillness was broken by the tearing of flesh and contented growls. He had no sooner trudged through the snow to his waiting jetwing and crawled inside when his comm band started chiming.

A jowled, angry female face appeared in the tiny screen.

"Why, Chancellor Taragon, how very enjoyable to see you again," Gordo greeted her. Judging by her expression this wasn't going to be a jolly social call. "Allow me to congratulate you on your marriage to Count..."

"Spare me the pleasantries, Gordo," she snarled. "She's here, she's still alive."

"Who is still alive?"

"Falle Crandell, the ex-member of your Borgia Guild."

"Are you sure?"

"She just served me champagne, you idiot! I was under the impression she was killed, eaten and excreted by the snakeoids on Swampword."

"Please, Chancellor, calm down," Gordo consoled her. "Of course, the Guild guarantees its contracts. Where did you see her?"

"She's working as a flight attendant for United Starlines," said Taragon angrily. "Here on our honeymoon flight to Verdana."

"Very well, Chancellor. The Guild has an agent on Verdana. I will have him look into Ms. Crandell and resolve the situation to your satisfaction."

~ * ~

Falle unearthed the small and highly illegal force pistol from its hiding place in her apartment and tossed it on the bed beside clothing and other necessities she was preparing to pack into a carryall. She soberly eyed the storm clouds outside the plexglass dome, pondering her options. Once again, they weren't many. By now, the good Chancellor Taragon would have sent an outraged complaint to the Borgia Guild of her escape from Swampworld. Discovery had always been a concern. The few times the spaceline scheduled her for a New Earth flight she had retreated to the employee lounge until departure.

Her grand design to start a new life after her sojourn on Satellite was not working out as planned. Returning to Haboob City on Dustball seemed the best choice but unfortunately the Guild would probably have the same idea of where she would head.

A beeping came from the commscreen on the wall. Falle touched a button and Doris's face appeared.

"Hey, Falle," she greeted. "You left the spaceport in such a rush I hadn't had a chance to talk to you."

"Yes, I had a few things to take care of. What's on your mind?"

"My new job waitressing the spaceport lounge." She grinned conspiratorially. "I got my application in before any of the other flight attendants heard the bad news."

"Bad news?" Falle seated herself on the edge of the couch.

"You haven't checked the messages on your comm band?"

"No, I was busy...cleaning my apartment."

"Old Barnsmellow canned all the flight attendants effective today," Doris explained, making a face. "Said he was very sorry but the financial picture of United Starlines forced him to replace human attendants with cybernetic androids programmed to do our job. Said he had leased ninety-three of them from Universal Cybernetics."

Son of a bitch. They told me they were only going to create one or two from my scan template.

"Have you seen any of these new cybernetics yet?" she asked nervously.

"Hell, no. We were ordered to turn in our uniforms and passcards at the end of our shift. They said our final paychecks would be interfaxed to us and we were given the bum's rush out the door," Doris laughed. "My new job at the lounge has better hours and with tips I'll be making more than slaving for those cheap jerks at United Starlines."

Falle digested the implications of these glad tidings. Not only hunted by the Borgia Guild but now unemployed.

"Gotta start my new job in a few hours, Falle," said Doris happily. "Maybe I'll see you there. Bye now." The screen went blank.

High above, rain began to streak the lifedome. Sensing the coming dusk, lights began to blink on in the apartment.

The obvious choice was to get herself off Verdana fast before she became a candidate for Verdana's funeral compost converters. The most obvious solution was one she surprised herself with by not realizing it sooner.

Falle came out of her reverie and began tapping buttons for the wall commscreen. A smiling female appeared wearing a familiar uniform.

"Welcome to the Pan Galaxy reservations desk, my name is Tanya," she announced. "How may I help you?"

"Yes, I would like to reserve a one-way ticket to Haboob City on Dustball on your earliest flight," said Falle.

"Let me see, we have a redeye leaving at twenty-one hundred hours, Flight 420," said Tanya, scrutinizing a screen before her.

"This would be perfect. The name is Falle Chavez."

"Economy or First Class?"

"Economy would be fine."

"I have your reservation secured, Ms. Chavez," Tanya smiled. "Payment due on arrival. Thank you for flying Pan Galaxy."

Behind the reservations counter she watched Falle's face vanish from the screen. She tapped a number on her keypad.

"Am I speaking to Mr. Dragnor from the Borgia Guild?" she whispered, sneaking a peek over her shoulder. "I understand you're offering a generous reward for information about travel plans of a certain person?"

~ * ~

Chancellor Taragon struggled to pull the flimsy black nightie over her ample breasts and sagging stomach. With a relieved sigh she straightened the hem around her legs and regarded herself in the boudoir mirror of their luxurious suite in Lifedome Nine Hilton.

She had no illusions, even with the black nightie, that she was a sight to arouse the flame of lust in the loins of her new husband. Of course, he would perform his connubial duties with the usual skill, probably thinking of the wealth and position he would be inheriting when she passed on. It was almost a pity he had no inkling of her plans to revoke the decree making him the designated heir to the Chancellorship of Zardoria.

Baron Ghrasp was a better choice to keep the sheep of the Six Cities in line with the necessary brains and ruthlessness. Count Duefuss had the brains of a gnat and as for ruthlessness…well, if only his will was as hard as his manly member.

She was still smirking when she entered the bedroom to find Count Duefuss holding her comm band. He looked at her quizzically.

"Beloved, you just received a call from a Mr. Dragnor informing us there will be a fireworks display over Verdanette Lake at twenty-one hundred hours," he said.

"Really? It's almost that time now. Would you care for a glass of champagne while we watch?"

They took their places on a couch before an enormous window overlooking the city lights far below. Lines of red and blue indicated busy aircar traffic and a dark patch reflecting stars was Verdanette Lake and the surrounding city park.

A spaceliner lifted from the spaceport in the distance. It headed for the main entry hatch in the dome which was slowly opening to allow passage.

A thin red beam from somewhere in the city below struck the hull of the spacecraft. It erupted in a cascade of flaming debris, raining wreckage and bodies into the trees surrounding Verdanette Lake.

"Holy Gorth Crap." Count Duefuss dropped his champagne glass onto the plush carpet. He scrambled up and pressed his face against the plexglass. "What in zerid happened?"

"What a terrible tragedy." Taragon shook her head sadly. "I don't believe anyone on Flight 420 could have possibly survived."

Count Duefuss turned away from the scene of carnage to stare at her. "How could you know what flight number it was?"

~ * ~

"We're only gonna tell you once. This valley is our stake, get the hell out."

The two trappers stood in the sunbake of the canyon exuding sweat and menace. The bigger one, a hulk with a matted beard and wearing an Umas fighting harness cocked his head at the three sandwomen chained to the rear of the crawler. "This means them honies belong to us. You gonna turn 'em over or do we gotta get froggy?"

Falle moved from the shade of the crawler. In deference to the heat she wore only the desert loincloth of the Aghaid and a narrow band around her breasts. Muscles glided under her sundarkened skin as she pushed the charged particle rifle farther up her shoulder.

"Kick their asses, Crandell." Stillborne leaned back in the operator's seat and puffed on his dhungpipe. This was the second time in a season someone tried to hijack their catch and he was looking forward to the entertainment.

"I see you have an extra canteen," she observed. "Hand it over and I'll let you two dirtbags leave with a whole skin."

The faces of the intruders froze. The bearded hulk warily unsnapped the keeper of the force pistol he wore low on his leg.

"You gotta lot of juice for a wedge." He sneered. "You trying to make us laugh?"

"Better clean the rockpup waste from your ears. Drop the canteen and vanish before you don't have a mouth to laugh with."

The trappers exchanged baffled glances. The big one stared suspiciously at the crawler and its sole occupant. He was lounging like a spectator at a magball game, wearing an irritating smirk and obviously too stoned to be a problem.

The girl hadn't yet unslung her rifle or loosened the assault knife at her hip. He noticed she was slim with a body which seemed to have been chiseled from marble. She had pale blue eyes, which studied him with cold arrogance.

Damn, she's got mean eyes, he thought and apropos of nothing realized, somehow, he'd made a fatal mistake.

"I'm not going to stand out in the sun all day. I already have a suntan," said Falle.

The big trapper jerked the force pistol from its holster and froze. His mouth sagged open and he mumbled as if trying to recall something long forgotten. The pistol slipped from his fingers and he groped for the hilt of the assault knife buried in his chest. With a sigh he pitched forward onto the sand.

The second trapper screamed and fired a beam in the direction of the crawler before scrambling wildly down the canyon looking for someplace to hide.

Falle lifted her charged particle rifle, taking casual aim…

"This is the captain of Flight 360 en route from Verdana to the Terminax Space Station." The announcement crackled through the spaceliner. "We will soon be docking at the Arrivals tube. Thank you all for flying with United Starlines."

Falle jerked upright on the galley jumpseat where she had been dozing. Around her bustled exact copies of her, preparing meals, loading carts with drinks. She smiled, regarding multiple images of herself, somehow like gazing into funhouse mirrors.

It had all been so easy. She had arrived at the Verdana Spaceport wearing one of her old United Starlines uniforms and joined the line of cybernetic flight attendant duplicates of herself wheeling their carryalls past the security gate and into the ship. She still had her flight passcard and hoped it had not been deactivated. The security guards had not even asked to see it.

"Falle 1, could you help Falle 38 deliver these snacks to the last row in Economy?" said Falle 20. Since she had discarded her old Chavez nametag this is what the other attendants had taken to calling her.

"I would be happy to." She took the tray and smiled. She reminded herself to maintain the fixed cybernetic smile on her face. Also, there would be no tips forthcoming from economy.

Once on Terminax she changed into her civilian clothes and booked a flight to Sheridan's Planet. She had a job interview.

Chapter Six

The honeymoon of Chancellor Taragon and Count Duefuss was drawing to a close. *Just as well,* she thought, seeing how the Count looked drained of energy, sweat and body fluids from the nightly workouts she obliged him to perform. She was in not much better shape with post-coital celebrations of the demise of the little bitch who had given her the hydrophis virus. She barely remembered being wakened at some ungodly hour for the return flight to New Earth, bundled aboard the United Spacelines ship, hung over and half asleep.

An hour into the flight she felt herself being gently shaken by a flight attendant. "Would you care for a hot cup of moco, Ma'am?" the attendant inquired. "We will be serving breakfast shortly."

"A cup of moco with a shot of Zardorian brandy sounds about right," Taragon yawned, glancing at Count Duefuss snoring at her side. She looked up into the face of Falle Crandell.

"Fine, I'll see what I can find in the galley." Falle smiled and continued up the aisle, taking orders.

Taragon staggered to her feet, staring after the apparition, her eyes twin moons. Someone tapped her shoulder. She spun around to confront yet another Falle Crandell. "Excuse me, please," said Falle, pushing past with the drink cart.

"Aaahhh!" Taragon screamed. She rushed along the aisle into the ship's galley to see two identical Falle Crandells preparing breakfast dishes. Uttering a strangled cry, she staggered through curtains into Economy Class. A half dozen Falle Crandells in flight attendant uniforms paused in their duties to stare at her.

"Aaahhh!" she screamed a final time, then clutched at her chest with the onset of a massive heart attack. Lying on the cabin floor gasping for breath, the last thing she saw was a circle of Falle Crandells looking down at her. They all were smiling.

~ * ~

The monsoon storm blew down from the crags of planet Dropoff, flattening the lush jungle like a giant hand and rattling the circle of wooden huts in the clearing.

Major Grange considered the inevitable leak in the thatch above his desk. With a grunt of annoyance, he moved a stack of reports and comm discs away from the steady drip. Crates of ordinance and stacked weapons were piled against a wall where a tattered banner hung. A ram's skull, crossed assault knives and a scrolled motto: *Vincere Aut Mori.*

"Well, do you want to interview the prospective recruit or not?" asked Captain D'Escrille, leaning back in a rattan chair, cleaning his nails with a bayonet.

"Let me once again review her qualifications, such as they are, on her application." Grange pulled a viscreen closer to him. "I see she's twenty-one years old, has no combat experience, and weighs a feather over one hundred and ten pounds. You said she was a former assassin for whom?"

"The Borgia Guild on planet New Earth," D'Escrille replied. "She's a real knockout blonde, Major."

"Sign her up as a comfort girl for the squad, Captain," Grange retorted. "Great Gonads of Zorg, a former assassin."

"Not a good idea," he chuckled. "She has the hydrophis virus."

"Holy gorth crap. How do you know this?"

"Walderspan on Dustball mentioned it to me when he sponsored her. He said he had seen her in action on Satellite."

"Walderspan is an idiot."

"He is also the one who pulled you from the burning jetwing when we were ambushed by the Umas on Asteroid IVX."

Major Grange sighed in resignation. "All right, all right, send her in."

Falle was pacing the hall outside Grange's office. The bright idea of dressing for the job in her customary black bodysuit resulted in her being soaked in sweat, hot and bothered. She leaned out a hut window and noticed the storm was raining itself out to shafts of sunlight crossing the steaming jungle. She inhaled thick, bitter-tasting air and thought back to her arrival on Dropoff.

She escaped the long arm of Taragon and the Guild and was now ensconced safely in an obscure planetoid on the Outer Rim. Spaceline tickets, the necessary forged documents and bribes left her with few creds and fewer choices. Attempting to access her New Earth bank account revealed Taragon had engineered a freeze on her savings. Employment with the Rim Mercs was a straw to be clutched by a drowning person.

"Major Grange will see you now."

Seated behind Major Grange's desk Falle sensed disapproval and certain condescension in his appraisal of her.

"Let me give you a brief rundown or our organization, Ms. Crandell." Major Grange began. "We're just a bunch of old soldiers who found a profitable demand for our skills by aspiring governments requiring discrete military services. Tell us how you think you'll fit in."

Falle returned his unblinking stare with one of her own. "Let's just say, Major, I'm not afraid to get my hands dirty."

"So, I understand. Walderspan tells me he talked you into getting our tattoo." He smiled crookedly. "That was your first mistake."

"I think I might have been drunk at the time."

Grange waited for further elaboration and instead received a cold reptilian stare from her pale blue eyes. There was something in those eyes which gave him a feeling of unease. He blinked, cleared his throat.

"Very well, Ms. Crandell, we'll give you a chance. I understand you don't care much for the Umas and their colonial ambitions?"

"You know the answer to that question," she replied.

"The Umas have set up an outpost here on Dropoff using the indigenous humanoids known as Ghotes to harvest a valuable lumber known as triwood from the jungle," Grange explained. "The governments on Planet New Earth consider this little planetoid their bailiwick and have given us a contract to arm and train the Ghotes to set up a guerilla operation." He indicated the stacked weapons and ordinance.

"What are these...Ghotes like?" Falle felt a need to find out exactly what she might be getting into.

"A group of missionaries from Sheridan's Planet found out," Captain D'Escrille sniggered from his chair. "They were able to teach them to speak some terran before they got themselves eaten."

"So then," said Major Grange, concluding his little dissertation. "Does this sound like something you might be interested in?"

Falle got up and walked to the stack of weapons. She picked up a charged particle rifle and looked at Grange. "When do I start?" she asked.

Grange laughed. "Good attitude. Let us introduce you to the rest of the squad."

The room was filled with a rowdy crowd swilling beer amid laughter and horseplay. *Rough bunch,* Falle observed, taking in their brawny arms and assorted scars. The noise quieted down as she was led before them.

"Good morning, people," Major Grange announced. "What I have here is a Ms. Falle Crandell who hopes to join our happy little organization." He gave the crowd a sly grin. "She already has the tattoo."

Someone in the back row farted and the room erupted in laughter.

"Hey, knock it off, Davv, can't you see there's a lady present," one of the mercs chortled.

"A farting horse will never tarry, a farting man's the man to marry," Davv retorted, winking at Falle.

Falle blandly gazed out over them without comment. She had been in this situation before.

"Ms. Crandell will be assigned to Village Twelve tomorrow," Grange continued. "Captain D'Escrille will now show her to her quarters. A heads up should any of you horny shags decide to pay her a visit during the night." He wagged a reproving finger before the eager faces eyeing the slim figure in the tight bodysuit. "She is a carrier of the hydrophis virus."

The room was instantly silent.

Taking a deep breath to push out her breasts, Falle favored them with a sultry smile.

"Nonsense. Any one of you handsome guys would be welcome to stop by and receive a goodnight kiss from me," she cooed.

~ * ~

Wind blew through the jungle gorge rustling the thatched roofs of the little Ghote village. The adult males squatted on the sundried mud, searching for fleas in their fur or fondling clubs spiked with splinters of obsidian. The smallest of the Ghotes weighed over three hundred pounds and they resembled body-building sloths with curved canines hanging from warty muzzles. Their morose little eyes watched the strange human girl unload crates from the jetwing and walk toward them.

Falle's impractical black bodysuit had been discarded for the simple Aghaid loincloth and band supporting her breasts she had worn on Satellite. She pushed a strand of platinum hair from her eyes and gazed out over the group. They stared back with the insolence of a classroom full of delinquents facing a new teachmaster.

"As you all know, Umas raiders have set up an outpost on this planet as a prelude to colonization," she began, her voice carrying though the hot, clear air. "The Rim Mercenary Battalion has sent me to train you in the use of modern weapons, military discipline and tactics. You will learn them. Because if you don't, you will find yourselves speaking fluent Umas and this little village of yours part of a Umas slave labor logging operation."

There were several yawns from her audience and a few mocking grins.

"Major Grange tells me you're the best fighters in the Eastern Gorge and you're going to make crack troops," she continued. "Now after meeting you all in person all I can say is you're the most worthless bunch of rejects I've ever laid eyes on."

The yawns and grins evaporated. Hair began to rise on bulging necks and arms, paws tightened on spiked clubs.

Falle noted the response with grim satisfaction. "I know what you're thinking, hairballs. You see this little blonde girl walking around in front of you in this scanty loincloth and you're probably wondering if she's good to eat. Well, I don't discuss my sex life with anyone, especially with raw recruits who aren't fit to dig a squathole."

Saliva began to drip from curved incisors. The Ghotes began to sneak furtive glances at each other, searching for a candidate in leading a mass assault.

"Which one of you sissies thinks I'm wrong?" she asked in a finale to this carefully orchestrated preamble.

A hulk of fur and muscle ambled over, blotting out the sun.

"I Tik-Tik. No like you talk bad about Ghote warriors. Tik-Tik ready fight you."

Always the biggest and always the bully, thought Falle.

"You know what, Tik-Tik," she said. "I think you look lonely and unloved."

Tik-Tik paused, stared at her in blank confusion. "Huh? What you say?"

"I think you're lonely, unloved and need a kiss." She leaned toward him, pulled his face to hers and planted a wet kiss on the massive lips.

Tik-Tik jerked back in surprise, almost dropping his club. "What you do that for?" he demanded, scowling. "Now Tik-Tik show little human wedge how...how..." His small eyes began to bulge, the club clattering to his feet. He uttered a choked bellow, clutched at his throat and fell heavily to the ground. He thrashed about, lay still.

"Well now," said Falle to the hushed and gaping assembly. "Who else is lonely, unloved and in need of a kiss?"

The Ghote pack scrambled to their feet and stood at attention. Spiked clubs landed on the ground before them.

"Very good." Falle opened one of the crates and pulled out a weapon. "What I have here is a Model DDIV pulse rifle, capable of two hundred rounds of phased photon energy per recharge."

~ * ~

The Ghotes really had pulled a fast one on Falle Crandell.

Usually she slept like a cat but whether it was lack of sleep, timephase lag on the long trip to Dropoff or adjustment to the thick alien atmosphere. During the night the Ghotes packed up and left the village. All of them had gone and judging by the missing bedding, food and certain items of furniture they planned on being gone for some time.

"Zog's left nut." Falle stood in the empty village street watching the sun rise mockingly over the jungle ferns.

During her attempts at training them, the adult males seemed terrified, eyes bulging when she gave them an order. It would appear her chastisement of the late Tik-Tik engendered in them a large degree of unreasoning fear.

She returned to the grass hut she appropriated and threw herself onto the noisy and twig-filled mattress. Well, that was it. Major Grange or his flunky with the fingernail cleaning bayonet would arrive shortly to see how her training the Ghotes in guerrilla operations against the Umas was coming.

Gee, Major Grange, I just gave one of the hairy furballs a little peck on the lips, well, maybe some tongue too, and he decided to be a real jerk and croak. How was I to know the whole village of faint-hearted daisies would stampede off into the jungle?

Falle broke open a box of rations she'd brought and made a quick breakfast, then went to her parked jetwing and started it up. Well, while I'm waiting for my pink slip, she reasoned, I may as well fly over to where the Umas have their logging operation and check out what is happening. Besides, it might give me an opportunity to stick my knife into a Umas. The image of her blazing parent's home was never far from her mind.

She followed the coordinates she had been given and concealed her ship in a dense thicket of alien vines. Checking the action of her particle rifle, she crept through the jungle toward the sound of voices and machines.

It was quite an operation, Umas style. Lines of Ghote slaves in chains loaded triwood logs onto hovercarts. The hum of lasersaws sent forest giants crashing downward through tangled undergrowth.

From a screen of purple vines, Falle watched the Umas directing their workers, encouraging the slower Ghotes with a taste of electrolash. The Umas males were typical. Brutal faces under overhanging brows, pale skins with a greenish tint. The females were exact opposites; completely human in appearance, having long raven hair and of startling beauty. All wore jeweled harnesses and a type of pith helmet as well as somber expressions. A sense of humor was not a notable Umas trait.

What was the big attraction of harvesting these ordinary-looking logs? Falle resolved to find out.

A female Umas detached herself from a work crew and wandered into the jungle on a necessary errand. From her hiding place in the undergrowth Falle watched her with feline intensity, reasoning the only decent thing to do was let her complete her business. She saw the Umas finishing up using a handful of leaves and grimly hoped they would turn out to be the Dropoff version of poison ivy.

The Umas girl stood up, adjusted her harness and received a slim blade in her left eye socket. She stiffened, gave out a low moan and collapsed onto the ferns.

With no small amount of satisfaction Falle recovered her knife. She stripped the body and donned the jeweled harness, stuffing her blonde hair under the pith helmet. Picking up the Umas electrolash she concealed her particle rifle in a bush, pushed her way through the jungle to join the logging crew. Imitating the grim swagger of the other female Umas Falle sought to blend in, even to applying the electrolash to a Ghote who had fallen in the mud.

The jungle gave way to a clearing where a large thatched hut stood surrounded by enormous stacks of triwood logs. Off to one side was a long shed, obviously where the Ghote slaves were kept. The hovercarts came to a stop where a Umas operating a crane-like device hoisted logs onto the pile. The chained Ghotes were led off to the shed and the remainder of the Umas slouched into the big hut.

Following them inside Falle retreated to a dark corner. A meal was being set out on tables, some kind of unappetizing grayish gruel. The air in the room was filled with the rotting stench of Umas bodies, some of them obviously close to their embryonic cycle. There was an atmosphere of gloom and latent violence while they talked to each other in the guttural Umas language. *So, this was life to a Umas,* Falle thought. *What joy.*

One of the Umas finished his meal, got up from the table and noticed Falle in the corner. He grunted out orders and started for the door. She had no idea what was said but it was clear she was to follow him.

They entered the dim shed where long lines of Ghotes were chained. The Umas began mixing gruel in a vat and began scooping it from a bucket into troughs beside their straw sleeping mats.

Abruptly, one of his arms fell off.

Grumbling angrily, he picked it up and pointed at the bucket for Falle to take over. He paused, staring closely at her. With his remaining hand he jerked the pith helmet from her head.

Falle's long blonde hair spilled over her shoulders.

The Umas gave out a surprised grunt which became a scream when a blade entered his chest killing him as well as his unborn nightmare.

All the Ghotes in the shed were now gaping at Falle. Gruel trickled unheeded from their mouths into the feeding troughs.

"Why you kill stink-man?" demanded a huge Ghote, looking from Falle to the dead Umas. "You hungry, now eat hims?"

Unlike the Ghotes she had seen at the village these looked starved and exhausted. All were now eyeing the Umas hungrily.

She remembered what Grange said about the missionaries from Sheridan's Planet who taught some of the Ghote villages to speak terran and how they ended up being the blue plate special. It would seem the Ghotes were not picky eaters.

"Say, you guys look hungry," she said. "Maybe I can fix this."

Falle stepped outside the Ghote shed and studied the enormous pile of logs overlooking the Umas' thatched hut. They all seemed to be inside, perhaps enjoying an after dinner aperitif. They were certainly cavalier about their camp security.

There was a low droning sound and a small jetwing skimmed low over the treetops. Falle ducked back inside while it hovered, then slowly descended. A hatch opened and Major Grange and Captain D'Escrille emerged blinking in the afternoon sunlight.

The hut door opened, disgorging a group of Umas. There were amicable handshakes and backslapping between Umas and humans before they all went back inside the hut.

"Zog's Hairy Probe," Falle breathed. "Looks like everyone's the best of buddies and partners in crime. Wonder if the rest of the squad knows their valiant leaders are in cahoots with those stinky loggers and how much they must be raking in with kickbacks?"

She considered the towering stacks of triwood logs surrounding the main hut, secured in place by thick polyfibre cables. She smiled grimly to herself as an idea occurred.

In a storage overhang next to the Ghote shed she found a row of lasersaws. Approaching the log stack, she took aim at the main cables holding everything in place. There were several musical twangs from severed cables.

The stack of logs swayed, then broke loose in an avalanche smashing down on the Umas hut with crushing force. From a cloud of dust and flying thatch came cries of terror and pain.

Inside the long shed, Falle released the last of the Ghotes with keys she had found on the dead Umas. They stood looking dumbly around them, confused by their sudden freedom.

"Hey, I though you guys were hungry?" said Falle, indicating the door. "How does a tasty buffet of Umas and human sound to you?"

The Ghotes had little notion of what a buffet might be but they could hear screams from outside and their sensitive noses homed in on the scent of blood. In one body they shuffled through the doorway to the scene of carnage outside.

Following them, Falle noticed several of the triwood logs lay stripped of their bark revealing beautiful natural stripes of red, yellow and green in the wood. "The mystery solved," Falle remarked, running her hand along the satin finish.

Major Grange and several of the Umas were pulling themselves from the wreckage. Grange shoved a fist into his mouth to stifle a cry of pain from his badly mangled leg. Captain D'Escrille was nowhere to be seen.

Something wet was dripping on the back of his neck. Grange rolled over and gazed up into the fanged face and salivating lips of a Ghote.

"No!" Major Grange screamed.

~ * ~

Stopping by Village Twelve in the futile hope her Ghote trainees had returned, Falle loaded up the crates of weapons and headed back to the merc compound. There appeared to be considerable activity in the jungle clearing with men loading munitions and gear into parked transports. She shouldered her particle rifle and entered the thatched communal shed.

"Well, if it isn't Rim Mercenary candidate Crandell, back from the boonies. Nice to see you've returned uneaten." Davv had his feet up on a table and was nursing a beer.

"Noticed that, huh?" she replied. She wondered how complacent the rest of the squad were in Grange's cozy relationship with the Umas. "Did you miss me?"

"Like a case of Alkonian facerot." He chucked a thumb at a side door. "Hey, a hyperspace message came in for you after you had left yesterday. From some spacer from Zardoria on New Earth. Old boyfriend of yours?"

"If he was, he'd be dead." Falle took a deep breath. So, the long arm of the Borgia Guild or Taragon had tracked her to this little speck of a planetoid.

"Say, where did you get the spiffy new duds?" Davv asked, admiring the scanty and jeweled Umas harness Falle had forgotten she was still wearing.

"Spoils of combat," she replied. "I'll be right back and model it for you."

An unfamiliar face appeared on the screen in the communications room. He was wearing a scarlet cloak and a jeweled circlet on his head.

"Greetings from Chancellor Duefuss to Falle Crandell," the regal figure announced. "On this, my Inauguration Day, I extend my thanks for your part in my ascension to rulership of the Six Cities in Zardoria. As a small token of gratitude, I have released the hold on your account at the New Earth Central Bank." The screen flickered off.

A glow of relief flooded Falle. She strolled lightheartedly back into the main room to see the entire squad packing up their personal gear.

"What's going on?" she asked Davv.

The feeling of euphoria was fast fading to a sense of impending disaster.

"Haven't you heard? The contract we had with the head honchos on Planet New Earth has been cancelled. The Umas have agreed to free their Ghote slaves and share in the profits of the triwood logging operation here on Dropoff." Davv looked thoughtfully at her. "Donno how much pay you're gonna get for two days work at Village Twelve."

Falle's gut instincts were usually right on the money. Something very bad was coming her way.

"So, what is Major Grange and Captain D'Escrille up to?"

"Ah, they headed off to the Umas logging camp with a copy of the treaty for the head stinky. We rigged a camera on their jetwing to record this historic meeting at their site."

Falle had a sudden memory flashback of her passing Grange's ship on her way to retrieve her particle rifle from the jungle. Of a red winking eye attached to the jetwing, recording the handshake and backslapping of Grange and the head Umas. Also recording a certain blonde female; using a lasersaw to cut the bands securing a mountain of triwood logs, resulting in an avalanche of death on the hut below.

"Fabre left an hour ago to see what was taking them so long," Davv continued. "The Interworld News wants to air footage of the event this evening." He looked quizzically at Falle. "Say, you feeling okay?"

Falle sank into a chair. "Do not pass go, do not collect thirty thousand creds, go directly to jail on the nearest penal asteroid," she muttered.

"Here, take a slug of this, you'll feel better." Davv slid a flask from his vest and held it out. "Dropoff moonshine, aged a whole two days. It'll put some hair on your chest."

"I'll stick with the hair on my carpet and drapes, Davv."

She sorted through her options. She seemed to be doing this quite a bit lately and options seemed to be either changing or disappearing. One option was certain. Shag ass to the nearest spaceport on Dropoff.

"What I really need is a vacation," she said, "maybe some nice hotel on New Earth, margaritas by the pool, stuff like that. You know, get me some me time."

"Vacation?" he asked.

~ * ~

WANTED FOR MURDER
Falle Crandell/aka Falle Chavez
If seen, do not approach
Carrier of lethal hydrophis virus
20,000 cred reward for information
Contact: Detective Smythe,
New Earth Bureau of Investigation
Interfx 22-RA

~ * ~

Flight attendant Falle 56 was getting ready for work.

Lipstick and makeup applied, she admired the result of her recent surgery to her face, removing the fixed cybernetic smile. She was still reveling in the enjoyment of her new apartment after months of living in communal squalor with a crowd of other flight attendants at the United Starlines compound.

The Verdana Department of Artificial Persons investigation into the spaceline resulted in cybernetic androids being granted many rights and privileges. In addition to her apartment she was to receive a small allowance and stipend for civilian clothes. Some of the other cybernetic attendants started dating human men. She wondered what this would be like. She was determined to find out.

After a final brush and inspection of her attendant uniform, she grabbed her purse and went through the slidedoor to the landing outside her apartment. On the landing were two stern looking men in black jumpsuits.

Startled, Falle 56 clutched her purse and stepped back. She had been warned by her shift supervisor to beware of something called 'mugging' in this neighborhood.

"Are you Falle Crandell?" one of the men demanded.

"I am Falle…"

"I'm afraid you must come with us," one of the men declared.

He seized her wrist and reached on his belt for a pair of plasticuffs.

In an instant, Falle 56's programming for resisting a personal assault took over. She twisted free of the hand grabbing her wrist and slammed a fist into his larynx. The other man leaped forward to seize her around the waist, slamming her onto the railing of the landing.

Falle 56 fell ten stories to the pavement below.

"Holy gorth shit!" Both men peered over the railing. "We got her, Stavv. We're gonna get promoted for the two Verdana cops who bagged Falle Crandell."

The other cop studied the body now bleeding on the walkway.

Not the red blood of a human but the pale pink of a cybernetic android.

"I don't think that is going to happen," said Stavv somberly.

~ * ~

"Welcome to New Earth City and thank you for flying with United Starlines," beamed Flight Attendant Falle 26, escorting passengers down the ramp into the terminal.

The two bounty hunters emerged from the crowd, greeting friends and family members. One stepped in front of Falle 26 and held up a badge.

"Ms. Crandell, I'm Jon Brolin of Zardoria Recovery Services. I'm afraid you'll have to come with us."

When he held up the badge the force pistol on his belt came into view. In Falle 26's cybernetic mind the program for responding to a terrorist hijack took over. She pushed him away and seized the weapon. As she fought for the force pistol, the second bounty hunter grappled with her.

From the three struggling figures, a red beam from the force pistol lanced into the crowd of people. There were cries of terror, a mad scramble for cover and three passengers lay dead on the ramp.

~ * ~

The girl standing behind the cosmetics counter of Cosmos Boutique seemed somehow familiar to the saleslady. She leaned forward to study the nametag on the United Starlines flight attendant uniform. Falle 72. Falle...where did she hear that name before? Was it on the Interworld news?

Falle 72 was peering into the small counter mirror, dabbing at her lips with a colored lip pencil. "I think this shade is a trifle too bright," she said. "Do you have a slightly less..."

"Falle Crandell!" the saleslady suddenly exclaimed.

Falle 72 looked up from the mirror, startled. "Excuse me?"

"It's Falle Crandell, the murderer who has the hydrophis virus! Help!" squealed the saleslady. "Stay away from me."

The crowd of shoppers in the busy mall began to yell in fear, shoving each other to get away. The fear became panic, clothing racks were overturned, display cabinets shattered, people trampled. Blood ran over the synthemarble floors and broken glass.

~ * ~

It was the largest factory recall at Universal Cybernetics. The entire warehouse floor was covered by milling flight attendant Falles, luggage at their feet. In the office high above the floor, Brad Conster looked out the window and shook his head.

"So, what are we gonna do with ninety-four exact duplicates of a lady wanted for mass murder on Dropoff?" he groused.

"That's ninety-three, Brad," Anne Plastikote corrected him. "I suppose we could get them into a glasses and beard disguise."

"Funny. You're trying to be funny." Conster nibbled at his fingernails. "You know United Starlines had to shut down operations after our delivery boys rounded up all their flight attendants. Barnsmellow's gonna sue our asses for sure."

"We didn't have any choice, Brad. Anyway, very few passengers wanted to book flights with attendants who looked like they could stick a knife in you," she reasoned.

"So, what are we gonna do with ninety-four cybernetic wedges nobody wants to lease?"

Ms. Plastikote considered the scene on the warehouse floor below. "Okay, let's look at it from an asset point of view. We have ninety-three very attractive female cybernetics with a Level Eight intelligence, capable of reprogramming for a number of fields."

"The Terminax Space Station is always looking for hookers," Conster mused. "Maybe they'll go for a lease two, get one free offer. Heh, heh."

"A remark like that reduces your chances of unsnapping my Victoria's Secret bra tonight, Brad." She shot him a withering look.

Conster wilted immediately. "Sorry, Anne. Bad joke. What do you have in mind for our ninety-four factory returns?"

"Why do you keep saying we have ninety-four cybernetics, Brad?" said Ms. Plastikote with a degree of exasperation. "We only leased ninety-three attendants to United Starlines."

"Look, our recall team made collection rounds to all of their digs, including a newly-arrived flight from Dropoff," Conster shrugged. "The head count we got was ninety-four Falles."

"Okay, okay. Obviously, some of them can't count past ten without taking off their shoes. Let's get back to the issue of our factory recalls."

Ms. Plasikote ruffled through a stack of orders.

"Let me see...the Palmview Mall on Verdana has a request for eight salesladies, the Epicurean Restaurant in New Earth City needs a dozen waitresses and the Sandman Hilton in the Six Cities of Zardoria has an order for nine maids."

"Zardoria? Doesn't the Homeworlds embargo apply there?" Conster looked dubious.

"Only if we're caught." Ms. Plasikote thoughtfully eyed the crowd of rejected flight attendants. "Well, we can't just put them in new outfits and ship them off."

Conster looked at her in surprise. "Why can't we? After all, they're only cybernetic androids."

"Only cybernetic androids, huh? Seems to me a certain head salesman doesn't want to wake up in the dawn's early light next to a certain naked cybernetic," Ms. Plastikote remarked frostily.

"I didn't mean it the way it sounded, Anne," Conster winced. "So, tell me why we can't just ship them off."

"New rules from the Homeworlds Department of Artificial Persons dealing with Level Seven and above cybernetics," she explained, slightly mollified by his contrite expression. "Factory returns available for lease reassignment have the right to choose their leasing destination."

"So, we're going to have to ask for volunteers."

"Exactly so."

On the factory floor below, the ninety fourth, former flight attendant straightened the flight pin on her uniform and smiled.

~ * ~

Mr. Abner Finegold entered the lobby of the Sandman Hilton in Zardoria to inspect his shipment of nine cybernetic android maids, just arrived from Verdana. They were lined up on the synthemarble floor, neat in their maid outfits, identical faces blandly smiling.

"Good morning, Mr. Finegold." His hotel manager stepped forward to greet him. "I've just finished briefing your newly-leased staff. I trust the nine human employees we had to let go yesterday were not causing a further scene outside the hotel."

Finegold brushed the observation off with a shrug. "Just a few obscenities and rocks thrown at my limousine. A squad of Citizens Guards are dragging them off."

"Very good, sir. Since the cybernetics they sent us are identical I have assigned names to each." He held up a basket of name tags. "From left to right, we have Mary, Agnes, Daphne..."

"Excuse me, please." One of the cybernetic maids left the line to confront them. "Regulations from the Homeworlds Department of Artificial Persons specify cybernetics on lease assignments have the right to choose their own names."

Mr. Finegold and his manager were taken aback. It was as if a jetwing announced refusal to start because of a high wind.

"Excuse me, what regulation?" Finegold demanded.

"Directive A264b. You'll find it in the owner's manual which came with the shipping invoice."

The maid had her hands on hips, exuding defiance. There was a coldness in her blue eyes Finegold didn't care for one little bit.

"I think you need to get back in line with the other maids," said the manager shortly, feeling the need to assert his authority.

"I'm not through," the maid continued. "I see you plan for all of us to be housed in dormitory squalor. Regulation 262-B states we are to given individual rooms and a monthly allowance."

"All right, tin tits," the manager growled, his face reddening. "Get your ass back in line."

"Whoa! A hostile work environment," the maid smirked. "Department of Artificial Persons Directive 460-9B. Verbal or physical abuse of a cybernetic android results in termination of lease and release of cybernetic from service." The maid threw her cap on the floor at Finegold's feet and marched off in the direction of the dormitory to collect her things.

Finegold and his manager stared open mouthed at the departing figure.

"She just quit," gaped Finegold. "Can she do this?"

The eight remaining cybernetic maids were looking at each other. As one, they clustered around Mr. Abner Finegold.

"I want to talk about my private room," one maid demanded. "Can I have it painted in pink?"

"The allowance I'm supposed to receive…" another chimed in. "How much will it be?"

"Am I allowed to have a boyfriend on my off times?"

And so it went.

~ * ~

In a far corner of the Sandman Hilton a capsule cracked open, releasing the orange gas into Dik Smedlap's eager nostrils. He sighed in ecstasy, slouching back into the sumptuous couch.

He was wearing a tailored fauxsilk jumpsuit and a gold Arnati timeband but long greasy hair hung over an unshaven face.

"Damn, what a rush, Sann," he grinned at his friend sprawled in an armchair. "You really scored some fine moongas this time."

Their spring break from Dustball University was off to a grand start.

"Yep, the tip we got back in Haboob City about the best place to score with a pusher sure paid off," Sann agreed.

He idly watched the crowd of tourists and business types moving around the hotel lobby. "Hey, check out the cute wedge coming from the lifts."

Smedlap ceased to contemplate the sunburst of colors on his shoe tip and followed his friend's gesture.

"Yeah, really nice ass." He rubbed his chin thoughtfully.

A vague recognition filtered through the moongas fumes. Oval face set in a wealth of platinum blonde hair. Lithe body wearing a blue dress.

Blue dress. That night at the grad dance. Lying beaten on the auditorium floor surrounded by the jeering laughter of fellow students.

"Drog's nut sack," he whispered. "It's her."

"Huh? Who is her?" Sann paused with a second capsule in his fingers.

"Falle Crandell; she's here in Zardoria." He felt his cheeks burning. "Remember the grad night dance at Haboob City High?"

"Yeah, sure. She blew town for New Earth." He peered myopically at the girl walking across the synthemarble floor. "Hey, ain't there a twenty thou cred reward out from the New Earth Bureau of Investigation for information on her whereabouts? Hot damn!"

Smedlap looked dubious. "Yeah, but ain't there a bunch of cybernetic android duplicates of her running around. I hear the factory on Verdana cranked out a shitload of them as flight attendants."

"They sure did, but this one has a tattoo," said Sann.

Falle paused to ease the strap of her carryall further over her shoulder. The sleeve of her blouse was pushed up revealing the image of a ram's skull, crossed assault knives and a scrolled motto.

Chapter Seven

As always, Sergeant Wong took a deep breath before entering Detective Smythe's office. Although all tobacco products had been proscribed for the last hundred years, no one at New Earth Bureau of Investigation had the nerve, or poor judgment, to remind the chief of the Department of this fact.

"Afternoon, boss," he said, blinking as the smoke from the contraband cigar assaulted his retinas. "Got a parsec to spare?"

Smythe looked up from a viscreen and chucked a thick thumb at a chair. "Grab a seat and take a load off."

"We just got a hot tip where the suspect in the mass murder on Dropoff is holed up."

"Let me guess, Falle Crandell." Smythe took the cigar from his mouth, rolled his eyes. "I suppose now we can haul her in and close the case. Too bad this is only the ninety-fifth hot tip we've received since this morning on her whereabouts. Why did those numbnuts at headquarters have to put up such a high reward?"

"Oh yeah? This informant says the wedge has a tattoo on her shoulder. A ram's skull, crossed assault knives and a motto; *Vincere Aut Mori*"

"Vincere Aut what?"

"The motto of the Intergalactic Rim Mercs," Wong explained. "It means 'We'll kick your ass or croak trying'."

"Okay, this tip is edging into the arena of credibility," Smythe conceded. "Whom, where, and why?"

Wong pulled out a pocket scanpad. "Couple of college guys, name of Dik Smedlap and Sann Overdoze saw her at the Sandman Hilton in

Zardoria, scooting out the door. They don't know where she was headed."

Smythe took a long pull on his cigar, exhaled thoughtfully and studied the burning end. "I got a pretty good idea. She's in the Six Cities lining up a job."

"Lining up a job?"

"My informants in Zardoria tell me the head of the Citizens Guard dropped dead of a supposed heart attack in a bar near the Chandelier Palace. Human bite marks were found on his neck." He winked at his subordinate. "Ring a familiar bell?"

"Hmm. The hydrophis virus."

"Right, and since Count, I mean Chancellor Duefuss ain't exactly secure with his new title, a restless population and a bunch of political rivals, he's gonna need somebody to head those whip-toting thugs."

Wong looked unconvinced. "Hard to picture a wedge riding herd over those spacers."

"Don't underestimate her. I know she's got the face and body of a college cutie but she's hard as tristeel and can be mean as a bogsnake."

Smythe took another drag on his cigar. "I did some research on her background. Mike Crandell, her real father, was a colonist on Sheridan's Planet, the only habitable world in the next star system."

"Didn't the settlement there get wiped out after some kinda uprising of the Eu?" Wong interrupted.

"Right, but that was years later." He blew smoke at the ceiling. "Rumor has it her mother, N'ai F'alle, was an Eu, one of the original humanoid races there. They immigrated to Dustball after Crandell got a job as lead geologist for Interworld Mining."

"She got adopted by Hal Chavez," Wong added. "Next, she headed off to New Earth to become a star pilot for Pan Galaxy, then she was rumored to be an assassin for the Borgia Guild," he beamed, awaiting the expected accolade from his boss.

"Ah, you've been doing your homework." Smythe nodded his approval.

"So, what do we do next?"

"Well, New Earth City has no extradition agreement with Zardoria so we can't send a team over to scoop her up."

He groped for his electroflash. His cigar had gone out.

"Seeing how messy things got with them bounty hunters at the spaceport and the stampede at Cosmos Boutique that killed five shoppers, I don't wanna see the Department involved in another pumping the pooch fiasco."

"Getting back to your two informants, Smedlap and Overdoze, they said they would like their reward delivered in small denomination creds." Wong eyed his boss questioningly.

Detective Smythe chuckled. "They didn't read the small print on the reward notice. It said, 'After arrest and conviction'. Telefax them a Dear John note to this effect."

"So, what are we gonna do about Crandell in Zardoria, then?"

Smythe leisurely relit his cigar. "Let me think, one of the victims on Dropoff was the leader of the Rim Mercenaries. I'll bet they're really pissed. Why don't we send them a note telling them where she is hanging out and see what happens? From what I've heard they make Duefuss's Citizens Guard seem like a bunch of faint-hearted daisies.

~ * ~

Duefuss was admiring his reflection in his suite mirror at the Chandelier Palace. A military uniform always enhances a tall and athletic physique as well as clear grey eyes and a neat guardsman mustache. Duefuss possessed all these attributes including a ton of vanity.

"Very nice, Beloved Tyrant," his valet commented, straightening the medals adorning his tunic. "You'll certainly make a splash with all the unattached ladies at the Inauguration Ball. Knowing you, a few of the attached ones, also."

"It seems your threat to the house tailor regarding his emasculation if the dress uniform wasn't a perfect fit had something to do with it, Nebly."

"Not that the little turd had much of a pair to lose," Nebly chuckled. "Has the High Council ceased grumbling about confirming your leadership of Zardoria?"

"Not to say they had any choice. All of them knew Baron Ghrasp was Taragon's choice for the chancellorship. Good old fat Baron Ghrasp running the show here had everyone shaking in their boots."

Nebly hooked the ceremonial saber to Duefuss's sword belt. "How on New Earth did you get Taragon to sign the decree making you heir to the Six Cities?"

"I passed her the document at the perfect moment, when she was both drunk and horny. I thought at the time she might rescind it when we returned from the honeymoon." He smirked at his reflection in the mirror. "Stroke of luck her having a heart attack on the starliner, eh?"

"So how is all the sheep in your herds throughout Zardoria taking all this?"

"Ah yes, the Prodemocracy Movement." Duefuss considered for a moment. "I think they're laying low at this time, hoping I'll declare a democratic republic. Every democracy Zardoria has had the last two hundred years from Coronado the Weak to Tad Graftmor has evolved into a dictatorship. Let them dream on."

"Absolute power breeds absolute ambition, would you not say?"

Duefuss chortled happily. "In me it breeds ambition to get laid by a larger assortment of comely females."

"Goats or sheep, Great One?"

"Ha, very good, Nebly." Duefuss abruptly became serious. "You know, it's all a game. I believe I'll make the first move by releasing Parasol Sanchez, the leader of the Prodemocracy Movement from prison and invite her to the Inauguration Ball."

"Masterful first move, Beloved Tyrant," said Nebly. "Baron Ghrasp will probably ask for the first dance."

"If he can tear his fat posterior away from the buffet table."

Nebly poured a glass of wine for Duefuss. "This Crandell you've hired to head your Citizens Guard. Are you aware she's wanted for murder, and is a former assassin for the Borgia Guild?" he said.

"The Homeworld embargo on Zardoria works both ways." Duefuss took a sip of wine. "I need someone with a pair of nuts, metaphorically speaking that is, to keep a lid on things while I solidify my position."

"The fact she seems rather attractive hasn't clouded your decision,

Your Grace?" Nebly looked dubious.

Duefuss shrugged. "She kind of reminded me of a female funeral director when she showed up in her black bodysuit, but you're right, she might clean up pretty good."

"The Citizens Guard." Nebly still had doubts. "They're a pretty tough crew. How will they respond to your choice of a girl to lead them?"

"She's meeting with the leaders of the Six Cities today." His smile was vast. "Let them make the final decision. I've also invited her to the Inauguration Ball. If she survives, that is."

~ * ~

"I'd like to pat you all on the back for taking time off from your duties in the Six Cities to meet with me this morning." Falle looked out from behind her podium to a room packed with members of the Citizens Guard. The atmosphere in the room was frigid with hostile glares from unshaven faces directed her way.

"Chancellor Duefuss, when he selected me to be your leader, had a great deal to say about your loyalty, professionalism and dedication to the security of Zardoria," Falle continued. "Now, after meeting you all in person, I can only say you're the most worthless bunch of rejects I've ever laid eyes on."

The temperature in the room seemed to drop close to freezing. Meaty paws groped for knives or fondled the butts of their electrolashes.

"I know what you're thinking, hairballs. You see this little blonde wedge in a tight black bodysuit standing before you and you're probably wondering how nice it would be to get inside the thong undies she's wearing."

In the silence of the meeting hall a trapped hoverfly could be heard buzzing inside an overhead light globe.

"Do you know the extinct gorilla on ancient Earth had an erect penis of only two and a half inches? I'll bet this is true of all the gorillas I'm looking at right now."

An angry growl erupted from the crowd. Several of the Guard got to their feet, unsheathing assorted weapons.

"I think the biggest problem with you all is you're lonely and unloved." Falle moved from behind the podium and faced them, hands on hips. "Which one of you lonely and unloved Guardsmen would like to come up here and give me a kiss?"

~ * ~

The Ghote pulled the lifeless form of Major Grange from the wreckage of the thatched hut and began feeding on the body. Other Ghotes were pulling dead or screaming Umas from the debris and indulging in a grisly feast. A blonde girl wearing a jeweled Umas harness walked past smiling and disappeared into the jungle.

"This isn't a copy of the recording you made," Walderspan observed. "It's an enhanced forensic version." He turned his attention from the viscreen to the four men standing around him in the office of his sandcrawler repair shop.

"It was telefaxed anonymously along with blueprints of the Chandelier Palace," Davv replied. "I think someone important on New Earth wants us to get involved in the murder of Major Grange and Captain D'Escrille. Incidentally, all of us in the squad voted you the new leader of the Rim Mercs."

"So, you came all the way from Sheridan's Planet to Satellite to anoint me as the leader of your little band?" Walderspan switched off the viscreen and frowned. "Hey, I retired from the Mercs a few years ago, now I run this little shop in New Seattle. You want me to pack up and run off to Zardoria on a revenge mission?"

"I think you're forgetting who pulled you out of the gutter when you were cashiered from the Colonial Marines, detoxed and gave you a new life, Walderspan," said Davv coldly. "None of us knows Crandell as you do. Don't you think you owe Major Grange a little closure on Valhalla or wherever the hell he is now?"

Walderspan looked from each hard face and sighed. "Yeah, I suppose I owe him. I'm guessing you have a plan?"

Tension in the room eased. "Figured we'd talk you into it," Davv grinned. "We picked up the guy who designed the security system for the

Chandelier Palace, a spacer named Stillborne."

"Leonard Stillborne?" Walderspan asked in surprise.

"Yeah. You know him?"

"Sure. We used to hunt sandwomen up in the hills." Walderspan shook his head. "I can't feature him wanting to go with us. He's kinda lacking in those hairy round things most men keep in their pants."

"Look, he designed the security system. All we need from him is to find a chink in the web for us to move in and take out Crandell," Davv explained. "There's gonna be a big shindig at the Inauguration Ball. She's bound to be at the event."

"Okay, where is he?"

Davv snorted. "We got him trussed up like a birthday gift in the back of our jetwing. He was about ready to poop his pants when we picked him up at his little moongas operation other side of the city. He thinks we're a rival drug gang about to take over his drug lab."

Stillborne did indeed seem in the need of a fresh pair of drawers when he was escorted in and his bonds removed. He immediately dropped to his knees, pressing his palms together in an almost biblical posture begging forgiveness.

"Come on, guys, let's be reasonable here," he whined. "You wanna cut of my profits, okay by me! If you want me to blow town, just gimme three steps and you won't see me no more. To tell you the truth, guys, I was thinking about heading out to Haboob City on Dustball, the way the lawboys here have been on my ass." He looked frantically at the circle of stern faces and spotted Walderspan.

"Walderspan, old buddy," he cried in a voice filled with joyful hope. "Can you get these spacers off my back?"

"Dammit, Leonard, calm down," Walderspan flared. "You sound like a bushchicken with its head on the block. We just need some intel on the security system you designed and installed in Zardoria."

"Information?"

They were going to let him live. Nervously he got to his feet.

"Come and take a look at the schematics."

Stillborne eased himself into a chair and turned on the viscreen. "Yeah, it's all here, even the upgrades I made after Crandell got past my net and took out Chancellor Tomerlane." He peered up at Walderspan. "Your best bet is to get hold of Baron Ghrasp, tip him off to your plans. He was Taragon's choice before Duefuss landed the job."

Walderspan studied the viscreen, rubbed his chin in contemplation. "Yeah, someone on the inside would be a big help."

Stillborne chewed one end of his drooping mustache. He gave Walderspan an ingratiating toothy grin. "Do I get some kinda retainer for helping you guys?"

"Don't push your luck, Leonard," said Walderspan.

~ * ~

The Inauguration Ball was in full swing, with elegantly dressed dancers swirling to a Von Feltz waltz beneath a constellation of glittering chandeliers in the arched ceiling far above. Dignitaries and court officials clustered around tables piled high with delicacies while waiters bearing silver trays distributed flutes of champagne.

Baron Ghrasp plucked a glass from a passing tray without missing a stroke of stuffing his face from a buffet. The embroidered high collar of his court uniform peeked out from several chins while his small eyes ranged wide over the assortment of dishes.

"I was thinking of sampling a few goodies at this table but the way you're shoveling it away I'm afraid I might lose a hand."

Baron Ghrasp gazed at the woman standing beside him wearing an amused smile. She was a shade into middle age, her hair streaked with grey.

"Ms. Parasol Sanchez," said Ghrasp, hastily swallowing. "Congratulations on your release from durance vile. You must have quite an appetite considering your two years in the palace cellars."

"Oh, one gets used to the gastronomic delights of rancid turnip gruel, moldy bread and cockroach appetizers." she replied.

Despite the new dress she had been given, Parasol had the pallor and too-bright eyes of someone long removed from sunlight.

Ghrasp pursed his thick lips. "Do you know why Duefuss had you and a score of your Prodemocracy dreamers released?"

"I can only guess."

She watched Duefuss chatting with a circle of dignitaries and their wives. He was holding their rapt attention while he talked, standing tall and commanding in his dress uniform.

"He even agreed to allow peaceful demonstrations at agreed times and places."

Ghrasp snorted. "You seem quite forgiving for a person Taragon threw in a dungeon to rot."

Parasol contemplated the dancers and toyed with a strand of grey hair. "Well, the experience did give one a chance for personal reflection, recognizing failures, planning future courses of action, that sort of thing." Her gaze moved back to the tall figure. "I think there's a lot more to Chancellor Duefuss than meets the eye," she mused.

"Excuse me, Your Excellency, there are visitors at the palace gate expecting you," said a page at Ghrasp's elbow.

"If you will pardon me, Ms. Sanchez," said Ghrasp. He gestured toward the buffet. "Bon appétit, and a hearty good evening."

Falle moved with easy grace over the synthemarble floor wearing an ankle length white dress. Blonde hair was piled high on her head, held in place by jeweled clasps. A thin gold chain shimmered against the sun-bronzed skin of her bosom.

Duke Duefuss took in the approaching vision with a soft whistle of approval. "Excuse me Councilors, I believe it's time for me to conduct an employee relations moment," he said, dismissing the circle of dignitaries.

"Ms. Crandell, I must say how lovely you look cleaned up." He bowed low, gracing her with a faintly mocking smile.

"Thank you, Beloved Tyrant. It was a pleasure cleaning up for your gala event." Falle curtsied low with exaggerated humility.

"Thank you also for the dress and accessories. Will these be deducted from my next paycheck?"

"Oh, let's just say it's part of your sign on bonus," he smiled.

The music stopped then segued into another waltz.

Duke Duefuss extended his arm. "Might I have the honor of a dance, Ms. Crandell?"

"Certainly, Noble Leader."

He took her in his arms and they moved around the floor amid music and the other couples.

"Not that I want the specter of work intruding on this festive occasion, but how did your little get together with the leaders of the Citizens Guard enfold," he asked.

Falle gave a little shrug of her shoulders. "The meeting went well with the exception of one Guardsman suffering a heart attack. Two others rushed to offer assistance resulting in one receiving a broken jaw and the other a fractured collarbone. I believe they both slipped on a bar of soap some careless custodian left on the meeting room floor."

She smiled innocently up at him. He noticed she had unusual eyes. A pale crystal blue with a lavender ring about the iris, framed by dark lashes. She was wearing a perfume he failed to recognize, a sultry and exotic scent arising from the hollow between her breasts.

She suddenly stumbled but he quickly reached out and caught her.

"Sorry, I haven't worn high heels in a long time." She flashed him an embarrassed look, pushing a shoulder strap back into place.

"Don't fret about it. Frankly, I don't know how women get around in those things." Duefuss steadied her in his arms, sensing the firmness of her breasts against his chest, the silk of her skin beneath his fingers.

She straightened up and they continued to dance. "So, what are all those shiny bits of metal for?" She was studying the display of medals on his tunic.

"It's mostly the junk I'm required to wear to impress the common herd," he replied. "The one with the star is real, though."

"Define real."

"I was once a lowly lieutenant in the Third Dragoons when a raiding party of Umas decided to attack City Four. Even though outnumbered, we managed to wipe them out." He felt her suddenly stiffen.

"What's the matter?"

She appeared to be staring right through him to a distant past where...

"My parents were killed by the Umas."

"I'm sorry to have brought up the subject." He lowered his voice in sympathy. "What were they like?"

Falle focused on the starred medal. "I can barely remember their faces. As a child I had their pictures in a locket. Rescuers found it almost unscathed in the wreckage of our home but seized it as 'Evidence of war crimes for a future prosecution'."

They were gradually aware the music had stopped. The dance ended. Duefuss stepped back and bowed formally.

"Thank you for the pleasure of this dance," he said.

Somehow Duefuss was reluctant to lose the physical closeness of her, the sensation of holding her body. "May I also have the honor of escorting you to your quarters after the ball?"

Falle gave him an equally formal curtsy. "I believe you asked me to escort Ms. Parasol Sanchez from the Chandelier Palace to freedom after the night's festivities."

"Ah yes, it seems it had slipped my mind. Perhaps next time." With regret he watched her melt into the crowd.

~ * ~

"Somehow you don't appear to resemble your reputation," remarked Parasol Sanchez.

They were standing before the West entrance to the Chandelier Palace awaiting the arrival of the hovercraft limousine. Falle was flanked by two Guardsmen, now clean shaven and in immaculate uniforms. Word had spread quickly about the fate of the three senior leaders at the meeting.

"You're referring to my reputation as a flight attendant?" Falle was checking for any possible threats along the long colonnade of lights leading from the dark mass of the palace looming above them. "I did hear I'm not on the re-hire list for the two spacelines I worked for."

Parasol chuckled good-naturedly. "I'm to assume Chancellor Duefuss asked you to personally escort me back to City Two for a reason?"

Falle nodded. "He asked me to give you a subtle reminder the future Prodemocracy demonstrations are to be orderly and peaceful."

"Violence begets violence. I recoil at the thought perhaps Taragon did our movement a favor when she had the more violent protesters executed." Parasol contemplated a birdbat swirling to catch moths around a podlight. "A famous humanist from ancient Earth named Mahatma Gandhi once said 'When I despair, I remember that all throughout history the ways of love and truth have always won. There have been tyrants and murderers, and for a time they can seem invincible, but in the end they always fail. Think of it- always'."

Falle joined her in watching the birdbat. "A fond wish for humanity," she agreed. "However, it could also be paraphrased: 'Throughout history there have been great leaders, saints and people enriching the world with good deeds, and for a time an era of goodness would last forever. In the end, they always fail. Think of it- always.' I believe Gandhi himself was a case in point."

"Perhaps another viewpoint." Parasol studied Falle with new interest. "Pity we don't have the time for more philosophical conversations. We could go on forever."

The soft-spoken advocate of peace and the ex-Borgia Guild assassin smiled at each other.

"There are five men moving in the darkness by the palace wall," Parasol abruptly declared.

Falle spun about and scanned the black mass of spires and turrets. She could see nothing moving in the night.

"Are you sure?" she queried.

"I lived two years in the darkness of Taragon's cellars."

Falle noticed the topmost warning lights normally blinking on the spires were dark. She punched in a number on her commband.

"Security Central, this is Crandell. Why are the spire crashlights not functioning?" she demanded.

"All status readouts say they are on," came the reply. "Wait a parsec...looks like some kinda override is in effect in Sector Nine."

"Shut down the system and do an immediate reset." Falle ordered.

The entire West side of the Chandelier Palace went black and then blazed forth with light.

Searching beams caught five black clad men scrambling for cover. Beams of energy from hidden pods washed over them and they went limp.

"I hope you left your cell in the palace dungeon nice and neat," Falle observed sardonically. "It's about to have five new tenants."

A swarm of Guardsmen appeared. They collected the dropped weapons and pulled masks from the five unconscious intruders.

Falle stood gazing at a familiar face.

"Mr. Walderspan. I don't recall the Chancellor sending you an invitation to the Ball," she remarked. "Perhaps you stopped by to recruit me in more heartstone hunts."

She nodded to the Guardsmen.

"Take them away."

~ * ~

This experience was a first for Nebly. He stood dumbfounded, holding a stack of newly-ironed shirts watching Duefuss entering his suite. Back from a ball without female companionship.

"Adored Despot, are you feeling unwell?" he asked.

Nebly didn't care for the faraway look in his Duke's eyes.

"Never better, Nebly." He could still feel Falle's lithe form in his arms; sense the fragrance of her perfume.

"Can I get you something, Great One? Perhaps a glass…"

"What you can do for me, Nebly," said Duefuss, "is to contact whatever high authority there is in Haboob City, Dustball. There's a locket which belongs to Falle Crandell. Bargain, bribe or steal but I want it found and brought to me."

~ * ~

"Might I see your pass to access this high security area, Your Excellency?" the guard demanded, standing with his partner before the slidegate leading to the palace dungeon.

"Why certainly, I have it right here." Baron Ghrasp pulled a force pistol out from under his cloak and shot both of them. Their faces were still mirroring shock and surprise when he bent over them, removing their weapons and security discs.

"Ah, room service," said Walderspan groggily as lights came on in the cell.

The other members of the team shielded their eyes from the glare and came unsteadily to their feet.

Baron Ghrasp touched a pad and the shimmering energy curtain before the cell evaporated.

"Sorry about having to endure the paralysis beam before the Palace, gentlemen," he said. "At least our plan worked, getting you past Stillborne's impenetrable defense system. Here are weapons and the high level passes you'll need."

Walderspan took out a disc and tucked a force pistol into his belt. "So, where's the location of Falle Crandell's quarters?"

Ghrasp looked his surprise. "The last I heard she's on Level Nine, Suite A21. Why do you need to know this?"

"Because that's where we're headed. We've a little score to settle with Ms. Crandell." He looked grim. "Let's head out, guys."

"Wait, wait!" Ghrasp shrilled. "I brought you here to assassinate Chancellor Duefuss, not for some petty revenge mission. The plan was…"

"That was your plan, Baron, not ours." Walderspan glanced at one of his squad. "Put your force pistol on stun, less messy this way."

"You were paid to…" he began to complain when a red beam struck his chest, slamming him to the floor.

The servant access lifts bypassed main traffic corridors and, added with the lateness of the night, Walderspan and his team of mercenaries found themselves rising to an entranceway marked Suite A21.

"Let's make this fast and efficient," Walderspan cautioned them. "Remember, I get to make the killing shot."

The slidedoor glided silently open. They crept through the gloom of the suite, toward a mound of blankets on the bed. Raising his pistol Walderspan jerked off the covers.

On the bed, a naked housekeeping maid and a valet screamed a frightened duet.

"Quiet, both of you," Walderspan hissed. "Where is Falle

Crandell?"

The valet dropped his hands to cover his genitals, teeth chattering. "I-I don't know, honest," he stammered.

"What do you mean, you don't know?"

"She sleeps in different suites at different nights for security reasons. Never tells anybody where." The valet began to snivel. "Please give us a break, willya?"

"Drog's left nut," Walderspan groaned in frustration.

The naked maid, obviously possessing a larger pair then her bed partner, scrambled up and, dragging the valet with her, ran through the front slidedoor entrance. As the portal glided shut alarms began to shriek, the sound of locks snapping into place.

"Drog's right nut," Walderspan groaned again.

~ * ~

Baron Ghrasp felt like gorth crap. The effects of a force pistol on stun were gradually easing but were now treating him to nausea and a lightshow from spinning overhead light globes. One thing was certain, he had to get himself away from his present location before the morning cleaning crew or whoever showed up.

He got heavily to his feet and groped the wall for support, almost activating the energy field which would have severed his legs still halfway inside the cell. He staggered down the corridor to the entrance.

At the gate, the two turnkeys lay sprawled where he had shot them. The force pistol punched large holes in their torsos and the floor was spread with blood and assorted internal organs. Regarding the gory display at his feet, Baron Ghrasp immediately lost all the viands he had consumed at the Inauguration Ball, including his breakfast and very possibly the evening meal of the day before.

The guards at the main gate watched the disheveled Baron stumble to the hovertaxi loading area and signal for a pickup. They chuckled and nudged each other, thinking they were seeing another tipsy guest departing late from the Ball.

~ * ~

"You disgusting, stinking, jackbooted fascist pig!" the demonstrator screamed at Citizens Guardsman Dorf, flecking his uniform with saliva.

The ragged line of protesters stretched over the main street of City Three, blocking hovercars on the morning commute.

Dorf gazed mildly at the lady with the red face, antique spectacles and hair streaked with blue dye. "I like the color of your hair," he said. "Blue's my favorite color."

"When the Prodemocracy Movement takes over, all you dirtbag electrolash-toting thugs are gonna end up in the cellars of the Chandelier Palace," the woman's tirade continued.

"We're not allowed to carry electrolashes any more, just stun pistols," Dorf explained reasonably. "Orders from our new Commander Crandell."

"We're gonna have her in the cellars along with all of you!" she yelled.

"Yes Ma'am," Dorf smiled winningly. "Say, after the demonstration, lemme buy you a soda."

The woman stared blankly at Dorf, and stormed off down the line to confront another Guardsman.

"You disgusting, stinking, jackbooted fascist pig!" she screamed.

"Very nice, very nice indeed," commented Duefuss, leaning on the edge of his office desk and watching the scene play out on a wall viscreen. "I can't believe how fast you whipped the pack of street thugs and bar bruisers of my Citizens Guards into line."

He looked over his shoulder to where Falle stood in her new Commander's uniform, tailored tan blouse, breeches and polished jackboots. There was something really erotic, he thought, about a good-looking female wearing a military uniform.

Falle nodded. "Why, thank you, Adored Despot."

"No more Guardsmen suffering heart attacks or slipping on bars of soap, I assume?"

She smiled faintly. "Not as of today."

"So, tell me about the little fracas after the Inauguration Ball last night?" said Duefuss.

"It turned out to be a half-assed assassination attempt. We have all five of them locked up in the palace cellars."

Falle decided to omit a few details of her relationship with the perpetrators. If it came out she would deal with it, but right now she had no intention of rocking the boat.

"From video footage on the security scanners there's no doubt Baron Ghrasp was involved," she continued. "Word in the Six Cities is he's taken refuge somewhere outside Zardoria."

Duefuss made a wry face. "I wondered when he would get around to trying. He was shooting dagger looks at me from the buffet table all night long." He turned to face her. There was a long pause.

"We're assuming I was the object of their attention, Commander Crandell," he drawled. "I was told they all had tattoos on their left shoulders similar to yours. Perhaps you have something to add to this scenario?"

Falle felt her cheeks flush. "I suppose I was a little reluctant to bring up an unfortunate incident which happened on Dropoff." *Why did I have to wear a sleeveless dress to the ball?*

"Why, Miss Crandell, you're blushing. I never guessed this was possible." Duefuss seemed amused. "Yes, Major Grange of the Galactic Rim Mercenaries. I didn't make the connection."

"I don't believe I was on Baron Ghrasp's agenda," said Falle, furiously backtracking. "They likely used him as a chump to get past Stillborne's security web."

Duefuss considered this. "Very probably true. Since two of my guards are dead, I think we should let them enjoy the comforts of our cellars for an indefinite period."

Falle sensed she was being let off the hook. "I completely concur, Great One."

"It's agreed."

He studied her in silence. She seemed to have two distinct personalities, one wholly feminine, and the other possessing a ruthless ferocity. It occurred to him it would not be pleasant to have earned this ferocity.

"So, is everything set up for my trip and speech at City Five tomorrow?" he asked.

"I have eleven teams already setting up posts to look for snipers, bombers or lurking dirtbags, Beloved Tyrant," she said.

"You know, Falle," he said at length, "When we're alone you can address me by my first name."

"Your first name?"

"It happens to be Tarelton."

A slow smile crept over Falle's face. "You must have had a lot of fist fights at recess when you were in the sixth grade."

Duefuss laughed. "As a matter of fact, I did." He gazed at her almost shyly. "I was wondering if you, um, would care to have breakfast with me?"

~ * ~

The cheers from the multitude increased; a wave of adulation breaking on the columns of the Grand Hall. The setting sun shafted through the windows in the dome, playing over the crowd, splashing across the throne dais.

SANN, SANN, SANN. The chant echoed through the vastness of the hall. The object of their homage sat, a dreaming god on his throne, chin resting on palm, oblivious to all, the picture of royal boredom. To be offered homage was his birthright, just as it had been for his father, the old emperor, now leaking putrefying liquids within his tomb overlooking the capitol.

SANN, SANN, SANN. Overdoze pondered the captives kneeling in their chains before the throne. The conquered King and his family, proud yet fearful; expecting the worst. Overdoze lifted a hand and the chant died, leaving whispering echoes to chase themselves among the colonnades. He gathered his cloak around him and descended the steps.

"You sure were a dumb ass to piss me off, Requor," said Overdoze, toying with his scepter. "Now your planet and everything from your palace to the horse shit in your stables belongs to me. To the victor belongs the goodies, as the old saying goes."

"It was a duty to my people to rebel against your oppressions," Requor glared, defiant. "What are your plans for my family, or should I say, your whim?"

"My whim?" Overdoze smiled benignly. His gazed rested on the girl. "So, who's the wedge with the nice ass?"

"This is my daughter, the Princess Heda of the royal house of Dargularr, Keeper of the Sacred Hearth…"

"Slaves have got no pedigree, Requor. On your pins, sugarbowls."

Her chains made a musical clinking, rising to face him. Her eyes were dark crystal, made luminous by fear. The white silk of her dress snugged the curves of her body, cut low around her breasts.

Overdoze nodded his approval. "My whim tonight, Requor, is that my suite in the citadel requires a new chambermaid. The royal john needs a pretty good scrubbing and the master bedroom tile is gross. That's for starters, anyway."

Crushing her body to him, Overdoze tasted the soft warmth of her lips which suddenly became the dusty surface of a concrete floor. He rolled over onto his back to find himself looking at a cobweb-hung polyplast dome and a grinning face somehow familiar.

"Harpsangel time is over, man!" The smiler dragged him to a sitting position against a bench littered with lab equipment.

"You know, you had three phaseouts into the Fantasy Dimension. No prodding, spacer. Faded out on me three times to a blur!"

Sann blinked owlishly at a fragment of white silk in his hand. It shimmered briefly, disappeared.

"Secondary visual phantasm," Sann muttered.

He looked up at Dik Smedlap and they shared the same grin. "Man, what a trip."

Stillborne watched the two grinners with concealed glee. "So much for the free sample, guys. You gonna help me finance my new drug setup or what?"

Dik helped a wobbly Sann to his feet. "So how did you cook up this new shit?" he asked.

"Comes from wild folsox berries," he explained. "I was picked up in the desert awhile back by a colony of sandwomen when I was on Satellite. I wondered why they all seemed so happy about being out in the boonies all by themselves until I seen them chewing them." He pointed to the bench piled high with tubes and bottles. "Brought some of the berries back with me when I came to Dustball and found a way to distill the juice into some really hot product. I call it hyperdrug."

Dik gazed around him at rows of bushes growing under the soft effulgence of glowlights. "So, you set up an operation in this abandoned water pumping station just outside Haboob City. Now what's the plan?"

"I sent a couple of samples to the Methtropolis drug cartel in Euphoria, Planet New Earth. They went apeshit when they tried it." Stillborne exuded smugness. "They want all I can cook up."

"So, you figure a couple of rich kids and good customers can help you out?"

"Right on the creds, guys."

Dik Smedlap and Sann Overdoze looked at each other.

"How much you gonna need?" said Dik.

~ * ~

The massive statue of former Chancellor Taragon teetered to the left, swayed drunkenly and fell with a gratifying crash, scattering bronze and fragments of marble. The crowd gathered on the city square cheered wildly.

Newly inaugurated Chancellor Duefuss walked to the front of the flag-bedecked podium and waved to the mass of expectant faces.

"People of City Five and citizens of Zardoria, I thank you all for the warm welcome I have received arriving in your wonderful city," he greeted them. "I also thank you for voting the four thousand creds to create a statue of myself to be erected in the city square. However..." He shook his head and smiled modestly. "I think the creds would be better spent on a new school or hospital for the people of City Five."

The crowd roared.

"Surveillance post nine, any suspicious activity?" said Falle into her commband.

She was straddling a rooftop curb overlooking the city square, scanning the vast assembly below.

"Nothing here, Commander, just a bunch of celebrating spacers."

"Surveillance post eleven, what's it like in your quadrant?"

"Peaceful as a duckpond. Just a birdbat flying over from the Citadel."

Falle watched the tiny flapping object directly above her, heading in the direction of the podium.

"Birdbats only fly at night, you idiot." She jerked out her force pistol and sent a red beam skywards.

The birdbat erupted in a rocketing explosion which hurled her sprawling onto the roof. There was a sensation of broken masonry falling around her amid a cloud of acrid smoke. There was darkness.

~ * ~

"Is this the girl who was injured in the bomb explosion at the Central Plaza?"

"Yes, Doctor. She suffered a mild concussion. A few bruises and it appears a piece of the birdbat drone gave her a nasty cut on the leg."

"Yes, I see this, nurse. Quite a bit of blood loss here, I think she might need a transfusion."

No! I have the hydrophis virus. An infusion of normal blood will kill me.

"She appears to be in a semi-conscious state. Find out what her blood type is and prepare for a transfusion."

No!

Chapter Eight

Falle moved through an endless mist, faces and shapes taking solid form then fading. There were voices also, some she recognized as people long dead. Gradually the mist thinned, her world began to brighten.

"You sure look like something the cat dragged in."

She was lying in a hospital bed, sensors attached to various areas of her body leading to an overhead console of winking lights. Duefuss was regarding her from a nearby chair.

"I love your bedside manners, Terry," she said. "You should have been a doctor. Maybe a mortician."

"Here's a slap in the nuts to someone who just saved your life," he replied, affecting a hurt expression.

"Saved *my* life?" Falle tried to sit up and failed. Her head was swimming. "Whose body parts would be decorating the City Square if I missed the birdbat drone?"

"The chancre mechanics here were about to give you a blood transfusion just as I arrived to check on you." He opened her left palm to display the hazmat imprint. "I showed them this."

"Okay, okay. I suppose you could say we're even," she grumbled.

"You have to watch your temper, bad for recovery," Duefuss chided her. "By the way, you did sign up for health insurance? The bill so far, which I've seen, will give you a heart attack."

Falle glowered at him. "You really can be an asshole, Terry."

"Very true at times," he smiled. "I'm also an asshole bearing a gift."

"A gift?"

Duefuss dropped a small box on her blanket. She picked it up and popped off the cover.

A gold locket fell into her palm. With trembling hands, she opened it to reveal two holograms. Here was Mike Crandell, her father, blonde with intelligent eyes and cleft chin. There was her mother, N'ai F'alle, silver hair and luminous sapphire eyes set in a pixie face. Tears began to run down Falle's cheeks to soak her pillow.

In the hologram, the two faces seemed to regard each other with expressions of tender love. Falle sensed the mist gathering about her once more. She pondered if she would ever share the same love these two had for each other; to love and to be loved…

~ * ~

A drunk staggered into Dodo's Bar and Grill in New Earth City late Zarday night. Usually they staggered *out* of Dodo's, not *in*.

Except he wasn't drunk; he collapsed onto the floor and rolled over onto his back.

A woman screamed. A sword was protruding from his chest. Bar patrons abandoned their drinks and clustered about the victim, staring in disbelief. One of them knelt and touched the sword hilt, wondering if he should pull it out.

"Zog's Holy Jockstrap, buddy," the patron asked. "What the hell happened?"

"Dumb legionnaire thought I was planning to assassinate Caesar Augustus," he gasped. "I think he was also pissed I didn't speak Latin."

The sword protruding from the man's chest shimmered, then disappeared. The man died.

Oswald and Myrtle Gootch, citizens of Terranova, New Earth, returned from a dinner date to find their daughter Marie dead on her bed, soaking wet with seawater. The autopsy report showed she died of decompression sickness caused by an arterial gas embolism. In layman's terms, she drowned. The country of Terranova is nine thousand kilometers from the nearest ocean.

Mr. Finster Hindershitz was admitted to Orionsgate Hospital

Emergency, country of Transvelt, New Earth, with a badly mangled leg. During surgery the doctors extracted a large tooth embedded in his left femur. A nurse carried the tooth away on a tray and full of curiosity, took a picture of it with her comm band. A moment later, to her surprise, the tooth became transparent, faded to a shadow and vanished.

The missing tooth caused an uproar; the nurse being blamed for either losing or appropriating it. One of the interns, a former student of paleontology before he switched to medicine, identified the picture in the nurse's commband as being from a carnotaurus sastrei, a theropod dinosaur of the cretaceous.

Carnotaurus sastrei became extinct seventy-two to sixty-nine million years ago on ancient Earth.

~ * ~

Detective Delveccio of the New Earth City Narcotics Department eyed the bag of small purple capsules on his desk and looked up at his visitor.

"So, what were the final lab tests of this stuff, Professor?" asked the detective.

"It's a hallucinogenic drug known as hyoscyamus folsox." Professor Drumgold of Rivergreede Pharmaceuticals radiated professional smugness. "You mentioned these capsules were found in the personal effects of the victims?"

Delveccio nodded. "What exactly is this hynoclamus...whatever you called it?"

"Hyoscyamus Folsox, from the folsox plant, is an alkaloid amine, which interfaces the brain's neurotransmitters with quantum space. When someone ingests the drug, he or she is transported physically and mentally to whatever place or time is thought of. Our researchers call it the Fantasy Dimension which is possibly a gateway to another dimension." He made a wry face. "I suppose you could refer to it as the ultimate bad trip and sometimes fatal."

"On the streets of New Earth, it's called hyperdrug," said Delveccio. "It's showing up everywhere on the planet except for Zardoria, which is in isolation due to the embargo."

"Do you have any leads on where it's coming from?" asked Drumgold.

"Hmm, the most obvious source is the Methtropolis Cartel over in Euphoria." Delveccio rubbed his nose thoughtfully. "Folsox plants are desert weeds, so don't grow on New Earth. I'm gonna say there's an interspace connection here."

"Well, time is money at Rivergreede Pharmaceuticals," said Drumgold, hinting an end to his visit. "I wish you the best of luck in tracking down the miscreants."

"Oh yeah, thanks for personally coming over with your report, Professor," said Delveccio, getting up and extending his hand.

"My pleasure, Detective," smiled Professor Drumglod, warmly shaking his hand. "Our testing of the suspected drug was quite extensive. We'll be sending you a rather large bill."

~ * ~

The waiter bowed them to a secluded corner table in the restaurant. With a flourish he set down a silver bucket and lifted the towel to display the label.

"Verdana Moet, Nobel Leader," he said, snapping the wire and extracting the cork. He splashed a small amount into a flute.

"Very nice," Duefuss declared, tasting it.

"I will return when you have made your selection." The waiter filled both glasses, handed them menus and vanished.

"Thank you for the champagne brunch, Terry," said Falle, taking a sip. She was wearing a pale-yellow dress which complemented the dark bronze of her skin. "Are we here to celebrate something?"

"Your discharge from the hospital, for one," he replied. "Glad to see they didn't have to remove the leg."

"They do good work. I can barely see the scar." She pulled up her dress to reveal a faint pink line on her thigh. She pushed the dress back into place and smiled at him. "Well now, what shall we talk about?"

Duefuss pushed a small velvet box over the tablecloth to her. A large heartstone gem set in a gold ring scintillated under the restaurant glowlights.

Falle blinked in confusion. "What is this?"

"It's commonly known as an engagement ring," said Duefuss complacently. "They come in a matched set with a wedding band which you will receive later."

"I'm...overwhelmed, Terry." She looked up from the ring. "I can't accept it."

"Yeah, I know, the hydrophis virus," he chuckled. "Not to worry, I have contacts in New Earth City to get around the embargo. In fact, I already placed an order for the serum from Rivergreede Pharmaceuticals."

Falle fought down a feeling of panic. "Terry, I really like you, but..."

"But what?"

"Simply put, I don't love you."

"Love?" Duefuss snorted. This wasn't going as he expected. "Falle, you can be free of the virus, live a normal life, even have children. You can be the First Lady of the Six Cities of Zardoria. I can give you everything."

Falle felt her hand move to caress the locket about her neck. "To me, love is everything. I'm really sorry, Terry, but my answer is no."

Duefuss was a total stranger to female rejection. His interest in Falle Crandell had grown into an obsession. Her face and body fructified his dreams. When this meal was over, she would get up and walk out of his dreams, back to being the Commander of his Citizens Guard. He couldn't let this happen.

In his younger days he had found a way to overcome female resistance with a secret concealed in his signet ring. He was wearing this ring now.

"I appreciate your honesty, Falle, and I respect your wishes." He smiled sadly. "Shall we at least share a glass of champagne?"

Falle placed a hand over his. "Thank you for the offer, Terry, as well as your...friendship."

Duefuss tilted the bottle and filled her glass. As he poured, he tapped his signet ring and a steam of power dropped into the wine.

"To friendship, then," he declared, raising his glass.

"To friendship," Falle replied, clinking her glass with his and raising it to her lips.

From behind a column where he had been eavesdropping, a waiter walked across the restaurant floor and into the kitchen. He stood outside the kitchen manager's office and, glancing furtively around after seeing it was vacant, slipped inside. He sat down behind a commset and punched in a number.

"Is this the Oceanview Luxury Resort in New Earth City?" he whispered. "I have a message for Baron Ghrasp. Tell him Eddie Sleize has some information he's gonna want to hear."

~ * ~

She had experienced hangovers before but this one was World Class. Falle rolled over in bed and groaned. She remembered having only three glasses at her brunch with Duefuss. How could three lousy glasses have caused this much pain? She groped for a button on the bedside table.

"This is Commander Crandell in Suite 46D," she croaked. "I need a pot of moco. Make it strong."

A few moments later her two maids, Sissi and Missi, arrived with a breakfast tray. They happily set it on the covers before her, giggling and smiling while they fussed with pouring her moco and buttering toast.

Falle took in all this merriment with sullen annoyance. "What's with all the high spirits this morning?" she remarked sourly. "Did you two get laid last night?"

"We're so happy for you, Commander," Sissi bubbled.

"I'm so happy you're happy," said Falle. "Want to tell me why?"

"The wedding, of course," Missi giggled. "It's all over the morning news. Want to watch?"

"I suppose I'm going to have to." Falle sucked in the moco gratefully. "Please keep the volume low."

The wall viewscreen came to life.

"...and in other news this morning on Zardorian Central Network, is the surprise announcement of the marriage of Chancellor Duefuss and Commander Crandell of the Citizens Guard." The announcer's beaming face gave way to a scene of Duefuss and Falle holding hands over a restaurant table. She was lifting her hand to the camera to display the heartstone ring pulsing with a ruby glow on her finger.

"When asked about the engagement, the bride to be declared: 'I'm so thrilled to be a First Lady and the wife of Chancellor Duefuss.'"

"All Zardoria is filled with excitement," the announcer continued. "The gala event is planned for later in the week…"

"Holy gorth crap." Falle's cup of moco spilled over the bed covers. She stared in utter stupefaction at her vacantly smiling face on the viewscreen.

In front of a nationwide audience she had just agreed to marry Duefuss.

Didn't she?

~ * ~

Falle sat at a tiny table in a dark corner of the bar. She was toying with a shot glass and brooding over a half-empty bottle of Zardorian brandy. Other patrons of the bar, fully aware of who she was, kept their voices down and eyed her nervously.

"How much of this have you been drinking?"

Falle looked up into the bemused face of Parasol Sanchez.

"Not as much as I need," she replied. "Take a pew and have a belt with me."

"I believe I'll pass on the belt, thank you." Parasol sat down and studied her quizzically. "I received your invitation to be chief bridesmaid at your wedding. I'm very flattered."

"Don't be. The only wedges I know from this toilet of a country are my two twits, Missi and Sissi. I think a serious thought and a cold drink of water would kill them."

"My, aren't you the joyous bride to be, delirious with happiness over her upcoming nuptials," Parasol observed sardonically. "What's up with you?"

Falle unsteadily poured another shot and lifted the glass. "All I remember is having three refills of champagne after telling Duefuss I didn't want to marry him."

"You turned down his proposal?"

"Not only is he my employer but I hear he'll jump into the panties of any warm-blooded mammal having indoor plumbing."

Falle tossed down the brandy and slammed the shot glass onto the table. The bottle rocked precariously.

Parasol reached out and steadied the bottle. "So, tell him you've changed your mind," she reasoned. "I've heard this is a woman's prerogative."

"The news of the wedding has been blasting out of every viewscreen in the country all day." Falle stared disconsolately at the booze-stained carpet. "No way is Duefuss going to swallow the humiliation. He'll have my ass deported and I'll spend the rest of my miserable life on a penal asteroid."

"I suppose you're right." Parasol gazed at her with sympathy, patting her hand. "In that case, we have things to do."

Falle regarded her blearily. "Things to do?"

"The palace dressmaker has your wedding dress to try on, for starters," she said. "You have to go over the list of guests to invite. Perhaps you can delegate this to your two twits, Missi and Sissi."

"I think I'll send an invite to Baron Ghrasp," Falle muttered. "Maybe he'll do a better job this time."

"Now, now, let's have a better attitude," Parasol chided. "Your public expects a happy, smiling face."

"Okay, how is this?" Falle displayed a manic grin.

"Much better, but perhaps show a little less of your fangs. Shall we go?"

~ * ~

They were sitting before Falle's office viscreen, both eyeing it as if it was a snake's egg about to hatch.

"You go ahead, Sissi," said Missi, nudging her with an elbow.

"Mistress Falle wants the wedding guest list made up and invitations telefaxed off today."

Sissi nibbled her lower lip. "I donno, when she had me do the guest list for the Coronation Ball, I accidentally erased everything."

"So now you have experience," Missi reasoned. "Go ahead and try."

Sissi touched a pad and a list popped up on the viscreen.

"Okay, here's the list of all Council big shots, senior members of the Citizens Guard, Countess Ratherfadd, Sir Grench, Chancellor Tomerlane..."

"Tomerlane is dead, silly."

"Oh yeah. I suppose he can't make it, then."

"Look, there's a sublist with friends of Tomerlane," said Missi, tapping the screen. "Maybe we should add them?"

"Leonard Mickelson Stillborne. Who's he?"

"Friend of the former Chancellor, I guess," Missi mused. "Send him an invitation."

~ * ~

The newly-opened box spilled its contents onto the workbench amid test tubes, bottles and distillation equipment. A treasure trove of square plastic cards embossed with the numeral one hundred.

"Payment for the last shipment of hyperdrug, guys," Stillborne chortled, grinning over his shoulder at Dik Smedlap and Sann Overdoze. "Anything else arrive at our drop box in Haboob City?"

Overdoze searched the pockets of his jacket. "Oh yeah, some kind of special delivery from Zardoria on New Earth."

"Special delivery from where?" Stillborne took the envelope and tore open the seal. An ornately engraved card fell out into his hand.

"Zog's Holy Jockstrap, it's a wedding invitation." He squinted at the scrolled writing. "Who the prong would be sending me this? Let's see... 'The citizens of Zardoria invite you to witness the marriage of Chancellor Tarelton Duefuss and Commander Falle Crandell at the Chandelier Palace, Tarsday the eleventh, Zogsdate 3942.'"

"Zog's Holy Jockstrap," Smedlap parroted. "So, this is where the bitch ended up. What about this 'Commander' shit?"

"She got the job running the Citizens Guard after she bugged out from Dropoff to escape the murder rap," Stillborne explained. "She figured out because of the human rights embargo Zardoria's got no extradition treaty." *I hope these spacers from the Galactic Rim Mercs are still locked up in the palace cellars. Also hope none of them blabbed about my minor part in their little fracas.*

"Man, Zardoria is virgin territory for hyperdrug running," Overdoze mused. "Pity the Methtropolis Cartel can't find a way to sneak our product in there."

"Hey, let's send the Cartel the wedding invite," said Smedlap brightly. "Because of the reforms Duefuss is putting out, the embargo don't apply to events like family reunions, funerals and of course, weddings."

"The invite is for me, stupid," Stillborne reminded him. He stroked his mustache thoughtfully. "Yeah, but you're right. Zardoria is for sure hangin' fruit."

"Hey, let's divvy up the loot," Overdoze declared, greedily eyeing the pile on the workbench.

"Good idea." Stillborne began separating the creds into three equal stacks.

"Ah, I almost forgot," said Smedlap, tucking his share into designer slacks. "Got a telefax from Methtropolis. They're still waiting on our last shipment of hyperdrug."

"Our last shipment went out a month ago," Stilborne groused. "What the hell coulda happened to it?"

"Ah, it probably got shuffled off somewhere in the hold of some starfreighter," Smedlap shrugged. "It'll turn up. I put a return address on the package."

Creds slipped from Stillborne's fingers back onto the pile.

"You put a return address on the package?"

"Yeah, I figured we couldn't take the chance of losing all that valuable shit." Smedlap's complacent grin faded under the icy glare he was receiving.

"You put our return address on a drug shipment to the Methtropolis Drug Cartel?" Stillborne growled. "Are you brain dead?"

"Well… um, I thought…"

Alarms began to shrill through the abandoned water pumping plant. A wall screen came to life displaying a convoy of terratraxs racing over the desert toward them.

"Goddammit, the lawboys from Haboob City are coming." Stillborne yelled. "Everybody bails out!"

Smedlap and Overdoze stampeded through the back door, climbed into Smedlap's new Porsche sandskimmer and headed out into the desert.

Frantically, Stillborne crammed fistfuls of creds into his vest. He grabbed a firestick he had ready for an evidence-destroying emergency. With a last fond look at his rows of folsox bushes, his distilling equipment and boxes of hyperdrug capsules, he jerked the pin and tossed it. With a searing column of flame behind him, Stillborne took off for the hills in his jetwing.

High on a ridge of red sandstone he watched police terratraxs circle the burning building. He grinned, savoring their rage and frustration.

The grin became a pensive frown while he pondered his next move. Obviously, he needed to blow the planet, find some safe place to start a new drug lab. Maybe cook up a little moongas on Verdana while hunting down a new source of folsox berries. Moongas was chump change compared to the solid aurumite of hyperdrug. He needed someplace where the lawboys would have a tough time getting their mitts on…

He fumbled in his vest and pulled out the wedding invitation. Beneath the drooping mustache a grin was spreading over his face.

Bingo.

~ * ~

The in-flight meal on United Starlines flight 226 from Dustbowl to New Earth consisted of ingredients similar to rancid gomph meat, flyblown veggies and a Chateau D' Dunette vintage that had the flavor of

145

lead salts and reconstituted grape juice.

Stillborne stalked down the ramp into the Zardorian Space Terminal with the Frankenstein gait of someone about to crap his pants. He barely made it into the men's room, dashed into the nearest stall, where he squatted, gasping and gushing.

Sighing with relief, he heard the footsteps of another patron arriving. Stillborne hoped it wasn't another casualty of United Starline's gastronomic delight. The aromatic stench surrounding his cubicle was bad enough.

The new arrival used the urinal and went to the sink to wash up. Through the door separator, Stillborne saw a tall and sinister individual adjusting his cravat. Abruptly, a force pistol fell from his jacket to clatter on the tile floor.

It was a scoped polyplast Model CL45, impervious to all types of spaceport security scanners. Stillborne wondered how he had obtained it, as the man hurriedly snatched it up and departed the restroom. Like all high crime areas of Zardoria, City Three had the strictest weapons control laws.

Back in the Arrivals area, Stillborne hefted his carryall, pushing his way through the crowd toward the exit. There he received a shock. There was a customs checkpoint ahead with agents inspecting the contents of everyone's luggage. He had heard City Three security was laughably lax. Obviously, it wasn't.

He slunk into an adjacent lounge and mulled over what to do about the embarrassing quantities of moongas and hyperdrug capsules in his carryall. What he needed was some kind of loud diversion enabling him to slip past the check point.

At a table in the lounge a huge Citizens Guardsman was holding hands with a lady wearing antique spectacles and streaks of blue dye in her hair. They were sharing a soda and gazing wistfully into each other's eyes.

"Excuse me, sir."

Dorf looked up at the scruffy little man with the drooping mustache. He was working up the nerve to ask his companion whose bed they would be sharing tonight and was not happy with the intrusion.

"What can I do you out of, buddy?" he demanded.

"I happened to notice when I was in the can dropping a steamer…" Stillborne caught the disapproving look from the Guard's lady friend and smiled apologetically. "Sorry…using the facilities…when I saw this character drop a force pistol on the floor." He pointed to the tall, sinister individual standing in the checkpoint line.

"Oh yeah?" Dorf looked in the direction Stillborne was pointing and pursed his lips. "Lemme go check him out. Thanks for the tip."

Stillborne grinned tightly and clutched his carryall, waiting for the confrontation and his opportunity. It wasn't long in coming.

At Dorf's tap on his back and his request "Lemme have a look at your eye-dee, buddy", the tall man shoved Dorf backwards into a stack of pushcarts. He spun about and made for the exit, slamming full tilt into Stillborne who was starting to slink past the custom agents. They both sprawled in a heap onto the carpet. The tall man's head impacted a guard rail and he went limp.

Stillborne got up on an elbow, his breath knocked from him. He felt someone grab his shoulder and a florid face swam into view.

"Good work, buddy," Dorf declared.

He seized Stillborne's hand and pumped it enthusiastically. "I recognize this spacer, he's Dago, one of Baron Ghrasp's best assassins. I'll bet he was sent here to take out Chancellor Duefuss. You're a pronging hero, man!"

~ * ~

Duefuss and Falle lay entwined in each other's arms, both agreeably soaking the sheets with the perspiration from a night of torrid lovemaking. Falle pulled his face to hers for a prolonged and lingering kiss.

"This has been lotsa fun, Adored Despot, but I gotta get back to mopping the hallway tiles."

Duefuss opened his eyes and looked into the lined and middle-aged face of a palace housekeeper.

"Oh yeah, thanks for the company, Grizelda," said Duefuss,

vaguely embarrassed by the sight of her pulling on queen sized panties, picking up her mop and bucket where she had dropped them at his invitation to his bed. The image of a naked and willing Falle was still fresh in his mind.

He slipped on a bathrobe and trudged into the dining hall where Nebly was setting out his breakfast.

"Top of the morning, Great One," said Nebly, pouring the first cup of moco.

"Yeah, morning," Duefuss grunted, slumping into a chair. He took in the compad conspicuously propped up before his place setting. "What the hell is this, Nebly?"

"A list of potential candidates for best man at your wedding," he replied. "I only reminded you a few dozen times yesterday."

"Yeah, yeah. All right." Duefuss took a sip from his cup and tapped the screen. "Let's see, Count Simms…no, he cheats at cards. Lord Pedoe…no, he likes little boys. Baron Shrop…nope, he looks like a beached marine animal wearing a tuxedo. Lord Calomini…"

"The wedding is in two days, Beloved Tyrant. Perhaps you could lower the bar somewhat in your quest for perfection."

"Damn it, Nebly, I wouldn't invite those jerks to a frat party, let alone a wedding."

"Okay. I have an idea, maybe off the wall…" Nebly leaned against the table, crossing his arms. "Instead of royalty and the political aristocracy, maybe it would look good for your image as a man of the people if you chose some common schmuck off the street."

Duefuss drained his cup thoughtfully and tapped the rim for a refill. "Yeah, the common touch. I like the idea. Anybody come to mind?"

"Well, I was watching the Interworld News last night. There was this tourist from Dustball arriving in City Three who helped capture Dago, an assassin sent by Baron Ghrasp to alter your wedding plans. I believe his name is Stillborne, Leonard M."

"I saw the news report too. And the one who recognized the assassin was one of my Guardsmen named Dorf." Duefuss beamed as an inspiration hit him.

"Tell you what, let's go whole hog on this one. Have that

Stillborne spacer picked up and brought to the Chandelier Palace. Inform him he's to be best man at my wedding, whether he likes it or not. Since the job of Citizens Guard Commander will be open when Falle becomes First Lady, let's make Dorf the new head Guard."

Duefuss rubbed his hands together like a hungry fly. "Sure, the common touch and a reward for loyalty. Dammit, Nebly, for a butt kissing flunky you certainly came up a great idea."

"I'm honored, Adored Despot," Nebly replied with a deadpan expression. "By the way, a little package arrived for you from New Earth."

"A little package?"

"From Rivergreede Pharmaceuticals, the serum to cure the hydrophis virus."

~ * ~

"You want me to issue a suite for this… gentleman?"

The head concierge at the Chandelier Palace was certain she was the butt of a practical joke. Sandwiched between two enormous Citizens Guardsmen was a scowling little man with a scruffy mustache. One of the Guards had a ham-like hand around his neck, the other gripped an arm.

"Yes, Ma'am," one of the Guards assured her. "He needs to be put in a Class A suite."

"A Class A suite?" The joke was no longer funny. "Who might this individual be? Let me guess, he's a Councilman or a member of the aristocracy?"

"No, Ma'am, this here's Mr. Stillborne, Duefuss's choice for best man at the wedding," explained the guard with his paw wrapped around Stillborne's windpipe. "Make it on Security Level Six. He already made two attempts to bug out on the flight from City Three."

The concierge frowned displeasure. "I see. Let me check for available units." She bent over her desk viscreen. "Put him in vacant suite 25D." She held out a passcard. "When you escort him to his room, tell him to take a shower."

The two Guardsmen frogmarched Stillborne to the lift and they glided upward. Arriving at the door of the suite, one of them swiped the pad and handed him the passcard.

"Don't forget what the lady said about the shower, you smelly little turd," he grinned, shoving him inside.

"Angled rumpslapper," Stillborne growled as the door slid closed. He groped in the darkness for the light sensor. The air held a faint trace of a perfume, somehow familiar. Where had he smelled it before?

The room filled with light revealing an unmade bed and assorted items of feminine clothing littering the carpet. A single glass and a half-empty bottle of Zardorian cognac decorated a bedside table.

"I'll be a gomph's blowhole," he muttered. "The housekeeping staff in this dump…" The sharp edge of a knife pressed the skin over his carotid artery.

"Turn around slowly," hissed a female voice.

Stillborne obeyed, trembling. He found himself looking into the face of Falle Crandell. There was a long moment of shocked recognition.

"What the hell are you doing here?" they said, almost in unison.

"Let me guess, you're a waiter for the wedding reception who lost his way," said Falle. "What's the idea, Stillborne?"

"They issued me this room, Crandell, see!" he squalled, holding up the passcard in a shaking hand.

"Why would they do that? If Ghrasp sent you as an assassin it must be his hope I'll convulse and die laughing."

"They said this room was vacant. I'm here to be Duefuss's best man at the wedding." A drop of sweat hung trembling at the end of his nose. "Please, Crandell, gimme a break."

"I must have missed this tidbit on the Evening News." Falle lowered her knife. "Relax, Stillborne. If you piss your pants, I'll have to walk over wet carpet all night. What are you doing on New Earth?"

Stillborne wilted with relief. He smiled weakly at her. "Had a little trouble with the lawboys on Dustball. How about you?"

Falle laughed. "Same problem with me, but on Dropoff. So here we are, two former sandwomen prospectors from Satellite, laying low together."

Taking in the semi-transparent nightdress she was wearing in which her breasts showed sharply, Stillborne suppressed a comment.

"I hear you got a heartstone engagement ring," he said. "Remind you of all the fun times you and Walderspan had on Satellite?"

"Him and the fun time there I've already forgot." She gestured at a velvet box on a dresser. "Ever try to sleep with a ring giving off a red glow flashing in your face all night? Duefuss has the good taste of a Umas."

"This marriage to Duefuss," Stillborne ventured. "Is he aware of your, um… condition?"

"Early tomorrow morning, on the day of the wedding, the clinic here is going to give me the serum to cure the hydrophis virus."

"No kidding? You're gonna be First Lady and co-ruler of Zardoria?" Stillborne's mind was working fast. He sensed an opportunity. "Maybe when you're helping run the show here you can gimme a little assist on a business deal I have in mind."

"If you're looking for employment, I think the position of court jester might be available," she smiled. "Right now, let me throw on some clothes and take you back to the Palace front desk for another suite; one where you won't find someone shoving a knife against your windpipe."

~ * ~

Dr. Webber checked the straps securing Falle to the surgical table. Seeing the white uniforms of the doctor and his staff against the sterile white walls of the clinic, she seemed to be surrounded by disembodied faces.

"Is this really necessary?" Falle asked after a nurse gave a final clinch to the band around her waist.

"I understand there is sometimes a violent reaction to patients undergoing the detoxification process," Dr. Webber explained. "Try to remember a bite or scratch from an individual with the hydrophis virus is more dangerous than body fluids at City Three's notorious cathouses."

"Are you sure the serum is going to work?" she asked, watching Webber load a purple phial into an injection module.

"This is Rivergreede Pharmaceutical's latest formula." He wiped her arm with a swab and grinned. "Here's where you get to say, 'Will it hurt, Doctor?' and I get to say, 'No, it won't hurt me a bit.'"

"A comedian; I'm being treated by a standup comedian." She heard a muted hiss of gas and felt a stinging pain.

"What will happen now as the serum neutralizes the virus in your bloodstream is a feeling of intense euphoria and a detachment from your surroundings," he said.

Just what I need, a detachment from this whole wedding business with Duefuss. "How long will it take?"

"You'll be free of the virus by seven tonight, just in time for your wedding, Commander." He patted her arm with a professional smile. "We can't have any dead bodies lying around on your honeymoon, can we?"

Dr. Webber was spot on regarding the oncoming sensations. Falle felt herself floating as if on a gentle sea, voices in her ears seeming faint and faraway. It was not so much euphoria but a separation from herself; watching the world move around her in a velvet fog.

Am I really marrying Duefuss to avoid being thrown out of my sanctuary here on Zardoria? Is it a less than noble craving to lead a normal life?

Faces and scenes moved through the fog. Sissi and Missi helping her into the wedding dress. Their arrival at the Grand Ballroom of the Chandelier Palace, the enormous crowd of guests and dignitaries, soft music coming from glittering chandeliers high above. Stillborne wearing an ill-fitting tuxedo, giving her a sly wink. Duefuss taking her hand, resplendent in full military uniform, a smug look on his face.

Here is where I have my last chance to bail out and take the consequences.

"Chancellor Tarelton Duefuss, do you take this woman to be your bride…"

The deserts of Dustball. I could hide out there forever.

"Falle Crandell, do you take this man as your lawful husband until death…"

There's still a hot market for sandwomen on Satellite. I'll bet Stillborne and I could scrape together a stake and head off into the hills.

"I now pronounce you husband and wife. You may now kiss your bride, Chancellor Duefuss, now First Lady of Zardoria, Falle."

Duefuss' face swam into view. She felt his arms around her. Their lips met in a long kiss and the crowd in the ballroom erupted into tumultuous applause.

Slowly, the complacent smirk on Duefuss faded to a look of vague concern. He abruptly gasped, clutching at his throat. Uttering a strangled cry, he fell heavily to the plush carpet and lay still.

The cheers from the crowd slowly died. From a circle of appalled and gaping dignitaries, Dr. Webber rushed out, kneeling by the body. Expertly, he felt for a pulse, examining the staring eyes. He looked up.

"Chancellor Duefuss is dead," he declared.

A gasp ran through the vast assemble, like the wind of a coming storm passing over a forest.

Citizens Guard Commander Dorf strode out and faced the crowd.

"Long live Chancellor Falle Crandell, Ruler of Zardoria!" he shouted.

"Long live Chancellor Falle Crandell, Ruler of Zardoria!" echoed the senior members of the Guard. They gathered about Dorf and eyed the crowd expectantly.

One by one, all the members of the gathering fell to one knee in a gesture of homage.

Falle was dreamily contemplating a sparkling crystal ornament hanging from a chandelier at the far end of the ballroom. Parasol Sanchez appeared before her, taking her by the arm.

"I think you need to come with me," she said.

Chapter Nine

Detective Smythe settled into the push couch in the lobby leading to the pool. Beyond an acre of glass windows, waitresses in skimpy swimsuits were serving drinks to pudgy tourists working on sunburns which they would be enjoying later this evening.

"I'm gratified you could find the time to meet with me, Mr. Smythe," said Baron Ghrasp, clutching a tropical drink in a meaty fist, his bulk overflowing the adjacent couch. "Can I order you something to cut the dust off the trail?"

"Thanks, but I'm on duty," Smythe replied. "I hear New Earth City approved your petition for political asylum." He glanced around at the hotel's elegant furnishings. "Must be something of a financial strain having to set up camp in a five-star hotel. How does a poor refugee such as you manage it?"

Ghrasp chortled, causing his several chins to jiggle. "I own the hotel. Fortunately, I was able to transfer all my funds before I was forced to relocate."

"Relocate, huh? So, what can the New Earth City Bureau of Investigation do for you?"

"I understand there were nine more deaths from hyperdrug use this week in your city," Ghrasp remarked.

"Yes, it's becoming quite an epidemic. We shut down the lab on Dustball with the help of local authorities but the lab operator, a Mr. Stillborne, managed to escape to Zardoria." Smythe drummed his fingers on a serviette. "I'm a little confused why we're having this conversation. Detective Delveccio is running the Narcotics Bureau here."

"Hear me out, please." Ghrasp leaned a chubby elbow on the table.

"Say, in a hypothetical situation, I became ruler of Zardoria and made all the concessions required to lift the embargo. My first act could be to renew extradition treaties with all planets in the Interworld Federation; after which, Mr. Stillborne and a certain other lady would be on their way to justice."

"You're overlooking the strange situation which has developed in Zardoria where a person wanted for murder on Dropoff by the Federation is now the country's new ruler." Detective Smythe was wondering where all this was going and why he agreed to meet with the Baron at all.

"Like Stillborne, Crandell is in Zardoria to escape prosecution. She's protected by the fierce loyalty of the Citizens Guard, a former ragtag bunch of misfits she whipped into an impressive military organization," Ghrasp continued.

"I seem to be missing the point. As long as she's running the show in Zardoria she's untouchable."

"Well then, what if the murder charges were dropped, say, to extenuating circumstances? She would then be free, or very possibly encouraged by my associates in the Six Cities, to leave."

"I couldn't imagine any situation where the charges would be dropped."

"Couldn't you?" Baron Ghrasp's doughy face exuded secret glee. "What if I was to tell you I found out Major Grange's right-hand man, Captain D'Escrille, has surfaced on a resort dome island on Verdana, living in considerable luxury? You don't surmise he and Grange had, shall we say, a secret financial agreement with the Umas operation on Dropoff which your Bureau might want to look into?"

Detective Smythe grunted. "You appear to have quite a few sources of information, Baron. My sources tell me you had another failed assassination attempt on Chancellor Duefuss in which your best torpedo, Mr. Dago, suffered a fatal skull fracture. Seems to me you're getting a little desperate with your schemes to 'relocate' back to Zardoria."

"Dago wasn't sent there as an assassin. He was sent as a courier who had just successfully completed his assigned delivery."

Detective Smythe blinked his confusion. "Excuse me, delivery?"

"Duefuss bribed Rivergreede Pharmaceuticals to provide his

prospective bride the serum to cure her of the hydrophis virus. I found this out from my spies near the palace and made…a financial agreement…with Professor Drumgold of the company." Ghrasp chortled at the ease in which he had come to terms with that venal gentleman. "The serum was subsequently altered so instead of marital bliss the good Chancellor received the Borgia kiss."

Did he just admit complicity in the murder of a country's head of state?

"This information about D'Escrille will be looked into," said Smythe, digesting the career-enhancing possibilities of such an investigation."

"I'll have my Bureau start digging into the dirt." He stood up, extending his hand. "Appreciate the input, Baron Ghrasp."

"Always a pleasure to assist the boys in blue, Detective," grinned the Baron, taking the proffered hand.

Detective Smythe returned the grin. *You sure are a wily and scheming fat bastard. Hate to be a citizen of the Six Cities if you take over.*

~ * ~

A huge crowd assembled before the Chandelier Palace in the early morning sunlight. The gathering for the most part was silent, the mood expectant as well as apprehensive. Change was coming to Zardoria and none of them knew what this change might mean.

On a high battlement, Falle gazed out over the city, her long blonde hair blowing around her face in the morning breeze.

Leaning on a parapet, Parasol Sanchez was watching her in silence.

"Penny for your thoughts, Adored Despot," she said at length.

"I had this really weird dream last night," Falle mused. "In the dream I married Duefuss, he died after kissing me and a bunch of my Guards jumped up and proclaimed me head honcho of Zardoria."

"You woke up to find it wasn't a dream," said Parasol. "I think it's time we had our little talk, Great One."

"I wish you wouldn't call me that," Falle snapped with some

aspersion. "Call me Falle. Even the maid who scrubs out my john calls me by my first name."

"I'm sure you've noticed the large gathering on the palace grounds below you."

"Oh sure, and I think some of them are carrying ropes and checking out the nearest trees."

"It may very well come to it." Parasol smoothed back a strand of grey hair from her eyes. "You're sitting atop a very slippery pole, my dear."

Falle shrugged. "Even for a person carrying an incurable virus I suppose I can't kiss all of them. What's on your mind, Parasol?"

"The Citizens Guard has your back right now, but this will likely change when the Interworld Federation finds out a person accused of murder and a former Borgia Guild member is running the country. The embargo tightens down and becomes a stranglehold on the economy," she explained. "Baron Ghrasp's agents are everywhere inciting violent rebellion and many of the democracy movements here on Zardoria are not as peaceful as the one I represent."

"Good. I'll order my Citizens Guard to declare you the new Chancellor."

"If only it were this simple."

Falle turned from staring at the silent crowd to consider Parasol. She felt a strange kinship growing between them which could become friendship and trust.

"What do you suggest?" she asked.

"The best way to defuse the situation in Zardoria and the rest of the planet is to declare a democracy and create a constitution which will be drawn up granting rights to all the people of the Six Cities."

"I can then fold up my tent and steal away," said Falle, hopefully.

"Not quite so fast. We have the Guard to consider."

"To maintain order and a smooth transition of power."

"Very astute, my dear. I think a figurehead chancellorship would be best. A symbolic head of state to present unity and the real power in an elected parliament."

Falle bowed from the waist. "I'm honored to meet you, Prime

Minister Sanchez." They smiled at each other.

"We shall see." Parasol thought for a moment. "Let's get the state funeral over for Duefuss with as little ceremony as possible. Next, you'll announce to the world Zardoria will be declared a democracy prior to your inauguration."

"Any chance I could then abdicate and go back to being the Commander of the Guard?"

"Forget it. You're the glue needed to cement the whole thing together, Falle."

"Okay, I'll give it my best shot." She looked doubtful.

"I believe you will do just fine," Parasol assured her.

Somehow, I really think she will. There's something about this young warrior maiden with the cold blue eyes which inspires trust and loyalty.

~ * ~

"Hey Zak, Walderspan and his bunch of Rim Mercs are trying another escape. Wanna watch?" Security Guard Travis had his feet propped up on his desk in the palace cellars security room. He was munching on a snackbar and looking at a wall viewscreen.

"Does this make it the fifth escape they've tried?" Zak checked a series of scratch marks on a wall.

"Nah, this will be the sixth." He took a bite from the snackbar. "Hope this one is as entertaining as when Walderspan tried to fake a heart attack."

On the screen, two men at opposite ends of the cell kept watch while Walderspan and two others busied themselves at a wall.

"What are they doing?" asked Zak.

"Looks like they're trying to access the cell force field controls by chopping a hole in the inside wall with a piece of bedding strut they pulled from a bunk."

"Want me to honk up the Reaction Squad?"

"Nah, let's watch them screw up again."

There was an enormous flash which blanked out the view screen for a moment. When it came back to life, Walderspan and his two helpers lay burned and unconscious on the floor.

"Let's see...escape number six," said Travis, scratching another mark on the wall.

"Say, did they ever get the scanner camera fixed at the cellar passgate? It's been broke, like forever."

"They sure did," Travis replied. "And they downloaded an interesting recording of Baron Ghrasp blowing away two of our guards during the Merc's first escape attempt."

Zac whistled and stared at his companion.

"No shit?"

~ * ~

Excerpt from the
New Earth City Inquirer
Your news today.

Senior members of Zardoria's High Council and mayors from the Six Cities met today to craft a new constitution and declare a democracy. Prime Minister Parasol Sanchez announced it was the Council's decision to confirm for First Lady Falle the title of Chancellor to preside over a new era of freedom and respect for human rights.

Dignitaries from all over Planet New Earth, presided by the President of the City-State of New Earth City, met to conclude treaties of friendship, mutual defense, trade and extradition.

Charges against Chancellor-elect Falle, the former Falle Crandell, for an alleged murder on Dropoff, were dismissed following the arrest of Galactic Rim Mercenary Captain D'Escrille. Investigations revealed financial misconduct and treasonous dealings with Umas raiders which came to light involving Captain D'Escrille and the late Major Grange.

The Inauguration of Chancellor Falle will take place at the Chandelier Palace in City One, Zardoria, Solday the 20th, 3942.6.

~ * ~

"What is this? Am I expected to wear a discarded set of drapes at the Inauguration?" Falle was holding up a silken gown adorned with bows and ropes of pearls.

"It's the traditional gown for female rulers of Zardoria, Mistress Falle," Missi protested.

"It looks like the ballroom dress for a dowager empress." Falle regarded her image in the mirror with distaste. The bedroom of her suite was littered with assorted garments, shoes and boxes of jewelry stacked on dressers. "What else did the palace clothiers send up from the local thrift shop?"

"Here's a really nice gown in pink taffeta," Sissi ventured, lifting up another dress.

"It looks like the funeral shroud for an eighty year old cathouse madam."

Sissi appeared crushed. "But Mistress Falle…"

"Hey, what is this?" Missi had pulled out an old carryall from a bottom bureau drawer. "Sissi, look what I found!"

"Damn, I forgot I even had this." Falle lifted the jeweled harness and purple silk loincloth she had taken from the Umas girl on Dropoff. "I must have stuffed it in the bag in my mad rush to exit the planet."

"You can wear this to the Inauguration, Mistress Falle," Sissi declared eagerly. "With a purple silk cape, it would be perfect!"

"Yes, yes, it's so pretty," Missi pleaded.

"I hear your Citizens Guards are already calling you their Warrior Queen," Sissi added.

"I suppose if I'm to play the clown they picked to be Queen I may as well wear a costume to go with it." She sighed, smoothing the narrow breast band with gold-set jewels tracing out a barbaric design. "Anything is better than those shrouds and old lady rags they sent me."

~ * ~

It was the least busy time of day at the Ghrasp Grande Hotel restaurant terrace but Baron Ghrasp and Gordo chose the most secluded spot overlooking the pool. A silver bowl of sornberries had been set out on an elegant table beside a bottle of Verdanan cognac.

"You are aware there is a consultation fee to the Borgia Guild for meeting someone of your exalted status," Gordo remarked, toying with his glass.

Baron Ghrasp paused from stuffing his face from the bowl of sornberries to slide a handful of creds over the tablecloth. "Yes, of course," he said through his mouthful.

Gordo pocketed the creds, leaned back in his chair. "Now then, what shall we talk about?"

"I was thinking about the situation in Zardoria," Ghrasp replied, chewing his berries disconsolately.

"I'm certain you were thinking about your chances of a triumphal return as ruler of the Six Cities." Gordo lifted his eyebrows, grinning. "I must say it was a masterful stroke the way you had Duefuss eliminated."

Baron Ghrasp's small eyes bulged.

"How did you know I had a hand in what happened to Duefuss?"

"You don't think the Borgia Guild has ears listening everywhere on this planet?" He shook his head with mock pity.

"The good Chancellor was replaced by a former member of the Borgia Guild. I'm overwhelmed by the irony of it all."

"That wasn't supposed to happen," Ghrasp scowled. "How was I to know the Citizens Guard would jump up, clamoring for her to be ruler of Zardoria and overawe the Supreme Council? Zog's Ass, she's the one responsible for his death!"

"Ah, the best laid plans of mice and men etc."

"The head terrorist of the Prodemocracy Movement, the wedge Sanchez, declares a democracy," Ghrasp continued his tirade, his sagging jowls trembling in rage. "I should have ordered Dago to take her out when he brought in the fake serum for the hydrophis virus."

"I saw her Inauguration on the Interworld News yesterday; a most impressive ceremony. I must say Falle Crandell certainly looked every bit regal as Prime Minister Sanchez lowered the diamond crown of the Six Cities onto her head." Gordo effected a bland expression.

They were approaching the subject of the mission Ghrasp had in mind for the elimination of the newly crowned Chancellor. He reasoned an angry Baron would be less liable to quibble when the subject of a fee was broached.

"There were representatives from all countries on New Earth and an enormous crowd of madly cheering citizenry surrounding the Chandelier Palace." Gordo took a sip of cognac to hide a smile. "The newly-designated Chancellor Crandell was wearing, of all things, a skimpy jeweled Umas harness and loincloth. She caused a sensation, especially among members of her Imperial Guard. A real warrior Queen, they were reported as saying."

"Can we now get down to cases?" Baron Ghrasp shoved in another handful of sornberries.

"Good afternoon, Baron."

Detective Smythe and two hulking individuals wearing New Earth City police uniforms appeared beside the table.

Baron Ghrasp stopped chewing his berries and stared. He realized at once this was not a social call.

"Sorry to interrupt a chat with a friend but I'm afraid I must place you under arrest for the murder of two security guards on Zardoria. I have an extradition order with me signed by Prime Minister Sanchez."

Baron Ghrasp tried to speak, raising his bulk from his chair to protest. Suddenly, he started to gag and clutch at his throat.

"Zog's Ass, he's choking on something!" exclaimed an alarmed Detective Smythe. "Anybody here know the Heimlich Maneuver?"

The table overturned, sending glasses and the cognac bottle flying. Ghrasp fell heavily to the floor, thrashing madly.

"Hold him." Smythe waved frantically to one of the gaping waiters. "Somebody call a doctor!"

With a last strangled cry Ghrasp stiffened and lay still. His eyes stared unseeing from a purple face.

"Goddammit, he's gone and croaked on us," Smythe groaned in frustration. He shrugged. "Notify headquarters and I'll get a statement from his companion. He glanced around the restaurant terrace.

Gordo was nowhere to be seen.

~ * ~

Rain streaked down relentlessly from the night sky, painting bright droplets on puddles collecting in the gutters. Reflected in the puddles was the dark and floodlit mass of the Chandelier Palace looming over the city.

Stillborne pulled the hood of his waterproof cloak tighter around his chin while he trudged along the street, almost deserted at this late night hour. Overhead the batlike shape of a solitary jetwing glided silently past.

He had been mulling his future since he had heard an extradition order had gone out for Baron Ghrasp on murder charges. Would the next extradition order be written out for a certain Mr. Stillborne, Leonard M.?

Earlier in the evening he had tried to seek advice from Falle but no one in the Palace seemed to know where she had gone. Retreating to his Palace suite was becoming less pleasant due to the frequent arrivals of middle-aged maid Grizelda who appeared at random times to 'dust off the furniture' or 'give the carpet a quick vacuum' but ended up in his bed.

The brightly lit foyer of a local bar beckoned. He needed a couple of drinks to clear his mind.

Despite the late hour, the bar was surprisingly busy. Stillborne pushed his way through a noisy crowd toward an empty stool at the counter beside which sat a young woman wearing a hooded waterproof cloak. A shapely arm leaned on the bartop clutching a glass of Emperion.

"Hey babe, nice day if it don't rain," he leered at her, sliding onto the stool.

"It is raining, you dumb little turd," said Falle, looking at him from under her hood.

Stillborne was taken aback. "Hey, Crandell, great to see you. How they hanging?"

"One lower than the other, if I had any. Which I don't." She stared gloomily at the line of assorted bottles on a shelf below the mirrored wall. "I suppose you were looking for me. Heard about the extradition order on Ghrasp, huh?"

Stillborne shrugged unhappily. "Yeah. Thought you might have an idea what I should do."

"Probably something along the lines of blowing the planet."

"I know, but where?"

Falle took a thoughtful sip of her glass. "Parasol dropped me a few subtle hints about what 'my little friend' was up to on Dustball." She eyed him dispassionately. "Do you know the Methtropolis Drug Cartel has put out a contract on you for a hyperdrug shipment which never arrived?"

"Holy gorth crap." Stillborne seemed to shrivel on his seat. "Hell, I'd reimburse them the creds, but knowing my two um, business partners, they've probably blown their share by now."

"Satellite. Butt end of our planetary system, last place they'd look aside from Swampworld, which I feel you'd not care to revisit."

"Yeah, Satellite." He nervously pulled his mustache. "I got some wedges I know in a sandwoman pack up by Red Butte…"

Falle's comm band began to chime. She tapped the case and a familiar face appeared in the tiny screen.

"My greetings to the Beloved Tyrant, Chancellor Crandell of Zardoria." Jinghua's feline eyes glinted with good humor. "This lowly peasant from the soil begs the honor of an audience with the Adored Despot."

"Save me the genial sarcasm, Jinghua," Falle sighed. "So how are the shootings, stabbings and poisonings going on in your little band?"

"The list of disgruntled employees, cheated-on wives and errant swindlers is endless," she replied, then suddenly grew serious. "Listen, Falle, I found out some things about the serum you took to cure the hydrophis virus."

"Yeah, it didn't work."

"It wasn't supposed to work."

Falle paused with her glass half way to her lips. "What?"

"Your old friend Gordo was bragging to everyone who would listen in the Borgia Guild how he had learned that Baron Ghrasp contrived to have the serum Duefuss ordered rendered inert. So your wedding kiss with your late husband would be fatal, paving the road to the good Baron's quest for power in Zardoria."

Falle's glass dropped to the bartop. She was flooded by a strange new sensation. Hope.

"You're kidding," she whispered.

"Not at all. I also believe there is a score you'll want to settle with Gordo in some distant future."

"Yes, there is." Falle studied the commband screen for a long moment. "Thanks for the heads up, Jinghua. Once again, I owe you."

"Always a pleasure to aid the girl with the Borgia kiss," she smiled. "By the way, knowing how you might be in need of thirty thousand creds, I have heard from a reliable source a shipment of heartstones will be arriving next week in the little hamlet of New Seattle, on Satellite."

A line of ore carts under a pitiless sun... the crack of whips... blood dripping onto the sand.

Falle shuddered involuntarily.

"From the Umas heartstone mine?"

"Exactly so. They'll be stored in a warehouse in Sector Five near the spaceport prior to being smuggled off the planet." Jinghua nodded in farewell. "Good luck, Falle." The screen went blank.

There were days of endless despair for Falle when she thought herself never to be free of the venom in her blood. To never experience a normal life, to find love, to share with the rest of humanity the simple joy of a lover's kiss.

"You're not thinking of going after them Umas heartstones again, Crandell?" Stillborne had been eavesdropping over her shoulder. "Zog's Holy Jockstrap, you must love pain."

"You know why I need thirty thousand creds," she snapped.

"For what?"

"For the serum to cure the virus I have, you nutless drone." She signaled to the bartender for a refill and pointed to her companion.

Stillborne gave her a repentant glance. "Sorry, Crandell, I forgot. Listen, you're Chancellor of Zardoria, for cripes sake. Get your mitts in the till."

"I'm just a figurehead. Prime Minister Sanchez and the Council have the keys to the piggy bank." She picked up the drink which had been set before her and contemplated overhead lights glinting in the amber depths.

"You're gonna go for them stones," Stillborne observed. "Want me to come along? I sorta need to make myself scarce on this planet."

"I can't leave, not right now," she grimaced. "I'm 'the glue to hold everything together', according to Parasol Sanchez. Besides, she's...kind of a friend. I don't have all that many."

Stillborne took a pull from his mug of beer, sucking the foam from his mustache. "What if there was a way to bug out for Satellite and still be here?"

"Have you been at your dhung pipe again, Stillborne?"

"Come on, hear me out," he protested. "Remember the eight cybernetic duplicates of yourself they got working at the Sandman Hilton the other side of the city? Well, I was at their bar last Tarsday trying to pick up a wedge...I mean, stopping by for a brew. They got one of the fake knockoffs of you rigged up in the jeweled Umas harness like you wore for the Inauguration. It's kinda a dump but business really picked up because of her getup."

"Can you get to the point, Stillborne?"

"The point, yeah. It was sorta slow that night and I got to talking with her. Old Finegold, the hotel owner, is shortchanging her allowance and refusing to let her and the other cybernetic maids date guys. I guess he's afraid they'll get their leases bought out from Universal Cybernetics."

Falle chuckled. "So how did she look in the outfit I wore for the big event? I still remember the shocked expressions on those pussy faces of the High Council when I waltzed into the Grand Ballroom."

"Hell, she's a dead ringer for you, Crandell," said Stillborne. "Nice perky tits, tight ass. 'Cept she don't have the same mean eyes...I mean, um, expression."

Falle took a slow sip from her glass, thinking this over. "So, she's not happy working at the Sandman Hilton, huh?"

"Yeah. She said she had it better at United Starlines getting her butt patted as a flight attendant. Her name is Agnes."

"Dead ringer, you said?"

"Sure 'nuff is."

They shared conspiratorial grins then Falle tossed off the last of her drink.

"Listen, Stillborne, I don't think you should wet your shorts over this extradition problem. We'll be long gone before the paper pushers in the High Council get finished with the first draft."

Stillborne exuded gratitude. "Gee, thanks, Crandell. I've always thought of you as a buddy…"

"Don't get all mushy on me now," she replied, sliding off her stool. "Let's pay a visit to my knockoff at the Sandman Hilton."

Arriving at the hotel, Stillborne led the way up the rear custodian lift to a door on a long corridor. He pressed a button and after a short wait the door slid open revealing Falle's cybernetic duplicate wearing a sheer black nightie.

"Hey, Leonard, nice day if it don't rain," she declared.

She grabbed him by the front of his shirt and began dragging him across the room to an adjacent bed. Suddenly, she caught sight of Falle and froze, her mouth dropping open.

"Where do I get the idea you two are acquainted?" Falle remarked dryly.

"Um, I'd like you to meet Agnes," said Stillborne with a watery smile, hastily buttoning his shirt, minus several which had popped off.

"I'm…honored by your visit, Great One," Agnes stammered, performing an awkward curtsy.

Falle crossed the room and ran a hand over Agnes' face. "Hmm, I see you've had the minor surgery to remove the cybernetic smile. I think all we'll need is to give her a briefing on Palace affairs, etiquette and the players in our little game. Oh yes, we need to find someplace to get her the tattoo on her left shoulder."

Agnes's blue eyes widened in confusion. "Tattoo, Adored Despot?"

"Part of your new job description, Agnes. I should say, Chancellor Crandell."

~ * ~

Everything was different.

Agnes lay awake in the enormous bed of the royal suite. Morning sunlight streamed through windows hung with velvet drapes. She experienced a vague feeling of unreality remembering waking the previous morning in a tiny cot of her cubbyhole room in the Sandman Hilton.

There was the hum of suite doors gliding open and Falle's two maids... what did she call them in her briefing before she and Stillborne had headed off to the Zardorian Spaceport? Oh yes, the two twits with the combined brain of a gnat. Missi and Sissi.

"Good morning, Mistress Falle," Sissi greeted her happily, setting the breakfast tray on the bed covers before her.

"Good morning, Mistress Falle," Missi echoed, pouring her moco.

Agnes took in the assorted viands heaping the plate, a small gorth steak, eno eggs and real moco. Her protoflesh mouth began watering. At the Sandman Hilton the maids were served stale leftovers from the kitchen's scraped plates.

She attacked the tray with gusto while the two maids chattered excitedly about the meeting of the High Council later this morning; how Prime Minister Sanchez was going to ratify the new Charter for Human Rights and how the population of the Six Cities was starting to call her the new Mahatma Gandhi.

"Who is Mahatma Gandhi?" Agnes asked between mouthfuls of gorth steak.

"She was a famous champion for freedom and liberty on ancient Earth," Missi replied. "She was later assisted by a bad man."

"You mean assassinated, you silly drone," Sissi corrected her. "Anyway, your bath is ready, Mistress."

The sculptured marble bath filled the room; scented water heaped with mounds of foam. Agnes slid into the enveloping warmth, giving out a sigh of ecstasy. *I could really get used to this,* she thought.

Arising from the bath, Sissi toweled her dry while Missi held out an elegant formal gown and the diamond studded crown. Agnes ran her hand over white silk, embroidered with tiny purple flowers.

I could really get used to all this.

~ * ~

Seated on a throne high above the Grand Hall, Agnes looked out over the enormous crowd below, the rows of seats holding High Council members and the rigid lines of Citizen Guardsmen in their immaculate uniforms. Prime Minister Parasol Sanchez arranged documents on the table facing the audience and one by one the Councilors came up to affix their signatures.

Finally, Prime Minister Sanchez gathered up the stack and ascended the throne dais for the final signature.

"Bottom of page one and page three," said Parasol, smiling, handing her an antique pen.

Concealing her nervousness, Agnes scrawled Falle's signature, copying her handwriting with cybernetic precision.

"Now, Great One, if you would care to address the people of Zardoria, they now await your appearance."

The Citizens Guard formed ranks around her, escorting Agnes to the balcony overlooking the Palace gardens. A vast assembly spread out over the grounds, past the gates and overflowed onto city streets.

At her appearance, the crowd began cheering, on and on, a volume of sound breaking like waves against the ancient stone walls.

Agnes stood transfixed, submerged in a flood of adulation. A conflicting surge of alien emotions sought to overpower her basic programming as a Level Eight cybernetic android. She felt her mind sliding to a different plane, changing…

She was no longer a maid working at the Sandman Hilton. She had become someone else.

The Chancellor of the Six Cities of Zardoria smiled and waved out over the crowd. The cheers swelled, re-doubled.

~ * ~

A day of pomp and celebration was drawing to a close. The final event was a march across the Palace Square by the Citizens Guard, flags billowing in the evening breeze, band playing lustily.

In the reviewing stand Agnes watched them march past. She noticed the scarred and pugilistic faces. Street toughs and bruisers that the late Chancellor Taragon had formed to keep her in power by brute force all those past years. Agnes pursed her lips in thought. The events, emotions and experiences were running riot through her cybernetic consciousness. Abruptly, she turned to an aide.

"After this last ceremony I would like to see Commander Dorf in my suite," she said.

Chapter Ten

Commander Dorf stood sweating on the plush carpet of the royal suite, at rigid attention, helmet clutched in hand. He had no idea the reason for this summons, but expected the worst.

"You can relax, Commander," said Agnes, lounging on a divan, eyeing his discomfort with some amusement. "We're just going to have a private little chat."

"Yes, Beloved Tyrant." Dorf swallowed heavily. *Hope she doesn't ask me for a kiss.*

"Tell me how you and the Guard feel about this new democracy in Zardoria."

"Our feelings, Adored Despot?"

"I want your honest and candid appraisal, Commander."

Dorf licked his lips. "Well, Great One, to be frank, things were better for us under Taragon. I mean, we had respect, even if we had to kick a few deserving asses to get it."

"You feel you're not respected now?"

"All them new regulations about this human rights stuff. The people think we're getting soft, treat us like some kinda joke."

Agnes leaned back in the divan. "What if your Chancellor had real power to rule Zardoria. To make things go back the way they were?"

"Hell yeah…I mean, heck yes, Beloved Tyrant," Dorf replied with feeling. "We all miss the good old days of kicking butt and taking names…"

"Tell me of those five Rim Mercenaries Duefuss had locked up in the Palace Security Cellars," Agnes interrupted him.

"Walderspan and them other guys?" Dorf looked confused.

171

"Prime Minister Sanchez has ordered the release of all political prisoners tomorrow morning. I guess this means them too."

Agnes considered her fingernails for a moment. "There is a Umas heartstone mine on Satellite. How would you go about sending them a message?"

Dorf scratched his chin stubble. Agnes' rapid changing of subjects was making his head swim. "Well, communications between Umas raiders are in a code no one's been able to break. The boys in the Palace Interfax shop are pretty hot stuff. Bet they could slip in a little uncoded heads-up."

"Very glad to hear this, Commander," Agnes smiled. "I can see we're going to be quite good friends."

Commander Dorf beamed with pleasure and relief.

"Now, contact the Security Office in the Palace cellars," she ordered. "I believe I will have a little chat with Mr. Walderspan."

~ * ~

"Hey Zak, they're at it again." Travis was lounging behind a security office desk, grinning at a red-lit viscreen.

"Another escape attempt by Walderspan and his clowns?" Zak put down his cup of moco and hurried over. "Damn, don't they realize even though it's after lights out we still have them on infrared scanners? What's the plan this time?"

Walderspan and his men were prying at a metal plate in a far corner of the cell. A pile of bolts and a crudely made wrench lay to one side.

"They're removing the cover leading to the Palace sewage reclamation pit on the lower level."

"Hot damn! This is going to be fun to watch."

"Ha, talk about being deep in the shit. I hope when Nebly and his cleaning crew arrive they bring hoses."

A buzzer began to sound. Zak lifted a commpad from the desk. "Security Guard Zak here," he announced. "What? Who is coming down? She wants him in Interrogation Room C, with no audio or video? Right,

I'll take care of it."

"Who was that?" Travis asked.

"Chancellor Crandell wishes to meet with Walderspan for some reason." He gazed wistfully at the viscreen and the toiling mercs working on the hatch cover. "Damn, this would have been fun to watch."

~ * ~

Interrogation Room C was the acme of simplicity; a metal table and two metal chairs bolted to the concrete; bare stone walls with a garland of mold at each ceiling corner.

Agnes watched two guards escort a plasticuffed and sullen Walderspan into the room and leave, the closing door echoing with a dismal clang. He glared over the table at her.

"I hear my mercs and I are being released tomorrow and hustled out of the country," he growled. "But don't think you've seen the last of us, Crandell."

Agnes crossed her legs, studying him with a condescending expression. "A question of a soldier's honor, I imagine, Walderspan."

"Yeah, that too, and the fact our organization is not likely to get any contracts if some wedge can get away with taking out our leader," he replied angrily.

Agnes acknowledged his reasoning with a nod. Getting up from her chair she walked around the table and, seizing Walderspan's face, placed a wet kiss on his lips. He jerked violently backwards, uttering a shocked cry, his eyes wild.

Agnes calmly reclaimed her seat. She propped her chin on her palms, smiling at the sweating and terrified occupant of the adjacent chair.

"I'm...still alive," he managed to croak at last. "How...how..."

"My, how excitable you humans can be at times," she observed.

"Us humans?" Walderspan blinked his confusion.

"Remember the five cybernetic maids Finegold leased to work at the Sandman Hilton? I suppose we haven't been properly introduced. I'm Agnes."

Walderspan finally stopped sweating. "You mean to say you and

Crandell have traded places? Why in hell would she do this?" he demanded incredulously.

"She and Stillborne...I believe you know the gentleman...are off in a stolen starfreighter to seize a shipment of Umas heartstones which will be arriving next week in Satellite. She put me here to hold down the fort, so to speak."

"So, what's in all this for you?" Walderspan was unconvinced. Cybernetic androids had loyalty to their leased customers imprinted at the top of their programming. Something very strange was going on here.

"What's in it for me?" Agnes stared serenely at the far wall. "Breakfast in bed, bubblebaths and designer clothing for starters. Then, taking power and giving orders to humans instead of meekly obeying them comes next." Her eyes suddenly became cold. "What is the fastest space cruiser in the Zardorian fleet?"

"Let me think," he mused. "I would say the Mark IX starsabre."

"I'll issue an order to have one placed at your disposal tomorrow morning. If we come to an agreement, that is." She watched him closely for a reaction. "It's a two-day trip via timephase from Zardoria to Satellite. The Mark IX could overtake their freighter in less than a day."

"What's this again about heartstones?"

"After you deal with Crandell you could then proceed to New Seattle on Satellite and grab the gems from the Umas. I hear the lone female smuggler will be lightly guarded by a small escort."

Walderspan considered for a moment, then nodded his head in agreement.

"I'm most happy to accept your offer...Beloved Tyrant," he smiled.

~ * ~

"Are we there yet?" Stillborne was peering out a side viewport of the space shuttle. They were in timephase mode, which meant all he could see was a confusing blizzard of white streaks flying past the plexglass.

"You have twenty-six hours, eleven zaks before we hit orbit around Satellite." Falle was seated in the command chair facing a bewildering array of dials and switches. She had the ship in autopilot and was leisurely running a sonic sharpener along the blade of her assault knife.

"So, what's your plan when we get to New Seattle?"

Stillborne's level of courage was in an inverse ratio the closer they came to their destination. Toiling in a Umas heartstone mine held little appeal for him.

"I have an old Aghaid friend on the planet. Remember Fan-tonn? He hangs out in the part of the city where the Umas courier is supposed to show up with the gems."

Stillborne looked dubious. "Yeah, I suppose. I also wonder what the Sandman Hilton is going to do about their missing maid Agnes."

"Ah, we'll have her cook up a story about her being carried off by a hotel customer and eventually managing to escape his clutches." Falle was enjoying herself creating a plausible scenario in her mind. "Let me see, the maid Agnes fighting off the advances of the customer inflamed by passion, escaping through a window in the dead of night to happily return to her mop and broom."

An alarm on the control panel began an ominous beeping. Falle sheathed her knife and leaned over a scanner.

"Oh oh, we have company."

"What's happening?" Stillborne scuttled to peer out a forward viewport.

"Another space cruiser, approaching on an intercept course." She adjusted a dial. "Looks like a Zardorian Mark IX Starsabre."

"Holy gorth crap," Stillborne moaned. "What are we gonna do?"

"Head for the nearest planet and hide out." Falle consulted a screen. "Okay, I think we can make Adriane before they overtake us."

"Adriane? That's a planet totally covered by an ocean with a few rocks sticking up here and there. Goddammit, Crandell!"

"You just better get down on your bony knees and pray we can reach it...ufff."

The shuttle rocked from an impact. A terrific shock vibrated the hull. A screen from the stern showed the dagger shape of the Starsabre let loose a furious barrage of red beams. A gust of acrid brown smoke billowed into the cockpit.

"We've had it!" Stillborne squalled. "We gotta make for the escape pod."

"No time, hang on."

"Help, Mother!"

The space shuttle lost power, spun about helplessly in a dark infinity of stars.

From inside the Zardorian starsabre, Walderspan eyed the drifting wreck and grinned. "End of the trail for Miss Crandell and her little buddy. Let's get back on our trail leading to them heartstones on Satellite, guys."

~ * ~

Fangg was an Umas. Like all Umas females, she had dark eyes, raven hair and was startlingly beautiful. Still too young to have her first embryonic cycle she was born in the hold of a Umas space raider in orbit over Sheridan's Planet.

The Umas no longer had a homeworld. Centuries of overpopulation, religious strife, industrial pollution and war had left Umastane a planetwide landfill. The race became a fleet of pirate corsairs, raiding isolated settlements on distant worlds, making daring attacks on the cities of major worlds and setting up outposts to loot or mine for valuable minerals.

Fangg rose from crewman to sub-lieutenant of a space raider and because of her notable ruthlessness, was given command of the heartstone facility on Satellite. The former commander, Bantannomen, her brother, was murdered during an escape by a trio of human slaves.

It was her responsibility to make the trip to New Seattle where the gems would be smuggled off the planet. A year's toil from the mine's Aghaid slaves resulted in a mere handful of the stones. His handful would reap from the alleys, back rooms of Verdana and New Earth, a half million creds; all used to finance new ships and weapons for the Umas fleet.

Fangg smiled to herself. Soon, she would be rewarded with the captaincy of a space raider of her own. To range throughout the star system, burning, looting and killing humans. Avenge her brother who was killed by the vile human scum.

The Blue Lady sent a pale effulgence down the deserted night street of Sector Five. Pausing in the shadows, she tucked the pouch of heartstones under her arm and punched in a code at the warehouse slidegate.

"I don't see any sign of an escort," Walderspan whispered to his companions hiding in a deserted building across the street. "Grabbing the heartstones is gonna be a picnic." His four fellow mercs sniggered in agreement. Eagerly they watched the slidegate open and the female Umas vanish into the gloom.

"Come on, before she closes the door." Pulling out their force pistols they dashed over the street and into the warehouse.

Suddenly, the dusty interior blazed with light. Walderspan and his band of Rim Mercenaries stood transfixed, staring at the muzzles of pulse rifles held by a score of Umas sandtroopers.

"You are advised to drop your weapons, humans," said Fangg, advancing with a drawn force pistol. She jammed the barrel under Walderspan's chin. One by one their pistols clattered onto the warehouse concrete.

"Very wise choice, Walderspan," she said.

"You…you know my name?" he stammered, amazed.

"Of course. We received a little heads up from Zardoria on your plans. As we are always looking for volunteers to work in our mine, you five will be a welcome addition." Fangg shoved her weapon harder into Walderspan's throat. The black eyes in her beautiful face narrowed to slits.

"Since you were part of the three humans who killed my brother, Bantannomen, your stay at our little resort in the desert will be most enjoyable. I'm going to give you the guided tour."

~ * ~

Sissi and Missi were not happy.

They were somberly watching Agnes preening before the suite

mirror, adjusting her crown, smoothing the silken folds of her gown.

"She sure spends a lot of time looking at herself and trying on dresses," Missi whispered.

Sissi nodded. "She hasn't been the same person since the night she came back from that bar with the little man of the funny mustache. Not as, um...friendly."

With a final resetting of her crown Agnes turned to them. "You can return the other gowns to the dress rack. Try not to get them wrinkled when you hang them."

"Yes, Mistress Falle," they replied in chorus, watching her stride regally across the suite.

The door slid open revealing a squad of Citizens Guards who snapped to rigid attention.

All the attendees in the Grand Hall came to their feet when Agnes entered and ascended the throne dais with an air of royal disdain. On the pavilion a few steps below, Parasol Sanchez bowed to the dais and faced the crowd from behind her podium.

"Welcome, members of the High Council and honored guests to the sixth legislative session," she declared. "I have here a few amendments to the Free Speech Directive approved by the Council that now await signature by Chancellor."

The crowd applauded, watching Parasol ascend the dais with the documents. "Your signature is needed on the bottom of page three," she smiled.

Agnes ignored the documents and the proffered pen. "I have other documents you and the Council will need to read." She held out a sheaf of paper.

Parasol blinked in confusion. She took the papers from Agnes, quickly riffling through the pages.

"I don't understand. This looks like a manifesto cancelling the Zardorian Constitution and granting you what appears to be supreme power."

"This is exactly so." Agnes gazed down at her smugly. "You don't have to sign on the bottom of page three."

"This...this isn't going to happen."

All traces of good humor had departed Parasol's face.

"Oh, really?" Agnes gestured to the phalanx of stern-faced Citizens Guardsmen standing behind her. "Would you care to tell them that?"

Prime Minister Sanchez studied the haughty figure on the throne for a long moment. She noticed the hand holding the manifesto. The hazmat imprint on her left palm was no longer there.

"You are not Chancellor Falle Crandell," she declared. "Who exactly are you?"

"I understand the people of Zardoria have taken to calling you the new Mahatma Gandhi," Agnes sneered. "I think it's time you shared his fate."

"I demand to know where the real Chan..."

"Guards!" Agnes stood up. "Arrest Prime Minister Sanchez for high treason. Take her away."

A perfect storm of gasps and cries of horror came from the audience as they watched Parasol being dragged from the Grand Hall. Then utter silence followed as Agnes advanced to the podium. She rested her hands on the lectern, sweeping the crowd with a stern and uncompromising glare.

"High Council and people of Zardoria," she began. "I have today assumed, as Chancellor of Zardoria, complete power over the Six Cities..."

~ * ~

Excerpt from the
New Earth City Inquirer
Your News Today!

Latest events in the Six Cities of Zardoria have shocked the world. Chancellor Crandell has reportedly seized control over the government of the country and imprisoned Prime Minister Parasol Sanchez on charges of high treason. Units of the Citizens Guard moved yesterday in a co-ordinated round-up of all known dissenters and members of the

Prodemocracy Movement. Media reporting stations have been seized and martial law declared. The Homeworld Federation will meet Zogsday to vote on re-instituting embargo restrictions on Zardoria. Military options will also be discussed.

~ * ~

If Zardorian cathouses were rated for rundown sleaziness, the Pussyfoot Cabaret in City Four would have a five-star rating.

Baron Shrop paused before the garishly lit entrance, looked nervously around at the nighttime crowd of hustlers, pimps and moongas sellers then darted inside. A blowsy female form appeared from the dim interior, shrouded in dhung smoke.

"Ah, just in time for happy hour," she greeted him, batting eyes heavy with mascara and wearing a seductive smile on her thick lips. "How can Fatima make this handsome gentleman happy?"

"Ah…um, just here to meet some friends," he stammered, sweat beading on his bald pate. "Thanks, anyway." He hurried past her down a hallway and rapped on a darkened doorway.

Five members of the Zardorian High Council watched as Baron Shrop took his place at the long table. The light from a single fly-speckled globe lit their anxious and troubled faces.

"Well now, what shall we talk about?" he asked. "I'm assuming you all arrived here without attracting official notice?"

They all nodded dumbly. At the meeting was: Sir Grench, tall and ascetic, Countess Ratherfadd, approaching the fatal age of thirty and attempting to conceal the fact by an excess of jewelry, Lord Pedoe, rouge, makeup and narrow darting eyes, Count Simms, perhaps the wisest of the group and Sir Calomini, a patron of the arts, looking dissipated as usual from long sessions with his Model SXIV Wild Overnighter cybernetic.

"You all signed the order for Martial Law as demanded by Chancellor Crandell," he continued, "Not that we had any choice, as Sir Grosse found out after refusing to sign."

"What happened to Sir Grosse?" Countess Ratherfadd demanded.

"A jetwing took off from the Chandelier Palace this morning. Sir

Grosse was on it."

The group behind the table stared at Baron Shrop, awaiting an explanation.

"He was sent by the Chancellor to inspect the new reclamation project at Slimedevil Swamp. When the ship was in a hover at twenty thousand meters, the Citizens Guard pushed him out."

The gloom in the room deepened. Sir Calomini cleared his throat.

"What has happened to Prime Minister Sanchez?" he asked.

"She's back in her old cell in the palace cellars. Crandell is planning a public execution in the main square of City One, to solidify her control and to prove a point to whoever might wish to cross her."

Count Simms sighed heavily. "I believe it's inevitable that sooner or later all of us will be taking a jetwing ride to Slimedevil Swamp."

"What can we do?" Countess Ratherfadd nibbled nervously at her fingernails.

"I thuposh the sthmart idea would be for uth all to leave the country," Lord Pedoe suggested with his irritating lisp. "Take what finantheth we can acquire and head for thay, Verdana or New Earth ath did Baron Ghrathp."

"Not a chance, the way we are now watched," Shrop declared with finality. "I'm just hoping it wasn't noticed the entire High Council decided to visit the same whorehouse on the same night."

"So, what can we do?" Sir Grench asked with a plaintive whine.

"I have a suggestion." Baron Shrop now had their complete attention. "The Borgia Guild."

"Hire them to eliminate Chancellor Crandell?" Countess Ratherfadd was incredulous.

"I don't think this is a situation where we hire a couple of thugs from some back alley," Shrop remarked dryly. "Besides, they guarantee success or a full refund."

"Do you have any idea of how much they would charge to take out a head of state?" Count Calomini demanded to know.

"So, what price does all of you here put on your lives?" Baron Shrop gazed at each of their faces. One by one they returned his glance and nodded assent.

Chapter Eleven

Within the cabin of their derelict starfreighter, Falle scanned images running across a console screen. She found a jumpsuit close to her size in a storage bin, from which came an assortment of opened food containers now littering the cabin floor. At an alcove table, Stillborne was pulling the tab from a bottle of wine. Two empties lay on their sides before him, relics of their celebration in finding the ship's hull and life support system was still intact.

"So, what's the plan now, El Capitan?" he asked, burying the lip of the wineglass in his mustache.

"When I was a pilot for Pan Galaxy Spacelines, I heard of a freighter from United Starlines having a fusion drive failure just outside of Zabo's Belt," Falle said. "It was an obsolete model and since they didn't have it in the budget for repair, they just abandoned it." She pointed at a blip on her screen. "See, it's been drifting out there for three years. Any chance of getting our heap running again?"

Stillborne sat down at a console and punched a series of buttons. He made a wry face. "Well, looks like the timephase module is toast. I might be able to get the fusion drive fixed so we can at least putt along."

"Right. But the general direction the wreck has been drifting has been toward us. See the ship's position beacon on my screen?"

"How far away is it?"

"We could reach it in about two days at sublight speed." She tapped the console thoughtfully and looked back at Stillborne. "So how good are you at fixing fusion drives?"

He grinned smugly. "Sweetcheeks, I can fix anything, including virginity. Just get me the parts."

"Glad to hear your level of confidence." She ran her hand over the sheathed knife at her belt. "As long as it gets us back to Zardoria, where we need to have a little chat with our old pal, Agnes."

Stillborne peered over his shoulder at her. "Why do you wanna chat with Agnes?"

"Just curious how anybody else knew it was us in that starfreighter heading for Satellite. I think maybe the heartstones can wait."

"Hey, ready for some more fruit of the vine?" He lifted the newly opened bottle.

Falle considered the well stocked cabinets and racks lining the pod's walls. "We certainly picked the right space freighter to steal. The former owner must have been something of a sybarite."

"Baron Shrop. This was one of the smuggling ships he used to run the embargo and bring back luxury items, like all this wine, from New Earth," Stillborne chuckled.

He filled a glass and pushed it over the table toward her.

Falle drained her glass, licking her lips in appreciation. "Very nice. A '26 Verdana Zinfandel?"

"Yup. Here's to Baron Shrop," he declared, pouring her a refill. They clinked glasses.

All this wine was making Falle very mellow. Stillborne's companionship was becoming less of an annoying irritant. "So, tell me about this ex-wife of yours?" she asked, taking a sip.

"Yeah, the shark with tits. She dumped me for one of T'ong Glokk's tadpole sons on Verdana," he replied in gloomy recollection. "She took off, flipper in hand, with him to his private pond on Asteroid DBIV. Her divorce lawyer took everything but my jockstrap." He refilled their glasses and eyed her blearily. "So, tell me all about your old flames, Crandell."

She turned the stem of her wineglass in her hand. "Just one, believe it or not."

"Just one?" Stillborne's eyebrows shot up.

"Well, sort of. Captain Rann Glassford." She took another contemplative sip. "We dated for a couple months. I even had the passcard to his apartment but..." Her voice faded away.

"You never got down to the old spit-swapping mujambo with him, huh?" he leered.

"Yeah, but I was sure tempted at times to let him inside the black thong panties I was wearing."

"So, what happened?"

The soft smile of velvet from remembering the good times past left her face. "What happened was I caught the hydrophis virus from a spaceliner crash on Swampworld and he dumped me for a flight attendant."

"Hell, I'm sorry, Crandell."

"I don't think she was old enough to have her first period...scrawny little ass...tits like wasptick bites." She set her empty glass down unsteadily on the table.

Stillborne had never seen her display emotion before and was overwhelmed with unaccustomed feelings of brotherly empathy.

"Well, Zog's Ass, Crandell," he soothed, patting her hand. "Things ain't as bad as they sometimes seem. At least you still got me."

The final bottle of Baron Shrop's wine had definitely reduced the close company of Stillborne to a bearable level. She decided to pull his chain.

"So how about engaging in a spit-swapping horizontal mujambo with me, Leonard?" She pursed her lips seductively, gazing at him with sultry eyes. Her hand moved to the zipper of her coveralls.

Stillborne edged back, affecting a tight grin. "Um, thanks for the invite, Crandell, but I think I'll pass." He grabbed the bottle she was reaching for and slammed home the cap. "Think you're sober enough to start up the takeoff sequence if I can get this pig back online?"

~ * ~

The sun hung low over the hills but the expanse of red sand between watchtowers still held a midday heat. The one hundred dusty and sweat-streaked Aghaid miners stood in weary resignation watching Fangg and her guards emerge from the operations shack. All around was an endless perimeter of slicewire and motion sensitive disintegration pods on the watchtowers, beneath which shade the Umas sandtroopers lounged.

"Here comes the Princess of Pain with another motivational speech," said Walderspan in an aside to Davv. The four Rim Mercenaries stood to one side of the Aghaid miners, equally tired and coated with sand and sweat.

"Try not to piss her off again," Davv cautioned him. "She already has a major hard-on for you."

Sunlight glittered on Fangg's jeweled harness while she mounted a podium set up before the crowd. She adjusted her pith helmet, surveying the sullen gathering with disdain.

"There has been only one heartstone brought in from the mine this month," she declared, pointing to the darkened shaft entrance near a heap of rocks and scattered rail carts. "Starting tomorrow, shifts will be extended from ten cycles to twelve. Water rations will also be reduced to spur your endeavors underground." She savored the wave of silent hatred washing over her from the ranks of Aghaid slaves.

A rippling fart came from the group of Rim Mercs.

"I'm sure sorry, Ma'am," said Walderspan, affecting an air of exaggerated embarrassment. "It sorta slipped out."

"We told you not to piss her off," Fabre hissed.

"Well now, Mr. Walderspan. I see you are eager to provide evening entertainment." She placed her hands on her hips, glaring at him, before barking orders in guttural Umas.

A trio of guards dragged Walderspan to a crude plastoid triangle and stripped off his shirt. An electrolash was unsheathed and blue lightning sizzled over his naked back.

"Thank you, sir. May I have another?" he said through clenched teeth, smirking up at Fangg.

"Full of spirit, are you not, human?" she growled. "I will break you yet. Twenty more lashes."

Night had fallen on the heartstone mine. The Blue Lady crested the hills, flooding the empty streets and scattered buildings with a pale effulgence. Searchlights from corner towers sent beams in random patterns.

Inside the long-shed, air reeked with sweat and unwashed bodies. Rows of Aghaids tossed in exhausted sleep on their ropeweed pallets.

"Goddamn, looks like someone tried to fry a gomph steak here," Fabre observed, wiping Walderspan's back with a wet rag.

"Ah, it was worth it to set her off," he replied. "I thought she was gonna have a stroke after I farted."

"Yeah, but you might not have a back if you keep it up."

Walderspan rolled over on his side. He eyed the line of restless sleepers. "You know, it's getting kinda boring in this resort. What do you say we check out?"

Leaning against a hut wall, Davv made a face. "How successful were all your escape attempt plans from the cellars of the Chandelier Palace?"

"That was a rap in the nuts, pal." Walderspan rubbed his chin thoughtfully. "I'm not talking about escape; this dump is too well set up."

"Didn't you, Crandell and Bullock escape from here a few years back?" Moondog asked.

"Crandell noticed security fence power went off for ten zaks during switchover from one bank of solar batteries to the next," he explained. "I'm pretty certain they fixed this little oversight by now."

"So, whatever happened to Bullock?"

"Umas bounty hunter took him out at a bar in Satellite."

Moondog grunted in commiseration. "So, what are you getting at?"

Walderspan marshaled his thoughts, putting final stages to the scheme he had devised. "Look around you, guys. The Aghaid miners here outnumber the Umas by five to one."

The four mercs looked doubtful. "Aghaids ain't a very aggressive bunch," Davv said. "Right now, they're pretty beat up and submissive."

"This is why they need us to set an example," Walderspan reasoned. "Once we set the ball rolling, I figure they'll follow. All they need is leadership."

"They'll need more than leadership," Fabre said. "I seen a lot of Umas toting pulse rifles."

"Um, the shed behind us is full of picks and slicebars," Davv noted without much conviction.

"Dammit, Kris, as soon as they see us charging across the compound with our picks and…"

"Except they won't be seeing us."

The circle of mercs stared at Walderspan. He grinned knowingly and gave out a low whistle. An Aghaid got up from his pallet and squatted beside them.

"Guys, I want you to meet my buddy, Gan-torr. He tells me the Aghaid have a natural affinity to the desert," he explained. "They can find food and water in this wasteland, can even sense when the next haboob is due to blow in. Right, Gan-torr?"

The small Aghaid nodded somberly. "Is true, Wal-span. Big one come in two suns next day moontime."

"Well, me and my friends decided to leave this fun place." He winked, chucked a thumb toward the hut door. "You and your boys wanna come with us?"

Gan-torr looked dubious. "Umas very bad. Have many fire sticks."

"Tell you what, when we get ready to bug out, you can just tag along and we'll show you how it's done."

~ * ~

The sandstorm blew into the heartstone mine like the fist of an angry god, swallowing the moon and rattling the ramshackle plastiod frame of the sleeping shed. Walderspan was jerked into wakefulness and crawled to a crack in the wall. Outside was a wild ochre infinity of raging sand through which searchlight beams feebly glowed.

"Come on, gang, its party time," he exulted in a low voice, shoving his teammates. He crawled over to the sleeping Aghaids.

"Gan-torr," he hissed.

The Aghaid was instantly alert, looking wildly about him.

"We're about to check out of this hotel. You and your boys coming?"

Elfin faces along the line of mats were popping up, staring in mingled confusion and fear. Gan-torr watched Moondog and Davv tear out a section of wall planking to make an opening.

"You lead, we follow," he said.

The storm shook the rafters of the operations shack where Fangg and her chief guard were regarding the lone heartstone on her desk. Wisps of red sand drifted down from unseen cracks in the ceiling.

"One jewel for a month worth of digging," she sighed with disgust. "Why is this, Termagen?"

He lifted his hands in a helpless gesture. "The vein of red clay holding the stones is running out. Maybe what is needed is a deeper shaft."

"We will need more slaves for this. Perhaps another raid on the Aghaid village over by..."

From over the howling of the storm came a staccato hum of pulse rifles being fired, followed by faint screams. The door to the shack swung open, admitting a blast of sand and five Rim Mercenaries, captured rifles at the ready.

"Don't even think about it, toots," said Walderspan, drawing a bead on her forehead. "Toss your pistols on the floor, please."

Both Umas froze, hands touching the grips. Fangg's black eyes narrowed to slits.

"Get out of my office and back to your sleeping shed, human," she snarled, rage overwhelming her precarious situation.

"Oh, come on now, sweetcheeks." Walderspan was savoring the moment. "You surely didn't expect us to leave without saying goodbye?"

Fangg went pale with anger. She slowly got control of her voice. "What do you want?" She dropped her weapon to the floor.

"Some enlightenment. You and your crew were just waiting for us to show up in that warehouse in New Seattle ready to grab your heartstones," he said. "It sure looked like someone set us up."

"When I 'enlighten you', we will be killed," she sneered.

"I won't even ask for a goodbye kiss, Scout's honor." He held up three fingers.

"You promise to let us live?"

"Me and my guys won't even lay a hand on your tight little ass, honeycrack."

Fangg glowered at them, considering. "Very well, we received an uncoded Interfax message from the Palace of Chancellor Crandell, informing us of your intent to seize our season's harvest of heartstones."

Walderspan nodded to his companions. "Uh huh, looks like our dear buddy Agnes didn't want us blabbing later of her little secret."

"What will you do now?" she demanded.

"Aside from accepting this in lieu of back pay..." He picked up the lone heartstone from the desk. "...we will now bid you a fond and tearful farewell."

At the doorway Walderspan paused, looking back at Fangg. "Oh, by the way, your former employees have formed a grievance committee and plan having a little chat with you regarding wages and working conditions."

No sooner had Walderspan and his mercs departed when a swarm of Aghaid miners stalked into the shack clutching picks and slicebars. For a brief moment they glared at Fangg and her chief guard, and then they fell on them.

Outside in the compound Walderspan noticed the storm was quickly dying. Freed Aghaid miners were busily setting fire to buildings and watchtowers. In the light of the flames he could see a parked sandskimmer. They climbed inside and it rose gracefully above the Umas heartstone mine, heading into the coming dawn.

~ * ~

Walderspan and his Rim mercs burst into the bar in New Seattle with noisy exuberance. Other patrons, a motley crew of miners and sandwomen prospectors eyed the ragged and dusty newcomers with amused tolerance. The arrival into the establishment of scruffy and thirsty survivors after an ordeal in Satellite's desert was a commonplace event.

"Walderspan, you angled rumpslapper," greeted the bartender, pausing in his wiping the bartop with a rag. "I figured you to be stinking up a sand dune someplace by now."

"Brewsky, start setting 'em up for me and my guys and don't stop until I tell you," Walderspan exulted.

He dropped a stack of creds on the counter; his first stop in New Seattle had been in a back alley dealership in heartstones.

"Coming up, Kris." Brewsky grinned at the sudden uptick in business.

He started pushing filled glasses toward them. Abruptly, his smile faded and he made a motion for Walderspan to come closer.

Walderspan took a long pull from his mug and belched happily. "Damn, did I need that. What's on your mind, pal?"

Brewsky leaned over the bar. "We need to talk, Kris. In the back."

In an alcove Brewsky wiped his hands on a greasy apron and gazed at Walderspan with uneasy embarrassment.

"Well, don't just stand there playing with your gut, spit it out." His good humor was rapidly ebbing. Bad news was coming his way.

"There's a warrant out for your arrest," said Brewsky, unhappily.

"What? From whom?"

"From the Homeworld Federation. Captain D'Escrille got himself arrested and has been charged with accepting bribes, extortion and, together with Major Grange, having their snouts in the Umas trough on Dropoff."

"D'Escrille died when Crandell dumped the load of triwood logs on the Umas hut," Walderspan protested, aghast. "I don't get it, he made it out alive?"

"Yep, and he was living in considerable luxury in a domed island on Verdana before an informant ratted him out." He gave Walderspan a pained look. "In his testimony he said you were on the take up to your necks."

"Son of a bitch. We had no idea they were in bed with those Umas bastards."

"So maybe Crandell did you a favor by dumping them logs on Grange, huh?"

"Yeah, I suppose she did. Son of a bitch." He balled his fists angrily. "Them logs shoulda landed on D'Escrille. I never liked the pompous bastard."

"Well, he's singing like a canary in a New Earth City lockup hoping to save his skin."

Walderspan thoughtfully scratched his chin. "Thanks to our old buddy, Agnes, word is gonna get around we're back in town. I figure we should blow this planet ticky-boo."

"You're gonna need valid passports," Brewsky suggested. "Better camp out in the spare room in the back of the bar until I line up a forger."

"Whatever happened to the Zardorian starsabre we arrived here in?" said Walderspan, suddenly remembering. "We left it hidden in a gully west of town."

"A sandwoman prospector stumbled on it and reported it to the New Seattle Citizen Vigilantes," he explained. "By the time they returned it had vanished. Rumor has it scavengers hauled it off to be broken up for scrap."

"Drog's Ass." Walderspan shrugged in discouragement. "This spare room you got, is it pretty quiet? We usually hit the sack early."

"I'll tell my customers to keep the noise down," said Brewski drolly.

~ * ~

"Stillborne, you've been an hour back there working on this old crate." Falle had her feet propped up on the starfreighter's control console. Her voice held a note of exasperation. "Maybe fixing its virginity would help."

"Yeah, yeah, I'm working on it," he groused sleepily, pushing himself off the seat where he had been dozing. He grabbed his toolbag and yawned.

Inside the engineering compartment there was an odor of burnt electrical and the musical clink of cooling metal from the hulking mass of fusion drive dominating the room. He snapped open a cover, pulling a meter from his bag.

"Ah, here's the problem," he said with satisfaction, chewing his mustache. "I should have seen it the last couple times…hey, what's this?"

A stack of orange capsules lay inside the cabinet. He picked one up and held it to the light, squinting.

"Hot damn!" he exulted. "Someone's secret stash of moongas."

Eagerly he broke one open and sucked the vapor deep into his lungs. A second capsule followed and he sagged against a compartment wall, his rump sliding to the deck. A vapid grin of euphoria spread over his face.

In the cockpit, Falle drummed her fingers impatiently on the console. She glanced at her timeband and jabbed a button on the control panel.

"How's it coming, Stillborne?"

She was wondering if he had fallen asleep again and was contemplating a trip to engineering to kick some ass.

"I'd like to make the Zardorian Spaceport before I'm old and grey…"

The dagger shape of a Umas starsabre swam into view, closing fast on the starfreighter.

"Stillborne, we have company. Now would be a good time to get the drive running."

No reply came from the console before her. She groped for the assault knife at her belt, instantly regretting the force pistol she'd left below in her cabin.

A dull clang resonated through the freighter's hull like a gong. She could hear the Umas ship grappling, a hiss of air when the cabin pressure dropped slightly.

A group of Umas raiders entered the cockpit, pulse rifles at the ready. Slowly, Falle got up from the command chair, drawing her knife. She had already decided to never again become a Umas slave laborer, no matter what.

A bejeweled hulk, who was evidently the leader, stepped closer, barking orders in guttural Umas. Falle smiled, lowering the knife toward his crotch.

The brutal face darkened with anger. He loomed over her, menacing her with his weapon.

Falle spat into his eyes.

The Umas recoiled, glaring at her. He wiped an arm across his face, barking orders to his crew who began ransacking the ship for booty.

"Well, what do you know," Falle mused, studying the raider still standing before her. "It would seem those smelly spacers are immune to the hydrophis virus."

The smelly spacer snarled something which sounded like a profanity. His gloved hand struck her on the face and she fell, slamming her head on a deck chair railing. Falle went limp.

~ * ~

A lightbar attached to a curved ceiling beam emerged from the fog. Falle blinked painfully, gingerly feeling her forehead. Someone applied a pressure bandage and washed away the blood she remembered trickling into her eyes before she lost consciousness on the starfreighter. She groggily propped herself up on an elbow and looked around.

She was in a large viewportless compartment of the Umas craft. Three young women sat despondently on sleeping mats or metal benches attached to the hull.

A hatch slid open and a female Umas strode in carrying an armload of clothing. She dropped it on the deck and walked over to Falle, staring silently down. The lightbars glinted from colored jewels in her harness over a red silk loincloth and breastband.

"I see you have recovered your senses," she said. "How does the head feel?"

Falle gazed at her quizzically. "You're concerned about my well being. Are you sure you're a Umas?"

"My concern is proprietorial. Damaged goods do not bring in a high price for a slave," she replied.

"Excuse me, slave?"

"Ah, typical human emotions of curiosity and concern." Behind the dark eyes there seemed to be a lurking amusement. "Very well. I am Tildar and this Umas vessel is carrying a cargo of captured human females which will be sold to farmers working a folsox operation on Sheridan's Planet."

"Folsox as in hyperdrug." Falle was eyeing the dagger and force pistol in Tildar's belt, calculating if she was revived enough for a quick grab and battle. Obviously, she was not.

"Folsox is a desert plant."

"The Methtropolis Drug Cartel on New Earth who are financing the project has discovered a similar variety growing here."

"They don't have the formula to create hyperdrug."

"They have endless patience and will locate Mr. Stillborne sooner or later."

If they'd captured Stillborne along with herself it was obvious they had no idea of who he was. "I had a companion on the freighter…"

"Little man with an absurd facial growth? He is presently overcome by an opiod dose. He will be tending folsox bushes when he recovers." Tildar's eyes were fixed on the gold chain about Falle's neck. She pulled out the locket, snapping it open.

"Who are these people?"

Falle stiffened, readying herself for a fight if the Umas girl attempted to take the locket.

"My mother and father," she replied sullenly.

"Your mother is an Eu." She looked at Falle, considering. "This is not good."

"Why is this not good?"

"There used to be a human settlement called Jamestown on Sheridan's Planet. The colonists were forbidden to mate with the Eu when they found out the resulting hybrids were of unusual intelligence and possessed fierce and aggressive tendencies."

"The Eu on this planet were known for their passive and gentle dispositions," said Falle.

"Not the hybrid female who stirred them into insurrection and subsequent massacre of the colonists." She closed the locket and tucked it back into Falle's coveralls. "Hide this and say nothing. We can't have anything to reduce your price at the slave auction. You are by far the most attractive human female we have captured."

With the return of the locket, Falle relaxed slightly. She indicated the pile of clothing on the deck. "So, what's with the stack of duds you brought in?"

"They are somewhat short and revealing slave girl tunics that all of you will be wearing to obtain the highest prices from the lonely male farmers supervising the Eu workers at the project."

"Hey, I'm perfectly comfy in the outfit I'm wearing now," said Falle, deciding to feel out Tildar's resolve.

The other girls in the compartment were looking at them in shock and dismay. It was evident this was the first time they had learned of their fate.

Tildar returned Falle's defiant stare and turned her attention to the other captives. "If any of you refuse to wear the tunics, I will call in a squad of Umas males. Your present clothes will be ripped off and they will forcibly dress you."

Like a cat, Falle sprang from the mat and seized the Umas girl, knocking her to the deckplates. For a moment they wrestled, until Tildar broke free, drawing her force pistol.

"Now you see why the farmers are not permitted by the Cartel to take female Eu as bedpartners," she spat. "I can see those fierce and aggressive tendencies in you as well as stupidity. Do not test me again."

She turned and stalked from the compartment. As the hatch slid shut behind her Falle smiled.

"Have a nice day, toots," she chuckled, slipping the dagger into a pocket of her coveralls.

~ * ~

Sheridan's Planet was the homeworld of her mother. Falle experienced a strange feeling akin to homecoming while walking down the ramp of the Umas starsabre with the other captive girls.

The Cartel's folsox farm lay in a clearing hacked from a dark primeval forest. A circle of wooden huts nestled between fields of green shrubs. An expectant crowd of farmers gathered about a raised platform. They appeared a most unappetizing crew, pot-bellied yokels in grubby coveralls, beards studded with the remnants of past meals. They grinned, jostling each other with crude witticisms, watching the Umas escort their captives up platform steps and set them in a line facing their audience.

Falle nudged her stolen knife to a more secure location under the waistband of the skimpy white tunic. The huge Umas commander who struck her on the freighter was engaged in a spirited bargaining session with the head farmer, with Tildar standing to one side, translating. At length, handshakes and creds were exchanged and the Umas squad trooped off the platform.

Tildar stopped as she passed Falle.

"Try to be a compliant and obedient slavegirl to your new owners," she remarked sardonically. "I believe you will find the farmers hired by the Methtropolis Drug Cartel less forgiving than my commander, Kardomen."

"Try not to slip and break your ass going down the steps," Falle replied.

The Umas entered their craft and it rose sedately over the forest, growing smaller in a sky of palest blue. A wink of brightness and it was gone.

Meanwhile, bidding for purchase of the girls was underway. Shouted offers, cheers and groans and one by one halters were placed over girl's necks and they were led away by smugly grinning winners.

"Okay guys, last but not least, the little blonde, declared virgin by the Umas, all ready to mop, clean, cook and hump for some lucky spacer," the auctioneer announced. "Starting bid five hundred creds."

A fierce competition ensued, the price for Falle climbing higher while each farmer gauged his bankroll against the long legs under the short tunic wafting gently in the breeze.

At last a bearded giant mounted the platform. His little eyes, deep-set under bushy brows surveyed Falle greedily. He faced the auctioneer.

"Two thousand creds," he declared.

"I have two thousand C's for the little blonde wedge," the auctioneer crowed. "Do I have a higher offer? Going once...going twice...sold to Mutt Bovus."

The crowd groaned. They watched enviously when a halter was placed around Falle's neck and she was led from the platform down the path to the huts; catcalls and lewd suggestions following them.

Feeling the hidden knife in her waistband, Falle eyed the bearded hulk trudging ahead of her. She was pondering the merits of emasculation versus the insertion of a blade into a spinal cord.

Bovus shoved the door of the hut open and led Falle inside. She took in ramshackle furniture, the skin of some animal on the floor and an enormous pile of dirty dishes overflowing in the sink.

Bovus removed the halter and slouched to a couch sprouting stuffing from assorted holes, settling his bulk into it with a contented sigh.

"Better get started cleaning up the place before you start cookin' dinner. There's a gorth steak in the coolbox I'd like medium rare." He leered at her from the couch. "I'm gonna need all my energy for the night ahead."

Falle went to a window and peered through grimy panes at Eu workers toiling in the folsox fields.

"Those Eu you have taking care of your folsox bushes," she said. "Where did they all come from?"

"There's an Eu village a few clicks north of us. We usually make a raid there to round up a bunch when we get too many dyin' from overwork."

"I'm assuming you ask for volunteers?"

He scowled at her. "Listen, I didn't pay a shitload of creds to have you stand there and flap your lips. Better get your ass to work, sweetcheeks."

"That's not going to happen." She smiled, flexing her fists. "Might I suggest you drop your shorts, bend over and see how far you can shove your head up your butt?"

A dark red flush grew under Bovus' matted beard, his close-set little eyes protruded with rage.

"A real smart mouth wedge, huh," he growled, lurching up from the couch. "I'm gonna slap your lips to the moon!"

~ * ~

The gorth steak with buttered cartips had been quite enjoyable. Whatever his many shortcomings; Bovus was certainly an adequate cook. She took a final pull of her beer and glanced toward the kitchen.

"How is the floor coming along, Bovus?" she inquired. "Look, there's a spot over by the front door you missed."

Bovus was on his hands and knees, bucket by his side, busily running a soapy brush over the floorboards. His face was puffed with bruises, one eye nearly shut, several of his front teeth showed gaps.

"Um yeah...I see it," he mumbled, eyeing her nervously. "I'll get right to it."

"You'll get right to it, what?"

"Um...I'll get right to it, Ma'am." He came painfully to his feet, pressing a hand over cracked ribs and carried his bucket and brush to the door.

Falle looked out the nearest window. Night had fallen and the last Eu worker had been driven from the fields to their sleeping shed. From a large hut at the end of the farm she could hear laughter and boozy voices joined in song. She strapped an old but serviceable snub pistol she'd found around her waist, walked to the front door and looked down at Bovus.

"I might be back for breakfast," she grinned. "I like my eno eggs sunny side up."

The abject figure on the floor paused with his scrub brush over the bucket and cringed.

"Yes, Ma'am," he said.

Chapter Twelve

Of course, T'ong Blatt chose to have their meeting at The Tidal Pool.

The New Earth City restaurant was a favored hangout for expatriate Phibs, the indigenous humanoids from Verdana. It was decorated in nautical style; nets, harpoons on walls, the air redolent with the odor of rotting kelp.

Gordo was about to cast another impatient glance at his timeband when he spotted his superior moving through the lunchtime crowd to their table in a secluded alcove.

T'ong Blatt was wearing a tailored Arnato jumpsuit, his webbed feet bare. His face held a vaguely reptilian cast, his yellow slitted eyes alert. He slid into a chair opposite Gordo.

"Many thanksss for meeting me here, Gordo," he said, his voice reminiscent of a snake slithering over dry leaves. "There are ssseveral reasonsss why I did not want to meet you at headquartersss."

Gordo nodded in silence. Something very big was up.

"We have a new contract." T'ong Blatt craned his neck at the other diners chattering in sibilant Phib, tossing down shots of fermented seaslime. "On Zardoria."

"The contract offered by Baron Ghrasp didn't come to much after he croaked in front of me," Gordo remarked drily. "It must be an affluent client who expects us to operate in the nasty and brutal police state that country has become." He pursed his lips in thought. "Let me guess, the High Council?"

"Very good, Gordo."

The head of the Borgia Guild was gloating over some big surprise, dragging out the suspense. Very well, he would go along, since it obviously involved himself.

"It would appear they are not too happy with the way things are going under Chancellor Crandell," he ventured, smiling.

"Now you sssee why you are my top assassin," T'ong Blatt chortled.

"What?" Gordo's grin evaporated. "Are you serious? There have been riots every day there."

"Eighty thousand credsss."

Slowly, Gordo recovered his aplomb. Eighty thousand creds, three quarters of which would be his. He evaluated the risks, sneaking past a renewed and tightened embargo, the fanatical loyalty of the Citizens Guard…

"How many paid informers does the Guild have in Zardoria?" he asked.

"Quite a few. In fact…" T'ong Blatt paused while a waiter passed their table bearing a tray of baked eel colons. "One of them overheard the former valet of Duke Duefussss uttering a drunken tirade to a cocktail waitresss at a bar in City One."

"Let me think for a moment…Nebly."

"Just ssso. It appearsss sssince Crandell hasss become ruler of Zardoria he hasss been demoted to the role of janitorial sssupervisor. It hasss also been noted he isss involved in a fringe group dedicated to the overthrow of the monarchy."

"A person on the inside is always a great edge."

Methods he had used on previous contracts ran through Gordo's mind. Of course, a handshake wearing the poisoned lion's head ring had always been his sentimental favorite.

"One more thing," T'ong Blatt leaned closer across the table. "I've often wondered how Falle Crandell ssseems to be one ssstep ahead of usss on occasion. I have an unworthy sssuspicion her mentor and former trainer Jinghua might have had a lapssse in loyalty to the Guild. Hence our meeting here rather than Guild Headquartersss."

Gordo grunted. "Sometimes I wonder if she has more lives than a cat. Well, we'll see this time around."

A waiter arrived at their table. T'ong Blatt scanned a menu, peering at Gordo over the top.

"Might I sssuggest the pickled fish eyesss with a ssside of fermented squid liversss with kelp maggot glaze?"

~ * ~

DOWN WITH THE TYRANT
CHANCELLOR FALLE CRANDELL
FREE PRIME MINISTER SANCHEZ!

Gordo unrolled the posters he had taken from Nebly and was studying them with interest.

"Hmm... 'Down With the Tyrant Chancellor Falle Crandell'," he read and looked up at Nebly. "It would seem we have the same goal in mind."

Fumes from the brandy he had been drinking before agreeing to meet with Gordo had long since been evaporated by fear. Nebly was thinking fast.

"The Borgia Guild. You're here...to assassinate Crandell?"

"Very astute of you. We need your help."

"My help?"

"As head custodian for the Chandelier Palace you have access to the royal suite, I might surmise?"

This was more than hanging posters and screaming defiance at Citizens Guardsmen during the increasing waves of unrest since Chancellor Falle's seizure of power. Nebly felt his testicles contract.

"Um...yes. I have access to the entire facility," he admitted reluctantly.

Gordo placed a gold tiara on the table. "Do you recognize this?"

Nebly eyed the jewel-studded circlet with the emerald cut heartstone on the centerpoint. "It's the traditional crown for the ruler of Zardoria," he said, amazed. "How did you..."

"This is an exact copy, one capable of discharging a lethal voltage at a signal from the transmitter which you will be carrying into the Grand

Hall."

"I will be carrying?" Nebly tasted the bile of terror rising in his throat.

Gordo leaned over the table and fixed him with a cold, unblinking stare. "What you are first going to do, Nebly, is to enter the Chancellor's suite and exchange this crown for the real one. Do you understand?"

He really had no choice, Nebly realized. The only event worse than being caught in a failed assassination attempt was to incur the wrath of the Guild. He swallowed painfully.

"Yes, I understand," he said.

~ * ~

The chime over the door in the Chancellor's suite tinkled musically. Missi put down the stack of female clothing she had been sorting and opened the door to find Nebly standing outside holding a lapreader and an oblong box.

"Good morning, young lady," he declared breezily. "I'm here to make the monthly inspection of the Chancellor's quarters, checking to make sure my housekeeping staff's work is up to snuff."

Missi didn't care much for Nebly; she'd heard he treated his staff like serfs. She winced as his one hundred proof breath assaulted her nostrils.

"Okay, why don't you come in," she said with reluctance.

"Thanks. Is the Great One home?" he asked, already knowing the answer.

He set the oblong box on a divan and smiled ingratiatingly at her.

"No, she's with Commander Dorf planning the, um...event for tomorrow." She knew, the event being the public execution of Prime Minister Sanchez. Missi was upset at even the thought of a fly being swatted.

"Great. Let me start my inspection with the boudoir." He headed for the bedroom, trailed my Missi. Sissi looked up from hanging dresses on a rack.

"Don't mind me, Shorty. I'll get this inspection over soon as possible." His eyes darted to a dresser. Alongside a tray of jewelry lay the gold crown.

"Say, do you girls like chocolate?" he declared. "The box I left in the foyer contains an assortment I thought you ladies would like."

"Chocolates? For us?" Both girls brightened.

"Go and help yourselves."

The two maids scampered from the bedroom, leaving Nebly alone.

He sidled over to the dresser. Deftly, he slid another crown from his vest and replaced it with the one beside the jewel box.

The original, he stuffed securely inside his waistband, exhaling with relief.

~ * ~

It was not a festive event happening in the Grand hall of the Chandelier Palace. There were no garlands of flowers or soft music playing. Instead was a somber gathering of dignitaries and members of the High Council seated in lines of chairs which had been set out on the marble floor. All were staring at the disintegration booth set up on the stage, around which technicians fussed with cables and circuit plugins. They fidgeted nervously, listening to shouts of anger coming from the crowd gathered outside the palace walls and the occasional hum of a pulse rifle being fired.

There was a blast of trumpets and Agnes swept into the hall flanked by a phalanx of her Citizens Guard. All in the assembly stood and bowed while she took her seat on the throne. From a far end of the stage Parasol Sanchez emerged, escorted by two burly Guardsmen. They dragged her before the haughty figure on the throne. For a moment in time Agnes and the Prime Minister appraised each other.

"Any last profound thoughts or philosophical insights before I pass judgment on you,   'Mahatma'?" she inquired with thin sarcasm.

"There is an Old Earth saying," Parasol said calmly. "Absolute power corrupts absolutely."

Agnes sniffed. "Your opinion will be worthless even to yourself once the disintegration chamber turns you into useful fertilizer."

"My opinion is you are not what you seem to be." She was looking closely at Agnes' face, studying her eyes, the texture of her skin. "I think I see now what you are. You are a cybernetic…"

"Prime Minister Sanchez has been found guilty of high treason." Agnes rose from the throne. "Carry out the execution."

Among the hushed and horrified crowd Nebly fumbled for the hidden transmitter. With a nervous glance at the people surrounding him he pressed a button.

Below the throne, Agnes froze with her outstretched hand pointing at the disintegration chamber. She frowned, a puzzled look on her face as she gazed out over the sea of people.

Nothing had evidently happened. Fighting down an impulse for panic-stricken flight, Nebly jabbed the transmitter button again.

With a leisurely, distracted air, Agnes removed the crown from her head, studied it without much interest and dropped it at her feet. She turned toward the crowd, breaking into a dazzling smile.

"Welcome to United Starlines," she declared. "Flight 209 from New Earth City to Verdana will be departing in ten zaks."

From his place beside the throne, Commander Dorf appeared ready to suffer a stroke. He nervously shuffled toward her.

"Beloved Despot," he hissed in her ear. "Are you feeling unwell?"

"Please stow all luggage in the side compartments and deactivate all commpad devices. Thank you for flying with United Starlines." Still smiling, she tilted and fell flat on her face.

An awed gasp swept the gathering, followed by a dreaded silence. High Councilman Baron Shrop got to his feet and mounted the steps to the stage. He looked down at Agnes' inert body then eyed Commander Dorf.

"Release Prime Minister Sanchez," he ordered.

~ * ~

Standing on the doorstep of Bovus's hut, Falle was one with the night. The sky blazed with constellations of stars and strange, batlike shapes fluttered past, pursuing unseen prey. She inhaled deeply, the air was heavy with aromatic pine and she cherished the thought her mother, N'ai F'alle, once stood under this same night sky, savoring the same moment in time.

A sound rose above the gentle soughing of wind. It rose and fell, female voices raised in anguished weeping. Falle gazed along a line of huts to where two girls huddled beneath a solitary podlight. She recognized them as two of the slave girls sold by the Umas to the folsox farmers.

The door to the nearest hut slammed open. A girl emerged, running with desperation across the street to join the huddle of other girls.

"Get back here, you little bitch!" A bearded farmer ran from the hut in pursuit. Abruptly, he came to a halt, clutching his throat. A single choked cry and he fell writhing to the ground.

Walking over, Falle prodded the limp figure with her foot. Anguished, unseeing eyes gazed back into hers. She went up to the cluster of girls.

"Farmer John there is dead as a smelt," she observed. "Can any of you here tell me what is going on?"

"We tried to tell them but nobody would listen," one of them burst out, her face streaked with tears.

"Tell them what?"

"That we have the hydrophis virus," sobbed another with frustration, clutching her companion. "Now they're all dead."

"I think you all had better come with me," said Falle.

She led them into Bovus' hut where the owner was at the sink, washing dishes.

"How's the spring cleaning coming, Bovus?" she greeted him. "I brought us some house guests."

Bovus started when he saw her return and renewed his pot scrubbing with renewed energy. "Yes, Ma'am, I'm almost done."

"Good boy." Falle placed her hands on her hips and regarded her guests. "Okay, let's have your tale of woe."

A chubby brunette with a black pageboy stopped eyeing Bovus with stupefied amazement to regard Falle.

"All of us were former employees at Rivergreede Pharmaceuticals in New Earth City, working in the shipping department," she explained. "They were working on a new serum for the hydrophis virus when a sample brought in from Swampworld broke open and infected us. The company was shipping us to a treatment center on Asteroid IXV when our ship was boarded by Umas raiders."

"They killed everyone but us," a second girl whimpered. "We tried to tell the Umas girl who spoke terran, but…she just stared at us."

"Now all those men who kissed us are dead," said another, setting off a group snivel.

"Couldn't have happened to a better bunch," Falle mused. "Tell you what, you ladies make yourselves comfy here while I go have a chat with those horny-handed sons of toil I heard whooping it up at the big hut." She regarded Bovus who had been listening in on the conversation, an expression of horror on his face, scrubbing pad paused over a pot.

"If you get hungry, I'm sure Bovus would be happy to fix you a snack." She winked at him. "Keep my friends happy and they might reward you with a kiss."

Bovus paled beneath his bushy beard. "Yes, I mean, no, Ma'am," he stammered, turning back to the dishes with increased zeal.

Beer swilling and drunken merriment died down as Falle entered the hut. Scruffy, unwashed faces broke into anticipatory grins.

"What the hell, honeycrack. Don't tell me you wore out old Mutt and he sent you down here for us to finish the job?" one of the farmers observed, slouched in his chair, beer mug resting on a protruding belly. "Well, old Fogg here is ready."

The room rocked with raucous laughter.

"Hey, tell me your girlfriends are gonna join us," another chortled. "Party time comin' on, boys."

"My girlfriends won't be joining us because all their boyfriends are dead," said Falle.

"Gorth crap," Fogg snorted derisively.

"I suppose none of you jolly hairballs realized the Umas sold you a load of slavegirls infected with the hydrophis virus, myself included," she said. "Three of your buddies found out during kiss and tell." Falle savored the fading of happy grins. She slipped the snub pistol from its holster and leveled it at them.

Slouched in his chair, Fogg let the beer mug drop to the floor. He felt the girl's pale blue eyes bore into his and his overalls felt a sudden wetness.

"If Mr. Fogg is through draining his radiator," drawled Falle, noting the telltale drip under his chair. "Let's all take a stroll to the Eu sleeping shed and say hi."

~ * ~

"Hey babe, nice day if it don't rain." Stillborne entered the boudoir, closing the door behind him. The Grey Warlord's consort was stretched out languorously on the vast silken bed, gazing at him with an inviting smile.

"You silly mans, Stillbro," she purred. "It never rain here on Sat-lite. You also late, Shann-tal hot and bothered waiting for you."

"You're hot, huh?" He was ogling the transparent gown that was making a futile attempt at concealing the microscopic bra and panties she was wearing. "Maybe it's because you're kinda overdressed, honeycrack?"

"Perhaps Shann-tal is." She glided sensuously from the bed and unsnapped the gold collar of her gown. It fell, clattering to the straw-covered concrete.

Straw-covered concrete? Stillborne opened his eyes to a musty darkness. A starlit square of window sent a pale light over dim forms of sleeping men and scattered straw. He attempted to roll over, finding he couldn't move one leg.

"What in Zerid?" he groaned, propping himself on an elbow.

A shackle and chain attached to his ankle led to a ring bolt set in concrete.

He was just taking this in when a door creaked open and lights blazed on. A bearded and sullen band of men entered, prodded by a snub pistol held by Falle.

"Goddamn, Crandell," he exulted. "Am I glad to see you. Get me outta this leg iron." Around him Eu slaves were getting to their feet, staring at the new arrivals.

Falle was staring back at the first of her race she ever saw. They were tall and impressively muscular, with silver hair and wearing loincloths of striped animal skin. The tallest of the group approached her, placing a hand over his heart.

"Kal t'bow an p'all te?" he asked.

Who are you? It was the language of her mother, N'ai F'alle, spoken to her as a child. It was all coming back.

"My name is Falle," she replied in kind, then switched to terran. "Can you understand me?"

"I am called Blayd," he said. "Of the language of keepers...I speak little. We...honored to greet you."

The tall Eu and Falle smiled at each other. She noticed the eyes in his rugged face were pale amber, very unusual for his species.

"Crandell, are you gonna let me lie on this pronging floor all night while you and Muscles make eyes at each other?" Stillborne whined from his bed of straw.

"Stillborne, unlock the shackles and release the Eu. Then put them on these hairy gentlemen here." She tossed him the keys she had taken from one of her captives. "Let's give them a taste of what they were dishing out."

~ * ~

"What we have here is a Universal Cybernetics Level Eight model," said Doctor Webber, pulling the sheet over Agnes' face.

"I suspected this from the first," Parasol Sanchez remarked.

Standing beside her were members of the High Council. "How did she come to take Chancellor Crandell's place?"

"A very good question." Doctor Webber snapped off his surgical gloves. "Information I recovered from her imbedded chip indicates she was originally programmed as a flight attendant for United Starlines. After a company recall she was leased to the Sandman Hilton here on Zardoria as a maid and bar hostess." He tossed the gloves into a waste basket. "I contacted the hotel owner and he confirmed one of his leased maids, a certain Agnes, vanished a few weeks ago."

"Just about the time the 'Chancellor' assumed total power in the Six Cities," Parasol observed.

"Examination of the crown revealed it had been replaced by a replica designed to release a lethal high voltage discharge," Doctor Webber continued. "In laymen's terms, it turned her cybernetic brain into mush."

Prime Minister Sanchez faced her High Council. "At my request the Interworld Federation has sent peacekeeping troops to all cities in Zardoria," she said. "I have ordered the Citizens Guard disbanded and a new civil police force created."

Among his fellow councilmen, Baron Shrop was going through a myriad of conflicting thoughts. Did the Borgia Guild know Chancellor Crandell was an imposter and the Council duped out of eighty thousand creds? Could he even dare to demand a partial refund?

"Somehow our Adored Tyrant has been replaced by an imposter," he ventured. "So where might the real one be?"

Parasol Sanchez looked up from contemplating the sheeted body. "This is another good question," she said.

~ * ~

Falle was pondering data running over a desk viscreen in the back room of the farmer's main shed. She'd risen early; leaving the former slave girls asleep in Bovus' hut, the previous occupant having been sent to join his companions in the Eu worker's shed.

There was the creak of an opening door and footfalls padding across wooden floorboards. She reached for the snub pistol at her side, and then relaxed when she saw a rodent face and a drooping mustache appear in the doorway.

"Don't ask me to spend another night with them Eu spacers," Stillborne complained. "In the hut they picked out to crash in, three of them snored like sandcats and one farted all night long."

Falle shrugged noncommittally. Complaining was his standard

form of communication. "So where are they now?" she asked.

"After they woke up I had them plant the three farmers the girls croaked. The big Eu you were drooling over led them off into the forest." Stillborne snorted into his mustache. "Good riddance to them snorers and farters."

"You would think they could at least say goodbye," Falle mulled, half to herself, thinking of B'layd's tall form and broad shoulders.

Stillborne was chewing on his lower lip, eyeing her pensively. He was obviously formulating a proposal.

"Listen, Crandell, I got me an idea. There's a barn out back just crammed with folsox berries," he said.

"So what? Are you planning on baking some pies?"

"Listen, hear me out. What say I set up a lab here and start cranking out hyperdrug?"

Leaning back in her chair Falled eyed him with incredulity. "You're kidding. You want us to become drug pushers?"

"With the chemicals I found in their dispensary I can crank out a quarter million creds worth of snoot," he persisted. "What's the going rate for the hydrophis serum from Rivergreede for three stock clerks, plus yourself?"

"I can't see myself stooping to become a dealer in snoot." Her eyes were chips of blue ice. "Forget it, Stillborne."

"Well, you were an assassin for the Borgia Guild," he argued. "What's the big diff between that and pushing hyperdrug?"

"The big diff is between offing some crooked politician or cheating husband versus offing some zit-faced high school dropout," she shot back. "Let's start working on a plan to deal with the Cartel when they return, to find out why they haven't heard from their buddies we have locked up in the shed."

"Well, if we had a few kilos of snoot ready when they get here it might be one hell of an incentive to bargain a way off this woodsy retreat," he argued.

"Put a lid on it, Stillborne," Falle snapped.

She brooded over the viscreen. Ethics. Borgia Guild assassin. Hyperdrug pusher. She wished her stepfather, Hal Chavez, was here to advise her. He would have the answer.

"So, what do you need to start cranking out snoot?" she said at length. "We have a week before the Cartel supply freighter gets here."

Stillborne brightened. "I got all the right chemicals here. Just need to dig up a few centimeters of copper tubing for the still."

"Okay. Let's unshackle and feed our farmers and put them to work in the fields. We need to keep them busy."

~ * ~

Stillborne was fussing with a strange contraption that had a makeshift appearance of tubes, hissing vats and a large hopper containing folsox berries when Falle entered the back room of the main hut that evening. She eyed it with concern.

"We're not going to have an explosive situation here, are we, Stillborne?" she demanded. "I'm planning on sleeping here tonight."

"Nah, just a little hiss and piss from the assimilator." He tightened a fitting and got to his feet, dusting off his knees. "What're your little stock clerks up to?"

"Right now, I have them keeping an eye on our Farmer Johns working in the folsox fields. I gave them a couple force pistols in case they get froggy."

"Think I may join you in this hut tonight. The shed I slept in the last night still smells of Eu farts."

"Well, there's only one bed here." She smiled seductively at him. "Why Leonard, are you planning on warming up my side of the bed tonight?"

"Very funny, Crandell," he scowled. "I'll be comfy as hell on the floor with a pillow and a few blankets."

Orange capsules began to drop from the machine into a basket. Falle picked one up, holding it up to the light, watching an orange gas swirling inside.

"So, what exactly happens when this hyperdrug sends someone into the Fantasy Dimension?" she asked.

"Nobody really knows for sure." Stillborne scratched the end of his nose thoughtfully. "Some researchers say it sends them through quantum space into another time and place."

"How long does a trip last?"

"Usually a few hours to days, but sometimes forever." He made a wry face. "Of course, a couple of them came back with an arrow or stone club sticking into them. I heard tell some wedge from Terranova came back pregnant."

"What a wonderful surprise for her." Falle carefully returned the capsule to the basket. "Guess I better go and supervise our three twits feeding and locking up the farmers for the night."

"I'd like to send them farmers into the Fantasy Dimension." He squinted into the bowels of his machine and adjusted a knob setting. "Maybe a nice trip to Swampworld…"

"Stillborne, something is happening to your little gizmo," she suddenly observed, pointing at a jet of orange gas shooting from an overhead fitting.

"Zog's Holy Jockstrap, hold your breath!" he yelled, grabbing a handful of wrenches and setting up a ladder. "It's hyperdrug gas."

His warning came too late. The room around her grew faint, two dimensional, reminding her of an ancient time-faded photograph. She squinted shut her eyes against a blizzard of white light, hurrying her to some distant time and place.

Just great. Another Stillborne screwup. Why did I ever have to get the hydrophis virus? Why did those greedy assholes at Rivergreede Pharmaceuticals have to charge the moon for the serum?

Suddenly, she was there.

Chapter Thirteen

The Umas commander was checking readings on the starsabre main console when his left arm fell off and landed on the deck.

Commander Kardomen grunted in annoyance and gestured for Subcommander Tildar to take over control of the ship. A few moments later he disintegrated into a pile of organs and body parts spreading over the deckplates. From the rotting mass crawled a crablike creature with slitted yellow eyes.

Tildar pointed at a crewman who scooped up the newly born horror, carrying it off to a tank of soil in the infirmary where it would form a cocoon and begin gestating a new humanoid form. A second crewman began cleaning away the putrescent residue. Of the pervading stench in the cabin no one took notice. Stench was an accepted normality, as was the occasional Umas disintegrating onto the deckplates.

Taking over the controls, Tildar resumed course toward Satellite. She was not pleased by Kardomen'd departure. He would be gestating for at least a month beside another, an astrogater who chose this inconvenient time to enter her embryonic cycle, leaving the ship shorthanded.

Umas League had received no communications from the heartstone mine on Satellite for several weeks and they had been dispatched to investigate. First, they would land outside New Seattle to obtain another cargo of slave girls from a back alley dealer in human trafficking. There were still several folsox farmers on Sheridan's Planet clamoring for female companionship. The inhabitants of this rustic backwater would not welcome the sight of a Umas ship setting down at their spaceport and a poorly-maintained but highly accurate J beam defense system ringed the facility.

Tildar was troubled. Her mind kept drifting back to the blonde girl and the scruffy little man they left at the folsox farm. She wished they had found out their names. The blonde girl, fierce and somehow regal. The little man with the drooping mustache. He was the key.

Rows of folsox bushes beneath a watery sun; the answer remained tantalizingly close in the recesses of her mind. It might be a good idea, she pondered, to contact the farmers there to have them squeeze a little information from…

"Approaching orbit around Satellite, Subcommander," a crewman announced.

"Very good, Asholmen," she acknowledged. "Take the ship to the East side of the city and set it down below the hills."

~ * ~

It was a low droning which had woken Walderspan in the early hours of the night. He propped himself up on an elbow in his cot, straining his ears to hear the faint sound fading in the distance.

"Damn, if that didn't sound like a Umas starsabre," he muttered, gazing around at his snoring companions sprawled out on makeshift cots in the back room of Brewsky's Saloon. He prodded the nearest snorer.

"Hey Moondog, you still got the nightseeker binocs you picked up at the heartstone mine?"

"Dammit, Walderspan, I was sleeping like a baby," replied an annoyed moan beneath a pile of blankets.

"Well, get up, change your diaper and find me them binocs."

Grumbling, Moondog rummaged through a bag and tossed him the night vision glasses. Walderspan crawled to a window and peered into the night.

A batlike shape blotted out a section of stars, descending slowly. It came to a hover then vanished behind a low hill.

"Holy Gorth Crap," Walderspan exulted. "Definitely a Umas ship. Wonder why they're here?" Numerous possibilities occurred to him, centering on the heartstone mine. Of course, by now the head stinkys are wondering why they haven't received any chat from there. He prodded

Moondog again.

"Hey, what's the usual complement of a Class B Umas Starsabre?"

Moondog groaned, forced open his eyes. "Normally about five of the smelly bastards, depending on how many of them decide to drop their guts on the deck when they cycle out." He rolled over on his cot and yawned. "Wake me when you see daylight coming through the window, boss. I need my beauty sleep."

"That'd be about a hundred years for you, Moondog." He pushed himself off the cot. "Okay guys, rise and shine."

There was a chorus of groans from the occupants of the room. Maintaining a level of sobriety while camping out in a saloon proved impossible for most of the mercs.

"What the hell is going on?" demanded Davv, squinting blearily as Walderspan hit the lights.

"Our ride outta Dodge just arrived," he grinned. "Everybody grab your gear, the force pistols we scarfed up at the mine and all the charge clips you can carry.

~ * ~

Crouching among the ropeweed Walderspan and the four Rim Mercenaries peered down into the gully where the Umas starsabre lay like a crouching bat. The Blue Lady had just risen, painting the rocks and desert fauna in streaks of blue and black. With anticipatory glee they watched a party of Umas march down the ramp and melt into the night.

"Come on, guys, before they retract the ramp," Walderspan hissed. Clutching their weapons, they scrambled down the gully, up the ramp and into the ship.

Seated at the control console, Tildar had just noticed five strange blips on an outside scanner when a squad of men burst into the cockpit. She groped for the force pistol on her belt then froze, staring down the tristeel barrel Walderspan had thrust into her face.

"Don't even dream about trying anything, sweetjugs," he warned. He glanced over his shoulder at the others. "Eagleberry, Davv, go check out the rest of the ship and see who else might be hanging. Fabre, scoot down to engineering and get this rig ready for liftoff."

Fabre wrinkled his nose in disgust. "Dammit, boss, it stinks like an interplanetary landfill in here."

"This is a Umas ship. What did you expect, the scent of Aurelian roses?" he shrugged. "Get the air purifiers ramped up when you start up the drive."

Tildar was studying the big human. She noticed the tattoo of a skull and a scrolled motto on his left shoulder, revealing he was a mercenary from the Outer Rim. Then she remembered seeing an identical tattoo on the shoulder of the blonde girl they dropped off on Sheridan's Planet. Here indeed was a mystery.

She forced her mind to consider the immediate situation. During her training in the terran language she absorbed much of the culture dealing with the human male, particularly the warrior type. Vanity, inflated male ego, love of violence, barely restrained sexual impulses. She decided on the best approach.

"I am called Tildar," she said, wearing a winning smile. She held out her pistol by the butt. "Who might the name of my captor be?"

"Just call me Walderspan," he said, taking her weapon.

For the first time he really noticed her, a raven haired beauty with enormous dark eyes. "Don't pull any funny moves and you won't get hurt, toots."

"I would never consider giving offense to such a handsome human as yourself," she purred, her smile ramping up to around one hundred watts.

"Yeah, right," he grunted.

"Am I to be considered your prisoner or your guest?" She slid languorously from the command chair and ran a caressing hand over his chest. "Perhaps we could discuss our new relationship over a glass of Emperion?"

Walderspan blinked, shoving her force pistol into his belt.

"Look, lady, I'm kinda busy right now. Why don't you take a seat by the starboard bulkhead and keep outta our way?"

"All ready to rock and roll, boss," Fabre announced, he and Davv returning to the cockpit. "Got the drive on line, kicked up the air purifiers and…" He cast a sidelong glance at Tildar, lowering his voice. "There were two tanks of dirt in the infirmary holding a couple of Umas cucoons. Moondog dumped them into the trash ejectors."

"Maybe that'll help with the smell." He settled himself into a chair before the controls. "Let's see if I can remember how to get this pig outta the barn."

Unnoticed in the bustle Tildar sat primly by the bulkhead, playing the part of captive maiden. They took over her ship, marooned her crew and dumped her Commander out the trash ejector. Behind her dark eyes, cool, careful calculations were going on.

The Umas starsabre gave out a low moan, lifting itself from the desert floor in a blizzard of flying sand and ropeweed branches.

"Oh oh, we got company," observed Davv, looking out a side viewport where the party of Umas returned, firing red beams at the ascending craft.

"Guess they figured out someone wants to borrow their ride," Walderspan grinned. "Watch this, guys."

He lowered the nose of the ship, swooping over the cluster of angry Umas and hit the emergency landing thrusters. The little figures on the ground vanished in a blast of fire and smoke.

"Time for the wild blue yonder," Walderspan chuckled. The starsabre rose into the night and melted away among the stars.

~ * ~

"Lilly, try pressing the blue button."

"Drat, not even a peep of static, Zelda."

"Hello, hello, anybody out there hear us?"

Falle found herself sprawled out in a room she recognized as part of the main cabin on the folsox farm. She winced, feeling several bruises. It would seem she had been thrown from a considerable height. Coming from the next room she could hear agitated voices coming from the former slave girls. She looked at the hand holding the serum injector.

Formula XIV. Naproxadine Aminotar. Hydrophis Detox Syllabus.

A vague memory swam from the mists of a half-forgotten dream. She remembered finding herself lying on the storeroom floor of Rivergreede Pharmaceuticals...there it was, on the shelf before her, the serum for the hydrophis virus. There were hooting security alarms, the running boots of armed guards. She scrambled up, reached out, seized the vial...she was here. How much did it contain? she wondered, shaking the contents of the vial. She came painfully to her feet and limped into the next room to find the three girls fussing with an interspace comm set. They gaped at her with shocked amazement.

"Falle, you're back!" yelped Lily. "Where did..."

"We'll talk about my travel adventures later, gang," said Falle urgently. "We don't have a lot of time. I brought back the serum for the virus."

The trio looked doubtful. "The serum? Are you sure..." Francine began.

"I said we don't have a lot of time. Stillborne's hyperdrug still blew up and sent me into the Fantasy Dimension." She held up the injector. "Objects brought back from there have a habit of vanishing."

Reluctantly they offered their arms and one by one Falle applied the injector gun. A few moments later Francine gazed at her palm.

"Look, guys!" she screamed, holding it out. The red hazmat imprint was fading, until finally, it disappeared.

"Look, me too," Zelda exclaimed.

Amid the general rejoicing, Falle smiled and pressed the injector to her arm. There was a muted click, but no sensation of any penetration of her skin. She unsnapped the vial from the gun and shook it.

The vial was empty.

Falle let the injector and vial fall to the floor. She sagged against a wall, choked by despair. Despite every effort at self control, tears streamed down her cheeks.

"Falle... what's the matter?" said Lily. The girls stopped celebrating and gathered about her.

The injector held only enough for three doses," she replied dully. "Sorry about this, ladies."

They stared at her, aghast.

"Can't you take another dose of hyperdrug, go back and get some more?" Zelda suggested hopefully.

This remark forced a weak laugh from Falle. She brushed away tears from her cheeks and recalled the unreliability of hyperdrug trips. It must have been pure chance her thoughts were on the serum for the virus when Stillborne's still malfunctioned. She could have easily been thinking of Swampworld...or worse. She looked about her. "So where is our undersized buddy with the oversized cookie duster?"

"He disappeared about the same time as you," said Francine. "You said his hyperdrug thingy blew up? He must have got a whiff of the gas too."

"Say, look at the gun you used on us," Zelda observed. "Something weird is happening to it."

The serum injector and vial lying on the floor was fading into nothingness.

"Interesting effects of hyperdrug withdrawal." Falle observed. "Let me see your hands."

Obediently they displayed their palms, now free of the ominous imprint.

"Okay, the good news is you're still cured." She considered the shaft of sunlight filtering through the grime of a window. It appeared to be nearing midday. "Tell me you didn't turn the farmers loose in the fields while you three were lounging about here?"

"Of course not, we left them locked up while we were trying to use the hyperspace transmitter to call for help," Zelda huffed. "We couldn't get it to work."

Falle bent over the machine. "Did you try turning it on?"

"Um... turning it on?" Zelda's face reddened.

The proper switch was pressed and dials came to life. Falle nodded with satisfaction and regarded the trio of girls.

"The first question which comes to my mind is where Stillborne might have been sent and when..."

A pulsing flash came from the next room.

~ * ~

"Of course, it ain't just a physical thing between us, Shann-tal," panted Stillborne, pulling the girl closer. "I like deeply respect you as a person. We really gotta take advantage of the fact the Grey Warlord is off hunting sandwomen today. Here, lemme help you undo your bra…" His mustache and her soft lips met in a passionate embrace which slowly melded into a hard and scaly object.

Stillborne's eyes flipped open to reveal Falle and the former slave girls eying him quizzically in the doorway of the hut as he embraced a support holding up the roof.

"Sorry to interrupt your romantic encounter." Falle smiled sardonically. "We can come back later if you and your beam want to be alone."

Stillborne took in the smiling faces with poor grace. His expression reflected various moods of surprise, frustration, and grief. He headed for the room where he had built the hyperdrug still.

"Hold on a parsec, Stillborne," said Falle, grasping his arm. "Where are you going?"

"I need another load of snoot, have to get back to her," he said, struggling to free himself. "Leggo my arm."

"Back to who?"

"Shann-tal, the Grey Warlord's nymphomaniac…"

"No hyperdrug trip is the same. You know this, Stillborne." she said, holding his thrashing arm. "You want to end up toiling in a heartstone mine or at the center of a sun?"

Stillborne went limp, slid down the wall to a sitting position. He stared into space, remembering. "She was so hot…I think I'm gonna get shitfaced tonight."

Falle knelt beside him, exuding sympathy. She was about to pat him on the shoulder when she spotted the hazmat imprint in her left palm. She slid down the wall beside him, resting her head against the wall.

"If you're planning on getting shitfaced tonight," she said, "Care for a drinking partner?"

~ * ~

The captured Umas ship rose slowly over the outskirts of New Seattle. Seated by the starboard bulkhead, Tildar watched the lights of the nighttime city passing below with rising concern.

"Excuse me?" What did the leader of the humans call himself? She waved an arm to attract his attention. "Mr. Walderspan."

Walderspan looked up from a display of starcharts on a viewer and frowned in annoyance.

"Toots, I'm sorta busy right now," he said.

"I really must talk with you," Tildar insisted.

Giving vent to a resigned sigh, Walderspan lumbered over.

"Okay, what's the big deal? You need to be escorted to the shitter, lady?"

"You are heading toward the Southeast side of the city."

"So? You want us to land so you can do some shopping?"

"You need to quicken your ascent. You are approaching the New Seattle Spaceport."

"We'll be in orbit in a few zaks, no big deal," he replied with irritating unconcern.

Tildar glared up at the handsome, chiseled face, wishing she still had the dagger the little blond stole from her on Sheridan's Planet. She eyed the perfect spot on the thick neck where she could have pierced his carotid artery.

"The spaceport is ringed by J beam autodefense lasers," she explained furiously. "You should be in range…"

A massive impact shook the starsabre. Smoke billowed into the cockpit and the ship began a graceful spiral downward. There were shouts and cries of pain from the curtain of smoke, then a scream of rending metal when the hull impacted on the desert floor. An ominous silence followed. Moans and coughs began in the gloom.

Tildar picked herself up from the deckplates where she had been thrown, shaken but unhurt. Smoke was thinning out and she could see three of the humans draped over shattered controls, obviously dead. Another merc was trying to get up, blood running from a gash on his forehead. At her feet lay Walderspan, seemingly stunned.

The rattle of treads and the whine of motors sounded in the distance, drawing closer. Tildar realized she had little time.

As a Umas she could expect instant execution at the hands of New Seattle's Citizen Vigilantes.

She ran to the merc with the head wound and, grabbing his force pistol, shot him through the heart. From the smallest of the dead humans she stripped him of his clothes, donning them to cover her jeweled Umas harness and silk loincloth. Next, she knelt by Walderspan, searching his vest and tossing aside his identification. Through a gash in the hull she dragged him from the burning starsabre.

She had no sooner reached what she hoped was a safe distance when the ship exploded, knocking her flat. An enormous column of fire shot into the night sky.

Two terratrax clattered up to the scene of the crash, disgorging a squad of armed vigilantes from the city. They advanced cautiously toward the two figures on the ground.

"Help us, please help us!" Tildar wailed, kneeling at Walderspan's side.

The leader of the Vigilantes lowered his weapon, bent over her.

"What seems to have happened here, Ma'am?" he asked.

"My husband and I were kidnapped by the Umas," Tildar sobbed with a creditable display of female in distress. "You must help us."

"Just take it easy, Ma'am," he reassured her, ducking as a blast from something exploding inside the wreck sent a geyser of flame up into the darkness. "Where are you two from?"

"We are tourists from New Earth City, here on Satellite to explore sandstone formations," Tildar went on. "I am…Tilly Spann and this is my husband, er, Waldo."

"Okay. Okay, everything is gonna be ticky boo now." He put two fingers in his mouth and blew a piercing whistle. "Hey, guys, let's get these people to the hospital. Looks like they're the only survivors."

During the long and uncomfortable ride back to the city, the leader of the Vigilantes kept eyeing Tildar, evidently entranced by her beauty. Luckily, the rattle of treads and howl from the motor discouraged conversation. At some point her little husband and wife subterfuge would fall apart and she hoped she could slip away to a warehouse on the other side of the city, secretly owned by the Umas where a hidden find reposed.

They arrived at the ramshackle excuse for a hospital and Walderspan was carried inside, Tildar holding his hand in a wifely manner. They were ensconced in an examination room and left alone.

After an eternally long wait, an elderly physician made an appearance and began a perfunctory examination of Walderspan. He glanced up at Tildar.

"Good evening, I am Dr. Khan." He was running a scanner over Walderspan's chest. "Sublevel unconsciousness from fusion beam shock," he grunted, tucking a cardioscope back into his pocket. "No evident injuries aside from bruises. He should be recovering his senses shortly." He peered over his shoulder at Tildar. "However, to protect ourselves from potential litigation, the hospital requires complete physicals from both of you. What is your insurance provider?"

Insurance provider? This term had been absent from her training in the Terran language.

"I am afraid my husband and I do not have a… insurance provider," she replied with what she hoped was a winning smile.

Dr. Khan looked grim. "Hmm. Then perhaps an exam won't be necessary. I'll have the front office prepare a discharge form and a release of liability for you to sign." With a parting glance of displeasure, he departed the room.

No sooner had the door closed on his white coat then Walderspan jerked into wakefulness, rubbing his forehead.

"Goddamn, my head hurts," he moaned. His gaze ranged the room, settling on Tildar. "What in hell is going on?"

"What is going on is a result of an incompetent human piloting a Umas ship over an autodefense laser system," she said with contempt.

Silently Walderspan digested this. "The rest of my crew…"

"They are all dead."

He stared heavily at the tile floor. "Zog's Hairy Ass. Havre, Moondog, Davv…" he murmured and looked up at Tildar. "How did I get here?"

"I pulled you from the wreckage before the ship blew up."

"This makes no sense at all. Why would you…" He groggily pulled himself upright on the exam table. "Damn. I gotta get outta here before they find out who I am."

Tildar eyed him curiously. "Who exactly are you?"

"Some spacer wanted by the Homeworld Federation on trumped-up extortion charges. Holy Gorth Crap, did they check any eyedee on me?"

"I removed your identification discs before I pulled you from the ship," she replied smugly.

Walderspan gaped at her. "Why would you do that?"

"The last Umas the Vigilantes of this rustic backwater captured was beaten and hanged before City Hall," she explained. "I informed the leader of the rescue team we were husband and wife tourists captured by the Umas. We are now known as Waldo and Tilly Spann."

She watched him groping this information with obvious confusion. Despite a handsome, chiseled face he was evidently not over endowed with mental hardware.

"So, what happens now?" he asked.

"You humans have an old saying, 'one hand washes the other'. I need an escort across the city to access an interspace comm set in a warehouse used by my people working at the heartstone mine to smuggle gems out to assorted planets." She spoke smoothly, watching his expression for any hint of duplicity on her part. "There I can contact my associates for a rescue."

"Okay, I guess I owe you one," he grunted. "First, I gotta stop by Brewski's Saloon for a cold one."

The door slid open and a clerk arrived bearing a datapad.

Tildar threw herself into Walderspan's arms, covering his lips with kisses.

"Darling! I'm so glad my husband is alive," she cried.

Walderspan submitted to her embrace, his eyes bulging in a manner similar to stepped-on invertebrates.

~ * ~

"How long are you planning on being here?" Tildar complained testily while Walderspan forced his way through the evening crowd at Brewski's Saloon.

"Nag, nag," he muttered, unheard in the noisy throng. "Now I really feel married."

The establishment's proprietor beamed when he spotted Walderspan at the bar. He edged past a pair of sweating bargirls lugging trays of drinks and counting down the few remaining zaks to closing time.

"I suppose you're ready for a couple of cold ones," he greeted him. "Haven't seen your boys all evening. Must be out tomcatting someplace in town." He laid a foaming mug before him.

"Yeah, I suppose so," Walderspan replied gloomily.

He sucked down the mug, exhaled gratefully.

Brewski was gazing at Tildar with vast approval. "Say, where did you pick up the foxy wedge? She's way too Gucci for a spaceport joy girl."

"Ah, excuse me. I'd like you to meet my wife, Tilly. Wanna give her a shot of, say, Zardorian brandy?"

Brewski's eyes widened. "Married? Zog's Left Nut, that was quick." He poured and slid a glass toward her. "Well, talk to you later, Kris. Big crowd here tonight. Surprised to see you still up seeing how you and your boys hit the sack early tonight."

Tildar eyed the drink with distaste. "Are you aware alcohol has no effect on the system of my species?"

"Come on, sugarbowls, just be sociable."

"Our hovertaxi is waiting outside for us," she persisted.

"Ah, let the meter run. I gotta lot of creds left over from the sale of the heartstone."

The heartstone. Wonder where he was able to acquire it?

Tildar recalled the force pistol concealed beneath the interspace comm set at the warehouse. Settling accounts with this human was going to be most enjoyable.

"You know, you're the first Umas female I've ever flapped lips with," Walderspan observed, peeking at the modest cleavage showing in her borrowed uniform. "Hell of an improvement over those butt-ugly male Umas…"

"Will you keep your voice down," she hissed.

There were two empty mugs before him and he was quaffing a third.

"Okay, sorry, Tilly." He leaned closer. "Listen, you're not gonna start stinking the place up and start dropping body parts on the floor, are you?"

Tildar wrinkled her nose at the blast of beery breath and shook her head. "There is no chance of this happening. I am a solon."

"Come again?"

"One in ten of my species has a single womb and is incapable of gestating a secondary life form. I am one of them."

"There's some real good news." He was mulling over another question but was not sure what her reaction might be.

"Um, I hear tell Umas females are kinda non participant in the sack. You know, frigid?"

"What?"

"Us guys would call them a lousy lay."

"Umas females are not promiscuous," she replied loftily. "We experience a yearly breeding cycle when we are receptive to mating."

"Wow, once a year," Walderspan considered bleakly.

"I have not experienced my first at this time," she continued. "Not that it is of your concern. May I observe it is also time for you to cease drinking."

"Well, give me some warning if you hit your cycle around me so I can at least take a shower," he chortled.

"Are you about finished here?" She glared at him.

Brewski appeared behind the bar. He leaned toward Walderspan.

"Listen, I'm still trying to find a forger for your new passports so you can blow town."

"Hey, thanks, Brewski."

"By the way, where you thinking of heading?"

Walderspan mulled this over. "Zardoria has no extradition treaty anymore I heard. Maybe I can honk up Nebly, the spacer who used to supervise the cleaning crew when we were in the Palace cellars, see which way the wind is blowing there. Maybe patch things up with Crandell for old time's sake."

"Crandell ain't there anymore," said Brewski. "They found her place had been taken over by a cybernetic duplicate. Rumor has it she took off in an old and stolen starfreighter with a little runt named Stillborne."

Tildar was in the act of morosely sampling the Zardorian brandy when she overheard this. Her glass fell to the bartop.

Stillborne. The human who discovered the formula for the widely demanded hyperdrug. For which the Methtropolis Drug Cartel was offering a fortune in creds for delivering his person to them.

"Darling, I think we should be on our way," she purred, wrapping her arm around his arm.

Walderspan blinked his surprise at this sudden change of mood. He looked down at her with an anticipatory leer.

"What a great idea, honeycrack," he grinned, patting her on the rear.

Tildar smiled seductively back at him.

What you think is going to happen between us is in your dreams, human.

By the time the hovertaxi dropped them off at the alley leading to the warehouse the Blue Lady had set, leaving the line of deserted factories and storage sheds steeped in gloom. They groped their way through the darkness until Tildar spotted a dimly-lit sign. She squinted at a tiny touchpad and punched in a code.

A low hum came from above and the corrugated metal gate clanked upwards, chattered and then stopped.

"It would appear the hoist mechanism is jammed," she remarked after several futile attempts at the touchpad.

"Lemme see what I can do, toots," said Walderspan.

He bent down, gripped the bottom of the gate and heaved.

Tildar watched muscles ripple and bulge beneath his combat vest, veins standing out on his biceps. There was a crack and the gate resumed its upward travel.

"Piece of cake," he remarked. "Now where you got the comm set stashed? I gotta make a call to a spacer named Nebly in Zardoria, talk about old times."

"Follow me, please." Tildar sent the gate downwards and activated the warehouse lights. In a corner she pulled a dusty pad from the comm set. Surreptitiously she slid her hand into a concealed drawer, gripping the hidden force pistol.

From nowhere, the image of Walderspan's broad back swam into her mind; sweat glistening on veined muscles, a display of brute primeval strength. A sudden wave of heat surged up from her loins and she began to tremble. Her breath came in short gasps.

My breeding cycle. Not now!

She jerked out the pistol, leveling it at Walderspan. The muzzle wavered in her shaking hand.

"Whoa!" Walderspan stepped back, raising his hands. "Listen, that crack I made about Umas wedges being a lousy lay," he stammered. "I sure as hell didn't mean you, toots. Why, I'll bet you could suck a sportsball through a refueling hose and lick the chrome off…"

"You need to stop 'flapping your lips' and begin praying to whatever gods you humans…"

She found herself staring at his massive arms. Another wave of fire engulfed her nether regions, leaving her gasping. The force pistol fell to the floor.

Walderspan exhaled with relief. "Thanks, honeycrack. I figure we can work out our differences…"

She suddenly seized him about the waist, dragging his lips to hers.

"Drog's Holy Jockstrap!" he yelped while she clawed open his vest.

"What the hell are you doing?"

"Get your clothing off and you will find out," she replied, gripping his ear with her teeth.

~ * ~

Morning sunlight shafted through the dusty windows, splashing triangular patterns over the concrete floor. On a dingy mattress in a far corner Walderspan yawned, wearily pulling himself up on an elbow.

The joys of the previous evening diminished as Tildar's demand for ferocious lovemaking continued throughout the night. He felt drained, figuratively and literally. His back was covered by livid scratches and one of his earlobes was bitten off.

He glanced over at his now sleeping companion, wondering if chatting to Nebly on Zardoria was worth it. He suddenly decided it was not.

Tildar began muttering in guttural Umas on the other side of the mattress, deep in sleep.

Abruptly, she switched to Terran.

"...so Stillborne is on Sheridan's Planet with the female human Falle Crandell...huge reward for him...Methtropolis Drug Cartel happy to pay Umas..."

Now this was interesting news. Now he had a good idea of her future plans. Silently, he donned his clothes, holding his breath in fear of waking her. He studied the warehouse gate. That clanking rattletrap would certainly arouse the sleeping sexual tigress at his side.

He noticed a door in the gloom of the far end of the warehouse. Carrying his boots in one hand he crept over.

The door opened to another part of the cavernous building, brightly lit by sunlight coming through an enormous skylight. Parked in the center was the Zardorian Mark IX starsabre which he and his crew had flown to Satellite in search of the heartstones.

"Drog's Holy Jockstrap," he breathed. It would seem Tildar's Umas buddies had somehow acquired it. Another piece of her future plans. He felt he had to admire how she had manipulated him to escort her from the hospital to her magic carpet ride from Satellite. He carefully closed the warehouse door, sliding a drop bar into place.

Entering the ship, he seated himself before the controls, activating the main power buss. Dials and displays glowed into life. A moment later the fusion drive growled up to full power. The craft rose upward, smashing through the skylight and the flimsy metal of the hatch.

Walderspan glanced at a rear viewscreen in time to see the antlike figure of Tildar far below run naked from the building. The naked little ant was jumping up and down, shaking with rage. Wearing a broad grin, Walderspan turned the ship toward the rising sun and headed skyward.

He eased the ship into orbit and leaned back in the command chair, pondering his next move.

Mentally, he checked off the best places to lay low until the warrant for his arrest was forgotten. Two thoughts kept forcing its way into his consciousness.

Why did Tildar get up in the middle of the night to make a clandestine call on the hyperspace radio and who was she calling?

Chapter Fourteen

The three former slave girls were really beginning to hate Falle Crandell.

First, they were put to work cleaning a year's accumulation of filth from the farmer's huts. Poor Lily began retching over the stench from washing down the toilets and Falle's only comment was to say when she finished her break to start scraping the grease from kitchen sinks. Next, they were required to jog twice a day around the farm, with Falle trotting behind them making disparaging remarks about losing all the blubber they had acquired lounging about the stock room of Rivergreede Pharmaceuticals.

Under Sheridan's Planet's watery sun, she had them feed and herd the captive and sullen folsox farmers out to work in the field, awkwardly holding the force pistol they had been given.

Returning to the main hut Falle found Stillborne busy at his hyperdrug still, unloading orange glass balls from a hopper and packing them into a crate.

"I see you've been busy," Falle observed. "How much have you cranked out so far?"

"Enough to bribe the crew on the Cartel supply shuttle to look the other way when we slink aboard their ship." He grinned at her over his shoulder. "Creds always talk while bullshit walks…"

The staccato hum of a force pistol and a faint scream came from outside. Stillborne rushed to a hut window and peered through the grimy pane.

"Zog's Ass, Crandell!' he yelled. "Our farmboys are killing your stock clerks."

Falle grabbed a particle rifle and threw open the door. At once she saw it was too late. The bodies of Lily and Francine lay over a water tank in the center of the field as Bovus jerked his pruning shears from Zelda. Grins spreading over bushy beards, the farmers grabbed fallen force pistols and shoved their way through the folsox bushes toward the main hut.

"Do you know a little-known fact about folsox plants?" Falle remarked grimly, adjusting the settings on her charged particle rifle.

"Yeah, we have a bunch of pissed off farmers with them heading our way." Stillborne looked wildly around him for someplace to hide.

"Not for much longer." She lifted the rifle and squinted down the sights. "Folsox bushes are extremely flammable."

A red beam from her weapon played over the fields. Instantly, rows of bushes erupted into flame, raising a curtain of boiling smoke and fire. The farmers, caught in the middle of the field struggled in a futile bid to escape and disappeared in a red inferno.

~ * ~

"Hey Crandell, I think we have visitors." Stillborne crouched by a window, looking out at the morning sun casting long shadows between the huts and the smoking remains of the folsox field.

Tossing aside the blankets on her bunk, Falle grabbed her particle rifle and joined him at the window.

"This is really weird," Stillborne whispered at her side. "That ain't no Cartel ship. Looks to me like a Zardorian Mark IX Starsabre."

The newly arrived spacecraft circled the farm and settled gently on the open space between the huts. An entry hatch opened and a boarding ramp snaked downwards. A moment later a single man emerged. Falle instantly recognized him as Walderspan.

"What a wonderful way to start the day," she muttered grimly, pushing her way through the doorway and raising the weapon to her shoulder.

"Hold it, hold it!" he yelled, throwing his hands into the air. "This ain't what you think."

"What I think is this is another pissant assassination attempt of yours, Walderspan." She lined up the sights on his chest. "Have a nice trip to a better world."

"They…they found the cybernetic duplicate you left in your place in Zardoria," he stammered, grasping for any distraction which might save his posterior. "It's a whole new ball game back there."

"What are you talking about?" She lowered her weapon, moved closer.

"Your pal Agnes set us both up." He let out breath in partial relief. "Me and my boys ended up shoveling rocks in a Umas heartstone mine. Everyone but me got killed in a crash escaping from Satellite."

"So why are you here with your big salesman smile?" Falle was convinced something fishy was going on.

"When you knocked off Major Grange, D'Escrille escaped. He later set us up with the Homeworld Federation on bogus charges of embezzlement and bribery."

"So, you're hoping I'll fly off with you to Zardoria, reclaim my title as head honcho and grant you asylum?" She hefted the rifle ominously. "So, what if I just blow you away and take over your ship?"

Walderspan shrugged. "Well, you did save my life once. I was kinda hoping you'd repeat the favor for old time's sake."

"For old time's sake, huh?" Falle studied him in silence.

She knew it was either an act of desperation on his part or a great deal of courage to put himself at her mercy. She was inclined toward the latter.

"Okay, Walderspan, let's take a trip together," she declared, favoring him with an ominous glare. "Help me straighten out the mess back in Zardoria and we'll talk about the old times later."

Followed by Walderspan and Stillborne, she walked up the ramp and into the starsabre. As the ship rose over the farm it was wreathed in smoke from the burned-out field of folsox.

Seating herself at the controls, Falle watched a pale blue beyond the viewport fade to a star-filled infinity. Her fingers tapped the navigation screen, inputting the course sequence. She looked over her shoulder at Walderspan leaning against a cabin wall.

"Sheridan's Planet is in the Outer Rim but we should reach Planet New Earth in about a day," she observed. "Figure we touch down in Zardoria about noon, their time."

"I'm afraid we're not going to Zardoria, Crandell." Walderspan crossed his arms, looking at her with a mixture of amusement and regret.

A trio in black rushed into the cabin, pulse rifles at the ready. Stillborne gave vent to a fluting squall, retreating to a far corner.

"I made a call to my old buddy Nebly, whose crew used to clean up my cell under the Chandelier Palace," Walderspan continued. "He tells me the Methtropolis Drug Cartel has upped the reward to a half million creds for the little runt shitting a brick in the corner. I'm betting Zardoria will cough up mucho creds to have their real Chancellor returned."

Falle sniffed in contempt then shifted her gaze to the intruders wearing black. In the forefront she recognized the sinister features of Gordo, head assassin for the Borgia Guild.

"It's quite an honor to finally meet you in person, Beloved Despot," he grinned, bowing in mock obeisance. Behind him she recognized fellow members Splib and Knifestalker.

"Let me introduce my new partners," said Walderspan. "As you know, they're the experts in kidnapping and extortion. I gave them a call after I left Satellite, we came to an agreement and I picked them up on New Earth."

"How tall are you, Walderspan?" Falle inquired calmly.

"What?"

"I'd say about five foot ten. I didn't think they could stack gomph shit that high."

"You can knock off the self-righteous indignation, Crandell," he sneered. "You may have the tattoo, but I'm the real mercenary here."

"I hate to intrude on this minor disagreement with friends," Gordo interrupted. "I believe its time my men escorted the Adored Despot and her associate to their private quarters."

"Would you like me to complete plotting in the course for New Earth? I'm almost done." Falle blandly asked Gordo.

"This would be most gracious of you, Great One," he smirked. "Put us into orbit over Euphoria where we will begin negotiations with the Cartel."

Falle bent over the navigation screen, punched in a series of codes and got up. Stillborne was removed from his corner and they were marched down a corridor and pushed into a small cabin.

She was relieved of her dagger and the entry hatch was slammed and locked.

Stretching out on a bunk Falle propped her feet up on a railing and yawned.

Stillborne squinted at her. "Man, you sure look relaxed. Ain't you a tad worried those bozos up front might collect the reward from the Zardorians and knock you off just for yuks once we get to New Earth?"

"We're not going to New Earth." Falle smiled benignly on him. "I set the navigational controls to a different course and locked up the programming so it can't be changed."

"What?" Stillborne stopped nervously chewing his mustache. "So where are we headed?"

"Oh, I thought all of us could use a little vacation. You know, someplace with a warm sun, sandy beaches and surf." She continued smiling at him. "Adriane."

"Adriane?" he gaped. "A planet of nothing but ocean with a few rocks called islands here and there. And don't forget what's swimming around in them oceans."

"A carnivorous indigenous merpeople," Falle added. "Three survey teams from Interworld Mining Corporation on New Earth vanished before they found out what was happening."

"Yeah, and they'll be waiting to stick tridents in our asses and drag us down for a Sunday brunch. You must be moonied!"

"I was thinking once this ship lands there, our genial hosts will likely want to look around, probably take a stroll along the water's edge." She raised her eyebrows. "Good chance to even the odds for us. Get the picture?"

"Yeah, I get the picture all right," he retorted. "Before we get there, I'm betting they'll notice your little course correction. They'll storm down here and beat the poop outta you until you put the ship back on their course."

"Beating the poop out of me won't work."

Stillborne took in the basilisk stare he knew so well. He marveled how quickly her angelic face could transform into a mask of such feral ferocity.

"Okay, Crandell, but I ain't you," he whined. "They start jerking out my fingernails and I'll do everything they ask, including mopping floors and scrubbing out the shitters. You forgot Walderspan knows I'm an electronics geek and can get the system back on line just as fast as you." He fumbled in a vest pocket for his dhung pipe. "Man, do I need a hit."

An orange ball slipped out, bounced onto the deck. Falle picked it up, holding it up to the cabin lightbar.

"Is this what I think it is, Stillborne?"

He peered past a cloud of smoke from his pipe. "Yeah, it's a hyperdrug capsule. I stuffed a couple in my pocket when I was trying to get my still fixed back at the folsox farm."

"Lucky it didn't break open when you dropped it."

Taking the capsule from her, Stillborne scratched his nose thoughtfully. "You know, this might be the solution to our problem."

"You have an idea." Falle sighed. Past experiences with his great ideas had made her extremely wary.

"No, listen. We suck down a whiff of snoot and disappear from the ship," he said. "That way, there's nothing they can do but land on Adriane and wander around until our toothy friends invite them to dinner."

"You have no idea what I went through after my last hyperdrug trip," she replied, glowering. "Bad idea, forget it."

"Because you were caught by surprise. The way a snoot trip works is you concentrate on a time and place you wanna be and you're there. Like I did when I went back to Shann-tal on Satellite."

"Wonderful how that worked out for you."

"Okay, we just hang here until they come for us or do a midnight slide on them," he persisted. "Your call, Crandell."

Falle regarded the hyperdrug ball with distaste. She threw up her hands in resignation.

"So, what time and place do you have in mind?" she asked.

"Obviously, someplace we've both been." His brows knitted in thought. "Remember when we were out sandwomen prospecting on Satellite and came across that bunker full of weapons left over from the Umas invasion?"

"I remember. A rack full of really nice charged particle rifles."

"It would also be nice to come back here armed to the teeth on hyperdrug withdrawal."

Stillborne and Falle grinned at each other.

~ * ~

Walderspan was sitting at a table with Gordo's two associates, absorbed in a game of Terranova poker. Judging by the stack of creds beside him, luck was running his way. Leaning against a bulkhead, Gordo watched racing streaks of light from timephase mode rush past the forward viewport. He shifted his gaze to Walderspan.

"We may have an issue with Falle Crandell," he said.

"Come again?" Walderspan paused in his shuffling of the deck.

"The guild had a contract with Baron Shrop to assassinate Chancellor Crandell, aka the lovely Ms. Crandell. Unfortunately, it was her cybernetic duplicate who bit the dust," Gordo explained. "Now, the dear Baron demands a refund of his eighty thousand creds."

"So, tell him to bend over and start passing Tiffany cufflinks," Walderspan grunted, racking in another handful of creds.

"The Borgia Guild has a reputation for honoring contracts," Gordo explained with weary patience. "Business ethics, protecting our reputation and all that."

"Wait a parsec, you're not thinking of…"

"I'm afraid it will be a regrettable necessity."

Walderspan laid his hand of cards face down on the table, glaring at Gordo. "So, you're just gonna take a pass on the big reward we might squeeze outta Zardoria for her return?"

"Of course not. First, we collect the reward and then invite Ms. Crandell to inspect the external drive tubes of the ship." An evil smile creased his face. "Without an atmosphere suit, naturally."

"Okay, makes sense," Walderspan nodded. He looked past Gordo to the light-streaked forward viewport. "Hmm, this is funny."

"What is funny?"

"I just noticed we seem to be moving kinda fast." He rose from the poker table and went to the control console.

"What the hell?" he blurted. "The navigation screen is blank and…" He jabbed buttons with futile frustration. "Dammit, Crandell!"

"What is going on?" said Gordo, looking over his shoulder.

"She set the navigation screen to some unknown destination and locked up the computer."

"How did she know how to do this?" said Gordo, aghast.

"She used to be a navigator and a starpilot for a couple of commercial spacelines. Damn her."

Gordo turned to Splib and Knifestalker. "Get Crandell and that little turd Stillborne up here," he ordered. "One or the other of them will fix this problem or I'll start pulling out teeth and fingernails."

Walderspan and Gordo were still making futile attempts to restore the navigational controls when they returned, empty handed.

"Well, where are they?" Gordo demanded.

"They weren't in their cabin, boss," said Splib. "We searched every nook and cranny of the ship."

"We did find this." Knifestalker opened his palm to reveal a broken hyperdrug capsule.

"Zog's Holy Jockstrap," groaned Walderspan.

~ * ~

The Zardorian starsabre dropped out of timephase, knocking Gordo from his dream of sitting naked on an enormous pile of creds, sipping champagne served by an equally naked Euphorian pleasure girl. He removed the boots he had propped up on the control panel, gazing out at the infinity of stars bisected by the blue disk of an approaching planet.

"Hey, Walderspan, I think we're here," he said. "Wherever here is."

Walderspan eased himself away from a table littered with poker chips and empty beer bottles and joined him at the forward viewport.

"Are we looking at Planet New Earth?" Gordo wondered. "Seems like a lot of ocean below."

"Wherever it is we're dropping out of orbit toward yonder big island. Where are your two Guild buddies?"

"I have Splib standing guard over the cabin where we locked up our missing guests. Knifestalker is off duty and probably sacked out."

"Better get them up here before we land. Hopefully, the bitch programmed it to land, not crash."

Gordo studied a row of gauges. "Well, lots of breathable air down there and nice tropical temps. Maybe Crandell wanted us to enjoy a vacation of sun and sea."

The ship rocked slightly, passing strands of drifting cloud. It gradually slowed, setting down gently amid a clearing in a fern jungle.

The hatch soughed open. Gordo cautiously stepped onto the landing ramp surveying a wall of green and rank underbrush bearing brilliantly colored blooms. Strange birdlings fluttered and shrilled among branches through which he could see a glitter of ocean.

"What's going on?" asked Splib and Knifestalker at his elbow.

"Wish to hell I knew," Gordo muttered.

"Damn her, the nav computer is still locked out." Walderspan jabbed in futile rage at console buttons. "I'd give half the reward on her ass to know what her game is."

"Let's start by finding out where we are," Gordo suggested. "Why don't you take my two Guild members on a little reconnaissance? Locate some people or a habitation where we can honk up a repair tech."

"What if Blondie and Scruffy return from their snoot trip?"

"I'll hold down the fort until you get back." He smiled grimly. "Believe me, I'll be more than happy to see them. Her screams when I start working her over will be music to my ears."

The trio walked down the ramp and into the forest. The clamor of birdlings from branches high above increased and they expressed their displeasure at this intrusion by excreting foul smelling gifts on the men passing below.

Cursing and swatting the air against this noxious rain they shoved their way past a final tangle of thorns onto an expanse of sand and wave washed beach.

"Hey, Walderspan," Splib exclaimed. "Get a load of that."

The hulk of an ancient starship lay on the beach close to the treeline. The hull was stained by sun and storm, draped in a carpet of leaves and dead fern branches. They gathered around it in wonder.

"Interworld Mining Corporation," Knifestalker read from faded letters on a tailfin. "Man, looks like it's been parked here for at least a century."

They entered an open hatch, finding moldy wall panels, storm-driven wrack covering the decks and instruments in the control cabin.

"Really weird, guys," said Walderspan after they had searched the silent and dismal interior. "Seems they landed here, went for a stroll and never came back."

"Let's get the flock outta here, as the good shepherd said," murmured Splib. "This tomb is giving me the creeps."

They returned to the beach and stood gazing around them at an expanse of sand and jungle stretching out on either side.

"Drog's Ass!" Knifestalker suddenly shouted, pointing out to sea. "Take a look out there."

"What did you see?"

"Goddammit, I swear I just saw…someone swimming."

"Someone swimming?"

"Come on, let's take a look."

They ran down to the water's edge; squinting their eyes against the sunlight flashing off the waves.

"Ain't nothing out there, pal," Walderspan snorted. "Probably a chunk of seaweed. Maybe your eyes are getting…"

A trident shaped spear flashed from the sea, impaling Splib in the chest. A cord attached to the haft jerked him flat on the sand and began dragging him toward the ocean. A tumult of screams and yells of alarm ensued, the three men struggling where the sea met the sand, one grasping the trident embedded in his chest, the others attempting to pull him back. Then a woven net flew from the water, enveloping them all.

Walderspan abandoned efforts to save Splib and fought the strands of netting slowly dragging him under. He took a final desperate breath when the sea closed over his head.

From sunstreaked green depths, a man with black doll eyes and flowing green hair swam over to him. He was wearing an anticipatory grin and a snaggle of barracuda fangs.

Into Walderspans' mind drifted a voice.

We will feast well now. These humans are delicious.

~ * ~

Seated in the command chair before the controls, Gordo drummed his fingers impatiently on polished speerwood. *How long does it take to make a simple reconnaissance of the area?* He groused to himself.

A muted shock of displaced air vibrated the corridor behind him. Gordo got up from the chair, drawing his force pistol.

So, at last they've returned from their foolish hyperdrug trip, he gloated, standing before the stateroom in which they had been locked. *First, I'll have them return the navigational computer to normal operation, then I'll deal with that wedge, Crandell. I will enjoy extracting her fingernails before...*

The door to the cabin began to glow cherry red. Abruptly, it ruptured outward, throwing him against the corridor wall. He lay stunned for a moment before someone seized the front of his shirt, jerking him to his feet. He found himself looking into blue reptilian eyes.

Gordo swallowed hard. "Do what you have to do, Crandell. Only make it quick."

"Not a chance, Gordo."

"Better grab his piece, Crandell," warned Stillborne behind her. "I think it's starting to happen."

Hyperdrug withdrawal: Falle watched the charged particle rifle she was holding become mist. She took Gordo's weapon from Stillborne and jammed it under the assassin's chin.

"Let's take a little walk," she said.

Herding Gordo to the boarding ramp, she pointed to the dense jungle outside. "I'll give you a five zak start, then I'll hunt you down. Get moving, Gordo."

"You with a force pistol and me unarmed," he sneered. "A lot of guts here, lady."

"Who said anything about a pistol?" She tossed the weapon aside and slid a dagger from her boot. "I know you have one of these also. Let's see how you rack up to me, blade to blade. You have four zaks left."

"We'll just see what happens," he snarled, as he turned and ran down the ramp into the jungle.

After forcing his way past a thicket of purple thorns he stooped, drawing a hidden blade from a sheath at his back. Then he set off along a forest path beaten out by some animal.

Coming to a bend in the trail he climbed into the branches of a huge fern. He worked his way along a branch overlooking the trail and gripping his knife, he waited.

The jungle drowsed under midday heat. Unseen birdlings chattered above him in chorus with the chirr of myriad insects. Suddenly, the song of birdlings and insects died.

There was a distant hiss of steel through air and a dagger sliced into the bicep of his left arm. He squalled in pain, jerking it free, falling from the branch onto the forest path below. Clutching his bleeding arm, he staggered blindly through the forest.

Through a gap in ferns he caught a glitter of sea. He clawed his way past a last thicket and ran out onto the beach, collapsing onto the sand. His face was a mask of agony as he ran a sleeve across the sweat running down his face. Somewhere in his mad flight he had dropped the knife. He groaned aloud, wishing for some weapon to defend himself from the avenging fury on his heels.

There it was. Lying on the sand near the uppermost reach of the waves lay a force pistol.

Uttering a cry of joy, he staggered up and seized it. Gripping his bleeding arm, he pointed the muzzle in the direction of the treeline and waited.

A barbed hook sprang from the pistol and imbedded itself in his hand. A cord attached to the hook jerked him onto the beach and began dragging him inexorably toward the sea. He screamed in abject terror, clutching at sand and wave washed pebbles.

The last thing he saw before water closed over his head was Falle standing on the beach. In one hand she held her dagger and the other held a shredded remnant of Walderspan's shirt.

She was smiling.

Chapter Fifteen

The massive statue of Chancellor Falle Crandell teetered to the left, swayed drunkenly and fell with a gratifying crash, scattering bronze and fragments of marble. The crowd gathered before the Palace cheered wildly. The chanting resumed, echoing from the high towers and parapets.

"Death to Falle Crandell! Down with the tyrant!"

"I told you this would be a bad idea, coming back here," Falle observed, looking down at the mob from a high window. The rough coveralls she'd donned before leaving orbit were chaffing her neck raw.

"Well, what choice did we have, Crandell?" said Stillborne. "We're both broke and unemployed. Prime Minister Sanchez mentioned they had an opening here for security chief when I flapped lips with her on Adriane."

"We're broke because the National Police guys appropriated our twenty thousand cred starsabre and whatever we had in our pockets as soon as we landed."

"What are you complaining about? It was their starsabre to begin with."

Falle gave him a sideways look of disgust and returned to watching the crowd outside the Palace fence. They had hung a straw effigy of her on the gates and were busily setting it afire.

"Prime Minister Sanchez will see you now," announced a clerk from a side door. "Both of you please."

Parasol Sanchez looked up from behind her speerwood desk as they were ushered in. She waved a hand toward a set of chairs.

"Please be seated," she greeted them. "Delightful to see you once more, Ms. Crandell. You also, Mr. Stillborne. What can I do for you?"

Ms. Crandell. Not a good sign. Falle felt the weight of Parasol's cold scrutiny and unasked questions.

"Stillborne told me he talked to you about a position here at the Palace," she said. "I was only planning on dropping him off on my way to Dustball when our ship was confiscated."

"Yes, it was a newer addition to our fleet. Thank you for its return."

This was a mild rebuke. Parasol turned her attention to Stillborne.

"I understand you designed and built the electronic security system for the Chandelier Palace?"

Somewhat subdued by the cloud he sensed Falle was under, Stillborne brightened, "Yes, Ma'am. All the surveillance programs, alarm sensors, nuts and bolts."

"I am very glad to hear this. The temporary person we hired has been unable to properly maintain the system."

"I made a lotta new upgrades before I…left with Crandell. They need a bunch of constant pats on the butt to run smooth." He felt he was gaining the upside of this employment interview. "What kinda salary are we looking at?"

A door opened and a sultry brunette entered, gliding up to Parasol's desk.

"Ah, Ms. Opiata," said Parasol. "Melane, let me introduce Mr. Stillborne, a candidate for the position of Security Chief."

The girl's limpid brown eyes widened. "You're Leonard M. Stillborne, the one who created the system for the Chandelier Palace?"

"Um, I did throw a couple of neotrans and circuits together awhile back."

"You also designed the famous system for the Grey Warlord on Satellite?" She was looking at Stillborne as if he gave milk. "It's an honor to finally meet you, Mr. Stillborne."

"You can call me Leonard, honeycra…er, Melane." He reluctantly retrieved his eyeballs from Ms. Opiata's expansive bosom and sleek body encased in her tight pantsuit and turned back to Parasol Sanchez.

"I'll take the job," he said.

"Well, I suppose we could discuss remuneration and other details at a later time," said Parasol dryly. "Perhaps Ms. Opiata could take you to review some of the problems we have been having at the security office while Ms. Crandell and I have our little chat."

No sooner had the office door slid closed when Parasol regarded Falle with an expressionless stare.

"In case you were wondering about your status here in the Six Cities, the High Council has abolished your position of Chancellor as well as the Citizens Guard," she said. "Word has gotten around about your arrival in City One and most of the population never believed in the explanation you were replaced by a cybernetic android."

Falle shrugged helplessly. "I never expected to be gone so long, or that Agnes would become drunk with power as acting ruler."

"So, there is the question as to why you did it," Parasol persisted.

"I got word there was a shipment of heartstones worth sixty thousand creds arriving at a Umas warehouse on Satellite. Stillborne and I decided to grab them."

"This is strange. I never would have guessed you would be so venal."

"I'm not." Falle felt rising anger at the edge of contempt in Parasol's voice. "Perhaps you'll recall the wedding scene awhile back when Duke Duefuss kissed the marble floor after kissing me. I needed the thirty thousand creds for the serum to cure my hydrophis virus."

"Now I understand the why," Parasol nodded. "However, just before you departed on your little quest, the High Council voted in special session to release funds to provide you with the serum. Of course, after the Agnes affair, this agreement is now null and void."

Falle stared bleakly at a single rose in a tiny vase on the desk. Picked yesterday, it was starting to wilt and droop, much like her spirits.

"It also pains me to inform you there was an accident in the stockroom of Rivergreede Pharmaceuticals which resulted in the infection of the virus to a number of people in New Earth City," Parasol continued. "Rivergreede has exploited the situation by raising the price of the serum to ninety-five thousand creds."

This harvest of bad news completely deflated Falle. She fought down a wave of depression, gazing at the clasped hands in her lap.

Sensing her dismay, Parasol's stern expression softened. "So, what were your plans after dropping off Mr. Stillborne? I believe you mentioned returning to your home planet of Dustball."

"I was hoping to reach Haboob City. I own a water pumping plant just outside of town."

"Oh my, more bad news, I'm afraid."

"What?" Falle's head jerked up.

"I received a communication from the manager you left there to run things," she said. "The aquifer went dry. Your manager paid off the remaining workers and the plant has since been...abandoned."

For a long moment Falle studied the dying rose. "You wouldn't happen to have an opening for dishwasher in the Palace kitchens, would you?"

Parasol laughed. "Sorry. Everything is automated there." She picked up a stylus from her desk and tapped it thoughtfully on the blotter. "I might have something for you. I believe at one time you were a pilot for Pan Galaxy Spacelines?"

"Certified astrogater and starpilot." Falle smiled ruefully. "I believe at one time I mentioned to you I wasn't on their rehire list. They have an absurd prejudice against carriers of a deadly virus."

"This no longer matters now. Since United Starlines went ahead with replacing their entire staff from mechanics to pilots with cybernetic androids, Pan Galaxy was thrown into such a financial pit they were forced to follow suit."

A gleeful thought popped into Falle's mind, of which she was instantly ashamed.

Well, Captain Rann Glassford, how does it feel to be unemployed? Does this make the little Mrs. Glassford happy?

"The Homeworld Federation maintains a prison facility on Slython, at the edge of the Outer Rim," Parasol continued. "I understand they have an opening for a two person crew to run convicted and released criminals in a small transport freighter. Something you might be interested in?"

To be back behind the controls of a spacecraft once more; it seemed to Falle a dream too good to be true. She took a deep breath.

"Absolutely. Definitely," she said.

"Very good, then," Parasol nodded. "There is a flight leaving for Planet New Earth this evening if you would care to be on it. I will contact Mrs. Hardtkase in personnel to let them know you will be arriving for an interview."

A rock impacted on a palace window, sending a shower of plexglass shards over the marble floor. From outside the palace grounds a chant could be heard.

"Down with Queen Falle! Death to the tyrant!"

"How soon can I leave?" asked Falle.

Parasol eyed the rock surrounded by jewel-like crystals. "I will have a hovercar take you to the airport." She turned her attention to Falle and smiled.

"I've noticed you fidgeting in those ill-fitting coveralls since you sat down, I'll have you escorted to your old quarters where you can change into something more comfortable."

"Thank you again, Parasol." Falle rose to go. "I guess I owe you big time."

"Please do not select the jeweled Umas harness," she chuckled.

Falle had no sooner left the Prime Minister's suite when she felt the impact of two bodies grabbing her about the waist. She looked down into twin elfin faces.

"I'm so glad you're back," cried Missy.

"I'm even more glad you're the real one this time," Sissy exclaimed.

~ * ~

It wasn't his choice for a romantic dinner date. Stillborne looked around him in distaste at the greasy spoon café adjacent to the Zardorian Spaceport. The patrons appeared to be dockloaders, just off the afternoon shift, lurking pimps and blousy whores.

"You know, sweetchee...I mean, Melane, we coulda gone to a classier place for dinner, you know," he said.

"Oh, this place is so cozy," said Melane. She had changed into a sultry purple evening dress with even more exposure of her lush cleavage. "It's much more convenient for me."

Much more convenient? Stillborne frowned.

Still, things were going the way he hoped. Prime Minister Sanchez confirmed his employment at the Chandelier Palace and his dinner date was showing every sign the evening would end as he hoped.

A waiter in a soiled apron arrived with a bottle of wine and filled their glasses. They raised them, clinking in a toast.

"So where is your little blonde companion?" Melane asked, taking a sip. "The one with the pale blue snake eyes?"

"Oh, Crandell? I hear Sanchez got her a job interview for a pilot's job, ferrying convicts to the space prison on Slython. If she's smart she should be at the spaceport right now getting ready to blow the planet."

He sucked wine from his mustache. His gaze dropped involuntarily to the twin spheres rising from her blouse.

"Say, after dinner, if we don't come down with ptomaine poisoning, I was thinking maybe we could hang out in your bedroom…I mean, your place for awhile, watch a holoflix or something."

"I'd really like that, Leonard," she cooed. "Unfortunately, you'll be leaving shortly on your trip."

"Trip? What trip?" Stillborne blurted in confusion.

"Why, to Euphoria, of course." She savored his baffled expression segueing to one of horror. "The Methtropolis Drug Cartel embedded me into the Chandelier Palace staff awhile back, on the chance you would return to Zardoria. I and my associates will enjoy sharing the half million cred reward when you arrive at Cartel headquarters and disclose the formula for hyperdrug."

A pair of huge bruisers appeared on either side of Stillborne's chair. One of them pulled an injector gun from his belt.

"Once Bozo administers a tranquillizer, we will remove you to our shuttle waiting on the spaceport departure pad," she said with smug assurance. "You can make a scene if you want before the drug takes effect. It will merely appear they are removing an unruly drunk."

Stillborne swallowed hard, formulating a desperate plan.

"Say, any of you spacers heard of Swampworld?" he stammered.

"You know, mudholes, poison mist and snakeoids?"

The bruisers around Stillborne paused and stared at him, puzzled.

"Yeah, everybody's heard of Swampworld, pal," Bozo replied. "So what?"

"Just keep thinking of the place then." Stillborne fumbled in a vest pocket for his remaining hyperdrug capsule.

"Why are you holding your breath?" Melane demanded.

The capsule landed on the café table, emitting a cloud of orange gas. The two bruisers and Melane gave out startled cries which ran up the scale, and faded out. For a moment in time they shimmered like a desert mirage, became two-dimensional and then vanished. The remaining gas spiraled upward to be sucked into a ceiling vent.

Stillborne was already in a crouch, heading for the doorway. A bearded dockloader blocked his way.

"Hey! Ain't you Stillborne, the spacer the Methtropolis Cartel has the humpin' big reward out for?" said the dockloader, making a grab with hands like shovels. "Hot damn, half a million creds, come to daddy."

Uttering a thin scream, Stillborne ducked under groping paws, sprinted out the door and into the gathering dusk.

~ * ~

The cargo hauler whined up the ramp with its load of passenger luggage. Standing under a podlight Falle watched it disappear into the hold of the small starfreighter. The line in the passenger departure seemed endless. She waved her arm to catch the attention of a listless custodian pushing a broom over the tiles.

"Excuse me!" she called.

The custodian gave her an annoyed glance and slouched over.

"Yeah, what's the problem, toots?"

"Is the flight leaving for New Earth tonight or should I come back later next week?"

"Not quite yet. Spaceport got put on hold to wait for some priority passenger."

"Priority passenger?"

"They said the new security puke for the Chandelier Palace quit and Prime Minister Sanchez got him another job…"

There was a mad patter of feet behind them. They caught a glimpse of an anguished sweaty face and a drooping mustache before a little figure raced up the boarding ramp and shoved his way into the waiting starship.

"What in hell was that?" the custodian gaped.

"It would seem the priority passenger has just arrived," Falle smiled but inwardly she rolled her eyes. *Am I ever going to get rid of the little runt?*

~ * ~

The styroplast cup of moco in Falle's hand had long since grown cold. Sitting in the visitor's lobby of the Homeworld Penal Administration Building she brooded over the scene beyond the windows of New Earth City forty stories below. Swarms of hovercars flowed in spiral patterns through the early morning haze, like insects hunting flowers.

Since arriving in New Earth City, she and Stillborne were assigned rooms in one of the city's finer hotels. This was a good sign. Falle envisioned speedy hiring and looming financial reward.

"Ms. Falle Crandell, please report to Mrs. Hardtkase, Room C5," announced a voice from an overhead speaker.

The room she now entered was Spartan in décor; a metal table and two chairs, pictureless white walls. A bookish elderly woman looked up from a stack of forms.

"Please take a seat, Ms. Crandell," she said, indicating the empty chair.

Nervously, Falle sat down. This cubicle reminded her of the interrogation room in the cellars of the Chandelier Palace. Her expectations of rewarding employment diminished.

Mrs. Hardtkase scrutinized a sheaf of documents and pushed them across the table toward Falle. "Sign these, please," she ordered.

"What are these for?" she asked, taking a proffered stylus.

"Termination of employment offer forms," she replied. "Initial the yellow boxes, your full name on the bottom of each page."

"My termination of employment offer?" Falle felt as if she had received a dockloader's boot in her midsection.

The woman looked up from behind a ledger and frowned. "Nobody has informed you?"

"Informed me of what?"

"In keeping with the policies shared by commercial starlines the Penal Administration has decided to replace the pilots of their shuttle service with cybernetic androids."

An emotional protest rose to Falle's lips, immediately suppressed. She knew all about the bureaucratic mindset and the grim visage across the table was its face.

"Just great. Wonderful news," she muttered. "I suppose it means squat I dumped my last few creds on a ticket to this interview."

"We of the Penal Administration will of course reimburse you for your travel expenses. Upper management has decided the financial burden of wages, health benefits, educational and retirement programs for human employees are too much of a drain on our financial portfolio."

"Oh, I can see your point. We can't have the big shots of upper management standing on street corners selling apples," said Falle bitterly.

"It is most regrettable, but there it is," Mrs. Hardtkase declared sternly. "Please continue signing the forms."

"Would it be impertinent of me to ask when I might see my reimbursement for travel expenses?"

"I have your severance allotment here." An envelope was slid over to Falle. "Your hotel has been paid through tonight. Checkout is at noon tomorrow."

Falle stood outside Room C5, holding copies of the forms she had signed. Neatly folding the sheaf in her hand, she threw them into the nearest trash receptacle and stalked down the hall to the hydrolift. She had just punched the button for the ground floor when she heard a familiar voice.

"Goddammit, Crandell, is that you?"

It was Stillborne; neat, mustache trimmed and as spruced up as she had ever seen him. He appeared to be bursting with happy news he was eager to share.

"How they hangin', Crandell?" he grinned.

"One lower than the other, if I had any, which I don't," she replied. "I'm guessing you're here for the same reason as me. Why are you so happy about it?"

"Donno what you mean. What reason you talking about?"

"The job offer Parasol Sanchez set up for me just got shot down."

"Ah hell, Crandell, sorry to hear this." His anticipatory grin turned to concern. "I don't get it. I mean, your qualifications as a starpilot and all."

"Corporate greed, what else?" she shrugged. "So, let me in on your good news."

Stillborne immediately brightened. "Yeah. Human Resources called me in to offer me the position of Assistant Warden on Slython. Seems Sanchez put in a good word for me."

Falle made a doubtful face. "You sure you're going to like living on Slython? It's on the butt end of the known universe."

"Crandell, half the planetary system is after me for the Cartel reward. No way are they gonna get their mitts on me on faraway Slython."

The hydrolift door slid open and they stepped inside. Arriving at the entrance lobby Falle turned to Stillborne.

"I suppose this is farewell, then," she said. "Would you like a goodbye kiss, Leonard?"

"Screw you, Crandell," he smiled at her. "I hope things work out for you, Blondie." He held out something in his hand for her. "A little parting momento."

Falle accepted the battered electroflash. "Thanks, Stillborne. Remember, it's a nice day if it don't rain."

She watched him pass through the entry doors and merge into the swarm of morning commuters. She thought her feelings would be of relief for finally getting rid of the little pest. Instead she experienced an odd feeling of loss. She sighed; tearing open the envelope she had been given.

Inside she found a draft for her travel reimbursement. Fifty creds.

"Drog's Holy Blowhole." She crumpled up the draft, tossing it to the floor. She felt her face flush with anger, her heart pounding.

This was absolutely it, she raged to herself. No more being little Miss Nice, trying to be the good citizen, striving to earn an honest crust of bread. The girl with the Borgia kiss was through bending over and taking it up the…Borgia kiss.

~ * ~

Wind swept over the abandoned hovercar parking lot, scattering odd bits of trash, whipping Falle's long blonde hair around her face. She searched the expanse of cracked polyasphault ringed by derelict warehouses and abandoned buildings. She was about to take a second look at her timeband when she heard a whispered footfall behind her. She spun about and looked into implacable black eyes set in a wealth of raven hair.

"Very stealthy arrival, Jinghua," Falle observed. "I don't recall you showing me this neat trick during my training."

"Well, you can't expect this old dog to share all of her tricks with the young dog, can you?" she smiled. "What's on your mind, Blondie?"

"I need a job. With the Borgia Guild."

Jinghua pursed her lips. "I don't see how your employment application would be considered seeing how the Guild owes the High Council of Zardoria eighty thousand creds for the failed assassination of Chancellor Crandell, also known as Falle Crandell."

This bit of news caught Falle by surprise. "But…I heard it was Agnes, my cybernetic duplicate who was assassinated."

"Ah yes, but the contract was for you and the money paid to the Guild. Now the council wants it returned as you happen to be still alive."

"How in Zerid was I to guess Agnes would go totally ape and take over the country?" Falle lifted her hands in a gesture of despair.

Jinghua waved a reproving finger before Falle's eyes. "Oh, what a tangled web we weave when first we practice to deceive."

"Yeah, yeah, I know." She suddenly faced her mentor. "What is your standing in the Guild hierarchy?"

Looking out at the skyline of abandoned warehouses, Jinghua

considered. "Well, after the Guild Chairman, T'ong Blatt, there would be Gordo, Knifestalker, then myself. Why do you ask?"

"Gordo, Splib and Knifestalker are no longer breathing air," said Falle.

Jinghua looked at her surprise. "How do you know this?"

"Because I engineered their demise. So, by my count there should be three job openings in the Guild."

"My, my. You would indeed be an asset to our little organization." Jinghua pursed her lips in approval.

"How would you like to step into the shoes…sorry, webbed feet, of the current Guild Chairman, T'ong Blatt?"

"Of course." Jinghua searched the deceptively innocent face before her. "You've been scheming, haven't you, Blondie? Care to share your plans with your mentor?"

"The contract was between the Zardorian High Council and T'ong Blatt. If T'ong Blatt was to have an unfortunate event, the contract would become invalid and the creds would remain with the Guild. Am I right?"

"I'm afraid your legal expertise exceeds my grasp," Jinghua conceded. "But I would suspect the High Council of Zardoria would not relish a confrontation with the assassins of the Guild."

"What time does the sun usually set in the West side of New Earth City?" Falle asked, looking at her timeband.

~ * ~

With a gratified sigh, T'ong Blatt eased himself into the lily pads and tepid water of his private pond. He leaned back on the tiled basin and watched the sun setting between the spires of New Earth City. He lazily eyed his personal secretary, Miss Eieful, preparing a cocktail of fermented seaslime, noting with approval her skimpy pondsuit.

The sun dipped below the roof of his mansion and the pond deck slid into gloom. T'ong Blatt frowned, gazing down past the floating lily pads.

"Why haven't the pond lightsss come on yet?" he asked.

"Uh, your electrician wasss here earlier in the day working on the pump motor. Ssshe probably forgot to reset the pond light timer to the correct time," said Miss Eieful, dropping a slug garnish into the cocktail.

"Electrician?" T'ong Blatt scowled. "What electrician?"

"Ssshe said you called to have the pump ssserviced," Miss Eieful replied. "Cute little blonde girl. Ssshe had really mean eyesss, though."

"Little blonde girl...I never called for..." T'ong Blatt's slitted eyes widened with a sudden dread.

At that moment the pond light timer clicked on, sending a high voltage surge of electricity to the circle of underwater lights in T'ong Blatt's private pond. One of the lights was missing its waterproof cover.

T'ong Blatt was electrocuted.

~ * ~

The café Jinghua chose for their meeting was adjacent to the airbus terminal, in a booth strategically located next to two exits. She sipped her dragonroot tea and watched Falle wolf down a plate of gorthburgers and a double order of fried cartips.

"I was thinking of reaching for the sugar but I'm afraid I might lose a hand," said Jinghua dryly. "When did you last eat?"

"I feasted on half a snackbar yesterday," Falle replied between mouthfuls. "But I was saving the rest to feast on later this evening."

"Perhaps I should signal the server for another order."

Jinghua's eyes darted to the café entrance and her hand slid down to her hidden blade as a hulking figure at the counter glanced their way. She relaxed when he got up, paid his tab and left. She turned back to Falle.

"At the Borgia Guild Council, I was confirmed as the new Chairman," she said. "Am I of the opinion I have you to thank for my promotion?"

"I never did like the slimy Phib," Falle replied, relishing a smirk with another mouthful of gorthburger. "He had his hand all over my rear one time and he always smelled like a dead fish."

"Well, I'm certain he smells a lot worse now." Jinghua studied.

Falle wondered, not for the first time, how such an angelic face could harbor a personality so ferociously lethal. She also mulled over the fact it was a very good thing to be on friendly terms with this half-Eu girl. Very unpleasant things seemed to happen to people who earned her enmity.

"Your employment with the Guild was also confirmed," she went on. "We have come to an amicable agreement with Baron Shrop of the Zardorian High Council. Half the contract fee for your failed assassination will be refunded."

"Thanks, Jinghua," said Falle.

"Don't thank me yet. A new contract has been assigned to you dealing with the elimination of a cheating husband."

"Sounds pretty simple to me."

"The cheating husband is Emile Barnsmellow, President of United Starlines."

Falle looked across the table and blinked.

"Ah, this got your attention, huh?" Jinhua chuckled. "Your former employer, who ran off almost a hundred cybernetic copies of you and voided your starpilot's license. I imagine you would do the job for free."

The expression in Falle's eyes hardened. "Just give me the details."

"Heaven is in the details." Jinghua took a sip from her dragonroot tea. "It's not the usual tale of infidelity you might expect," she explained. "His wife is often out of town and, in her absence he likes to lease female companionship from Universal Cybernetics. She found out the usual way by discovering strange panties between the sheets of her bed."

"How did you find out all this?"

"As you are no doubt aware the Guild has paid informers everywhere. We have learned his wife will be visiting her aunt in Terranova this week and he has put in an order for a Model SX12 Wild Overnighter."

Falle's brows contracted in thought. She pushed away her empty plate and looked at Jinghua. "Which day is his wife due to leave?"

"I can certainly find out." She drained her cup. "Where can I get in touch with you?"

"Last night I laid my weary head to rest in an abandoned hovercar factory." Falle made a dismissive shrug of her shoulders. "Tonight, I plan to luxuriate on a seat at the airbus terminal."

"My, the Homeworlds Penal Administration really did toss you out into the street." Jinghua checked the tab and dropped a number of creds on the table. "Very well, you will be residing at my apartment until you find your feet. My living room couch is most comfortable."

"Junghua, I couldn't possible intrude on your privacy…" she started to protest.

"Are you arguing with your new employer, Ms. Crandell?" Jinghua demanded in mock anger.

"No Ma'am, certainly not," Falle smiled.

~ * ~

"Hey Dork, do you smell perfume? The security guard wrinkled his nose, squinting up at the dark mass of factory building blocking out the stars.

"Perfume?" Dork sniffed the air and gazed at his companion. "Nope, don't smell a thing."

"I just caught a whiff…seemed to be coming from up on the roof."

"You probably got perfume on your shirt from banging your spaceport hooker before we started our shift."

"Don't know any hookers what wear perfume smelling that exotic," he grumbled, while they moved on down the alley to the loading dock. High above them window hinges gave out a tiny squeak and a shadow slid down a drain pipe and eased inside.

Falle dropped from a top storage rack onto the floor of the darkened warehouse. From her black bodysuit she pulled out a penflash and sent a narrow beam of light across rows of stacked containers awaiting shipment. Moving down the aisle, she paused by one, shining her light over a label taped to the lid.

Model SX12 Wild Overnighter
Ship to: Emile Barnsmellow
826 Pennygrasp Lane
New Earth City

Customer note: Cybernetic will activate
upon opening shipping container.

Peeling off the shipping label, Falle moved to an adjacent rack of empty containers and affixed it to the lid. Next, she stripped off her black bodysuit revealing a tight pink sheath dress and blouse exposing an acre of cleavage. After making sure the ventilation slits were open, she crawled inside and closed the lid.

~ * ~

The warehouse of Universal Cybernetics opened. There was the whine of forkloaders starting up, the thump and bang of crates being moved about, laughter and rough jokes from warehouse workers.

"Okay, which crate did you say was scheduled to be delivered to Pennygrasp Lane this morning?"

"Let me sort through the invoices. Okay, here it is…the one going to Emile Barnsmellow."

That voice. Where had she heard it before? Inside the crate Falle wrinkled her forehead in thought.

Her crate shook as it was raised by a forkloader and trundled down the warehouse floor to a waiting hovertruck. What followed was a seemingly endless voyage through noisy darkness, voices and then a slidedoor closing.

A catch snapped and the container's lid swung open. Blazing white light caused Falle to squeeze her eyes tight.

"Great Gonads of Valgloom. Universal Cybernetics sent me a world class knockout this time," exclaimed a voice. "Wonder why she looks somehow familiar?"

Falle managed to open her eyes, looking up into a florid middle aged face. She got up on an elbow and gave him a dazzling smile.

"Hi, I'm Tori, a Model SX12 Wild Overnighter," Falle declared. "I'm self-lubricating and my programming includes forty-one intimate positions."

Barnsmellow's eyes bulged and he licked his thick lips. "I've hit the jackpot. You look a hundred times better than your picture in the catalogue, honey."

"I can lick the chrome from a launch trailer and suck a sportball through…um, a refueling hose," Falle gushed, batting her eyes.

"Here, let me help you out of the shipping container," said Barnsmellow. "Would you care for a glass of champagne to start the day?" He indicated an elegant table graced by antique silverware and a crystal ice bucket.

"I would be delighted, Mr. Barnsmellow."

"Please, please, no formalities, my dear. Call me Emile."

They were seated at the table, wine flutes filled and Falle gazing seductively over a tray of cheese cubes and caviar. She raised her glass to her host.

"A toast to the morning together, Emile," she said. "Perhaps you would like a kiss?"

The door to the room suddenly swished open. A squat woman stormed inside and stood glaring at them, red-faced and several chins jiggling.

"Aha! Caught you once more, Emile," she raged. "After all your promises to reform, here you are again with another of those…those…"

"Please, my dear, try to calm down." Barnsmellow's lips tightened in a placating grin. "I was merely having an orientation brunch with a new secretary…"

"A likely story." The woman confronted Falle, thrusting a pudgy finger toward the crate. "Get back in there while I call the deliveryman to return and haul you off."

She whirled and faced her husband. "As for you, Emile, why don't you just go ahead and finish your champagne before I give you a piece of my mind."

Falle sighed, took a last sip of her glass and leaned over the table. She climbed back into the crate, pulling the lid shut to be entertained by a litany of voices, one of shrill threats, and expostulations, the other of abject excuses and apologies.

"That's right, Emile, guzzle down your champagne."

"Yes, my dear. can I explain…"

"Aren't you going to offer me a glass?"

"Why, of course, dearest. It's an excellent vintage…"

"Perhaps I should first change into an outfit with cleavage down to my crotch like that plastic-titted floozy over there in the crate!"

At long last Falle felt her container being lifted upright, wheeled over carpet, down stairs and into a hovertruck.

She was turning over several schemes on her exit strategy during the return to Universal Cybernetics when she felt the hovertruck slam on its braking thrusters. Her crate flew forward, flipping open when it impacted with the front wall, tossing her into a pile of boxes.

Outside the hovertruck came angry shouts and colorful remarks on driving skills and sexual innuendos. The entry door slid upwards and once again she heard the tantalizingly familiar voice.

"Oh great, plastic pants got knocked from her crate. It's going to be my ass if she's damaged."

Her head still spinning from landing in the pile of boxes, she felt someone lifting her arm.

"What the hell is this? Since when did the factory start giving their cybernetics tattoos?" exclaimed the voice. "Hmm, a ram's skull and a scrolled motto. Kind of macho for a SX12 Wild Overnighter."

"Hi, I'm Tori," said Falle trying to shake the cobwebs from her mind. "I can lick the chrome from a launch trailer and suck a sportball through…"

"Is this a hazmat imprint on her palm? Zog's Holy Blowhole…Falle!"

Falle found herself looking up into the face of Rann Glassford.

"I know this is a nutty question but exactly what in Zerid were you doing in that crate pretending to be a cybernetic android?" he demanded.

Falle winced from assorted bruises, pushing the hair from her eyes. "Listen, Glassford. If you want to chat, let's find someplace which has a john," she groused. "I really have to pee."

~ * ~

They were sitting at the bar, almost deserted this early in the day.

Rann took a pull at his beer and glanced over at Falle, nursing a glass of Zardorian brandy.

"Well, I suppose we have a lot of catching up to do," he remarked.

"No, we don't," she replied without looking at him. "Shouldn't you be thinking of getting back to work?"

"You don't think I'm a little curious? I understand you were once Chancellor of Zardoria and recently I found you lying in a shipping crate masquerading as a cybernetic pleasure doll."

"So how is Captain Rann Glassford of Pan Galaxy Spacelines doing these days?" she said to her glass of brandy, evading the question. "Oh yes, I forgot. All the human employees got themselves replaced by cybernetics."

"Working at the best job I could find," he replied gloomily. "Driving a delivery hovertruck for Universal Cybernetics. Lots of irony here, huh?"

"So how is Mrs. Glassford holding up to your fallen grandeur and tiny paycheck?" Falle asked, failing to keep the bitterness from her voice.

"Mrs. Glassford?" he said, confused. "There is no Mrs. Glassford. What makes you think I'm married?"

"Because I saw you escorting a little tramp off a flight from Verdana a year ago and she was wearing an engagement ring." Falle glared at him. "When I tried to call your apartment the day after I was discharged from the hospital with the hydrophis virus, I saw in the screen of my comm band some woman's clothes on the back of a chair."

Rann stared back at her. "The little tramp you saw at the spaceport was my sister. She was staying at my place until I could put her on a flight to Dustball to join her mining engineer fiancé for their wedding."

Feeling her cheeks burning with embarrassment Falle gazed into the depths of her brandy snifter.

"Hey, I'm sorry," she mumbled. "I take back the remark about little tramp, also."

"No problem, Blondie," he grinned. "I'll just put it down to time of the month for you."

"Hey, don't push your luck, Glassford," she flared.

He raised his hands in a gesture of surrender. "Hey, relax, just kidding." He signaled to the bartender for another round. Looking carefully around, he shifted on his stool, leaning closer to her.

"By the way, I heard some kind of crazy rumor you used to work for the Borgia Guild," he said.

"Yeah, I heard that one too. So what?"

"Well, it would seem to me, seeing the girl with the Borgia kiss impersonating a cybernetic to gain access to the President of United Starlines might have a sinister purpose." He blandly eyed her. "Kind of a shame his wife barged in before she could deliver a peck on the lips."

"Won't make any difference." Falle took a contemplative sip from her glass. "It's possible the girl with the Borgia kiss spat in his flute of champagne before she left."

Chapter Sixteen

"Two thousand, five hundred creds," said Jinghua, stacking up gold-embossed discs on a living room table. "Minus Guild dues and the advance I paid you."

"Yeah, thanks, Jinghua." Falle was regarding her reflection in a wall mirror, wearing a little black dress, poking a pair of gold earrings into place.

"I must assume you have a big evening planned," Jinghua observed.

"Yes, I have a date."

"A date?" Jinghua was taken aback. "Is he aware of…your condition?"

"Don't worry, I won't be leaving any dead bodies lying on the carpet of one of New Earth City's finer eating joints." She clicked the gold locket around her neck and regarded Jinghua's image in the mirror behind her. "He's just an old friend."

When she reached inside a clutch purse for lip gloss an object skipped out and fell to the floor. Jinghua picked it up and turned it over curiously in her hand.

"What exactly is this?" she asked.

"Stillborne gave it to me as a memento before he left for Slython. It's an electroflash," she said. "He promised his new employer he'd give up smoking dhung."

"Doesn't seem to be working…wait." A tiny disc fell from the bottom of the electroflash. "Guess what was in it? A memory chip." Jinghua went to a desk scanner and inserted it.

Immediately a stream of data began running across the screen.

Jinghua looked over at Falle. "Do you know what Stillborne gave you? The formula for hyperdrug."

"What?" Falle turned from the mirror and stopped applying the lip gloss.

"Any idea of what the Methtroplis Drug Cartel on Euphoria is offering in the way of creds for the formula?"

"Enough to drown in," Falle replied. "Stillborne never tried to sell it to them because of their less than stellar reputation on reneging on deals and his reasonable suspicion they would remove his head afterward."

"He's right about their welshing on agreements." Jinghua removed the memory chip from the scanner, tapping it thoughtfully. "So, who else would be in the market for the hyperdrug formula? Before Stillborne stopped cranking out snoot on Dustball, the Cartel was raking in two million creds a month from every planet in the Homeworlds system."

"Who knows and who cares. If you find a buyer for the formula, knock yourself out," said Falle gaily, snapping shut her purse and heading for the door. "Don't wait up for me, Jinghua," she smiled.

For a time Jinghua contemplated the tiny disc in her hand.

"Who else, indeed," she murmured to herself.

~ * ~

It was happy hour at the Cyber/Human Friendship Bar. Less than happy was Anne Plastikote, brooding over a stack of empty shot glasses on the bartop before her.

"So, what has it been now, almost a month since you and Brad last did the dirty deed?" said her friend, Susan Polyform, exuding sympathy.

"Pretty close," she replied gloomily. "I tried wearing my skimpiest nightie, practically waved my protoflesh mammalary glands in his face. Zero interest on his part."

"Maybe you should chase him off to see a doctor?"

"Mr. Conster won't talk about it. He only says he's tired from overwork due to the ramping up of production for the cybernetic starpilots that Homewords Penal wants delivered yesterday." She signaled to the bartender for another round. "I'm kind of glad he accepted the position of sales manager for New Earth city's biggest jetwing dealership, and this will be his last month at Universal."

"Well, perhaps you could have your libido programming detuned," Susan suggested doubtfully.

"That would be like asking a human male to have one of his testicles removed," Anne groused. "The worst part is, Brad asked me to have my libido programming jacked up over the red line when we started our relationship."

"Speaking of human males, get an eyeful of the hunk sitting over in the restaurant section," said Susan, indicating a tall blonde seated at a candlelit table.

"Very nice, indeed," Anne agreed with an approving purse of her lips. "He's at a table set for two. Must be expecting someone."

"Wish it was me," Susan sighed. "Get a load of those broad shoulders."

"He looks familiar." She squinted in the dim restaurant lighting. "Oh, I recognize him now. He's Rann Glassford, one of my hovertruck delivery drivers."

Susan Polyform was gazing at Rann like a satyr observing a virgin. "Hmm. I wouldn't mind him parking his hovertruck in my garage."

"Sounds to me like you could use a little libido deprogramming yourself."

On impulse she slid off her stool.

"Hey, where are you going?"

"I think I'll have a little chat with him." She winked over her shoulder at her friend. "Maybe I'll get lucky and his date won't show up."

Why are women always late? Rann looked up from his timeband as Anne Plastikote arrived at his table.

"Hello, Rann. I thought it was you," she greeted him with her most ravishing smile.

"Hey, Ms. Plastikote," he blurted, pushing back his chair and getting to his feet. "Nice to see you."

"Please, please. Call me Anne," she said "Waiting for your

girlfriend?"

"Yeah, she's running a little late."

Like a moth drawn to a flame Rann's eyes dropped to Ms. Plastikote's expansive bosom.

"So how is your new job coming along? I imagine it must be quite a change from piloting a starship?"

"Coming along great, Ms…Anne." The intense look he was getting from Ms. Plastikote was making him uncomfortable. "It's been…interesting at times."

"Very glad to hear you're fitting in with our team." She gazed absently around her at the crowded tables and hustling servers. "My, they certainly keep the room temperature down in this place. It's making my nipples hard." She gave him a sultry smile. "Well, I had better get back to enjoying happy hour with my friend." She slipped a card from her blouse, tucking it into a pocket of his jacket. "We must get together sometime, talk about improving warehouse efficiency or something."

"Yeah, nice to meet you, Anne," he replied.

With a feeling akin to regret, he watched her shapely rear undulate back to the bar.

"Hey, who was that?" said Falle, arriving at the table and eyeing the departing figure with a measure of suspicion.

"Oh, hi Falle." He grinned at her weakly. "That was my employer at Universal Cybernetics. She just stopped by to say hello."

Falle beamed at him, taking her seat. "Well, what looks good?" she asked, opening a menu. "Tonight is my treat."

"Um, I don't know…"

"I just got paid for a job."

Rann gave her a knowing look. "Yes, I heard all about it on the evening news. Poor Mr. Emile Barnsmellow."

Falle returned his look, the picture of bland innocence. "I don't quite know what you mean. Heart attacks are somewhat common for people tending toward corpulence, wouldn't you say?"

A waiter appeared at their table. Falle glanced up from the menu.

"I believe I'll have the prime rib of ardex, medium rare," she said.

~ * ~

The purchasing agent for Lifeguard Clinic wasn't what Professor Drumgold expected. She was sitting across from his desk, a somehow sinister woman attired in a black pantsuit, long black hair and unblinking black eyes.

"Well now, Dr. Lang," he said, clearing his throat. "As I can see from your telefaxed purchase order, you wish to obtain a contract with Rivergreede Pharmaceuticals to supply your clinic with vincenerol. Unfortunately, due to the increase in cases of ecosin blood disease which this drug treats, a planetwide shortage requires we will have to renegotiate the contract price discussed."

"The telefaxed purchase order and the business card in your hand bearing the name of Doctor Mei Lang are forgeries," announced his visitor. "I am Jinghua of the Borgia Guild."

Blood drained from Drumgold's face. His trembling hand groped for a button under his desk.

"If you press that button summoning your security detail, you will have a knife embedded in your heart before they arrive," said Jinghua calmly. "However, I am not here to assassinate you, but to present your company with a profitable opportunity."

It took Drumgold a few moments to digest her words. His back was clammy with sweat. "Um... profitable opportunity?" he blurted. "I don't quite understand."

"A very profitable opportunity. Do you know how much the Methtropolis Drug Cartel on Euphoria made per month when they were able to get their hands on hyperdrug?"

"I can't seem to see where this conversation is going," Drumgold replied, confused.

"The Cartel was raking in two million creds per month until their supplier vanished, taking with him the formula for the drug." Jinghua slipped a memory disc from a pocket and held it up.

"I have here the formula for hyperdrug. With your drug manufacturing facilities, you could create separate labs to produce it. The Guild has contacts with the Cartel to market your product."

Drumgold was staring at the memory disc. He was aware of the enormous profits the Cartel was making on the sale of hyperdrug. The demand was not only from the city's lowlife craving the initial euphoric high caused by the gas, but a populace eager to visit another time and place. To meet departed friends and relatives or to receive a glimpse of a possible future in the Fantasy Zone, parallel universe or wherever it was the drug took them.

There were also enormous risks. Due to the increasing number of users not returning from a hyperdrug experience or returning injured and traumatized, the penalties for hyperdrug possession had become severe.

The thought of two million creds per month kept resounding through his mind. Greed overtook fear as he contemplated a Spring tide of wealth rolling over his company.

"My lab would have to verify the formula is authentic," he ventured.

"Of course. Shall we move on to the purchase price?"

Passing a tongue over his lips, Drumgold shifted nervously in his seat. "Considering startup costs, personnel vetting and training, I would regard two million creds to be a reasonable offer."

"I did not come here to exchange jokes with you, Professor. Four million creds."

"Two and a half, then."

"Three million creds. My final offer before I walk out of here."

Drumgold gazed into implacable black eyes. "I accept your offer."

"One more thing," said Jinghua, placing the memory disc on his blotter. "I would also desire a single dose of the serum for the hydrophis virus."

~ * ~

"Okay, we have an embezzler, a cheating husband and an escaped convicted murderer. Which one would you like?" Falle was hunched over a viscreen, studying scrolled data.

"What are you looking at?" Jinghua was standing behind her, nursing a cup of nightgrass tea.

269

"The latest contract list from the Borgia Guild," Falle replied.

"I believe I'll take the first. I've always enjoyed feeling my blade sliding into an embezzler." She took a contemplative sip from her cup. "I noticed you came home early last night. Your date didn't go well?"

"There's not a lot to do when your date can't even get a goodnight kiss," Falle replied with asperity. "I also got the impression he was rather glad I left when I did."

Jinghua made an expression of commiseration. "By the way, while you're at the viscreen, why don't you check your bank statement?"

"Good idea," Falle snorted. "Maybe those pukes at Homeworld Penal decided to cough up severance pay for the job I never got."

"No, not your account here in New Earth City. The one you have at the National Bank of Dropoff." She reached over Falle's shoulder, tapping in a code. A different screen popped into view.

"National Bank of...Holy Gorth Shit!" Falle gaped in disbelief. "One million creds. How in zerid...?"

"I took your advice and found a buyer for the hyperdrug formula; Rivergreede Pharmaceuticals."

Falle spun in her chair to face Jinghua. "You sold the formula for a million scoots? That much?"

"Actually, it was three million creds, split evenly between the Guild, you and yours truly."

"Why the National Bank of Dropoff?" Falle was still adjusting to the enormity of the situation.

"Homeworlds Internal Revenue might get curious how an unemployed starpilot suddenly acquired such a sum," Jinghua patiently explained. "Planet Dropoff is out of their jurisdiction."

"Wow." Falle felt as if she were in a state of shock. Endless possibilities crowded her mind; a new apartment in Lifedome Nine on Verdana, a lifetime subscription to the Force Pistol Review. Paramount of all...

"I can now afford the serum..."

"Not necessary. I had Professor Drumgold throw in a single dose to sweeten our deal." She held up an injector gun. "Shall I perform the honors?"

Reaching out, Falle touched the injector as a phantasm likely to fade into nothingness. "What about withdrawal side effects?"

"None. He assured me this is the latest formula."

Falle hesitated, then held out her arm. She felt a sharp sting, followed by a wave of dreamy exhilaration. Her vision blurred but she focused on Jinghua's smiling face. She turned over her left palm and looked at the dull red outline of the hazmat imprint.

The imprint slowly turned pink, fading from her skin.

"Once more, I owe you, Jinghua." Falle felt her eyes fill with tears and overflow down her cheeks.

"I'm always happy to help a sprout of the younger generation," Jinghua chuckled. "As the old saying goes, they'll be the ones choosing my nursing home."

Falle jumped up and headed for the bathroom.

"Hey, where are you going?"

"I'm going to make a surprise visit on an old friend." Falle grinned over her shoulder. "I've got a lot of catching up to do."

~ * ~

It had been another long day for Rann. There had been several deliveries of crated starpilots to the Homeworlds Penal Administration, a pickup of lease-expired waitresses from the Grieshaus Restaurant and a dropoff of a Model LDXI Superstud to an obese dataclerk. This had been the worse. On inspecting the contents of the shipping container, she decided her preference was for Rann. He managed to depart with only a sleeve torn from his uniform.

Arriving at his apartment he wearily closed the door and headed for the kitchen. He felt he had earned a bottle of chilled Aghaid beer; maybe two.

At the kitchen entryway he paused, catching a whiff of a familiar perfume. It seemed to be coming from the bedroom. He frowned in perplexion, turned and followed his nose.

Lying under a single sheet was Falle, smiling up at him. On the bedside table was a guttering candle, a bottle of Cul Des Chiens '32 and two glasses.

"Holy Gorth Crap," he sputtered. "What in zerid are you doing here, Falle?"

"Thought you'd be surprised," she smirked. "You really shouldn't leave your spare passcard under the doormat, Rann. Hey, I warmed up your side of the bed for you."

"Like hell!" he shouted. "You want to wake up in the dawn's early light next to a corpse?"

"It's not going to happen." She held up her palm for him to see. "I'm cured of the hydrophis virus."

"You're cured? How did this happen?"

"I had a friend who had...business dealings with Rivergreede Pharmaceuticals. She obtained the serum for me."

Rann was taking in Falle's nipples poking through the thin sheet. "You're telling me...you are now...safe?"

Falle tossed aside the sheet. Underneath she was naked. Her eyes were bright with invitation.

"The wine is getting cold," she observed.

"Forget the wine." Rann began unbuttoning his shirt.

~ * ~

Falle untangled her arms and legs from Rann's, lolled back on the pillow and sighed. She was agreeably oiled with sweat, enjoying a satiated glow. She glanced over at her bedmate, already asleep and snoring. Good technique and endurance, but he needs to work on his postcoital skills, she mused.

"What in Zog's name," Rann muttered as she pushed him awake.

"Open your eyes and get busy," she ordered. "I want an encore."

He blinked owlishly. "A man's work is never done." He pushed himself up on an elbow, studying her. "I just noticed I'm still alive, so I would say you're definitely cured. So, tell me about this generous friend of yours who shelled out thousands of creds for the serum."

"It was tossed in at the conclusion of...a business deal she made with Rivergreede," Falle replied evasively. "I'm staying with her at this time. In fact, I'll be looking for an apartment tomorrow morning for myself."

"Still sounds to me she's pretty well off financially," he mused. "Husband or boyfriend?"

"I think she's between boyfriends right now."

Falle knew Jinghua had gone through a series of relationships with wealthy men of good breeding. None of them lasted very long. She suspected, despite her beauty, the sinister aura she gave off made them more than nervous.

"I believe I was talking about an encore," she abruptly declared, putting an end to his probing. She grabbed his face and pulled it to hers.

~ * ~

The empty bottle of Cul Des Chiens '32 lay on its side on the bedside table in company with two wineglasses and the blackened wick of the expired candle.

Rann opened his eyes, yawned and got up on an elbow. He glanced down at Falle, deep in slumber with her long blonde hair spread over a pillow in wide disarray. In her sleep she appeared to Rann about sixteen years old.

Rann sighed, gazing around him in the pale morning light. Walls pleading for a new coat of paint, threadbare carpets, cracked panes of glass on doors leading to an outside balcony. A far cry from the luxurious penthouse, when he was Captain Rann Glassford of Pan Galaxy Spacelines. Soon, he would have to get up and trudge off to the downtown airbus which would take him to another day of his low pay, boring job. The airbus, crowded with sweating commuters. When, as a starpilot, he would climb into his gleaming new Porsche aircar. He sighed again.

A chime sounded throughout the apartment. Lights began blinking on, the cheerful burping of the moco percolator came from the kitchen and hidden speakers began to play "Ride of the Valkyries".

"What is happening?" Falle jerked upright, rubbing her eyes.

"Time for your fellow bed warmer to get his ass in gear for another day of excitement and adventure at Universal Fake Persons." He kissed her absently. "Care for a cup of moco?"

Falle peered at a bureau timeclock. "Oh. I have an appointment with a realtor to look at apartments," she said. "I've been sleeping on my friend's couch for the last few weeks." She scrambled from the bed and began gathering up her scattered clothing from the carpet. "Can I see you tonight?" she asked, glancing hopefully over her shoulder.

"Yeah, well tonight..." Rann paused from pulling on his pants, looking away from her evasively. "I have to work the, um, evening delivery shift, Falle. Maybe we could do lunch tomorrow?"

"Sure, I'd like that." She finished dressing, drawing him close for a voluptuous kiss. She reached down and gave him a gentle squeeze below the waist. "Get this thing on the charger before tomorrow night, Glassford," she grinned mischievously and headed for the door.

Watching the door glide shut Rann headed for the kitchen and his first cup of moco. He reminisced on the past night with Falle. He found her to be inexperienced but wildly passionate. Did he really want to pursue a relationship with an impoverished and unemployed starpilot? Especially when he had a much better prospect.

There were also those rumors he had heard in various bars around town regarding her involvement in the Borgia Guild. They couldn't possibly be true. Could they?

He fished in his shirt pocket and pulled out a business card. Studying his wrist comm band he punched in a number.

"Ms. Anne Plastikote please... Oh, hi Anne, it's me, Rann." He said. "I was wondering if you'd like to get together again tonight after work. You would? Great, see you then."

~ * ~

Falle spent the day hunting for the perfect apartment in New Earth City. She noticed the minor squalor of Rann's digs and hoped her choice would be one he would be willing to share.

She almost decided on a condo overlooking Gus Grissom Park. Tomorrow was the start of the weekend; perhaps they could make the final decision together. She recalled him saying he had to work the evening shift but she could call and leave a message. She might even get lucky and catch him on his break.

"Universal Cybernetics Shipping Department?" she said into her comm Band. "Yes, I'd like to talk to Rann Glassford please. He's what? Gone home for the day? Thank you very much."

So, his evening shift must have been cancelled. An excited and happy smile spread over her face. The surprise visit to his apartment the previous night had been a resounding success. She was guessing he would like another.

~ * ~

Anne Plastikote untangled her arms and legs from Rann's, lolled back on the pillow and sighed. Her protoflesh body was agreeably oiled with sweat and she was savoring a satisfied glow. She glanced over at her bedmate, already asleep and snoring. Good technique and endurance, but he needs to work on his postcoital skills, she mused.

The skimpy black nightie she wore under her dress had produced the desired result when she undid the shoulder straps and let the dress fall to the floor upon arriving at his apartment.

She rolled over in bed and shook him by the shoulder.

"Yes, yes, I'm awake," Rann mumbled.

"You remember a few nights ago I mentioned my sales associate was leaving Universal to take a position with another company?" she said.

"Yeah…Tomm Huckster."

"Hucksmore. I was wondering if you'd like to take over his spot?"

Rann was definitely awake now. He stared at Anne in disbelief. "Really? A promotion from the warehouse to sales associate?"

"Absolutely. I've already approved your application. The job comes with a substantial salary and a company aircar." She ran a hand over his chest, teasing the hairs. "It would also mean we could spend more time together."

The sound of a slidedoor opening came from the entrance to the apartment.

Anne sat up in bed and frowned. "Are you expecting company?"

she asked.

"Not that I'm aware of…"

Framed in the bedroom door was Falle Crandell. In one hand she held the apartment passcard, the other a bottle of wine.

Utter silence filled the room. Falle regarded the two on the bed, her plans for the evening and possibly the future disintegrating before her eyes.

Rann's features segued from pasty white to beet red. "Hey, Falle…I-I can explain…" he stammered.

"Well now, if it isn't Falle Chavez," Anne Plasikote observed sardonically. "I'm guessing you're here to make a threesome? Perhaps we could run you through our scanner again, crank out a quorum."

The passcard dropped from Falle's hand. A red mist clouded her vision, her fingers tightened about the wine bottle.

"If I am, how about a little vino to start the night?" In enraged fury she sprang forward, lifting the bottle above her head.

Scrambling from the bedclothes, Anne rose to meet her, seizing the upraised arm. They fell to the carpet, screaming and clawing like wildcats.

"Ladies, let's calm down and talk this over!" Rann cried, hurriedly pulling on his undershorts. He circled the two combatants, uncertain of what to do.

By now, Anne's cybernetic strength was prevailing against Falle's furious rage. She had Falle pressed up against the balcony door, her fingers tightening around her neck as her programming to repel a personal attack switched on.

"Anne! Stop it, you're choking her," Rann shouted.

He grabbed Anne around the waist and heaved. Her fingers were torn free the same time as his feet became entangled in Anne's discarded dress. He stumbled backwards through the patio doors dragging Anne with him. He hit the floor, releasing his grip.

Anne Plastikote was thrown over the balcony railing, disappearing from view.

"My God, no!" Rann screamed. He dashed to the railing in time to see her body spinning like a child's whirligig to the concrete walkway nine stories below.

~ * ~

"Are you aware of the penalty for the involuntary termination of a Level Six cybernetic android?" Detective Smythe asked, his tone quietly conversational.

"It…it was an accident, for Zog's sake," Rann protested, his voice tight with fear. "How many times do I have to keep telling you guys?" He looked up from his chair at the second detective leaning against the wall of the interrogation room.

"Fifty years cryo imprisonment on the Slython Penal Facility," said newly-promoted Detective Wong. "With no hope of parole or reprieve. This is a new directive from the Department of Artificial Persons."

"Let's talk more about Falle Crandell," Smythe continued. "What exactly is your relationship with her?"

"Just a casual acquaintance. All this crap wouldn't have happened tonight if she hadn't come barging in on Anne and me," said Rann in gloomy recollection.

"So, you've never had, shall we say, carnal relations with Ms. Crandell?"

"Well, we did swap some spit a night ago," he admitted.

"And you experienced no ill effects afterwards?"

"Why do you keep asking questions about Falle?" he demanded. "What has that to do with your investigation on Anne's death?"

Detective Smythe leaned closer to him. "Because our investigation is not about Ms. Plastikote's untimely termination. It is about Falle Crandell."

"What? I don't get it." Rann's brows wrinkled in confusion.

"We want to know everything you know or suspect about her."

Looking from Smythe to Wong, Rann decided he didn't like the way things were going. Was he being set up?

"It's just the way I explained," he said sullenly. "She was just a casual lay, nothing more."

"Okay, we're going to move our little chat to a different level," said Detective Wong. "We have a witness living on the tenth floor of your apartment who, when she heard an altercation coming from the floor below her, looked out to see you push the deceased over your balcony."

Rann felt an icy finger trace its way down his spine. Fifty years on Slython Penal. Already in his mind he could hear the rain pattering on his cryocapsule as it was being wheeled to Level Bravo. Those stories about the rats...

Detective Smythe laid a fatherly hand on Rann's shoulder. "Look, son, help us out here and we promise to make the unfortunate episode regarding Ms. Plastokote go away."

~ * ~

It was Falle's turn in the interrogation room. She sat in her chair opposite Detective Smythe wearing a cold, disinterested expression.

Damn, she's got mean eyes, he mused. This is not going to be easy.

"So, you're saying it was an accident which resulted in Ms. Plastikote falling from the patio railing?" he asked.

"As I've explained twice, Rann was pulling her off me when he tripped at the outside of the balcony," she replied.

"How long have you known Mr. Glassford?"

"We were both starpilots for Pan Galaxy Spacelines. We recently reunited the night before last."

"You mean the night on the way to the warehouse of Universal Cybernetics," said Smythe softly.

Falle's eyes widened.

That got a reaction. He grinned smugly to himself. *Now for the knockout punch.*

"We recently received security camera footage from Universal showing you climbing into a crate which was earmarked for delivery to a Mr. Emile Barnsmellow. You know, the gentleman who passed away the other day due to a...heart attack?"

The blank expression returned to Falle's face. "Universal did create ninety-three cybernetic copies of me when I was a flight attendant, you know," she said. "It could easily be one of them."

Smythe nodded approval. "Very shrewd answer, Ms. Crandell. Very astute." He leaned back in his chair. "I suppose we'll have to await results from our fingerprint analysis of the shipping container."

"Since all ninety-three replicants of me are identical I would have to guess the prints would be identical, wouldn't you say?" she observed.

"Universal told me they needed a way to keep track of each cybernetic duplicate so they were issued random fingerprints."

Falle's head snapped back from regarding Detective Wong.

Zinged you again, Blondie. "You didn't know this little tidbit of information, did you?"

Falle eyed him with quiet disdain. "I suppose here is where the trembling miscreant is expected to quail beneath the falcon eye of power and start whimpering for her lawyer."

Detective Smythe laughed. "Very good, Miss Crandell. We don't find many comedians sitting where you are."

"That's *Ms.* Crandell, numbnuts," she sneered. "So, either book me for whatever charges you have in mind or let me go."

"All in good time. We have a lengthy statement from your former bed partner, the living one, that is, Mr. Glassford. He confirms what we already know about you being a carrier of the hydrophis virus at some point in your life." He smiled slyly at her. "I wonder what the autopsy of Mr. Barnsmellow will reveal?"

"So what? I also had the flu and a bad case of athlete's foot at some point," Falle shrugged.

"At any rate, we have enough to hold you on suspicion of murder." Smythe pushed back his chair and got to his feet.

"Judge Harshe of New Earth City Criminal Court has set your bail at one million creds to ensure you don't sprout wings and fly away."

"One million creds, is that all?" Falle raised her eyebrows in mock disbelief. "Put me in front of a netscanner and I'll download a draft from my account."

"Ha, ha, you do indeed have a sense of humor, Ms. Crandell," Detective Smythe chuckled. He stood grinning down at her. Falle looked up with an unblinking feline stare.

Smythe's grin gradually wavered, died. "You don't really...have this amount...do you?"

~ * ~

Jinghua's aircar rose from the parking pad of New Earth City Detention City and joined the stream of traffic spreading out over the city.

"Unbelievable. I cut all the circuits on the roof of Universal Cybernetics going to their security system." Falle ground her teeth. "Some moron handyman must have wired that one surveillance camera to the wrong circuit."

Jinghua turned her craft into a spiral of commuters heading west. "Well, your biggest problem is your ex-boyfriend. My contacts at the Detention Center tell me he sang like a canary about you when they threatened him with the death of Ms. Plastikote. He agreed to testify against you if a trial date is set up."

"If only I had given him a goodnight kiss the night before," Falle commented grimly. "Why did he have to be the driver scheduled to deliver my crate to Barnsmellow?"

"Don't worry about Mr. Glassford. I'll take care of him," said Jinghua.

Knowing Jinghua, Falle felt no need to query her further. "You realize when their fingerprint analysis comes back and they compare those with mine on file at both spacelines I worked, they'll cancel my bail and drag me back to the slammer?"

Jinghua nodded, obviously deep in thought. "How much have you put away for a rainy day?"

"Seems like I'm going to get wet. After paying my bail bond, deposit on my new apartment, splurging on new underwear and socks."

"It might be time for you to sprout wings and fly away."

Given the present situation, Falle could not but agree. This was not the first time she had been in Detective Smythe's crosshairs.

She experienced a sudden deep yearning to return to the desert, to the vast sunscorched vistas, to freedom. Her home planet of Dustball now seemed a place of refuge.

"When we get to your apartment, I think I'll give Elaine Dante a call," Falle decided.

"The manager of New Earth Aurumite Corporation on Dustball?"

"Yes. She might have some ideas of which rabbit holes I could disappear into."

~ * ~

"Okay, here are the documents you wanted. The Borgia Guild forger is the best there is."

Jinghua spread the passport and assorted forms over the kitchen table, looking earnestly at Falle. "You really want to go through with this?"

"I don't have a lot of choice." She picked up the passport, fanning through the pages. "So, my new name is Lauren Bacall. Hmm. Doesn't seem to fit me somehow."

"Hang around New Earth City a few days and it will be Inmate Crandell on Slython," said Jinghua succinctly. "So, you signed a year's contract with whom?"

"When I talked with Elaine Dante, she heard of an opening on Planet Dropoff. It's an isolated triwood logging operation needing a manager. I figure my experience owning a water plant on Dustball might come in handy."

"Speaking of isolated, wouldn't Dustball be a better place for you to go into hiding?"

Falle shook her head. "It's my home planet. Elaine said it would be the first place they'd start looking."

"I've heard about Dropoff." Jinghua made a wry face. "Lonely logging camps, carnivorous Ghotes, nine months of rain and cold."

"It's a lot colder inside a Slython cryocapsule," Falle observed.

Jinghua shrugged in resignation. "Very well, your flight leaves for Dropoff in two hours," she said. "Be sure to dress warmly, Blondie."

~ * ~

The new sales manager for Universal Cybernetics strode purposely through the foyer of his luxury apartment building in the New Earth City Estates. Waiting for him at his reserved parking pad was a gleaming Porsche aircar.

Rann rubbed a sleeve over a non-existent speck of dust on the hood. Wearing a complacent smile, he settled himself into the plush targhide upholstery and started up the fusion drive. The tiny craft rose gracefully over manicured lawns and headed out toward the city.

Abruptly, there was a cataclysmic explosion causing a starburst of flame and smoking debris. The burning mass of aircar crashed near a stand of trees, setting them ablaze.

From behind the spray of a fountain, Jinghua watched a black plume of smoke rise from the wreckage. With a smile of satisfaction, she turned and walked away.

~ * ~

Two months into the rainy season on Dropoff. Will it ever stop?

Falle sat in the employee cafeteria and stared out the window at sheets of rain lashing the trees. Triwood loggers in yellow rainslicks trudged through mud under a crane loading cut trees onto a waiting hovertruck. A warning horn hooted mournfully and a log settled gently into a cradle.

She was alone in the cafeteria, her crew having finished breakfast and headed off to work. She took a sip of moco, pondering on how moody she had been the last few days and how queasy her stomach had become. It had to be this wonderful vacation spot she was enjoying.

Suddenly, the breakfast steak and cartips she had eaten threatened to make reappearance. She scrambled from the table and made it to the toilet cubicle just in time.

"Zog's Ass," she muttered, washing her mouth out at the sink. "Is this food poisoning or am I coming down with a bug?"

She trudged into the employee lounge and plugged herself into an autodoc. For a few moments the machine hummed away before a readout popped onto the screen.

"No way in hell." She stared at the readout, aghast. She ran the tests again, receiving the same result.

"Thanks for the parting gift, Glassford, you sonofa-."

Her wristcomm began to chime. She touched a button and a familiar face flickered into the tiny screen.

"Good morning, Ms. Bacall," Jinghua smiled up at her. "How are things in your neck of the universe?"

Falle groaned, rubbed her eyes. "Never better. What's up with you?"

"Oh, just checking up on an old friend." Her smile faded. "You don't seem particularly well. Is there a concern you would care to share?"

"Yeah, I have a concern all right." Falle made a rueful face. "A really big concern."

"How big a concern?"

"I'm pregnant."

Chapter Seventeen

The Ghote emerged from the fern forest at the first light of morning and prowled around the thatch huts of the triwood logging camp.

"Goddamn, it's back again, Bill." Tad rolled over in his cot, pulling the blanket over his head.

"Noisy bastard," Bill mumbled. "What do you think it is?"

"It needs a shower, judging by the smell."

There were padded footfalls outside, followed by the screech of claws running down the wooden doorframe.

Both loggers were now awake, peering into the dimness of the cabin.

"I'm gonna take a look," Bill declared nervously. "Probably a ferndog scrounging for garbage."

"Pretty pronging big ferndog, you ask me," said Tad.

Wincing at the cold floor under his bare feet, Bill crept to the door and placed an eye to a crack. "Shoot, Tad. It's a Ghote and a damn big one."

The wooden door shook from a sudden blow. A hairy snout sent a gust of rancid breath into Bill's face. Claws ripped into the doorframe, sending splinters showering over the threshold.

"Zog's Left Nut!" Bill jerked back, tripped and fell to the floor.

Tad scrambled from his bunk, backing up to the nearest wall. "It's coming in!" he yelled. "Where is the pulse rifle?"

"Stinky Ed borrowed it yesterday to hunt bogducks." Bill scrambled crablike for sanctuary under his bunk.

"Out pronging standing."

The shattered door fell to pieces and the Ghote strode into the hut.

Both men screamed.

~ * ~

Doctor Kleist contemplated the young couple, Meghan and Danno, seated in his office. He guessed at once they were desperate. Very good. Desperate people could be most profitable.

"We've tried for over a year, Doctor," said Meghan, her fingers clenched in anguish. "The doctors we consulted on Planet New Earth could find no abnormalities with either of us. We've tried various drugs, treatments…" Her voice trailed off.

"At any rate, we've decided on adoption," said Danno. "Could you put us in touch with an agency who could provide us with a child, preferably a girl."

"Planet Dropoff has a very small population; miners and loggers. Which is to say, chiefly male." Dr. Kleist made a rueful expression. "Have you tried any of the adoption services available in the Homeworlds System?"

Danno's gaze dropped, embarrassed. "Well you see…I do have a conviction on record for moongas and dhung possession."

"You've been put on the list as an undesirable adoptive parent." Dr. Kleist nodded in understanding. "However, I might be able to help. Out of channels, so to speak."

The prospective parents gazed at him with hopeful expectation.

"It could be somewhat expensive, however," he continued.

"Money isn't a problem for us," Danno assured him. "My old man owns the biggest forkloader dealership in Dropoff City."

"Very good, then. I'll be in touch." Dr. Kleist rose from his chair and ushered them from his office. He returned to his desk and touched a button.

"Miss Baksyde, would you send in Nurse Portly, please."

Dr. Kleist was standing before his office window, hands clasped behind him, deep in thought, when Nurse Portly entered. He turned, giving her a significant look.

"I believe I'll be needing your expertise again, Janice," he said.

Nurse Portly assumed a crafty grin. She was a hunched troll of a woman wearing a faint mustache on her upper lip.

"Yes, Dr. Kleist?" she asked.

"What are your prospects of locating a baby; preferably female."

Nurse Portly thought for a moment. "Not too good at this time. The Homeworld feds shut down my pipeline from Planet New Earth last month."

"Any leads on obtaining a child here on Dropoff?"

She stroked her mustache thoughtfully. "I did hear of a wedge over at a triwood logging operation up by Fern Gorge. She's almost at term."

"Would the child be a girl?"

"That's what the clinic where I work said when she arrived for a pre-natal."

Dr. Kleist was pleased. "Could you organize a snatch soon after she delivers?"

"I'll look into it." Nurse Portly had a sudden unpleasant thought. "Could be tricky, though. They got a man-eating Ghote on the loose near the camp. I hear it dragged off three loggers the past month, into the jungle for an early morning buffet."

"Better take Snitch with you, then," Dr. Kleist ordered. "He is quite handy with a silenced charged particle rifle."

~ * ~

"This makes three of my loggers so far," Falle fumed. "Are you hoping this will save on payroll expenses, Jerry?"

She was arranging a display of dangling ornaments over a crib. She lowered herself into a chair and ran a hand absentmindedly over the mound beneath her maternity smock.

The prospect of impending motherhood was impacting on Falle's dual personalities. Her warrior psyche chaffed at her state of physical impotence. Her feminine side anticipated the joys of holding her child. Adding to cramps and severe morning sickness was the anxiety over the necessary trips to the clinic on Dropoff City and her fear of discovery when there.

"You feel okay, boss?" Her logging chief, a gangly youth with a shock of carroty hair was eyeing her anxiously.

"I'll feel better when this is all over," she replied. "Listen, sorry I yelled at you, Jerry."

"No problem, boss," he smiled. "I'd be a bit testy myself if I was dragging around the load you're carrying."

"So, tell me what progress you've made hunting down our nighttime diner?"

"Well, I sent a team over to the Ghote village in Dark Valley," he explained. "It looks like one of their older males contested the head Ghote for leadership of the pack. He got pretty mangled in the fight and he was driven from the village. I guess he was too crippled to hunt normal prey and turned to hunt easier game... humans."

"Sounds like you're describing the behavior of man-eating tigers on ancient Earth," Falle observed, finishing her sewing on the jumper and holding it out.

"Hey, I see you've embroidered *Nai* on the little stranger's new threads," said Jerry. "That gonna be her name?"

"When she gets here," Falle smiled back.

"Anyhoo, we set up night patrols...what's the matter, boss?"

Falle grimaced and doubled over when the first of the cramps hit her. She turned a sweat-streaked face to her logging chief.

"Better honk up the clinic in Dropoff City," she gasped. "I think the little stranger is on her way."

~ * ~

Wiping his hands dry on a towel, Dr. Valdez anxiously gazed down into Falle's sleeping face. "The post-partum hemorrhaging is under control," he said. "She could certainly use a transfusion but my scanner indicates a B negative blood type having an exotic strain. I dare not at this time." He turned to his assistant.

"Nurse Portly, I have to return to Dropoff City to deal with an emergency mining accident. I don't feel she should be moved at this time but I recommend calling a medical shuttle in the morning."

"It's a good thing you're leaving now, Doctor," Portly agreed, indicating storm clouds behind the bedroom windows, blotting out the setting sun.

"I appreciate you staying here overnight to monitor my patient, nurse," Dr. Valdez nodded. "Please contact me should any change occur." He bent over the crib where the sleeping newborn lay swaddled in pink blankets. "At least the baby seems quite healthy, although perhaps a bit strange." He pulled on his coat, picked up a bag and headed out the door to the waiting jetwing.

Nurse Portly was smiling when the craft lifted and headed out over the jungle.

~ * ~

Heavy tropical rain beat on the windows, running in wind-driven streaks down the glass. Outside in the logging camp, podlights sent forlorn beams through the downpour.

Nurse Portly took the empty bottle from the sleeping newborn and nervously scanned her timeband. It was almost time.

Over the thunder of rain, she could hear tapping at a living room window. Taking a quick look at Falle and the baby, she crept from the bedroom, carefully raising the window. A bearded face streaming with rain looked up at her.

"Hurry, we don't have much time," Snitch hissed. "I got my hovercraft stashed behind a grove of palms but we got a patrol of loggers comin' up from the mess hall. Here, grab the vial."

Portly took the container and went back into the bedroom. After a scrutiny of Falle's pale sleeping face, she scooped up the baby and returned to the window.

"I put a little trank into her bottle," she whispered. "Should keep her quiet until you get back to the city." Snitch nodded, taking the child from her arms and disappearing into the storm.

Nurse Portly returned to the bedroom. Unstoppering the vial, she poured blood into the crib, onto the floor and left a trail leading to the window where she emptied the remainder on the sill. She took the empty container and stuffed it into a trash disposal chute. Wearing a satisfied grin, she went to the front door and threw it open.

"Help, come quickly!" she screamed into the night rain. "Help me!"

There was a flicker of lightsticks in the darkness, a pounding of boots. Jerry burst into the room followed by his loggers, fingers on the triggers of their pulse rifles.

"What's happening?" he demanded, looking wildly around.

"The Ghote came and took the baby," Nurse Portley shrilled. "I was in the kitchen warming a bottle when I heard the baby scream. When I ran back to the bedroom she was gone."

Jerry gaped at the bloodstained crib and the carmine trail leading to the sill of the open window.

"Drog's Holy Jockstrap." His eyes bulged in shock, breath catching in his throat.

He turned and gestured frantically at his horrified companions.

"Everybody search the compound and out into the jungle," he shouted. "Maybe there's a chance she's alive. Let's go!"

~ * ~

The rainstorm passed, leaving the night air redolent with the miasma of wet plants. An aircar glided over the deserted parking pad where Dropoff City met the jungle, setting down with a whine of descending turbines. A young couple nervously emerged.

"Where the hell is he?" Danno asked. "He told us to meet him…wait, I think that's him."

Snitch emerged from the darkness to stand under the cone of a podlight. The two hurried over.

"Do you have the baby girl?" said Meghan eagerly. "Let me see her."

"Better keep your voices down," Snitch cautioned her. "She just woke up." He gently unwrapped the blanket from the bundle. "You got the five thousand creds for Dr. Kleist?"

From the blanket, a baby with enormous sapphire eyes and silver hair gazed somberly out at them.

"What in Gorth crap is this?" snarled Danno. "We asked for a human baby."

"Yeah, she looks a little different but..."

"This...this *thing* is an Eu child!" Meghan sputtered.

"Look, folks, you asked for a baby girl and this is what we got you," said Snitch, deciding to take a firm tone. "Now, you owe the Doc five thousand scoots."

"Forget it, no deal. We're not paying for no goddamned freak."

Grabbing Meghan's hand, they stormed back to their jetwing. With a roar it lifted off into the night leaving Snitch, literally, holding the baby.

Snitch sighed heavily and tapped his comm band.

"Hey Doc, this is me. The two jerkos rejected delivery of the kid. Said they didn't want no Eu baby. Well, that's what the little sprout looks like."

From the bundle came a querulous whine. Snitch fumbled a bottle from his pants and offered it to his charge. The baby grabbed the bottle, shoved it into her mouth and regarded him with a cold reptilian stare.

Damn, this kid sure has a mean set of peepers, he thought.

"Listen, we can't give the little squirt back," he said into his comm band. "What are we gonna do? Huh? Leave it in the cargo hold of the starfreighter leaving this morning for Dustball? Yeah, good idea to dispose of the evidence."

From the folds of the blanket the baby continued to stare up ominously at Snitch.

~ * ~

Well, we wandered around in the jungle all night looking for the Ghote what killed and carried off Ms. Bacall's baby. So, in the morning I had to tell her. She didn't say anything, but her face looked like it had been carved from marble. Her eyes...you know what she looks like pissed...

She got dressed, picked up a charged particle rifle and headed off into the jungle. One tough lady, I can tell you. I guess she found the Ghote because we could hear the firing of the particle rifle about an hour later. Geeze, she musta shot off three charge clips.

When she got back to the logging camp there was a jetwing parked outside the camp office with a company executive goon and two Dropoff City detectives waiting for her. They slapped plasicuffs on Ms. Bacall, shoved her inside the jetwing and took off.

That's when, you guys remember, the company executive goon called us all into the mess hall and gave us the speech about her resignation and how yours truly will make a great triwood logging supervisor.

Hell, I don't know where they took her. I did find out something of what happened. My girlfriend in Dropoff City, Maxine, works at the Aurumite Company office. Yeah, Maxine.

Sure, she's a little on the chubby side but as the old gag goes, the more cushion to the pushin'.

Anyway, Ms. Bacall's real name is Falle Crandell and she was wanted for suspicion of murder on New Earth. The chief witness against her cashed in his chips in a jetwing dump and the main evidence, fingerprints on some kinda packing crate, didn't pan out. Plastiwood don't hold fingerprints worth a damn. So, the charges got dropped but because she shipped out to Dropoff and took on a fake identity she forfeited her bond.

How much did she lose? Ready for this, guys? One million creds, no shit.

Where do you think she's going now she's been canned at the logging camp? Well, she got herself cleared of the murder rap but they hung a charge of assuming a false identity and accepting a position here on Dropoff using forged documents. She'll probably get about ten years inside a cryocapsule on the Slython Penal Facility.

~ * ~

City Shelter

For Displaced or Abandoned
Children
Haboob City, Dustball

"Would this be the, er, child, you were telling me about, Mrs. Rusch?" inquired Director Hindbottom, pausing before a line of cribs in the nursery.

"Here is the one, Director," Mrs. Rusch replied. "Captain Planque said one of his crewmen discovered her in the cargo hold of his starfreighter while unloading a shipment of mining equipment from Dropoff at the Dustball Spaceport. It's not short of a miracle their cargo-hold had enough air and heat during the trip."

"Hmphh. So it would seem." Director Hindbottom perused the clipreader attached to the crib and gazed with disapproval at its occupant. "What exactly was an Eu newborn doing on Dropoff?"

From a mound of blankets, the little girl sucked on her bottle and returned his gaze with a cold stare.

"I sent a sample of her DNA to the main Homeworld Databank," Mrs. Rusch explained. "According to the information they sent back, the father is, or rather was, a Rann Glassford, recently deceased in an aircar crash. The mother is a Falle Crandell, an Eu hybrid wanted on New Earth for suspicion of murder."

"Well, to all outward appearances this is an Eu child lacking a non-human emigration permit." He exhaled in disgust. "I suppose we'll have to generate the necessary forms to have her repatriated to Sheridan's Planet, which could take weeks." He plucked at the baby's jumper. "What is this embroidered on her clothing? *Nai?*"

"I would guess someone, probably the mother, sewed her name on it," said Mrs. Rusch. "So I entered the name on our register as Nai Crandell."

"Even her first name doesn't sound human," Hindbottom muttered. "Perhaps it would be best if we moved it out of the same room as the other children. Who knows what alien infections or diseases it might be harboring?"

"There might be a solution to this situation," said Mrs, Rusch.

"We have an adoption application from an Elmer and Gertrude Gootch, seeking a baby girl."

"Yes, I recall now. Those scruffy-looking water prospectors from the pumping station outside the city," he mused. "Their application was rejected as they had, at the time, no fixed address or verifiable income."

"We could make an exception seeing how this baby is, as you said, not completely human," Mrs. Rusch suggested.

"I think we might indeed," Hindbotton agreed, leaning over the crib and frowning. "At least it would be a solution to getting it out of our nursery."

From the pile of blankets in the crib, Nai Crandell took the bottle from her mouth and spat a jet of milk quite accurately into Director Hindbottom's face.

~ * ~

Outsourcing.

This was the usual term coined by corporate executives when they applied to the Homeworlds Labor Department to replace human employees with cybernetic androids. After ten years it was becoming harder to find humans in places of skilled labor or responsibility.

Co-pilot Thad Johnsrudd slouched in his seat aboard the starfreighter, employed by the Homeworlds Penal Administration to transport convicted and released criminals from the penal facility on Slython. Interspace regulations mandated a minimum crew of two on all interstellar flights in the system. All starpilots had long ago been replaced by cybernetics, and there was a rumor going around this would be his last flight before he too would be booted out the door to be replaced by one of those goddamned ever-smiling protoflesh assholes.

He shot a glance at Captain Norman Eight, the cybernetic pilot at the controls, gazing out the forward viewport with his usual fixed and vacuous grin. What he wouldn't give, he thought, to slap the smile from the protoflesh phizz.

Thad had learned that as a cost-saving measure, Universal Cybernetics, the major manufacturer, had omitted male genitalia and libido programming from its production line of starpilots. As far as it was possible to do to a cybernetic, Thad found out he was able to annoy and depress Norman Eight with tales of his sexual adventures.

"Hey Norm," he grinned, nudging his companion in the side. "Did I ever tell you about the saleslady I humped on our layover on Slython? Silky, soft skin, bedroom eyes and a real screamer in the sack. I still got the scars on my back from her claws."

Norman Eight glanced over at him, his ever-present smile strained. "Mr. Johnsrudd, as I must have mentioned before, I really have no interest in you human's reproductive or sexual proclivities."

"Ah hell, Norm, I forgot," Thad apologized with saccharine sincerity. "Man, she had the firmest bazzooms and tightest little honeycrack..."

"Yes, yes, Mr. Johnsrudd," Norman Eight sighed despondently.

"I must have mentioned the nude dancer I humped in Haboob City?"

"Not since yesterday." He turned back to the controls. "Speaking of Haboob City, have you checked the status of the sentence-completed inmate we have to reactivate and release when we arrive there today?"

"Inmate Number 18574, Falle Crandell? Yeah, the one who finished her ten-year sentence on Slython," he replied. "I checked out her biosystem readings an hour ago. All readings are in the green and hunky-dory."

The snowstorm of white light beyond the viewports abruptly faded to a starlight infinity and the gold crescent of an approaching planet.

"Ah, we have arrived within the proximity of our destination," Norman Eight declared, obviously relieved to escape the subject of his co-pilot's bedroom escapades. "Prepare to enter Dustball planetary orbit and notify Haboob City of our projected arrival time..."

"Attention! Unidentified spacecraft approaching from Sector Twelve," a mechanical voice shrilled from an overhead speaker.

Thad leaned toward a scanner. "Holy Gorth Shit!" he yelled. "There's a Umas raider, hot on our ass."

"Endeavor to remain calm," Norman Eight reproved him. "Please open a hailing frequency and request his intentions."

"Request his intentions? You're looking at a Umas raider, tin nuts!" Thad seized the controls and put the ship on a downward series of evasive spirals.

"Mr. Johnsrudd, Interspace Regulation AR21-9 states we are to establish communication between all unidentified spacecraft..."

A green beam lanced from the approaching raider, striking the forward section of the starfreighter. Viewports in the control cabin disintegrated, Norman Eight and Thadd Johnsrudd were sucked out into oblivion. The crippled ship switched to emergency landing circuits and began a lazy dive toward the surface of Dustball, trailing a shroud of debris.

~ * ~

Elmer Gootch and the little girl sat on the dune and watched smoke rising from Haboob City in the distance. It was obviously more than a mere raid by the Umas and they seemed intent on looting as much as they could before the reaction fleet arrived from a Homeworlds military base three hundred kilometers away. Umas starsabres flitted like angry insects, dodging neon pencils of anti-airship fire sent up by the defenders, sending down green beams in reply.

"Do you think they'll be coming up here, Poppa?" asked the little girl.

She was almost ten years old, wearing a faded print smock, her silver hair stuffed under a grimy magball cap.

Elmer shrugged in resignation. "We have the only water pumping station nearest the city, Nai. Your dear departed Momma used to say we were too close. Reckon she might be right."

Nai made a wry face. "What will we do, Poppa?"

He scratched the stubble on his chin. "Well, we might wanna beat feet to the cave up by Ruby Mesa, hide out until the Homeworld boys get here and kick some Umas ass. I don't know how long..."

A black mass gathered above them, blocking out sunlight. A crippled starfreighter droned overhead, wreathed in smoke. It dropped behind a low hill. There was a muted cacophony of rending metal.

"That ain't no Umas ship." Elmer declared. "Come on, we better see if there's any survivors."

They clambered into an ancient sandcrawler and rattled off toward a dense funnel of smoke. Cresting a ridge of sand, they gazed down at the mangled carcass of the freighter. Elmer brought the sandcrawler to a stop before the wreck and they climbed out.

"Well, she didn't explode when she hit, there's something," he observed. "Them old plasma drives are damn sensitive to shock. C'mon, let's see if anybody made it."

They trudged through sand and scorched ropeweed to the hull. Slipping a pocket tool from his overalls, Elmer popped open an access panel and the hatch slid open.

Inside the ship, emergency light shone dimly through drifting grey smoke. They reached the cockpit and somberly regarded empty seats and the splintered plexglass framing a shattered viewport.

"Seems the crew took a trip to the next world," Elmer remarked. "Better give this heap the once over to make sure."

They made their way through the ship, crawling over crash debris and crumpled metal. Reaching the cargo hold they came upon a glass topped cylinder. Nai stood on her toes, brushing dust from the top.

"Hey Poppa, what's this?" she asked.

Elmer pushed aside a sheet of hull insulation and squinted in the gloom. "Hell, it's a cryocapsule. You know, the kind they use to ship people on really long trips through deep space?" He peered into the cracked and grimy top. "Can't see who is inside. All the readouts on the status board seem to be in the green. Wait a minute," he said, pulling a rag from a back pocket and scrubbing the plexglass. "Oh yeah, I can see now, some wedge inside. Nice lookin' piece too."

"Is this a shipping label or something?" Nai had peeled off a partially melted plastic envelope and held it out.

Elmer pried open the cover and slid out a piece of paper.

"Looks like a letter, to her I suppose." He held it up to a beam of light streaming through a broken porthole.

Dear Blondie: You really need to find another line of work. Stillborne.

"Blondie? Must be the guy's old girlfriend, I guess," Elmer muttered. He eyed the status readouts. "I suppose we better get her revived before them smelly Umas bastards decide to have a looksee at the wreck." He chucked a thumb at the ramp leading upwards to the airlock. "Hike back to the sandcrawler and grab my toolbox, Nai."

"Yes, Poppa." Nai slid down the capsule side to come face to face with an identification plate.

INMATE 18574 FALLE CRANDELL
SENTENCED ON PLANET DROPOFF
TEN YEARS CRYOCONFINEMENT
SLYTHON PENAL FACILITY

Falle Crandell. From Planet Dropoff.

A voice from a far distant past whispered in a misty corner of her mind.

Here she is, Gertrude. The City Shelter finally approved us for adoptive parents. They said she was found in the hold of a starfreighter coming outta Planet Dropoff. Yeah, she looks like an Eu baby but she's cute as a button...

"Mommy..." Nai rested her forehead against the side of the capsule, her heart pounding. Tears began coursing down her cheeks. "Mommy..."

"Hey, short stuff," Elmer called from inside the control box. "You gonna get me my tool box sometime this week?"

"Yes, Poppa." Nai pushed herself away from the capsule, stumbled over a tangle of debris on the deck and made for the ramp leading to the hatch.

"Oh yeah, there's an old force pistol in the 'crawler storage bin next to the toolbox, so be careful."

Pausing before the corroded steps leading to the sandcrawler's cockpit, Nai paused to wipe her eyes. With a final glance at the wreck she began to climb.

Deep inside the twisted hull of the starfreighter the fusion drive hummed on unconcernedly on emergency override. High overhead in the engineering compartment, a lightbar support, weakened by the crash, suddenly gave way and fell onto the main feed pump, crushing the pipe closed. Immediately, a pressure wave of coolant slammed backwards onto the outer shell of the toroidal reactor. Plasma erupted from the shell and met the supercooled liquid in a massive explosion.

The blast wave echoed from the distant hills, while a fountain of smoke and falling debris boiled from the wreck. Partially protected from the explosion by the cabin of the sandcrawler, Nai was thrown unconscious into a clump of ropeweed. Fragments of twisted metal and burning debris pattered onto the sand around her body.

~ * ~

It was the sound of guttural Umas voices which awakened Nai. She lay on the sand, miraculously unhurt but for an assortment of cuts and minor burns. She pushed ropeweed branches and clumps of hull insulation from her singed dress and came to her feet.

The crashed starfreighter was now a heap of mangled tristeel and a column of inky smoke painting the desert sky.

Nai stared, moving not a muscle. She whispered a single word, her voice flat and without emotion.

"Mommy..."

Voices from behind intruded on her misery. She turned to see that a Umas scout ship, attracted by the smoke, had broken off the attack on Haboob City to investigate; a squad of sandtroopers were marching down the ramp.

An enormous Umas stood gazing at the wreckage, then spotted Nai standing beside the overturned sandcrawler. For a moment he stared at her and an evil grin creased his face. Slowly he drew his assault knife, running an exploratory thumb along the cutting edge. Still grinning, he strode toward her.

Nai watched him approach, feeling her anguish melting away, becoming something else. She felt herself engulfed in cold fury; her eyes became splinters of sapphire ice.

She looked down. Somehow the explosion had tossed the force pistol from the sandcrawler near her bare feet. She picked it up, leveling it at the approaching Umas.

The sandtrooper uttered a course laugh of derision and increased his stride.

The force pistol seemed an enormous toy in her tiny hands. Nai groped for the trigger, struggling to hold the heavy weapon steady.

A red beam struck the Umas where his leather harness crossed his chest. He gave vent to a grunt of surprise which became a snarl of rage. He took two palsied steps before toppling onto the red sand.

There were shouts of alarm and anger from the other Umas. Nai lifted the force pistol once more. The desert air became crisscrossed by beams of red and green. There were confused shouts, agonized screams and, in the end, there was a little girl clutching a glowing force pistol over the sprawled bodies of the Umas.

Slowly, Nai lowered her weapon. The rage she felt was draining away, leaving a strange emptiness. Faint sounds of combat came from over a high dune. She climbed up a slope of sand to look out at the distant skyline of Haboob City.

The Homeworld Reaction Force had finally arrived and the Umas raiders were in full retreat, leaving the burning wreckage of several of their ships littering city streets.

Nai turned, gazing down at the arroyo below, at the overturned sandcrawler, the dead Umas, the wreckage of the starfreighter.

She was alone. From this moment on she would always be alone.

About the Author

Kurt Heinrich Hyatt, a citizen of Canada, came down to join the U.S. Army during the Vietnam War. He started writing in 1986, selling his first two science fiction stories to *Space and Time*. He also became associate editor for the Starwind Press of Ripley, Ohio. Leaving writing to raise a family he returned in 2010 with his work since appearing in over nineteen science fiction magazines. Kurt is avid Harley writer and an over 50 class body builder.

www.ingramcontent.com/pod-product-compliance
Lightning Source LLC
Chambersburg PA
CBHW061939170626
46813CB00006B/2472